*f anyone can show just
*ause why this couple
*hould not be
*oined together
n matrimony...

"You can't do it!"

Christian reached out and grasped Annabel's arms, wishing he could shake some sense into her stubborn brain. "You can't marry Rumsford. If you marry him, you'll be making the biggest mistake of your life, trust me."

"How do you know?"

"Because he doesn't love you. Because he's a fortune-hunter, and an ass. And because . . . damn it all . . . because there are things you'll never know with him, things he'll never be able to make you feel."

She groaned and started to pull away. "There you go, talking about love again. If you mention love one more time, I swear I'll—"

"I'm not talking about love. I'm talking about something else, a feeling I'd wager my life Rumsford has never given you."

"What feeling is that?"

He let go of her arms and cupped her face in his hands. "This one," he said, and kissed her.

By Laura Lee Guhrke

TROUBLE AT THE WEDDING
SCANDAL OF THE YEAR
WEDDING OF THE SEASON
WITH SEDUCTION IN MIND
SECRET DESIRES OF A GENTLEMAN
THE WICKED WAYS OF A DUKE
AND THEN HE KISSED HER
SHE'S NO PRINCESS
THE MARRIAGE BED
HIS EVERY KISS
GUILTY PLEASURES

Laura Lee Guhrke

Trouble at the Wedding

ABANDONED AT THE ALTAR

AVON

An Imprint of HarperCollinsPublishers

This is a work of fiction. Names, characters, places, and incidents are products of the author's imagination or are used fictitiously and are not to be construed as real. Any resemblance to actual events, locales, organizations, or persons, living or dead, is entirely coincidental.

AVON BOOKS
An Imprint of HarperCollins*Publishers*
10 East 53rd Street
New York, New York 10022-5299

Copyright © 2012 by Laura Lee Guhrke
ISBN 978-0-06-196317-9
www.avonromance.com

First Avon Books mass market printing: January 2012

Avon Trademark Reg. U.S. Pat. Off. and in Other Countries, Marca Registrada, Hecho en U.S.A.
HarperCollins® is a registered trademark of HarperCollins Publishers.

Printed in the U.S.A.

10 9 8 7 6 5 4 3 2 1

For Aaron, who really knows
how to give a girl a birthday party.
Thank you, sweetheart. I love you.

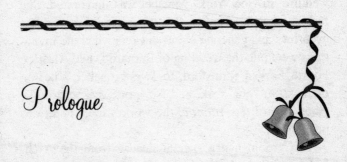

Prologue

Somewhere in the Northern Atlantic
April 1904

The middle of the ocean wasn't the usual location for a lavish, high society wedding, but if anyone could make that wedding a success, it was Miss Annabel Wheaton.

First, she was an American, which meant she had no doubt that anything she wanted to achieve was possible. Second, she had money, which always helps transform impossibilities into realities. Third, she was a Southern girl, which meant that underneath the honeyed words and charming smiles was a stubborn streak as wide as the Mississippi. And if all that wasn't enough, Annabel was the bride, with all a bride's determination that her wedding day would be perfect no matter what.

So, when her desire to be married in England clashed

with the desire of her British fiancé's family to have the wedding in New York, Annabel was undaunted. She fashioned a compromise, and though it did raise a few eyebrows and generate a few snickers when the invitations went out, the wedding of Bernard David Alastair, Fourth Earl of Rumsford, to Miss Annabel Wheaton of Jackson, New York, and Newport, was set to take place aboard the *Atlantic*, the world's most luxurious ocean liner.

The groom had a special license from the Archbishop of Canterbury, the bride selected a white satin wedding gown from Worth, and on April 9, 1904, more than one hundred guests from the highest echelons of society gathered in the grand ballroom of the *Atlantic*, the most unorthodox location for a wedding any of them had ever heard of.

The bride had no illusions about why some of New York's most influential people had come to her wedding. Her daddy might have struck it rich in the Klondike and left all those gold mines to her when he died, but New York Knickerbockers wouldn't have crossed the street to watch a jumped-up, New Money nobody like her get married. No, they were here because of Bernard, and she would always be grateful he was making her most cherished dream come true.

Fifteen minutes before the wedding, as her maid attached the elaborate train to her bridal gown, Annabel stood before the mirror in her stateroom taking the shine off her nose with a discreet dab of powder and thinking with a hint of amazement that she'd come a long way since her first foray into good society.

An image of the ballroom from their house in Jackson flashed through her mind—its gleaming electric wall sconces that looked like candles, its crimson wallpaper that had flecks of real gold dust, its refreshment tables laden with food, its polished—and empty—dance floor.

They'd sold the house in Jackson shortly afterward and moved to New York, but the painful disaster of her debutante ball had proved to be only one of the many social snubs for her family, and Annabel had soon figured out that the Knickerbockers of New York were no different from the society matrons of Jackson. After three years of being ostracized, she'd almost given up hope her family would ever be accepted. And then Bernard had come along.

She smiled, remembering that night six months ago at Saratoga, and the shy, fastidious man who'd crossed a room full of Knickerbocker girls to dance with the redneck girl from Gooseneck Bend, Mississippi. An image of his face came before her eyes, a handsome, proud, very English face, and Annabel felt a rush of affection and fondness. It wasn't hot, passionate love, not by a long way, but Annabel didn't mind. She and Bernard understood each other, they had companionship, and mutual affection, and a shared vision of the future.

Fifteen minutes from now, she would become his countess, and the people she loved would never again be whispered about and shunned and laughed at. In the coming years, when she had children, no one would treat them like dirt. Her children would be part of the privileged class, and everything life could offer would be at their fingertips. And Dinah—

A fierce wave of protectiveness washed over her at the thought of her baby sister, and above the powder puff she was using, Annabel met her own eyes in the mirror, vowing that Dinah would never, ever know how it felt to have a coming-out ball where nobody came.

But what about love?

Annabel paused as a voice went through her mind, a male voice that spoke in the clipped, well-bred accents of a British aristocrat but was not the voice of her fiancé.

Lowering the powder puff, she watched her own reflection recede as another image took its place—an image of smoky blue eyes in a dark, lean face, of unruly black hair against swirls of gray mist. She frowned, feeling uneasy as elusive, hazy memories of last night suddenly came into clearer focus, memories of moonshine and steaming heat and the desire she'd seen in Christian Du Quesne's face.

Annabel stared into the mirror, seeing that man's reflection before her instead of her own. She watched his mouth curve in a half smile and his black lashes drop a little as he gave her that look—the sleepy, seductive look all bad boys knew, the look that threatened to send a girl's common sense sailing right out the window and ruin her life.

That look of his wasn't the only thing about last night she remembered. Annabel closed her eyes, remembering his wide palms cupping her face and his warm fingertips caressing her cheeks. And his mouth tasting like moonshine.

Her lips began to tingle, and heat flooded through her body. Desperate, Annabel opened her eyes and reminded herself that Christian Du Quesne was like the serpent in the garden, offering temptations, whispering doubts. But none of it was real.

Bernard, she thought, was real. Bernard was a gentleman. Bernard wanted to marry her. Marriage was the last thing on Christian Du Quesne's mind.

Don't you want love?

She scowled at the mirror and the memory of that man. No, she didn't want love, at least not the kind offered by bad boys with hot kisses and dishonorable intentions. She'd had that kind of love once already, from Billy John Harding back in Gooseneck Bend, and all it had gotten her was heartache and humiliation. No girl needed love like that.

You're making the biggest mistake of your life. Christian's words from last night echoed through her mind. *Trust me.*

Trust him? She'd sooner trust a snake. Annabel made a sound of derision that caused Liza's hands to still behind her. The little Irish maid peeked around her shoulder, a frown of concern on her piquant face. "Are ye sure you're all right, Miss Annabel?"

"I'm fine, Liza," she answered, working to make it

true as she put the powder puff back in its silver case and replaced the lid. "I have never been finer."

Those words fair reeked of insincerity, but Liza didn't seem to notice. The maid returned her attention to her task. So did Annabel, trying to put that man out of her mind and quiet the doubts he'd been trying to plant in her head for the entire week she'd known him.

Respect? You think Rumsford respects you?

His derisive words rang through her mind, as clear as if he were standing right in front of her, but thankfully, the door to her stateroom opened just then and her mother came bustling in.

"Heavens, child," she cried, closing the door behind her and eyeing Annabel with dismay, "aren't you finished dressing yet? Liza, what's the delay?"

"I'm almost finished, ma'am," the maid assured Henrietta, and after one or two more adjustments, Liza stepped back, carefully spreading out the train. "Sure and you're ready now, Miss Annabel."

"Well, darlin'," Henrietta said, moving to stand beside her at the mirror, "it's time."

Her stomach clenched, whether from nerves or from the aftereffects of last night, she couldn't be sure. But Annabel turned away from the mirror, turning her back on any memories of last night, that man, and all the temptations he'd stirred up. She faced her mother, but she ducked her face as she smoothed duchesse satin and Brussels lace. "How do I look?"

"Beautiful. So beautiful, it hurts my eyes." Henrietta lifted her chin and kissed her cheek, then moved toward the door, stepping carefully to avoid the sweep of the long bridal train. "Now, we'd best be gettin' on with this. If'n we don't, all the guests will think this wedding's called off."

Annabel followed her mother out of her stateroom to join her uncle Arthur, who was frowning like thunder; her stepfather, who was smiling like he'd had a nip or two from the jug already today; and her half sister, Dinah, who was looking far more serious than usual, and older than her eleven years. The five of them left the suite together, with Liza following behind to carry her train. They paused at the first mezzanine by the grand staircase, joining Bernard's three sisters, who formed the remainder of the bridal party.

Liza pulled the veil down over her face and straightened her train. Lady Maude, Bernard's eldest sister, handed over the enormous bridal bouquet of pink magnolias, then moved behind Annabel to take her place in line with her sister Lady Alice beside her, and her older sister Lady Millicent behind her with Dinah. Mama and Uncle Arthur moved to the back of the line, Mama signaled to the organist, and the prelude to *Lohengrin*'s Wedding March began.

On her stepfather's arm, Annabel started down the stairs, the bridal party behind her, and as she made the slow descent to the ballroom below, a strange sense of unreality enveloped her.

This was her wedding day, the moment that would give her what she'd only been able to dream of a year ago, and yet suddenly it all seemed superficial, like a stage setting or a dream. She couldn't smell the flowers or hear the music, and through her filmy veil, the Knickerbocker faces she passed as she started up the aisle seemed hazy and indistinct.

Only one thing seemed clear to her—that man's eyes and all the desire she'd seen lurking in their smoky blue depths.

There are things you'll never know with him, things he'll never be able to make you feel.

A throb of fear touched Annabel's heart.

Her steps faltered a little, but she recovered and kept walking. She looked straight down the aisle, squinting through her veil, searching for Bernard. The sight of him standing on the dais at the opposite end of the ballroom, waiting for her, was like a soothing balm to her jangled nerves.

With his slender build, long nose, and fair coloring, he was every inch the aristocratic English gentleman, and as she came closer to him, as his grave, dignified face became clearer and clearer, Annabel's doubts and fears slowly faded away. Yes, she thought, looking at her husband-to-be as she halted before him, this was a man with whom she could build a new life.

When George's arm slid out of hers and she moved to Bernard's side, it once again felt like the natural place for her to be, as if she'd never met Christian Du Quesne.

"Dearly beloved," the reverend began, "we are gathered here in the sight of God, and in the face of this company, to unite this man and this woman in the bonds of holy matrimony . . ."

With those words, Annabel sent Christian's bad-boy blue eyes and last night's momentary madness to oblivion. She cast off the past, all of it. Her future with Bernard was what mattered.

Annabel took a deep breath, stepped up beside Bernard, and readied herself for the vows that would transform her life forever.

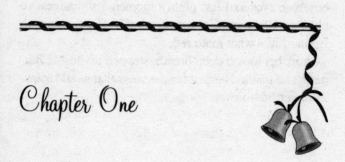

Chapter One

New York City
Seven days earlier . . .

Everyone in society knew Christian Du Quesne, the Duke of Scarborough, didn't have a heart. A block of ice, perhaps, or a steel plate of armor, or even a powerful pumping muscle used to circulate the blood. But a heart? A romantic thing that yearned and loved and broke? No. Christian had lost any such organ years ago, and much to the chagrin of the ladies, he had no interest in acquiring a new one.

Christian, had he been questioned on the topic, would have disagreed, at least on this particular evening. He had a heart. In fact, he had five of them, three in his hand, and two face-up on a green felt table at New York's notorious House with the Bronze Door—five hearts in perfect, beautiful, absolutely ripping numerical sequence.

He couldn't have asked for a better night to be blessed by good luck. This was a no-limit, open-stakes table with a pair of very wealthy men, and he was deuced low on cash these days. Still, to the other two gentlemen at the table, he might just as easily have been holding a motley assortment of rubbish, so coolly disinterested was his expression.

Hiram J. Burke, railway magnate, millionaire, inveterate gambler, and the man who had invited Christian to join the game this evening, had an ace on the table, but unless it was part of a royal flush, Christian's straight flush would take the pot.

"Call," he said, reaching for chips. "And raise five thousand more."

The bet passed to the third man at the table, Arthur Ransom, a wealthy attorney whose only client was his even more wealthy niece. Ransom, who had a florid, benignant face and a thick, drawling Mississippi accent, raised an eyebrow, but he did not raise the stakes. "Call."

Christian raised the stakes again as the dealer went around for the draw, tossing chips worth ten thousand dollars into the pot, a bet that earned him a hard stare from Hiram.

"That must be one helluva hand you've got, Your Grace," he murmured, tapping his finger thoughtfully atop the stack of chips before him, a stack that was quite a bit smaller than it had been at the start of the evening.

Christian offered a noncommittal shrug and nothing more.

"I don't think you'll be gettin' any hints out of this fella with that steely stare o' yours, Hiram," Mr. Ransom said. "Englishmen are cool as cucumbers. Believe me, I know," he added, making a wry face as he tossed his cards into the muck. "Fold."

Hiram straightened in his chair. "Maybe you're right, Arthur, but I've got one helluva hand myself. In fact, Your Grace," he added, returning his attention to Christian, "I think my hand is better than yours. Call, and raise another ten thousand."

Christian knew the hand was his. All he had to do to claim the winnings was see the bet, but he hesitated, appreciating that there was more at stake here than a round of poker. Some men were not of a mind to discuss business after being defeated at cards, and business was the reason he was here. Perhaps he should fold and let Hiram win the pot. No, he decided. He was enough of a gambler to bank on the notion that Hiram wasn't the sort to sulk over a lost round of cards. "I'll see you," he said and matched the bet.

"Four aces," Hiram said, grinning as he fanned out the three aces in his hand beside the one on the table. But his triumph was short-lived.

"Straight flush," Christian said, laying down his own cards. "Queen high."

Hiram stared at the cards for a moment, but then, much to Christian's relief, he laughed. "Four aces, the best hand of my life, and I can't even win the hand." Still laughing, he sat back in his chair, shaking his head in good-natured disbelief. "You are one lucky son of a bitch, Your Grace."

Christian knew being lucky at cards wasn't enough. Thanks to the massive amount of debt his profligate elder brother had managed to accumulate before his death, Christian was not only the newest Duke of Scarborough, he was also required to find a more lucrative and stable way of earning an income than cards. How ironic, he thought as he raked in his winnings, that Andrew had always been regarded as the good son, yet had managed to spend a fortune into oblivion with nothing to show for it, while Christian, who had made quite a good living off his gambling over the years, was still considered by many in the family to be the black sheep.

Still, he was the duke now, and could no longer afford to gamble for his living. He'd arrived in America yesterday with one purpose in view: to forge connections with men who knew how to make money, prepared to offer his own British connections in exchange, in the hope that investment opportunities would follow. Drinks at the Oak Room and an introduction to Hiram through a mutual acquaintance had led to what was proving to be a very lucrative evening for Christian.

"You'd soon find this cash back in your pocket, Mr. Burke," he said as he stacked his winnings in front of him, "if you would allow me to buy shares in that new transatlantic telephone company of yours."

"How'd you hear about that? The shares haven't even been offered yet."

Christian smiled. "I do have some connections here already, Mr. Burke."

"Your sister, you mean? She was married to Roger Shaw, wasn't she? The architect?"

"She was, yes. And she manages to learn all the latest news here in New York, despite the fact that she is a widow now and spends most of her time in Paris."

"She's here now, I understand?" He paused, tilting his head to give Christian a thoughtful look. "And she probably has your social calendar completely filled with engagements already?"

Christian paused, considering, knowing he had to tread carefully. "Actually, no. My primary purpose in coming to New York is not social, but business."

Hiram gave a rather awkward laugh, tugging at one ear. "I see. When you accepted my invitation to play cards this evening, I'd hoped . . ."

Hiram paused, but there was no need for him to finish. Christian already knew what Hiram Burke's hopes had been, but his interest was in transatlantic telephone lines, not transatlantic matrimony.

"Alas, my goal is to forge business connections, Mr. Burke, and to perhaps discover some worthwhile investments. This company you're starting up seems just the sort of thing in which I'm interested. It sounds like an exciting opportunity."

"It would be." Hiram paused, meeting Christian's eyes across the table. "For the right man."

The inference was clear, but though he had no intention of providing Hiram's daughter, Fanny, with a duchess's coronet, he hoped to engage Hiram as a possible business ally. But before he could offer a reply that emphasized his desirability as an investor rather than his suitability as a son-in-law, another voice entered the conversation.

"At the card tables again, Du Quesne?" a pedantic, distinctly British voice entered the conversation. "Why am I not surprised?"

Christian looked up, and the sight of the man by his elbow rather dimmed his spirits. Like himself, the Earl of Rumsford was a British peer, they'd both gone to Eton and on to Oxford, and they both happened to be visiting America at the same time, but any common ground between the two men ended there.

Christian was a dark-haired descendant of Norman nobles and Irish peasants, with a caustic sense of humor and no reverence whatsoever for his newly acquired title. He'd been wild as a boy and was still a bit wild as a man, and he knew, when he had occasion to look in the mirror, that the faint lines at the corners of his eyes and at the edges of his mouth showed many nights of whiskey and cards. Too many nights, perhaps.

A greater contrast to Rumsford could not be imagined. The earl had pale green eyes, fair hair, and a face widely described as handsome—that is, if one ignored the weak chin. Rumsford also possessed an inflated sense of his own importance and a superior little smile, two traits Christian had always found annoying as hell.

Rumsford, he knew, had a similarly low opinion of him, and by tacit agreement, the two men avoided each other as much as possible. Thanks to Christian's aversion to the proper, respectable circles Rumsford moved in, avoiding each other wasn't usually difficult. He'd never have thought to encounter the earl here, in an illegal New York gaming club. Still, nothing for it but to be civil.

"By Jove, it's old Rummy," he greeted, donning a careless smile and a jaunty air. "What a small world it is."

"Du Quesne." Rumsford gave him a bow, then turned toward the other two men at the table, and Christian thought there was a fleeting hint of surprise in Rumsford's expression as he glanced at Ransom. But it was gone in a moment. "Good evening, Arthur," he said pleasantly.

"Lord Rumsford," Ransom responded, sounding much less inclined to be pleasant. He glanced at Christian, then back again. "So, you two Brits know each other?"

"School days," Christian explained. "Eton and Oxford, you know. We rowed on the same team. Been a long time since then, eh, Rummy? Fancy meeting up here, of all places."

Rumsford turned to him, his thin lips curving in that damnable smirk of his. "Our last encounter was the Derby. You were placing a sizable bet on an outsider. The horse lost, as I recall. Interesting how every time I see you, you seem to be gambling, Du Quesne," he said with a little laugh.

Having been elevated to his ducal title on̶ ̶ ̶ ̶w̶
months earlier, Christian was sometimes still addr̶ ̶ed
by his surname. It was not an uncommon mistake, and
one he usually allowed to pass without comment, for
etiquette was one of those things he really didn't give
a damn about. But then his mind flashed back to early
days at school, and how Rummy had been one of those
to belittle him for his French name, his Irish grand-
mother, and the fact that he was only the *second* son of
a duke. Since Rummy was such a stickler about these
things, Christian decided to make an exception to his
usual rule.

"It's Scarborough, nowadays, old chap," he corrected lightly. "Duke of."

He had the satisfaction of seeing the other man grimace at his own faux pas. "Of course. Forgive me,
Scarborough, and please accept my condolences on
your brother's passing. You must be . . ." He paused,
glancing at the poker table. "You must be shattered
with grief."

Christian kept his amiable expression firmly in
place. "Quite."

"So," Hiram said, turning to Rumsford, "what brings
you out on the town tonight, my lord? Celebrating, are
you?"

"Celebrating?" Christian echoed. "What's the occasion?"

The other three looked at him in some surprise.
"Don't you know?" Hiram asked him. "Lord Rumsford here's engaged to be married to Miss Annabel

Wheaton." He gave a nod toward Ransom. "Arthur's niece."

Christian vaguely remembered hearing his sister mention Rumsford's engagement in her last letter to him, but since he and the earl were none too fond of each other, he hadn't found the other man's impending nuptials particularly interesting news. Baffling, perhaps, that some young woman would agree to spend her entire future life with a poor stick like Rummy, but not interesting. What did interest him was the lack of enthusiasm about the match displayed by Ransom.

He turned toward the earl and raised his glass in salute. "My felicitations, Rumsford," he said, and took a hefty swallow of whiskey. "To you and Miss Wheaton."

Arthur Ransom jerked rather abruptly to his feet. "I need a drink," he muttered, and started toward the bar at the opposite end of the room.

There was a moment of awkward silence no one seemed inclined to break. After a moment, Hiram gave a cough and stood up. "I could use a drink myself," he said, and clapped Christian on the shoulder. "About those shares, Your Grace, I'll be bringing my wife and daughter to England in May. Perhaps we can talk more about it then."

"Of course," he said politely, but as he watched Hiram walk away, he suspected there would be nothing to talk about, not only because he avoided London during the season like the plague, but also because those shares were clearly reserved for Fanny's marriage settlement, and that was a business deal Christian would never make. Not again.

He picked up his glass and took a drink of whiskey as he turned to Rumsford, who, for some unfathomable reason, seemed inclined to linger. "Care to join the game, Rumsford?" he invited out of sheer politeness, heartily relieved when Rumsford declined.

"Thank you, no," he said with an anemic smile. "I'm not like you, I'm afraid. I've no talent for gambling."

Christian couldn't help laughing at that. "Then what are you doing in a gaming club?"

Rumsford gave a quick glance toward the bar across the room where Arthur and Hiram were standing, and then, to Christian's surprise, he leaned closer in a confidential manner. "There are . . . other distractions here, Scarborough," he murmured, and his gaze lifted to the ceiling, excitement reddening his pale cheeks, that arrogant smile curving his mouth.

Christian raised an eyebrow, studying the other man's flushed face and almost adolescent excitement. He was no saint, God knew, but bedding a courtesan in a gambling club just before one's own wedding was a notion that offended even his jaded sensibilities about matrimony.

He hadn't been the best of husbands, perhaps, but he had been faithful, though he doubted Evie would find much consolation in that fact, were she still alive.

At the thought of his wife, Christian's throat suddenly felt dry, and he downed another swallow of whiskey, forcing himself to don a smile. "So that's why you're here, eh?" He gave the other man a wink, one man of the world to another. "One last fling before the big day, eh?"

Rumsford winked back. "I didn't say it was my last."

They laughed together in man-of-the-world fashion, but Christian's laughter died the moment Rumsford walked away.

"Some things never change," he muttered under his breath, watching as the earl turned his head for one more furtive glance at Arthur before slipping out of the room to seek the feminine companionship upstairs. "All these years, and you're still an ass."

He felt a hint of pity for the fiancée. He knew nothing of Miss Wheaton, but the only conclusion he could come to was that she was an heiress in the mold of Consuelo Vanderbilt—sweet, biddable, probably a bit naive and under the thumb of an ambitious Yankee mother, forced to marry Rummy because she lacked the courage to refuse.

"I must apologize, gentlemen, for droppin' by your offices this way, but I am just so confused."

As she spoke, Annabel's voice was as sweet as sugar and her Mississippi drawl was more pronounced than usual. The wide-eyed gaze she gave the three men seated on the other side of the conference table was melting and filled with apology. She'd even brought her mama with her. To any man who knew a Southern girl, these were obvious signs that all hell was about to break loose.

Unfortunately, the lawyers of Cooper, Bentley, and Frye were native New Yorkers, and had little experience dealing with women from the Southern side of the Mason-Dixon line. They were accustomed to seeing Annabel only a few times a year and conducting any business matters surrounding her estate with her uncle Arthur, who was one of her trustees, and who was, like them, a lawyer. The fact that Annabel had come to their offices without her uncle and without any advance notice the day she was supposed to be leaving for England might have caught them off guard, but she could tell they had no inkling of what was coming.

Bless their hearts.

"Thank you for that prenuptial agreement y'all sent over to me last night, gentlemen," she went on as she leaned down to pull the document in question out of the leather portfolio she'd placed beside her chair. "You obviously put a lot of work into it, and I appreciate that so very much."

"We're always happy to assist you, Miss Annabel," Mr. Bentley assured her. "We hope you know that."

"I do." She pressed a gloved hand to her bosom, the picture of sincerity. "And I promise I won't take up too much of your time. I just have a few teeny little questions. I'm sure y'all will have me out of your hair in two shakes of a lamb's tail."

Her mother made a soft sound of derision at this pretense of sweetness and light, and Annabel gave her a gentle kick under the table. The last thing she needed was Mama rolling her eyes right now.

She placed the sheaf of papers on the table and began to rummage through them. From beneath the brim of her pink silk bonnet, she watched her lawyers relax, easing back in their chairs, clasping their hands on their substantial stomachs, the picture of indulgent, fatherly patience.

She stopped at the page she wanted and tapped a particular paragraph with her finger. "It says here that Lord Rumsford is to receive seventy-five thousand dollars per year for the maintenance of his estate, Rumsford Castle." She looked up and gave them her prettiest smile. "Gentlemen, that is just not going to be acceptable."

The fatherly patience faded. The three men sat up straight in their chairs and exchanged uneasy glances.

"I've read the reports provided by Lord Rumsford's solicitors," she went on, "and I know that seventy-five thousand dollars barely covers the shortfall between the expenses of the estate and the income from the land rents. Lord Rumsford's solicitors asked for one hundred thousand dollars, a provision I already agreed to. Why hasn't this been changed?"

Mr. Bentley, as one of her trustees and senior partner of the firm, took charge. "We have written many marital settlements of this kind, Annabel, and the annual sum offered in the agreement is adequate for an English estate the size of Rumsford Castle."

"Adequate?" Annabel echoed. "Is that all that you believe I am worth, gentlemen? Adequacy?"

The men exchanged glances again, and this time it was Mr. Cooper who chose to speak for the group. "The amount requested by Lord Rumsford's solicitors is well above the estate budget, and we understand some of it shall be spent to restore certain areas of the house and grounds, a waste of money."

"Mr. Cooper," she said, still smiling, "we are talking about my future home. My home, and that of my children. It must be taken care of properly."

"Yes, yes, of course. But you and His Lordship and your children will probably live at Rumsford Castle only a few months a year. The American wives of peers always seem to want to live in London. Based on that knowledge, we thought it best to keep the expenses of the estate to a minimum. And," he added before Annabel could reply, "we understand some of the funds requested would be used for social activities—balls, parties, and other extravagances."

"You gentlemen are about as much fun as a funeral," she said, noting their expressions of disapproval with some humor. "What's wrong with balls and parties?"

"British men of Lord Rumsford's position are notorious for excessively lavish entertainments. Such unnecessary expenditures can only drain your resources, my dear Annabel."

Annabel, who knew the extent of her resources down to the penny, disagreed. This wasn't just about big balls and lavish parties. Although she'd never had those things, and she wanted them, for sure, there was far more at stake here than entertainment.

In this world, social position was everything. And her family had none. There hadn't been a time in her life when they hadn't been looked down on, and having money hadn't changed that. Seven years ago, when her daddy had died and left her all that money, she'd thought inheriting a fortune was a blessed miracle that would change all their lives for the better. But though she might have prettier clothes now, and fancier houses, and a big, fine motorcar to drive around in, she and her family were still regarded as nothing more than poor white trash.

Annabel's hand tightened around the papers in her grasp. No girl ever forgot what it was like to be poor white trash.

She was determined to rid her family of that stigma once and for all, but the only way to do it was social acceptance, and she'd been hammering away at that particular stone wall for the past seven years without making a particle of difference.

And then Bernard had come along. Bernard would give her and her family the one thing they couldn't buy on their own. Bernard would be the reason her children would never be seen as trash. Her daughters, and her sister, Dinah, too, would have their pick of young men from the finest families. And Bernard would see that no one ever laughed at them again. This wasn't about being frivolous. She was using her inheritance to make an investment in the future, a future that was well worth one hundred thousand dollars a year. Especially when she had more money than she could spend in a lifetime.

"We have your best interests at heart, Annabel," Mr. Bentley said. "We don't want you wasting your money."

"Why, that's right kind of you, gentlemen," she said softly. "But it's my money to waste, now, isn't it?"

Without waiting for an answer, she pushed the sheet of paper with the terms of the estate maintenance across the table. "Rumsford Castle has been in His Lordship's family for over three hundred years. It's important to him, and it's important to me. I'd like this changed to one hundred thousand dollars, please."

Without waiting for an answer, she went on, "There is also the matter of His Lordship's sisters." Flipping to that part of the agreement, she once again shoved a sheet of paper across the table. "I'd like you to double the amounts for the pin money allocated to Lady Maude, Lady Alice, and Lady Millicent, if you please, as I asked before. Pretty clothes are important to a girl. And double their marital dowries."

The men started to interrupt, but she hastened on. "And about His Lordship's personal income, you have allotted only ten thousand dollars per year. I understand he asked for twenty thousand dollars. Is that right?"

Mr. Bentley again took charge. "Many gentlemen of the earl's position find ten thousand dollars quite enough for an allowance."

"What other gentlemen think doesn't really have much to do with it. I have the best clothes, jewels, and folderols money can buy, and I want my husband to have the best, too."

"Of course you do, of course you do, but my dear . . ." Mr. Bentley paused, pasting on his fatherly face again. "Perhaps you are letting your heart rule your head a bit here."

"Uh-oh," Henrietta murmured. "Now you've done it."

Unwisely, Mr. Bentley chose to ignore Mama's gentle hint of caution. "This engagement was very sudden, Annabel, and we would be remiss in our duty if we failed to protect your interests. Perhaps in light of these concerns, you would consider a longer engagement. Perhaps, say, a year?"

Annabel quelled that notion with nothing more than a look.

"Six months," he amended hastily. "Still plenty of time for you and Lord Rumsford to truly be sure you are suited to marry and can agree on how to spend your money wisely."

"First of all," she said, a note of steel coming into her sweet-as-pie voice, "my heart *never* rules my head, gentlemen. Second, Bernard and I have already agreed on how to spend the money. It's you three and Uncle Arthur who don't seem to be rowing with the boat here. Third, Bernard and I want to marry, and we see no reason to have a longer engagement. And I'd have thought you gentlemen would be happy for me." She paused deliberately. "Having my best interests at heart, and all."

"We are happy for you, my dear," Mr. Cooper hastened to say. "But we are . . . concerned. Your uncle is, too. We all only want what is best for you. Of course you want to be married, Annabel. Every girl does, but—"

"I am not a girl," she reminded, interrupting this condescending flow of words. "I'm twenty-five."

"Of course, of course," Mr. Frye assured her. "You are a fully grown woman, we know. But that's just it. You *are* a woman. And it's widely understood that women are not particularly skilled in matters of finance."

Beside her, Henrietta murmured something about Fort Sumter all over again. Annabel, however, had no intention of letting another Civil War break out. Nor did she have time for any more delays over the marital agreement.

She pulled a thick document out of her portfolio. "According to Daddy's will," she said, setting the sheaf of papers down smack-dab in the center of the table, "I have three trustees, but only two of them need to approve my marriage, isn't that right?"

They nodded—reluctantly.

"And, although Uncle Arthur has refused his permission, my stepfather, Mr. Chumley, has given his, isn't that also right? And you, Mr. Bentley," she went on without waiting for an answer, "the third trustee, also gave your permission. Do you intend to change your mind?"

He hesitated, and she went on, "You know, I'm starting to think maybe when I'm married and I have control of my own money, I should pick my own lawyers, too." She turned to her mother. "What do you think, Mama?"

Her mother gave her a wry look in response. "Does it matter what I think?"

Annabel ignored that rather unhelpful response and returned her attention to the men across from her. "After all, there are other lawyers besides the three of you. I'm sure I can find some that are just as capable, and a lot more cooperative."

She smiled into the dismayed faces across from her and decided it was time to stop pussyfooting around. "Gentlemen, Lord Rumsford and I are getting married aboard the *Atlantic* in six days. Since we don't have a lot of time here, let me tell you what's going to happen, all right? You are going to draw up the prenuptial agreement I want today, with all the changes I have asked for. You will get the proper signatures and give one signed copy to each party involved, including Uncle Arthur. Now, Mr. Bentley, you are still coming to the wedding, aren't you?"

Without waiting for him to answer, she went on as if he already had. "That's good. I'd hate for you to be mad at me over this little set-to we've had and not come to my wedding. If you'd be kind enough to bring my copy of the revised agreement with you this afternoon, you can give it to me aboard ship." She glanced around. "Now, gentlemen, are there any questions?"

Looking resigned, all three men shook their heads.

"I'm glad to hear it," she said, and stood up, indicating this meeting was at an end and bringing everyone else at the table to their feet as well. "Thank you for your time today. I do appreciate it. Now Mama and I will get out of your hair, and let y'all get started. You have a lot of work to do before this afternoon."

She turned toward the door and sailed out of the room in a cloud of soft, expensive French perfume, her mother right behind her, leaving a trio of very unhappy men staring after them.

"It's like herdin' cats," she muttered once they were out of the law offices and headed for the elevator. "This is the third time I've had to ask them to make these changes, and I just don't understand what's so hard about it."

"They are good men, Annabel."

"I know, Mama, I know," she said as they paused in front of the wrought-iron gate of the elevator and she pressed the electric button to bring it up to the tenth floor. "But they pat me on the head every time I talk to them and act like Uncle Arthur is the only one they have to answer to."

"I doubt they think that now," Henrietta said with a touch of humor. "Not after today."

Annabel smiled. "I did come down hard on 'em, didn't I, Mama?"

"Like a hammer, darlin'."

"I couldn't help it. All that stuff about how a woman can't manage finances just got under my skin. And then they had to bring up that whole business about waiting a year."

Henrietta was silent for a moment, then she said, "Would it be so bad to wait? A year isn't all that long."

Annabel groaned. "Oh, Mama, not you, too. Not again."

"Well, it's true you and Bernard don't know each other all that well. Maybe—"

"Now, Mama, we've had this talk already," she reminded, having no desire to revisit the subject. "Bernard and I know what we're doing, and we don't see any reason why we should wait another six months. It's plain as day those lawyers are dragging their feet because that's what Uncle Arthur wants them to do. He's never liked Bernard, and he's been against this marriage from the first. But I did think you were on my side."

"Annabel Mae, I am on your side! I'm your mother, and all I'm concerned about is your happiness. Arthur feels the same way. And your short acquaintance with Bernard worries us a bit."

"Bernard and I have known each other six months, and that's long enough for us to know what we're doing. So there's no need for y'all to be worryin' about me. I know you think I'm rushing in headlong, but I'm not. And anyway, the wedding's in six days. It's a little late to be having doubts now."

"Is it?" her mother asked, jumping on that like a duck on a June bug. "Are you having doubts, Annabel?"

"No! Heavens, how many times do I have to say it?"

"You're not in love with him."

She wriggled under her mother's gaze. "Bernard and I get along very well. That's enough for me, Mama."

"I'd like to see you marry a man you're in love with."

Like you did? The words were on the tip of her tongue, but she bit them back. She didn't say that Black Jack Wheaton, her mama's great love, had been a worthless, wandering rascal, and that divorcing him for desertion so that she could marry George was the best thing her mama had ever done. Nor did Annabel point out that Mama hadn't married her second husband because she felt a deep, passionate love for him. No, Henrietta had married George because George had always been the loyal, trustworthy, faithful friend who'd never come home drunk, gamble away the grocery money, or abandon her in search of goldmines.

And Annabel definitely did not bring up her own experience with love eight years ago, how she'd sobbed on Mama's shoulder after Billy John Harding had ripped out her heart, torn it to pieces, and stomped on it.

She didn't say any of those things. "I'm very fond of Bernard, Mama," she said instead, "and he's very fond of me. And I think that's a better foundation for marriage than love could ever be, because love doesn't last."

Henrietta looked at her with sadness. "Oh, Annabel." Just that, just that soft little sigh of her name, and she felt it like the sting of a bee. "Please, Mama, let's not talk about all this again," she said, and turned away from the disappointment in her mother's face.

She didn't understand, and she never would, why her mother of all people would want her to ever marry for love. Black Jack Wheaton had wandered off when Annabel was seven, never to come back, and she could still remember all the nights she'd heard Mama crying her eyes out after he was gone. And even though Henrietta was now married to another man, Annabel suspected that her heart still belonged to old Black Jack.

Her mother already knew her views about her father, and thankfully, the elevator came into view before she was tempted to offer them again. "I know Uncle Arthur means well," she said instead, as the liveried attendant slid back the wrought-iron door and she and her mother stepped inside the elevator, "but all he did by telling those lawyers not to make the changes I asked for was to get me riled up. I hate it when he does that."

"He wants what's best for you. He loves you."

"I know, Mama. I don't have a particle of doubt about that. But sometimes, it feels like he's just smothering me. First floor, please," she added to the elevator operator before returning her attention to her mother and the topic at hand. "I've already told him a dozen times that I'm going to marry Bernard. I've absolutely made up my mind about it. Land sakes," she added in exasperation. "He's known me since I was born. Doesn't he know by now there's no talking me out of something once I've made up my mind?"

"He knows," Henrietta assured her with a sigh as the elevator began sinking downward. "Believe me, darlin', he knows."

Chapter Two

The House with the Bronze Door was an illegal gentlemen's club, meaning that unless it was raided, it stayed open until dawn. And since Christian's luck at cards had seemed inclined to stick with him, he'd been happy to remain at the poker tables, so the sun was coming up over Manhattan by the time he tumbled into his bed at the Waldorf. He didn't awaken until midafternoon, and only then because McIntyre woke him.

"Verra sorry, sir," the valet's pleasant Scottish burr murmured beside his ear, "but Lady Sylvia Shaw is here."

Christian mumbled something he thought communicated his present lack of interest in that fact quite clearly, but caught in the heaviness of sleep, he must not have been clear enough. A few minutes after McIntyre departed the room, another person interrupted his slumber, a person far less inclined to consider his need for rest.

"Christian, wake up." He heard his sister's insistent voice, but he kept his eyes tight shut and tried to ignore her. Sylvia, unfortunately, was not the sort to ever be ignored. "Good heavens, why do you always sleep like the dead? Wake up."

"Leave off, Sylvia, for pity's sake," he muttered, and rolled over, turning his back to her. "I'd have called on you at the Windermeres later. Why are you bursting in on me at this hour of the morning?"

"It's not morning," she informed him as she gave his shoulder another rousing shake. "It's afternoon, and I can't believe you've come to New York without even letting me know. And to arrive the day before I'm leaving for home? What's in the wind?"

He wasn't quite awake, and he had no intention of satisfying his sister's curiosity right now. He shrugged off her hand and worked to hold on to sleep.

"And why this decision to stay at the Waldorf?" she asked. "You could have stayed at the Windermeres' house on Park Avenue as I've been. I could have arranged it before I leave, if only you'd written and told me you were coming. I'm sure Delores Windermere would have been delighted to have you. And her daughters would have been over the moon!"

"Exactly." He moved to pull the covers over his head, but he'd barely grasped the edge of the counterpane before she spoke again, her voice a soft murmur close to his ear.

"If you don't rise and attend me at once, dear brother, the headline across the next issue of *Town Topics* shall read, 'Newest Duke of Scarborough Ready to Marry Again. But Which Lucky Girl Shall Be His Bride?'"

"Good God." He sat up so quickly that Sylvia had to jump back to avoid being bumped in the nose. "You wouldn't dare."

"Wouldn't I?" She sat down in the nearest chair, settling her black crepe skirts around her and giving him a smile he knew well. It was the same smile she'd given him when he was ten and she was eight and she'd given his beloved puppy to the children of the local orphanage. He'd had the devil of a time getting old Scruff back again. This occasion, he feared, would be no different.

"All right, all right," he said, giving up on sleep altogether since he was now fully awake. "I don't know what's so damned important, but whatever it is, I have no intention of discussing anything with you without being dressed first. Have McIntyre ring for tea, then tell him to come and help me dress."

Fifteen minutes later, clad in black trousers, white shirt, and black smoking jacket, Christian entered the sitting room of his suite, where he found his sister seated on one of the two facing settees, pouring tea. He crossed the room, taking the cup she held out to him as he passed. "All right, Sylvia," he said as he sat down opposite her, "now that you've invaded my rooms, bullied your way past my valet, and dragged me out of bed, what the devil is so important?"

"How can you even ask me that? You've come to New York! And I had to learn this through gossip?"

"I only arrived yesterday, and you're leaving tonight, so I hardly thought it necessary to inform you, especially since I saw you at Andrew's funeral scarcely three months ago, and I shall see you again at Scarborough Park during Whitsuntide."

"Oh, Christian! Didn't it occur to you that after nearly three months here in New York, I might be missing you? Although why I should feel that way escapes me now," she added, frowning. "You weren't intending to see me at all before I left, were you?"

He shifted his weight uncomfortably. "I would have called on you later at Park Avenue, as I said."

"After I'd already departed for the pier! Don't deny it; that was your plan."

He took a sip of tea, meeting her eyes over the rim of the cup. "I haven't the least idea what you're talking about."

"Really, Christian, it never works with me, you know."

"What never works?"

"That innocent I'm-not-trying-to-pull-the-wool-over-your-eyes look. Other women may be fooled by it, but I know you too well. Whenever I see that look, I feel as if we're children all over again and you're trying to hide the fact that Scruff just chewed my favorite doll to bits."

He sighed, giving in. "I didn't want to see you because you'll want to hear all about my meeting with the land agent."

She bit her lip, studying him for a moment before she spoke. "It's that bad, is it? What did Saunders say? Did you go over the account books? What income do we have?"

"There is no income."

She looked at him in bewilderment. "But surely Minnie—"

"Minnie's income isn't tied to the estate. Since Andrew and Minnie had no children, the income the estate receives from her ended with Andrew's death."

"But I know our brother had funds, investments—"

"He did, worthless ones. Despite his lectures to me about my gambling, Andrew had a fondness for it, too, it seems. Instead of cards or horses, he preferred worthless gold mines in Tanzania and fraudulent cattle ranches in the Argentine."

"Then all the money we brought in from our own marriages . . ."

"Is gone," he finished when her voice trailed off. "All the estates not entailed are already mortgaged, and they'll have to be sold. They don't generate enough income to pay the interest on the debt, much less pay for themselves."

She pressed a hand to her mouth, her blue-gray eyes so like his own wide with shock above her black kid glove. "What about Cinders?" she whispered behind her hand, referring to her villa just outside London. "And Scarborough Park?"

"Cinders doesn't form part of the entail, but by the terms of our father's will, Andrew couldn't mortgage it. It's yours for your lifetime. Scarborough Park is entailed, of course, so it can't be mortgaged or sold. But to pay its expenditures, it will have to be leased. Indefinitely."

Sylvia was made of stern stuff. She lowered her hand and straightened on her seat, and it took her only a moment to gather her composure. "Well, it's far worse than I thought, but it does explain why you've come to New York, although why you thought you could handle this without my help, I can't think. Nonetheless—"

"No, Sylvia," he cut in before she could go any further. "I appreciate your desire to assist, but it isn't necessary. I don't need the sort of help you're thinking of."

"But you can't do this sort of thing alone. You haven't moved in American society for over a decade, and—"

"I'm not here for society. I'm here to investigate possible business investments. Not worthless gold mines or fraudulent cattle ranches, but sensible investments that might actually prove profitable in future. America is where to find those."

"Investments? But what about capital?"

"Finding capital is the difficulty. I have some cash of my own, but not near enough. So once I've decided what investments I might wish to make, I shall have to return home and survey the family valuables to see what can be sold—jewels, paintings, furnishings."

"I have my income from Roger, and I'd be happy to contribute what I can." She paused and reached for her cup. She stirred her tea, took a sip, and put the cup back down, each move conducted with slow deliberation, as if she were trying to decide quite how to say what he knew she was going to say. "But don't you think there's a better solution than selling off the family valuables?"

This was the real reason he hadn't wanted to discuss the situation with Sylvia. "No, I don't."

"Christian, you shall eventually have to marry again."

He set his jaw. "No."

She got up from her seat and came around to sit beside him. She slipped her hand into his, just as if they were still two lonely children in the nursery, and said, "Evie's been gone twelve years. Isn't it time to stop punishing yourself?"

He jerked his hand free. Suddenly in need of something stronger than tea, he stood, set aside his cup, and walked over to the liquor cabinet by the window. He yanked the stopper out of a bottle of whiskey, poured a generous amount into a tumbler, and took a hefty swallow. Resentment welled up inside him as the whiskey burned its way down.

"We both know a good marriage for you is the only viable solution," his sister said behind him.

"Is it a solution?" He turned to face her, glass in hand. "We all married rich Americans," he said with disdain, "selfishly thinking it would resolve the problems of our debt-ridden family. What you and I didn't know when we sold ourselves and handed over the spoils was that Andrew would make such appalling use of them. I married once to fatten the family coffers. I won't do it again."

"It's not just about the money, you know. It's also about producing an heir."

"Cousin Thomas is my heir. He can have the title. And Scarborough Park, too. He's welcome to that crumbling pile of stones with my blessing."

"Don't say that. It's our home."

"Is it? It never felt like home to me. Perhaps I'd feel differently if the family portrait in the gallery didn't have me, the second son, and, you, a mere daughter, shuttled off to one side, like some sort of afterthought, with Andrew and our father in the center like a pair of glorious sun gods destined to rule the universe. We weren't the least bit important, but we were expected do our duty by the family just the same after Minnie's father went broke. Well, you made Roger happy, I daresay. I, however, can claim no similar accomplishment."

"You've every right to be bitter, I know—"

"Bitter? You mistake me, Sylvia. I'm long past bitterness. I don't care about Scarborough Park. I don't care about restoring the south wing, or what to serve at the annual garden fete, or who's up for MP in the Commons. I just don't care."

"You have to care now," she said. "You are the duke."

Even though he'd already accepted that inevitable fact, he still couldn't stop the resentment roiling inside him. He cared, but damn it all, he didn't want to care.

"And because of that," she went on in the wake of his silence, "you now have responsibilities you cannot ignore."

"I will not whore myself to save Scarborough Park. Not a second time. What?" he added at her sound of impatience. "I know we're terribly well-bred and all that rot, but can't we at least call a spade a spade?"

"There's nothing wrong with allowing a pretty girl with a dowry to catch your eye! But you seem to prefer drinking and gambling and keeping company with women of low moral character. You sneer at Andrew for being irresponsible, but now that you're the duke, how shall you be better? Investments need capital and are not guaranteed to succeed. Our people are depending on you for a more secure future than that."

"Like they depended on Andrew?"

"Marry well," she said as if he hadn't spoken. "Invest the dowry wisely, prove yourself a better duke than he was, and carry on."

"For what purpose? To raise yet another generation of lilies of the field?"

"I think whether your children are lilies of the field rather depends on you."

Instead of answering, Christian turned toward the window, staring out at the traffic that clogged Fifth Avenue, thinking of Hiram J. Burke and how he'd built an empire worth millions in less than a decade. "Amazing country, America," he said after a moment, thinking out loud. "People seem to make fortunes here all the time, don't they? How do they do it?"

"Heavens, I don't know." She paused to consider. "Earn it, I suppose," she said, sounding doubtful.

"A task for which we English aristocrats seem uniquely ill-suited."

"Well, an English gentleman can't earn a living by pegging away at a job. It would be unthinkable."

"Yes, marrying for money is so much more honorable." He bent his head, pressing the cool glass to his forehead.

Oh, Evie, he thought, *if I could do it all again, I'd do it differently. I swear I would.*

"Christian?"

Sylvia's voice interrupted his thoughts, and he lifted his head, turning to face her. "Hmm?"

"I don't want . . ." She paused, looking at him with uncertainty for a long moment before she spoke again. "I shouldn't ever want you to marry someone you're not fond of."

"Fond?" he choked. "God, what a horrible word."

"I would like you to marry again, it's true, but it would grieve me if doing so were to make you unhappy. Fondness can grow into love, you know. I wish you could believe that."

Her voice was tentative now, conciliatory, and he knew his sister was offering up an olive branch. He also knew he'd take it. Her rosy view of marriage was due to the fact that although she and Roger had married for material considerations on both sides, she'd grown to love her husband. He'd never had the chance to love Evie. No, he corrected himself at once, he'd had the chance. He just hadn't taken it.

"Christian?" Sylvia's voice broke the silence. "I could change my passage and stay longer. I'm booked on the *Atlantic* tonight because I'm supposed to attend Rumsford's wedding. It's aboard ship."

"A most unusual choice for a ceremony."

"Rumor has it the bride wanted the wedding in London, not New York, but that Rumsford is too embarrassed about the match for such a public display. She's very New Money, I understand."

"I'm not surprised he's embarrassed," Christian countered with derision. "He's that sort. What does surprise me is that a member of our family actually received an invitation."

"Well, you and Rummy were at school together. And his sister Maude and I, the same."

"That's not why. You're a valuable connection for the girl, that's why."

"Possibly. But I don't have to go. I can express my regrets and stay here with you. Introduce you about and . . . and such."

"Hope springs eternal," he murmured wryly.

"That doesn't alter the fact that I know a great many people here in New York, and you don't. Even if all you intend to do is conduct business, I can still assist you. And besides," she added with an irrepressible smile, "American girls *are* uncommonly pretty. If by some chance, you happened to fall in love with one of them, you could make her your wife and keep your principles intact at the same time."

"I already had a wife. One wife. And she died. There won't be another."

"Evie's death was not your fault. It was only because she lost the baby—"

"There won't be another," he repeated. "And we won't discuss it again, Sylvia."

She studied his face for a long moment, then she nodded. "All right. Shall you see me off on the boat then?"

"Of course. What time do you sail?"

"Half past five."

He glanced at the clock on the mantel. "Plenty of time for a spot of lunch and a long visit. Shall we dine here? I understand the Waldorf has this smashing salad, something with apples and celery."

She made a face. "After what you've told me, I'm not sure we can afford lunch at the Waldorf. In fact, I'm not sure you can afford to stay here, either. Perhaps you should go to the Windermeres' after all? It would be less expensive."

"Only in some ways, Sylvia. As for what we can afford, we're so far in debt, a few weeks at the Waldorf won't make a damned bit of difference. Shall we go down, or have our meal sent up? They can do that here—room service, they call it."

Before she could answer, there was a knock on the door.

"Good Lord," Christian muttered. "My rooms are

as lively today as the Doncaster Races. If that's room service, I shall have to compliment the management on their perspicacity."

McIntyre entered from the bedroom. "Are ye in, sir?" he asked, pausing beside Christian.

He glanced at his sister. "If it's any young American woman with a mother tagging along, then no, I am not in."

McIntyre, a long-faced Scot with no sense of humor, simply bowed. "Verra good, sir."

Christian and Sylvia waited in the sitting room, which was obscured from the door by a painted Oriental screen, as McIntyre answered the knock. There was a low murmur of voices, then the door closed and McIntyre reappeared, a card in his hand.

"A Mr. Ransom to see you, Your Grace. He requests a few moments, if you are free?"

"Ransom?" he echoed in surprise. "Arthur Ransom? Show him in," he added as his valet nodded confirmation.

"Arthur Ransom is Annabel Wheaton's uncle," Sylvia murmured as McIntyre started back toward the door. "The girl we talked about, the heiress Rumsford is marrying. Why does her uncle want to see you?"

"I have no idea," he answered, and stepped forward to greet the lawyer as he was shown in. "Mr. Ransom, this is a welcome surprise." He gestured to Sylvia, who had moved to stand beside him. "Are you acquainted with my sister, Lady Sylvia Shaw?"

"I haven't yet had the pleasure." Mr. Ransom smiled,

then he took up Sylvia's hand and kissed it, making no effort to conceal his admiration. "Pleased to make your acquaintance."

"And I yours, Mr. Ransom," she answered. "Your niece is to marry Lord Rumsford, I understand, and the earl was kind enough to include me among the invited—"

She stopped, for there was no mistaking Ransom's grimace at the mention of his niece's upcoming wedding. Always sensitive to such nuances, Sylvia changed the subject at once. "Would you care for tea?" she asked, gesturing to the tray on the table.

"Thank you, ma'am, but tea's something I've never been able to cotton much to. Besides, this isn't really a social call, I'm afraid. I've come to see your brother on matter of business. That is," he added, turning to Christian, "if you're interested, Your Grace?"

"Of course," he answered, slanting a glance at his sister.

Sylvia took her cue.

"I shall leave the two of you to your discussions," she said, reaching for her handbag, "and I shall toddle off to pack. I look forward to seeing you aboard ship, Mr. Ransom. Christian, I'll send my maid to tell you when I'm ready to depart?"

He nodded, and with that, Sylvia left the suite, allowing him to give the American his full attention. "Shall we sit down?" he asked, and gestured Ransom toward Sylvia's vacated settee. Once the other man was seated, he started back over to the liquor cabinet. "Would you care for a drink? There's quite a fine Scotch whiskey here, a tolerable Irish—"

"If there's bourbon, count me in."

"Bourbon?" He rummaged a bit amid the glass decanters. "Hmm, I don't—"

"Allow me, sir," McIntyre interjected, stepping from behind the screen where he had just closed the door after Sylvia. The valet crossed the room to take his master's place at the liquor cabinet, leaving Christian to resume his own seat.

"Your visit intrigues me, Mr. Ransom, I confess," he said as he sat down.

"I hoped it would." The lawyer paused a moment as if thinking out precisely what he wanted to say, then he went on, "As you already know, my niece is set to marry Lord Rumsford six days from now. I'm a pretty observant man, Your Grace, and from what I could tell last night, I think it's safe to say that you and the earl aren't exactly friends."

"Put it that way if you like," Christian said cheerfully, leaning back in his seat. "You might also say we loathe each other to the core. That would be a less polite, but more precise description."

"Then you and I have something in common."

"Indeed?"

Ransom plucked his glass of bourbon from the tray McIntyre presented to him and downed a hefty swallow. "I can't stand him, either. Looking down his nose, giving me that little smirk every time I see him, acting like he's doing us all a favor by marrying my niece. Goddamn, it gets my back up." As if to demonstrate that point, he set his glass down on the table between them with enough force to rattle the tea things.

"So we agree that Rumsford is an ass," Christian replied, reaching for his own glass. "Rum luck for you, since he's about to become a member of your family. I fear your Christmas dinners will prove deuced awkward from now on."

"Which is why I'm here. I think you might be just the person to help me avoid that calamity."

Christian hoped he was not about to be subjected to more matchmaking schemes, but to be on the safe side, his brain began crafting polite but emphatic statements about his aversion to matrimony. "While it would delight me to see Rumsford set down a notch or two, I don't really see how I can assist you."

"I'm hoping you can stop her from marrying him."

He stared at the other man, astonished. "My good man, I've no cause to do so. If you somehow think I do, by breach of promise, or something along those lines, then you are quite mistaken. I've never even met Miss Wheaton, much less—"

"I'll pay you half a million dollars."

Christian nearly dropped his drink.

Ransom had the good sense to stop talking and let the offer speak for itself. Christian took a hefty swallow of whiskey, calculated the exchange rate, and took another drink. "I'm listening. How could I not with that much money on the table?"

"The amount I'm willing to pay shows you just how desperate I'm getting. I've done everything I can think of, but it's all been useless. Annabel just won't see reason."

"Is she of age?"

"She's twenty-five."

"Old enough to legally marry without your permission."

"Yes. But per the terms of her daddy's will, she doesn't gain control of her money until she's thirty, or until she marries. I'm one of her trustees, along with her stepfather, George Chumley, and another lawyer by the name of William Bentley. Two of the three trustees have to approve her marriage if she's under thirty. Bentley knows he'd better stay on Annabel's good side, unless he wants to be booted out after she's married and in control of her own money. And Chumley just can't bear to refuse his permission. He's known Annabel since she was knee-high to a grasshopper, and he never could say no to that child, especially now he's married to her mama. I'm the one holding out. I've tried to persuade Annabel to take more time and have a longer engagement, but the more I talk, the more she digs in her heels. Annabel can be mighty stubborn."

Studying the other man's hard, determined countenance, Christian found it easy to see from which side of her family Miss Wheaton had inherited her stubbornness. "Rumsford is urging a wedding straightaway?"

"No," he conceded with reluctance, "I wouldn't say that. He's mired in debts, but I'm told his creditors aren't pressing too hard yet. But he also doesn't see any reason to wait, and Annabel doesn't, either. I tried to tell her he's just after her for her money, but . . ." He gave a heavy sigh. "That didn't go over too well."

"I'm not surprised. Telling a woman that a man wants her only for her money conveys the implication that she is undesirable otherwise."

"Exactly. And Annabel doesn't seem to care about his debts. She feels it doesn't matter since she's got so much money. Besides, she says, all you peers have debts."

"Which is true, alas." He paused, thinking of last night. "What about women?"

"I set private detectives on him, and told her about his past mistresses, but that didn't bother her much, either. And if he's catting around now, he's not providing me with any proof that would convince Annabel."

"Is she in love with him?"

"She says she's fond of him." Ransom made a sound of derision. "I ask you, is that enough reason to marry somebody?"

"Some people say it is." He took a drink. "I have sympathy for your predicament, but I'm not quite sure what you think I can do to resolve it."

"Before I came, I did some asking around about you. Lots of rumors floating around."

Christian's hand tightened around his glass. "That sounds ominous. What is being said nowadays? My sister doesn't keep me informed of the gossip about me, I'm afraid."

"They say you have quite a way with women when you choose to, although you don't often choose to, at least not when it comes to marriage-minded women."

He lifted his glass in acknowledgment. "For once rumors have festered into facts," he murmured, and took a drink.

"They say you married for money a long time ago, a rich American girl, not someone of your own class. They say she was unhappy afterward, so unhappy that she . . ."

"Go on," he urged in a hard voice when the other man paused. "Don't stop now. What else do *they* say?"

"They say she was so unhappy she killed herself."

He sucked in his breath, surprised. Even now, even after twelve years, it still hurt. Like a blow to the chest, or a knife through the heart. He swallowed the last of his whiskey, put his glass aside, and stood up. "You really shouldn't listen to gossip. Good day, Mr. Ransom."

The other man didn't move to leave. "I don't know if any of that's true," he said, looking up at Christian, "but I know I don't want my niece to ever be that unhappy."

"Be damned to you. What have I to do with who your niece marries? It's not my business. And if you think waving money in my face will impel me to make it my business, you're mistaken. Some things can't be bought. But buying a title is easy, and if your niece is rich enough to do so, why not let her?"

"We weren't always rich. Her mama—my sister—

and I grew up poor. So did her daddy and her stepdaddy. We all lived in the same small town in Mississippi. Jack Wheaton always was a no-account wanderer, and my sister finally had to divorce him for it. He happened on a gold mine seven years ago and struck it rich, but that was just pure, dumb luck. He died right after, and left it all to Annabel even though he hadn't seen her since she was a little girl. As for me, I'm a country lawyer, self-taught. My daddy was a sharecropper, and my sister and I were raised in a tin-roof shack—Annabel was born in that shack. We're plenty rich now, but Anna-bel didn't even own a store-bought dress until she was fourteen. There's a term down South for people like us. We're known as poor white trash. The money didn't change that, but Annabel thinks marrying an earl will do what her money can't."

"It sounds as if she knows what she wants. And many people do marry for considerations other than love. You don't strike me as a romantic sort of fellow. If she doesn't care about marrying for love, why should you?"

"Because I care about her! Annabel has never been to England, never been around anybody English until she met Rumsford, and I don't think she understands just what living the sort of life you people lead really means. I don't, either, not really, but you do." He shot Christian a shrewd glance across the table. "I think you know better than most what's waiting for Annabel if she marries Rumsford. I'd like you to sit her down and explain it to her."

Christ. Christian gave a sigh and sat back down, reminding himself he couldn't afford to snub men with money. "Let me see if I understand you. You want me to strike up an acquaintance with your niece, tell her about my own experience, and persuade her that people who marry out of their class and without mutual love end up unhappy. Is that your idea?"

"Pretty much."

"I do believe you're serious. My good man, the intimacies of marriage are hardly a topic I can discuss with a young lady. It's not proper."

"You don't strike me as the sort of man who worries much about things like that."

"Are you being disingenuous, or do you truly not see the point? I can't discuss these things with her in front of others. I'd have to be alone with her."

"As long as you behave like a gentleman, I don't see a problem. Lord knows, I'm paying you enough to make behaving yourself worthwhile. Now, if I hear otherwise . . ." He paused and smiled, the benign face suddenly ruthless. "Not only will you not get paid, I'll shoot you dead."

"A useful thing to know, but that still isn't my point. If anyone saw us together, if anything were misinterpreted, I would be obligated to marry her, something I will not do."

Ransom gave a decisive snort. "Lord, I hope not! That'd be like trading a toothless horse for a lame one."

Christian didn't know whether to be relieved or insulted by that. "And if this doesn't work? If I can't talk her out of it?"

"You don't get paid, and I'll have to start boning up on annulment and divorce law in case I'm right about that fella."

Christian considered. "I only have six days? That's cutting it rather close."

"I'll pay you even if all you can get her to do is postpone it a few months. I just want her to take some more time, be sure she knows what she's getting into. Maybe tour around England, make some friends there, see for herself what it would be like to live in your world. If after that, she still wants to marry Rumsford, I'll . . ." He paused, frowning, and reached for his glass to take another drink. "I'll accept it."

"How do you know you can trust me? I married one girl for money. I could do it again. If I stained her reputation on purpose, I'd have the perfect excuse to marry her myself and I'd gain control of her money."

"There's a marital settlement, limiting Rumsford to a fixed annual sum. You'd get no better. Annabel may be stubborn, but she's got plenty of business sense. In fact, that's a big part of her trouble. She's thinking of this more like a business deal than a marriage. As for you, I've heard that you've said many times you'll never marry again, and though women never believe it, a man who says that usually means it. And if a rich American wife was what you were after, you'd never have passed up the chance to meet Hiram's girl, who's a beauty and even richer than Annabel."

"I can see you've thought this through."

"I have. Half a million dollars is enough to give you the capital for those investments you want, so you don't have to marry anybody for money. And if you want advice on American investments, I'd be happy to oblige. I've done a pretty fair job with Annabel's investments over the years."

Christian couldn't help admiring the other man's thoroughness. "There's still the risk someone will see me with her. Even if all we are doing is talking, if there's no chaperone present, it could still stain her reputation."

Ransom sighed. "I know, but I'm running out of options. And I say a tainted reputation is still better than a lifetime of misery with a man who doesn't love her and who's only after her money."

Those words jerked Christian to his feet. Walking to the window, he stared out again at the traffic, but in his mind, he didn't see Fifth Avenue or the faint reflection of his own face in the glass. He saw instead London's May Day Charity Ball, and a blond girl in a blue silk dress, a shy girl with a pretty smile and a sweet, terrible innocence, and guilt felt like a ten-ton weight on his shoulders.

Evie, I'm sorry. He touched his fingers to the glass, wishing he could touch her face, wipe away her tears, do it all again a different way. *I'm so damned sorry.*

He squeezed his eyes shut. If he could stop another girl from making Evie's mistake, perhaps—

He turned around. "You're sure Rumsford doesn't love her?"

"I'm sure."

He nodded slowly, for he was sure of it, too. Fortune hunters always recognized one of their own. "All right," he said. "I'll do what I can."

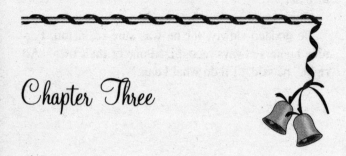

Chapter Three

Christian decided not to tell Sylvia he was hiring himself out as an obstacle to transatlantic marriage. She would never approve, even if the girl's own uncle was paying him an enormous amount of money to do it. No, she'd nag him about the propriety and the moral implications—interfering, risking a girl's reputation, that sort of thing—and she'd bring up again how much better it would be to find an heiress of his own. Clearly, keeping mum was his best option.

But when he told Sylvia he was returning to England straightaway so that he and Arthur could further discuss business on the ship and in London, her pleased little smile told him she still held out hope for his eventual capitulation in the matter of finding a wife. After all, there would be many heiresses in London for the season.

His sister was probably composing a list of possible candidates this very minute, he thought as he stood on the balcony of the stateroom suite they were sharing aboard the *Atlantic*.

While he was enjoying the beautiful late afternoon sunshine and watching the pier recede into the distance as a tugboat pulled the *Atlantic* out into New York Harbor, Sylvia was inside, supervising her maid and his valet in the unpacking of their things, and thinking of pretty faces, considering various names, and tabulating possible dowries.

To say his sister was mercenary wasn't quite fair, he reflected, turning to stare out across the harbor toward Staten Island. She was simply the product of her upbringing. Marriage without an appropriate alliance was unthinkable for people of their class. A hundred years ago, alliance meant the accumulation of lands and the preservation of the aristocratic bloodlines, but nowadays, it was all about survival. The land rents their ancestors had lived on were drying up in the face of agricultural depression and technological advancement, and for the past few generations of British gentlemen, marrying a girl with a fat dowry was as inevitable as a public school education and a tour of the Continent. He, like most men of his class, had been raised to think it perfectly acceptable, even honorable, to secure the future of the family estate by marrying money, without much regard for things like love and affection.

If Evie hadn't died, he'd probably think that way

still. But her death had revealed to him the sordid consequences that could result from such arrangements, and any notions he'd been stuffed with that marrying a girl for money was an honorable course had died with her.

"Sir?"

He turned to find his valet behind him in the open doorway. "Yes, McIntyre, what is it?"

"There's some confusion about Your Grace's things. Her Ladyship is insisting that you shall need two suits of evening clothes during the voyage as well as your customary wardrobe. I explained that the private card rooms aboard ship do not require formal evening dress, but Lady Sylvia . . ." His voice trailed off tactfully.

"I understand," he said, appreciating the vital point. "When Sylvia gets a bee in her bonnet, there's no arguing with her. If you don't pull out two tuxedos, she'll do it for you. Besides," he added, "in this case, she's right. I doubt I shall be much engaged in cards during this voyage."

To McIntyre's credit, he showed no reaction to this most unexpected development beyond a slight raising of his fiery red eyebrows. "Verra good, sir," he said, and returned inside to accede to Lady Sylvia's wishes, and Christian returned his attention to the view from his balcony.

Leaning forward, he rested his forearms on the rail and looked back toward the stern where the enormous Statue of Liberty could now be seen. A fitting symbol for its host, he decided, for it rose up out of Bedloe's Island like a resounding shriek of triumph—a bold, brash statement for a bold, brash country. From here, he could also make out Ellis Island, where the immigrants came in to embark upon a new life. America was a country bursting with vitality and hope. England seemed like such a tired jade by comparison, and he wondered, not for the first time, why these American girls were so ready to leave their exciting homeland to live in a place of interminable boredom, where everyone, including him, got through their endless days in a state of perpetual ennui.

The door directly below him banged open, interrupting his contemplations, and a voice floated up to his ears, an unmistakably female voice. "Dinah? Dinah, where are you?"

American, he knew at once, American and Southern. Strange how that voice seemed to underscore his very thoughts, for despite its slow and drawling cadence, it managed to convey far more energy than Christian's clipped and proper British accents ever could. It reminded him of Arthur Ransom, and Christian wondered if it might perhaps belong to the niece.

He turned from the view of Bedloe's Island to that of the promenade deck below as a feminine figure dressed in buttery yellow wool emerged from the ship's interior. She paused only a few feet in front of him, planted the tip of her ruffled parasol on deck, and rested her white-gloved hand on the carved ebony handle, glancing up and down the promenade, which was nearly empty at this time of day. "Dinah?" she called again. "Oh, Lord," she muttered to herself when there was no answer to her call. "Where has that girl got to now?"

Though her face was hidden beneath her hat, an enormous, frothy confection of yellow straw, white feathers, and black and yellow ribbons, nothing blocked the rest of her from Christian's sight, and he was able to indulge in a long and appreciative study of her figure. If these hourglass curves did indeed belong to Miss Annabel Wheaton, and if she had a face to go with that body, then it was no surprise Rumsford had gone after her instead of an equally wealthy girl from the Knickerbocker set. On the other hand, she seemed willing to settle for Rummy quite gladly, so how pretty could she be?

The door banged again and the young woman below looked back over her shoulder. "There you are at last!" she exclaimed as a girl about ten years old came into view, her age evidenced not only by her more diminutive stature, but also by the shorter length of her skirt, the sailor motif of her dress, and the fact that her dark hair was not put up. It hung to her shoulders, prevented from tangling in the ocean breeze by the curl-brimmed boater hanging down her back.

"I've been looking everywhere for you," the woman in yellow went on. "Where have you been?"

"Exploring. Did you know they have a sweet shop on board?" The girl pulled a lollipop out of her skirt pocket. "Just down there," she added, flourishing the candy toward the aft end of the ship's cabins.

"So that's what you've been doing all day while the rest of us have been unpacking your things for you? Exploring the ship and buying sweets with your pocket money? Eating them all, too, I'll bet, and spoiling your supper."

The girl paused in her task of unwrapping the candy from its red paper covering. "You won't tell Mama, will you?"

"Tell her what?" The woman in yellow tilted her head as she asked the question, giving Christian a brief, tantalizing glimpse of delicate throat and jaw, but not much else. "Am I supposed to tell Mama something?"

Dinah laughed and stuck the lollipop in her mouth. "I love you, Nan."

The older girl sniffed, not seeming particularly impressed by this declaration of affection from the younger one, who was clearly a sister. "If you love me, then kindly act like you got some raisin', Dinah Louise, and take that candy out of your mouth when you're talkin' to me."

The younger girl pulled out the lollipop long enough to drawl a rather impudent-sounding "Yes, ma'am," and earned herself a hard jab in the ribs from her sister's elbow. "Ow!"

"Do you still have that map the purser gave you when we came aboard?" the woman asked. "Get it out so I can have a look."

Dinah shoved the lollipop back in her mouth and reached into her pocket. She pulled out the requested document and unfolded it, and side by side, their backs to Christian, each holding one side to keep it from being carried away by the stiff ocean breeze, they studied the map.

"What's this?" The woman reached up between them, tapping the handle of her parasol against the map, then she bent her head to read the minuscule print. "A Turkish bath. My, that sounds exotic, doesn't it? I wonder what it is."

"I know!" her sister said and once again removed the lollipop from her mouth. "I saw it earlier. A maid was there putting out towels, and she told me all about it. It's a tiled room with big radiators and no windows, and they fill it up with steam."

"No water?"

Dinah shook her head. "No, just steam, because it's not really a bath. There's no tub or anything, just big wicker chairs you sit in."

"But if it's not a bath, then why do they call it that? What's it for?"

"It's supposed to make you sweat, so that you . . . release unhealthy toxins from your body." She said the last part with care, as if to repeat what she'd been told as precisely as possible. "The maid said it's supposed to be relaxin'. Some people, she said, even fall asleep."

"That's all there is to it?" Her sister sounded a bit disappointed. "You just sit in a hot, steamy room and sweat and fall asleep? What's so special about that?

Why, we can have baths like that back home in Goose-neck Bend just by goin' to church in the summertime!"

Christian gave a shout of laughter, but fortunately for him, the sound was drowned out by the blare of trumpets announcing that dinner would commence in one hour, and because of that, neither of the young ladies below perceived they had an eavesdropper.

Dinah seemed to think what her sister had said was as amusing as he did. "I don't think it's like church, Nan," she said, giggling. "You're supposed to be naked, the maid told me. Nobody goes to church naked, do they?"

"Unfortunately not," Christian murmured under his breath, studying the shapely backside of the woman in yellow.

"What do you mean, Dinah?" she asked in lively astonishment. "You don't mean completely naked, do you?" As if realizing she'd raised her voice with that question, she glanced around to be sure no one was within earshot, but fortunately for Christian, she didn't glance up as she looked over her shoulder. Mistakenly reassured by the empty deck that no one was listening, she resumed discussion of the somewhat salacious topic of Turkish baths. "No clothes at all?" she asked, lowering her voice again. "Not even your unmention-ables?"

Dinah shrugged. "You might be able to keep those on, I suppose. The maid said 'unclothed,' so I think that means naked. C'mon," she added, jamming the lolli-pop in her mouth and pulling the map from her sister's fingers. She began refolding it as she started toward the door leading back inside. "That was the dinner bell. We have to dress or Mama will tan both our backsides."

She returned the map to her pocket and shoved open the door, but then paused as she realized her sister wasn't following. "Aren't you coming, Nan?"

The woman shook her head and walked away toward the starboard rail, staring out over the view of Staten Island in the distance. "You go on," she called back. "I want to stay out here a little bit longer."

Dinah departed. Christian, however, remained right where he was. He watched as the woman lifted her arms to pull out her hat pin and remove her hat, a move that only served to better show off the perfection of her figure. A shame if this was indeed Miss Wheaton, for such exquisite curves should never be wasted on a husband like Rumsford, for he would never appreciate them. Did she know that? Did she care?

He'd concluded the other night when he knew nothing about her that she must be one of those sweet, biddable girls who did what she was told, but after talking to Ransom, he knew there wasn't anything sweet or biddable about her. She seemed to have a mind of her own, and a will that didn't bend to anyone else's, not even her nearest and dearest. She was also, if her uncle was any judge, intelligent, with heaps of money, a voice like warm honey, and a body that was—obviously—splendid. So why would a girl with all that in her favor settle for Rumsford? Arthur's explanations didn't quite satisfy him.

She might be plain, of course. In the ruthless marriage marts of New York and London, a plain girl without connections had a devil of a time landing a titled husband, even if she were wealthy as Croesus. Miss Wheaton had probably taken a good, long look in the mirror, faced facts, and decided Rumsford was the best she could do.

"Annabel?"

She turned at the sound confirming her identity, and as she tilted her head back to look at the woman who had called to her from a balcony near his own, Christian stared at her upturned face and realized with some chagrin that he'd been wrong, utterly and completely wrong.

The girl was gorgeous.

With her hat off, her hair gleamed in the late afternoon sun, turning it from chestnut brown to deep, flaming red. She possessed the pale, luminous complexion that usually accompanied hair of that shade, though he couldn't tell from here if her eyes were the usual redhead's green. Nor could he discern if any freckles dotted her nose, but he could see that it was a nose so retroussé that one might call it impudent. Her mouth was lush and pink, with a wide, brilliant smile that made even Christian's jaded, supposedly nonexistent heart stop for just a second.

This was Rummy's fiancée? This vibrant, vivid, luscious creature was engaged to that stiff, pompous ass? It was absurd, nonsensical, one of Nature's great jokes.

"Yes, Mama?" She lifted her hat to shade her eyes

from the sun, a move that shadowed her face and prevented him from any further scrutiny, but Christian knew he hadn't conjured that face out of his imagination.

"Annabel Mae," the woman called down. "Put on your hat, young lady, and put up your parasol! Sakes alive, do you want to get freckles? And what are you still doing down there? It's less than an hour until suppertime. You've got to change."

"I know, Mama," Annabel called back, tucking her parasol under her arm long enough to don her hat and slide in her hat pin. "I'll be up in a few minutes. I promise."

She turned her back, returning her attention to the view of Staten Island and giving Christian the chance to draw a deep breath and comprehend what seemed incomprehensible.

He thought of Rumsford the other night—of his flushed face and naughty-naughty English manner as he'd winked and smirked about having a tryst with a courtesan. At the time, Christian had found Rummy's adolescent behavior both amusing and a bit repugnant, but now as he looked at Miss Wheaton's hourglass curves and thought of her stunning face, he began to understand why the fellow was visiting courtesans. Any man engaged to this woman was bound to spend most of his time prior to the wedding night in a state of acute desperation. Did she realize it? he wondered.

Christian studied her back a moment longer, considering, then he straightened away from the rail, smoothed his tie, and buttoned his jacket. It was time to meet the bride.

Annabel had never been on a ship before. The closest thing to it had been a rickety rowboat on Goose Creek, and that rowboat, along with about half a dozen more, would fit inside one of the lifeboats that hung along the sides of the *Atlantic*, with room to spare.

This luxurious ocean liner was as unlike that old rowboat as a ship could be, and she was a long way from being the girl who used to row along Goose Creek and lay catfish bites. But she still wasn't far enough away. Not yet.

The correct prenuptial agreements had been drawn up and signed, much to Uncle Arthur's chagrin. The final wedding arrangements had been made, her dress was pressed and ready, the flowers and the cake were in the refrigerated section of the ship's stores, and the names on the guest list included Maimie Paget and Virginia Vanderbilt.

Six days from now, she'd be a countess. Seven days from now, she'd step off this ship and into a whole new life. She'd be Lady Rumsford, and she'd live on an estate older than her country. Once married, she'd have control of her money, and she'd be able to do so many wonderful things with it. She'd run charities and help with the village school and hospital. She'd help Bernard return Rumsford Castle to the grand estate it had once been, and together, they would hold those lavish parties and balls of which her lawyers so heartily disapproved. Her children would have crumpets and Cornish pasties and English Christmas, just like in a Dickens story. More important, her children would have position and the respect that came with it.

Uncle Arthur didn't quite see it all the way she did, but that was because he had this notion to protect her. What he didn't understand was that she didn't need protecting. She knew what she was getting into, which was why she let all her uncle's arguments roll off her back like water off a duck. Every single thing that Uncle Arthur saw as a flaw in Bernard, she saw as just right.

Yes, he was sort of dull, no denying it. But that was fine with her. A dull man was safe and predictable and easy to manage. Her friend Jennie Carter had married a French marquess, and from what Jennie had written, married women in Europe had far more freedom than married women in America. Here, a woman managed her home and not much else, but over there, a married woman was free to manage near anything she wanted, just as long as she could manage one thing: her husband. Annabel intended to do just that.

And yes, Bernard had already had a mistress or two, but that was long before he'd met her. It wasn't as if she didn't have some peccadilloes in her own past.

She also knew Bernard wouldn't have asked her to marry him if she were poor. Poor girls from no-account families didn't get to marry the boys from the good families. She'd learned that lesson the hard way.

Marry you? Billy John's incredulous voice echoed through her mind from eight years ago, as clear as if it had all happened yesterday. It didn't hurt now, but she vividly remembered how much it hurt then. She couldn't change her past, but she had damn well been able to learn from it.

She wasn't in love with Bernard, and she hoped to God she would never be in love again. Girls in love were silly, and they made stupid, silly mistakes. She was a woman now, one whose eyes were wide open, and she was just fine with the way things had turned out. Bernard was offering her something more important than love, something she'd been seeking all her life: respect. There was no way she was turning that down.

A whole new world was about to open up. She'd have a husband and children to care for, and a house—castle, really—to manage. Her money would be in her control, and she had heaps of plans for what to do with it. Hospitals and orphanages and schools where poor girls could learn a trade. Yes, she was fair bursting with ideas, and she felt as if life was just beginning. She couldn't wait to get started.

A loud, exuberant whistle interrupted her thoughts and Annabel turned her head to see a ship every bit as grand as the *Atlantic* approaching the harbor from the open sea, black smoke spilling from its bright red smokestacks. To her, it was a magnificent sight, for these big ocean liners spoke of adventure and exotic far-off places that she couldn't wait to see. London would be first, of course, and then the rest of England. After that, Bernard had promised to show her Europe and Egypt, maybe even the Orient. A bubble of excitement rose up inside her, and she laughed out loud, anticipating all the wonderful things that lay ahead.

"Best not to stand there, Miss Wheaton."

She turned at the sound of her name. A man she'd never seen in her life before stood in the doorway that led to the first class cabins of A-deck, one shoulder propped against the jamb in a negligent pose, hands in his trouser pockets, watching her. His lean face, handsome in a dark and wild sort of way, was unfamiliar to her.

She frowned, puzzled. "Do I know you?"

He flashed her a grin. "Would you like to?"

Annabel stiffened. She wasn't unaccustomed to men who got fresh—she'd dealt with men like that plenty of times in the days before society and chaperones, men who thought they could take advantage of a girl.

"No, I wouldn't," she answered and turned her back, leaning out over the rail again to resume watching the approaching ship.

"I don't blame you a jot," he said, sounding not the least bit perturbed by her snub. "There are many people who know me who wish they didn't. Still, I have been on enough ocean liners to know you're better off inside with me than you are out there."

"I doubt it," she shot back, for she had no intention of putting herself in closer proximity to him than she already was, but when he didn't speak again, she couldn't help glancing over her shoulder, curious to see if he was still in the doorway.

He was, of course, and she watched as he leaned forward to glance at the approaching ship. "Best move quickly, love," he advised, straightening to look at her again. "You don't have much time. Two minutes at most, I'd say."

Despite his elegant clothes and well-bred voice, Annabel just knew this man was trouble. She could feel it, and when he shot her an inquiring glance and turned sideways in the doorway, beckoning her to join him in the corridor, she didn't move.

He sighed. "You're a very untrusting sort of girl, aren't you? I can see I shall have to better elucidate my point."

Stepping over the steel lip that protected the interior of the ship from any incoming water, he started across the promenade deck toward her as the cabin door swung shut behind him. With a hint of alarm, she glanced around, but there wasn't another person in sight. So as he approached, she faced him, lifting her parasol and pointing its tip at the place that would hurt him the most. "Come any closer, sugar, and you'll have to become a Catholic priest."

He stopped, staring down at where the metal tip of her parasol grazed his trousers, but when he looked up at her, he was smiling a little, a faint smile of amusement that tilted the corners of his vivid, gray-blue eyes and curved the edges of his mouth. "A fate worse than death," he murmured. "Celibacy, I fear, wouldn't suit me."

He moved to stand at the rail beside her, careful to maintain the distance set by her parasol, and reached into the breast pocket of his jacket. He pulled out a silver case, and from it, he extracted a cigarette and a match. He put the cigarette to his lips, returned the case to his pocket, and struck the match on the ocean-corroded rail beside him.

"Wind's coming southeast," he said, cupping his hand around the flame to light the cigarette. Tossing the match overboard, he pulled the cigarette from between his lips, tilted his head back and exhaled, sending a cloud of smoke upward. It caught on the breeze and broke apart, wispy remnants that sailed over his head toward the door he'd just exited. "See?"

She saw the smoke, but didn't see the point. What did it matter which direction the wind was blowing? "Do you do this all the time?" she demanded instead, taking the offensive. "Corner women when they're alone?"

"At every possible opportunity." He seemed unashamed by the admission. "But at this moment, I'm actually attempting to be chivalrous."

She made a sound of derision. "In a pig's eye."

"Have it your way." He took another pull on the cigarette, then flicked it overboard and glanced again at the approaching ship before he turned away. "You now have about fifteen seconds," he told her over his shoulder as he retraced his steps, resumed his place, and settled one shoulder against the open door to keep it propped wide. "At that point, the smashing Worth creation you're wearing will be utterly ruined, but it's your choice."

Comprehension dawned, and with an alarmed glance at the ship now directly to starboard and the black smuts pouring from its smokestacks, Annabel raced for the doorway. The man took several steps back, fingertips holding the door open for her, and she followed him inside. The door had barely closed behind them before a thick, black cloud poured over the promenade right where they'd been standing. She watched it through the door's pane of window glass, and she could only imagine how awful her beautiful yellow dress would look now, had she remained out on deck.

"That was a near shave, wasn't it?" he murmured behind her, his voice near to her ear.

Though he was not touching her, Annabel was acutely aware of how close he was to her. His body seemed to emanate heat she could feel even through her clothes, the kind of heat she hadn't felt for eight years, the kind of heat that fired up a girl from the inside out, flared out of control, and left her as scorched and empty as a burnt-out shack.

She would have hightailed it out of there as fast as she could, but for the moment there was nowhere to go. So she turned around, met his eyes, and kept a firm grip on her parasol, just in case it was needed again.

"Beastly stuff, coal dust," he murmured. "It penetrates right through your clothes and puts a dingy film on your skin." His lashes, thick and straight and as black as the soot he was discussing, lowered as he cast a glance over her, and the heat radiating through her body flooded into her face. She recognized that look. It was the same one Billy John always had, that slow, sliding sort of glance that could make her weak in the knees.

"In fact," he went on, returning his gaze to her face, still smiling a little, "I doubt even the steam of a Turkish bath would do the trick."

Those words doused her susceptibility to hot looks from heartbreakers as effectively as a flood of water doused a fire. "You were eavesdroppin' on me and my sister?"

"Sorry. Couldn't help it." He pointed directly above their heads. "The balcony of my cabin is right up there."

Annabel glanced up at the ceiling, then back at him, frowning. "That's my uncle's suite."

"It was, yes. Urgent business called me back to England unexpectedly, and because of your wedding, I could not obtain a stateroom in first class. Hearing of my difficulty, Mr. Ransom kindly offered his suite to us and agreed to take my sister's cabin in exchange."

"Uncle Arthur isn't kind, not kind like that, not to strangers."

"Ah, but I'm not a stranger, Miss Wheaton."

"You are to me, and how do you know my name?"

"I know your fiancé," he said as if that was an answer to her question. "It's not uncommon for a duke and an earl to know each other."

"You're a duke?" Annabel sniffed, not believing it for a second. Despite his fine suit of clothes, accent, and access to first class, he had a touch of the tar brush about him that seemed at odds with the high and noble rank he claimed. Besides, a duke surely wouldn't eavesdrop on a woman's intimate conversations, and even if he did, he'd never be so uncouth as to mention it to the woman afterward.

"Difficult to imagine, I know." He reached again into his jacket pocket, this time extracting a card. "The Duke of Scarborough, at your service," he said, presenting it to her with a bow.

She hesitated, not taking it. She knew who the Duke of Scarborough was, of course. His sister, Lady Sylvia Shaw, was one of the guests Bernard had included on their invitation list. But she found it hard to believe this man was the brother of a lady like that. Why, he wasn't even wearing gloves, she realized, staring at his long, strong fingers. How could he be a duke? How could he even be a gentleman? A gentleman, she knew, always wore gloves.

With skepticism, Annabel took the card, an elegant one of white linen edged with silver that supported his contention of a ducal title, not that an elegant card meant much. Hers were every bit as fancy as these, but they weren't what would make her a lady.

"Christian Du Ques—" She paused over his surname, sure she was about to make a mistake in the pronunciation, and when she glanced up, his widening smile told her she already had.

"Du-cane," he supplied. "If you intend to embark upon the life of a peeress, you'd best become familiar with the pronunciation of English surnames. Or, to be accurate, French ones. Most of us are of Norman descent, and therefore, French. Your fiancé is an exception, of course. Rummy's stout Saxon stock through and through."

She didn't quite like this nickname for Bernard. "You have me at a disadvantage, sir. You seem to be on very familiar terms with my fiancé and my uncle. But I can't recall ever making your acquaintance myself."

"It is a puzzle," he agreed.

He didn't elaborate, and she frowned, sensing that he was toying with her. "You don't seem very ducal."

"I shall take that as a compliment. And your skepticism is quite understandable. I wasn't supposed to be the duke at all, you see, so it's not surprising that I don't quite suit the role. I was the second son, the spare, the insurance, useless to the family in any other capacity. I have been groomed all my life to gamble, drink, carouse, and taint our good name, and until three months ago, I had been fulfilling that role admirably. Then my brother had the deuced poor judgment to expire and leave me in charge of things." He gave her a look of apology. "It shall be downhill for the Scarboroughs from now on, I daresay."

Annabel didn't know how to reply. His words about his departed brother seemed cruel and his disregard for his rank strangely cavalier. Bernard was very nice to his sisters and took his role as an earl very seriously.

"Though I am a duke," he resumed, "that won't be much use to you if you need any instruction on being a proper countess."

"That's no never mind to me," she countered at once, "since I don't intend to ask you for any instructions. Why should I?"

"In my opinion, you shouldn't. Proper countesses are very dull, and I should hate to see you become one, but it's inevitable, I fear. You see, I know Rummy, and his mother and sisters, too, and I can safely say they won't want you to stay the way you are. They'll want to change you, mold you into what they think you ought to be. They'll work to change the way you dress, the way you move, your voice—"

"What's wrong with my voice?" she demanded, but even as she asked the question, she could hear how she sounded, how *my* became *mah* and *voice* became *vo-iss*, and she stopped, biting her lip in frustration. A month's worth of diction lessons, yet she still couldn't stop drawing out her vowels, especially when she was upset.

"My dear girl, no need to scowl so fiercely," he said in amusement, watching her face. "There is nothing at all wrong with your voice. It's a luscious voice, absolutely splendid."

He was making fun of her. He had to be. Her accent was crude and uncivilized and came from eighteen years in a Mississippi backwater. There was nothing luscious or splendid about that.

"Unfortunately," he went on, "diction lessons will soon be part of your daily schedule, I daresay."

Annabel would have to be whipped within an inch of her life before she'd admit they already were, and at Bernard's request.

"Don't do it." He leaned closer, all trace of amusement vanishing from his face. "I meant what I said. You have a gorgeous voice. It's like warm honey butter oozing down over hot toast. Don't let them change it. Don't let them change you."

Annabel sucked in her breath, taken aback by the sudden fierceness of his voice. In the dim light of the corridor, his eyes seemed to glitter like silver, and they looked directly into hers, seeming to see right through all her attempts to be a lady, finding instead the awkward girl who'd never worn shoes in the summertime because she couldn't afford them. Looking at her as if he would have liked that girl.

A ridiculous notion. He didn't even know her. "I—" She stopped and licked her dry lips, feeling all muddled up. "I don't know what you're talkin' about."

"I think you do," he said. "And I think you want to be changed, which is the saddest part."

"And I think," she said, careful to enunciate her words, "that you are a very rude man."

"Oh, I am," he agreed amiably, "but I just can't resist talking to pretty women. And there's no question you fall into that category."

"What do you hope to gain, giving me compliments this way? I am engaged to be married."

"I know." He looked her over, a slow, lingering glance of regret. "Deuced shame, that."

The heat inside her deepened and spread. Lord, this man's eyes could melt a girl into a puddle. Billy John could take lessons from the likes of him.

She swallowed hard, trying to gather her wits. This was crazy. She'd never met this man in her life before, she knew nothing about him, and yet she knew what he was making her feel. Like she was seventeen again and gloriously unaware she was about to get dumped on her behind by Gooseneck Bend's biggest heartbreaker. This man was a heartbreaker, too, the sort who toyed with a girl like a cat toyed with a mouse and didn't care two bits that she belonged to somebody else. He might be a duke, but he was still trouble, the sort of trouble she never wanted to get tangled up in again.

She forced a smile to her lips, the charming, deceptively sweet smile her lawyers at Cooper, Bentley, and Frye knew very well. "And I suppose that if I weren't already engaged, you'd be interested in forming an acquaintance with me?"

"Love, any man with half a brain and one eye open would want to form an acquaintance with you. And my brain and my eyes function perfectly."

Annabel's smile widened. It was always reassuring to be proved right about a man's bad character, though a bit galling to think she could still find a man like that attractive. "My eyes and my brain work, too, sugar," she purred. "And they can see a man like you comin' from miles away."

If her perceptiveness unnerved him, he didn't show it. Quite the contrary. "Excellent," he said. "Then we both know where we are. A good beginning to our friendship, I think."

She opened her mouth, but before she could assure him there was no beginning and they were not friends, he spoke again. "But we shall have to wait until you've been married a few years before we can renew our acquaintance. The shine'll be off the tiara by then, I expect."

"What do you mean?"

"Well, it always happens." His voice became serious, his flippancy vanished. "You American girls always have these romantic dreams in your heads about marrying a lord and living in a castle, but a year or two after the wedding, you realize just how dreary it is to be married to one of our lot, how painful chilblains are, and how deuced cold a castle can be in December."

Though she might sometimes talk as if she was just off the farm, she wasn't. She might not know what the heck a chilblain was, but she did know a scoundrel when she met one. And she knew just what sort of friendship he had in mind.

"So when I'm married to Rumsford," she drawled, not bothering to curb her Mississippi vowels anymore, not with this man, "and I'm all lonely and homesick, you'll be willing to step in and console my disillusioned little heart?"

"I'd like to."

"Yes, I just bet you would."

Her knowing reply didn't put him off. Instead, it made him grin, a flash of white in a dark, reckless face. "But as I said, we shall have to wait at least several years. Every peer expects his heir to be his, you see, not some other bloke's, so I'm afraid I must valiantly resist your charms until then."

"How noble of you."

"Being noble has nothing to do with it, love. Rummy is one of those hopelessly old-fashioned chaps that might actually call me out for fathering the next Earl Rumsford, and he happens to be a decent shot. I like living too much to take the chance."

Without giving her any opportunity to reply, he spoke again. "Unfortunately for you, he's also as dull as a scullery maid's dishrag. So, when the heir and the spare are safely ensconced in the nursery, and Rumsford has become as boring to you as he is to everyone else, I hope you will call upon me, Miss Wheaton. You'll only have to say hullo in that gorgeous voice of yours," he added with a bow, "and I shall fall at your feet, and into your bed. Rummy, I assure you, won't blink an eye. It's the English way. All part of the rules, you see."

Annabel was torn between rebuking him for his presumptions and asking him what he meant about rules, but he turned away before she could decide which course of action tempted her more. He ducked out of sight around the corner, and a moment later, she could hear the tap of his footsteps as he ascended the stairs that led to the staterooms above.

Just as well, she supposed. Her virtue might be long gone because of a scoundrel just like him, but her reputation was intact, and she intended to keep it that way. Still, she did have to admit to a certain amount of curiosity about some of the things he'd said, and she decided to ask Bernard at the first opportunity. If there were some rules about British marriage she didn't know, it was best to find them out now. A girl like her couldn't afford to make any mistakes.

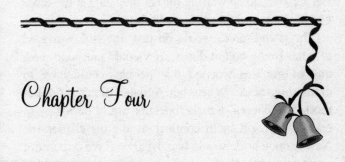

Chapter Four

The grand dining room of the *Atlantic*, a Baroque fantasy of meringuelike plasterwork and faux-marble columns was not only well suited to the formal dinners available for those in first class. It was also, much to Annabel's relief, the perfect setting for her wedding. Three stories high and capped by a skylight dome of stained glass, the room would lend a suitably cathedrallike air to the ceremony.

As Bernard escorted her down the grand staircase for dinner, she couldn't help imagining how it would be when she made this same journey in a cloud of satin and tulle. As she paused with him and her family near the foot of the stairs, waiting for an usher to escort them to their table, she pictured the elaborate bouquets of pink magnolia blossoms as well as the path of rose petals that would pave her way across the royal-blue carpet. Instead of standing beside her as he was now, Bernard would be waiting for her on a dais at the other end of the long, elegant room.

The round tables would do just fine, she was glad to note. Being bolted down, they could not be moved, and Mama had worried that people would have to crane their necks to see, but Annabel didn't share her mother's concern. Knickerbockers would be happy to endure that sort of discomfort on the off chance the New Money bride would trip over her gown or commit some other ghastly faux pas, something they wouldn't want to miss.

Annabel had no intention of obliging them. This was her opportunity to cement a place in society for herself and her family, and she was not going to let anything spoil it.

That thought had barely crossed her mind before she spied the Duke of Scarborough standing about a dozen feet away, and at the sight of his tall, lean body and rakish face, she felt her stomach give a nervous little dip. She hadn't been mistaken about him, she realized. He was every bit as attractive as she'd thought earlier, and, she suspected, every bit as dangerous.

Beside him was a tall, striking brunette whose resemblance to him was so marked, it was clear she must be his sister, Lady Sylvia Shaw. She was talking with a group of acquaintances that included Virginia Vanderbilt and Maimie Paget, and as Annabel watched, she couldn't help admiring the easy familiarity and animation the other woman displayed. Annabel was always so worried about pronouncing her vowels correctly or saying the wrong thing, that it was easier to speak very little around the Knickerbocker dragon ladies and leave them to do most of the talking. The duke's sister no doubt had the same sort of voice as her brother and Bernard, the voice of an aristocrat, the sort of voice that instantly garnered respect, the sort of voice that was never subject to ridicule. If only she could learn to talk like that . . .

She returned her gaze to Scarborough, and as she did, his words of that afternoon flashed through her mind.

Don't let them change you.

The intensity of his gaze as he'd spoken those words still surprised her. Why should he care? He didn't even know her. And how on earth could he think she had a nice voice? It had a twang in it as wide as the Mississippi. But he thought it was like warm honey butter oozing down over hot toast.

Annabel felt a sudden rush of heat, the same sort of heat she'd felt with him a short while ago, and though she willed herself to stop it, the duke chose that moment to look up.

As if sensing her scrutiny, he glanced past his companions and saw her. Murmuring something to his sister and the others in his immediate circle, he started toward her, and Annabel felt a jolt of panic, not only because the look in those eyes was just too unsettling for a girl's peace of mind, but also because she and Scarborough had never been introduced. She'd pored over enough etiquette books during the past seven years to know it wasn't proper for a man to approach a woman before he'd been given a formal introduction, and she suspected this man was outrageous enough to defy propriety.

She tensed as he came closer, prepared to deny any claim he might make to having already met her, but she needn't have worried. Though he gave an acknowledging nod to Rumsford, he walked right past her without a glance, and held out his hand to her uncle Arthur.

Chagrined, she watched as Arthur greeted him with warm familiarity. "Let me introduce you," Arthur said. "This is my sister, Henrietta, and her husband, George Chumley. And you already know Rumsford, of course. Have you met his fiancée, Miss Annabel Wheaton, my niece?"

Scarborough shook his head. "Alas, I have not yet had the pleasure. Miss Wheaton," he added with a bow.

She didn't know if that lie stemmed from politeness or expedience, but either way, she was quite happy to share in it. "Your Grace," she murmured with a polite curtsy, then turned to her uncle. "I didn't know you knew any dukes, Uncle Arthur."

"I didn't, not until last night," Arthur told her. "The duke and I met over cards. His Grace is quite the poker player. Took Hiram for a bundle."

"Merely a lucky flutter," Scarborough countered smoothly.

"Still hard lines though, old chap," Bernard put in. "They say a man lucky at cards is unlucky in love."

Annabel frowned, wondering if there might have been a hint of malice in her fiance's comment, but if so, Scarborough didn't seem perturbed by it. "Ah," he said with a smile. "That explains why my last amour ended with a vase of flowers being thrown at my head."

Everyone laughed at that, even Bernard, and Annabel feared they were becoming far too friendly with him. Next thing you knew, he'd be joining them for dinner.

"Care to dine with us, Your Grace?" her uncle asked. "I'm sure we could make room for you and your charming sister."

The duke glanced at her, and Annabel tensed, fearing the worst, but much to her relief, he refused the invitation. "Thank you, no. We have other companions to consider. Another time, perhaps. Now, if you will pardon me, I see the usher has come to seat our party."

With that, he bowed and returned to his own group and they were guided to a table. A few moments later, the usher did the same for her family, and she was glad when he led them to a table that was not in close proximity to Scarborough and his companions. But when the usher indicated a seat that put her directly in the duke's line of vision, she hesitated, glancing around.

There was no way she could move to take a different seat without drawing attention to the act, so Annabel sank into her chair, accepting the inevitable, and when a menu card was placed in front of her, she was glad to have something that would shield her from that man's smoky blue eyes.

She certainly didn't need the menu for its intended purpose. Bernard would order for both of them, as he always did. She'd learned on her first evening after becoming engaged that it was customary in a restaurant for a man to order not only for himself, but also for his fiancée. She'd accepted that, thinking nothing of it at the time, not only because it was customary, but also because menus were always in French, and though she'd taken two years of French lessons, she still wasn't comfortable enough to navigate the sophisticated dishes of a menu with a waiter whose familiarity with that language was probably better than hers. She hated making mistakes, and she didn't want to risk embarrassing herself in front of Bernard.

Allowing him to order for her had been an easy decision, but suddenly, it occurred to her that he never consulted her preferences before he did it. She watched him, and as he selected various hors d'oeuvres, potages, poissons, entrées, and entremets, another voice seemed to intrude on the conversation, invading her thoughts, imposing itself over his discussion with the waiter like a shout of rebellion.

Don't let them change you.

"Wait," she said as the waiter turned to go. "I would like the lamb rather than the beef."

Bernard stirred uneasily beside her. "Annabel,

choosing a saddle of lamb instead of an entrecote of beef changes everything else." He gave a little laugh, glancing at the waiter, then back at her. "I selected the wine, the salad, even the sorbet, to be in harmony with beef. Lamb would require wholly different choices."

"I know, darling, I know, and it just amazes me how well your choices harmonize, but I just feel in the mood for lamb tonight. Everyone else can have the beef if they like, but I would like the lamb. No mint sauce," she added, glancing at the waiter. "Just a bit of rosemary glaze. And I would like the peas instead of the asparagus."

She returned her gaze to Bernard, and saw that he was prepared to further debate the point, but Arthur spoke, interrupting any reply he might have made.

"You know, I believe I'll have the lamb and the peas, too," her uncle said. "I appreciate your talent with the menu, my lord, and I'm sure Annabel does, too. But lamb sounds mighty good. You don't have to change everything else just for us," he added. "Annabel and I don't mind being out of harmony every once in a while, do we, darlin'?"

When her uncle looked at her, he was smiling, and she winked back at him, feeling oddly pleased with herself. It was a little thing, she knew, but life was all sorts of little things added up. And as she went through the courses of the meal, she was unable to find the various dishes any less palatable just because they weren't supposed to be served with lamb. Who decided that only certain wines were appropriate for certain meats, anyway? she wondered. And on the same subject, who decided that Virginia Vanderbilt's money was more aristocratic than hers?

It's all part of the rules, you see.

"Bernard?" Impulsively, she turned in her chair to the man beside her. "What's a chilblain?"

"What?" He laughed, but he seemed astonished by the question rather than amused. Uneasy, he glanced at the others, but they were engaged in a separate conversation. "What on earth put that topic into your head?" he asked in a whisper.

"Oh, I just heard someone mention it earlier. What is it?"

"Nothing for you to worry about, Annabel."

"They said it was painful," she persisted, not really certain why she was pushing the point, except that she felt a hint of apprehension. If it was nothing to worry about, then why didn't he just tell her? "What is it?"

A slight frown marred his high forehead. "Something that is quite unsuitable for conversation, my dear. Especially at dinner."

Which still wasn't an answer. She opened her mouth to point that out, but she saw his frown etching deeper, and she stopped. She knew Bernard well enough by now to know that the direct approach wasn't usually the most effective. Like most men, he had the tendency to pat her on the head a bit, but like most women, she knew there was always a way to go around a man when he was like that.

She'd find out what a chilblain was without asking

him, she decided, and resumed eating dessert. The ship had a reading room with books and stationery supplies for use by the first-class passengers. There was probably a dictionary there as well. And though now was not the time, she'd find a way to ask Bernard when they were alone if there were any rules about British marriage she needed to know.

As for the Duke of Scarborough, she had the disquieting feeling he was not dealt with quite so easily.

Annabel took a peek at him past her uncle's shoulder and found to her dismay that he was looking right at her. When their eyes met, he smiled, and Annabel felt again that awful, nervous dip in her stomach and that rush of heat down to her toes. Lord, that man's smile was like moonshine.

She turned to Bernard again. "Darling? That man over there, the Duke of Scarborough, what do you know about him?"

Her fiancé made a face. "He's a bad lot, I'm afraid. A very bad lot. Always has been."

She nodded, not the least bit surprised, although this confirmation of her ability to discern a man's bad character by her own instinctive attraction to him was a bit disheartening. "That's just what I thought," she murmured. "He looks a bit of a wrong 'un."

"Excellent that you are so perceptive, my dear. He married an American girl, by the way. A Miss Evelyn Tremont of Philadelphia."

Annabel froze for a second, a spoonful of cream caramel halfway to her mouth. "Really?" she asked, a squeak of surprise that impelled her to set down her spoon and reach for her water glass. She took a sip, enabling her to ask her next question in an ordinary, disinterested sort of way. "Scarborough is married?"

"Was married," Bernard corrected. "His wife died in a drowning accident, poor soul. Scarborough was in Europe at the time. Gambling, drinking, carousing, I've no doubt."

"How awful. When was this?"

"It's been . . . oh, ten or twelve years ago now."

"So long?" Annabel set down her glass, returned her attention to her dessert, and strove to keep her voice as indifferent as possible as she asked, "He's never remarried?"

"No. Rumor has always been that he hated being married so much that he'll never marry again, although I don't see how he can avoid the prospect now. He's the duke, and he has no direct heir and he has no income. He has to marry and marry well. It's his duty."

"He might not care about his duty."

"True. Very true. Scarborough is just the sort to ignore his ducal responsibilities." Bernard smiled at her. "You and I seem to share the same opinions about so many things, my dear. He keeps well away from good society most of the time, but whenever he does choose to appear, there always seem to be women who find him attractive. Inexplicable to me, but there it is."

"Some women," she said with a sigh, "are attracted to bad men."

"Quite." There was a pause, then Bernard added, "I am glad you are not one of those women, Annabel."

"So am I," she agreed with emphasis, swirling her spoon idly in her cream caramel, peeking at the duke from beneath her lashes. "So am I."

Scarborough was handsome, wicked, and wild, a combination that was nothing but trouble, and it never did a girl any good to court trouble.

After dinner, the gentlemen retired to the smoking room for brandy and cigars, and the ladies remained in the dining room for coffee and gossip.

Annabel, however, decided to forgo the coffee. Excusing herself, she murmured something delicate to her mother and left the table. Exiting by a side door, she went straight past the ladies' retiring chamber, up the stairs, and into the reading room, where newspapers lay on carved tables and rows of books lined two walls. After a hasty scan of the shelves, she found the book she was looking for and lifted it above the two-inch lip that prevented the volumes from spilling onto the floor in stormy weather.

Flipping through pages, she soon reached the one she wanted, but what she found there was every bit as awful as she had feared.

Chilblain: inflammation brought on by repeated exposure to cold, sometimes accompanied by redness or painful lesions.

Horrified, she stared at the page. Inflammation? Painful lesions?

"Ghastly, aren't they?"

She jumped, startled, and turned to find Scarborough standing only a few feet away. "You again? Aren't you supposed to be in the smoking room with the gentlemen?"

"Aren't you supposed to be having coffee with the ladies? Neither of us, it seems, is good about doing what we're supposed to."

He leaned one shoulder against the bookshelf and nodded to the book in her hands. "Best to eschew those pretty little silk stockings that are no doubt in your trousseau," he advised. "Stout woolen socks will serve to protect your feet much better."

Fighting the urge to hide the dictionary behind her back, she strove for an air of nonchalant dignity. "I don't know what you're talking about."

"Piqued your curiosity, did I?"

"You're mistaken," she assured him, careful to keep the book positioned so he couldn't discern the title. "I was just looking for something to read."

"Of course," he agreed gravely. "And the dictionary is so entertaining."

She slammed the book shut. "You are like a bad penny," she said, glaring at him. "Or maybe you're just plain bad."

"My reputation precedes me, I see. But it's gratifying to know you've been asking about me."

"I didn't," she lied at once. "No need. I know a skunk without having to ask what the smell is."

"You're terribly prickly. Love, if you're going to

marry an Englishman, you'd best cultivate a sense of humor. God knows, you'll need it."

"I have a sense of humor." She paused, smiling sweetly. "I just don't find you funny."

To her consternation, he chuckled, not the least bit put out. "Point taken. You're cheeky, too. Has Rumsford seen these aspects of your character? On the whole, I'd guess not. When he does, he won't like it."

"I can manage him." The moment the words were out of her mouth, she wanted to bite her tongue off.

"Manage him?" Scarborough echoed, seeming quite entertained. "Well, I daresay you think so. He does have that weak chin. But I do think it's a bit unfair of you to correlate that particular physical trait to the lack of a spine. A few days from now," he went on, overriding her outraged protest about Bernard's chin, "you might agree with me about that, after you've said the part about 'until death us do part.' Men, even those with weak chins, are often much less willing to be managed once they've got everything they want, especially an iron-clad marriage settlement in a country where divorce is almost impossible."

Annabel felt a sudden, inexplicable jolt of uncertainty. Was any of what he said true? she wondered, and then immediately shook her head, banishing that question and her momentary doubt. "You're talkin' nonsense!"

"Perhaps I am. I often do. But your words do make me wonder—are you really the sort of girl who would be happy with a man she can 'manage,' as you put it?"

It was her turn to laugh, for she was beginning to see just where this conversation was going. "I suppose I'd be much happier with someone else, someone clever and charming who'll always try to spar and match wits with me? Someone like . . ." She paused, giving him her best wide-eyed look. "Someone like you, for instance?"

"Possibly. Even I can be managed. If a woman does it properly."

Something in those words sent a rush of heat into her face, and she quickly looked away, returning her attention to the books along the shelf.

"And," he added, "I like to think I'm a more interesting conversationalist than Rummy."

"Don't flatter yourself. You're not."

"Quite. You must adore listening to dissertations on the inner workings of Parliament. Now that I've been put most decidedly in my place, I shall banish all hope of winning you, my heart broken and my dreams crushed. But before I go to the garden for an aperitif of worms, might I suggest muslin as the best binding for chilblains?"

That reminder of what she'd just read was a bit sobering. "Is that what . . . what you're supposed to do? Bind them?"

"Don't worry, your new sisters-in-law will show you how. Like all British girls, they've vast experience with that particular ailment. Well, except my sister. We installed radiators ages ago, along with gas-lights, and bathrooms with hot water and flush toilets. Rumsford Castle, alas, is not so fortunate. They still use coal and candles up there. As to the matter of flush toilets, there aren't any. There hasn't been a hygienic improvement along those lines since they took out the moat."

She swallowed hard. No central heating? No bath-rooms? Bernard hadn't told her any of this. Lord, she felt as if she was going back to the primitive conditions of her Mississippi childhood, only at much icier tem-peratures. What was the point of being an aristocrat if one still had to use a privy pot and bathe out of a bucket?

Scarborough was watching her, smiling, as if he could read her thoughts like the pages of a book. She lifted her chin, rallying. "That's part of what the earl and I shall be doing. We intend to bring Rumsford Castle up to date."

That wasn't quite true, for she and Bernard had only discussed restorations at Rumsford. They'd never talked about installing any modern amenities, mainly because she'd assumed an earl's house would already have them. Still, now that she knew otherwise, she also knew where her money was going first. Bernard's res-torations could wait. "Our home shall have all the con-veniences of modern life."

"Hmm, I daresay you'll have your work cut out for you there. The Dowager Countess is a formidable op-ponent of all things modern. Tradition has always been far more important to that good lady than comfort." He leaned closer. "I think she wishes hair shirts and chastity belts were still in vogue."

"You're exaggerating."

With a shrug, he turned to the bookshelf. "You obviously haven't met her." He lifted out a book and began to scan the pages. "Perhaps you should," he added, the very nonchalance of his voice making her suspicious. "If you could manage that before the wedding, you'd avoid a great deal of heartache and a great many head colds."

"I find it hard to believe that any woman, especially an older one, would prefer to live in a house that's freezing cold when she shall be able to have central heating instead."

"I told you. Because it's tradition, and traditions cannot and shall not be broken." Marking his place with one finger, he closed the book, then he turned toward her, looking down his nose at her, the book pressed to his chest. "We have nev-ah had central heating, my lady," he said in a ponderous voice, managing to seem every bit as proper and stuffy as she'd always imagined an English butler to be. It was so uncanny, in fact, that she had to press her lips together to avoid a smile. Smiling, she feared, would only encourage him. "And we nev-ah shall, God willing," he went on. "Keeping our feet warm is what the dogs are for."

"Dogs? You mean foxhounds?"

"No, no, hounds are another thing altogether. They rather go along with the estate, like the entail, you know, and the leaky roof, and the inevitable dowager who always hates being usurped. No, I'm talking about Rummy's own dogs. He has nine."

"Nine?" She stared at him in some alarm. "Nine dogs?"

"Pugs. Fierce little fellows. I believe Lady Seaworth had to break with him because of the dogs."

She smiled. "If you're trying to shock me, you won't succeed. I know all about Lady Seaworth. Arthur already told me she was Bernard's mistress before he met me."

"You know about Lady Seaworth, but not the dogs?" He leaned closer, adopting a confidential air. "Rumor has it the dogs slept with them, and after a time, she just couldn't tolerate the snoring. Or the drool."

"You're making that up," she accused.

"Ask Rummy if you don't believe me."

"Rummy—Bernard," she corrected herself at once, "would have told me about any dogs."

"Perhaps he didn't want to frighten you off. If they're inclined to drool on you in the middle of the night when you're in bed—"

"They won't drool on me." Annabel set her jaw. "Not in my bed anyway."

"That's the spirit," he said with approval, resuming his former breezy demeanor. "You Americans are so full of verve. Bringing our English estates up to snuff, and braving Northumberland winters without so much as a pug or two to warm your feet. It's all very admirable. But I am curious about something."

He returned the book to the shelf and moved closer to her. "Why did you need to learn what chilblains are from a dictionary? You seem a confident, forthright sort of girl. Why didn't you just ask your fiancé?" He slanted her a knowing look. "Or perhaps you did ask, but Rummy wouldn't tell you?"

He was the most irritatingly perceptive man. Still, she wasn't going to admit he'd been right again. "This has all been very interesting, Your Grace, but I came in here for a book, so if you will excuse me?"

She tucked the dictionary back where it belonged, and moved to the set of shelves where the novels were kept, but of course he did not take the hint and depart.

"My guess," he added, following her, "is that Rummy thinks chilblains are much too crude a subject to discuss with a young lady. Rather like the lack of flush toilets at Rumsford Castle. I don't suppose he told you about the wandering hands of his uncle Henry, either? Best steer clear of the old boy, by the way. He's nigh on eighty now, but still quite spry. He'll be in the library, which is always the only room lit by a fire during the day, so if you stay away from there, you should be safe." He paused, tilting his head, looking doubtful. "Although, perhaps not. Henry tried to corner my sister in a stair cupboard once. She bashed him with a niblick."

"I don't think you're serious about anything," she said, and turned to peruse the shelves. "You're just havin' fun at my expense."

"Ask Sylvia if you don't believe me. I shall introduce you to her, and she can verify every word I'm saying.

Rumsford's uncle is a skirt chaser of legendary proportions. He's rather like our king in that respect."

Appalled, she stared at him. "The King of England is not like that!"

"Best to toddle off to the Continent whenever Rummy has His Majesty up to Northumberland for a shooting party," he went on with complete disregard for her protest. "You won't want to be anywhere in the vicinity. The king would take one look at you, my delicious little lamb, and start licking his chops. I've no doubt he'd make Rumsford step aside."

Despite herself, Annabel felt a hint of dread, for she'd seen photographs of England's pudgy, bearded king. "He couldn't do that. My husband wouldn't let him."

"My dear girl, Rumsford won't have a choice. Noblesse oblige, and all that. Another one of the rules."

"Rules, rules," she said crossly, at the end of her rope. "Just what are all these rules you keep talkin' about?"

"The rules we British live by. They are very specific, and they are unbreakable. Violate them, and you're out."

Annabel felt her dread deepening into alarm. She couldn't afford to commit some awful faux pas. On the other hand, she didn't know whether to believe him or not. Everything seemed like a joke to him, and his motives, she suspected, were obviously less than pure.

"I've been reading your society pages, etiquette books, and such, and I've learned a lot about England over the last couple of years." She folded her arms, studying him through narrowed eyes. "I've never read anything about these rules."

"I highly doubt anyone's bothered to write them down. Someone should, of course. It would save you Americans a great deal of heartache. I say, that's an idea," he added as if to himself. "If I wrote such a treatise, a guide to British matrimony for the American heiress, your lot would buy heaps of copies. I might actually make a living out of it, a respectable one. What a refreshing change that would make."

How he earned his living, respectable or not, was of no concern to her. "Bernard's never told me anything about rules. Wouldn't he tell me if we're to be married?"

"Doing that would be highly improper. Bernard, despite his one or two redeeming qualities, is much too proper to have a candid conversation on any topic."

Annabel chose to ignore this disparaging remark about her fiancé, not wanting to be distracted by side issues. "Damn it, stop toying with me. Are you going to tell me about these rules or not?"

"I don't know." He tilted his head, considering, and his hesitation confirmed everything she'd already decided about him.

"I suppose you want something in return for this information?"

"Why, Miss Wheaton, what a delicious suggestion."

"I should have known," she said. "A cad always expects something in return for doing a woman a favor."

"It was your idea," he pointed out. "But despite that, I shall resist the temptations of my baser nature. I am happy to give you these rules freely, without any expectation of recompense. The problem is that I don't see how such a thing can be managed."

"What do you mean?"

"I told you, it's not a proper subject, not one I can discuss with you in front of chaperones, particularly your mother."

Thinking of what he'd said about the king, she had to concede the point, but she didn't see why that should matter.

"So why don't you tell me right now?"

As if in answer to this question, the sound of voices floated through the open doorway, and Annabel glanced apprehensively in that direction, for the last thing she needed was to be caught unchaperoned with a man, especially this one. But though the couple talking passed by the reading room without pausing, it was a reminder not to linger here. On the other hand, she badly wanted to know what these rules were. What if she went into London society and made some horrible gaffe that got her shunned? Then all her efforts would be for nothing. If there were rules, and he wasn't just talking nonsense, then she needed to know what they were.

"Meet me the day after tomorrow," she whispered, and lifted a novel from the shelf. "Ten o'clock in the morning, by the second-class smoking room. Since it'll be Sunday, everyone will be at services, but I'll plead a headache. No one either of us knows is likely to be down in second class anyway."

"You're willing to be alone with me?"

He was surprised, she could tell. "As long as you keep your hands to yourself," she shot back, and departed, ignoring his laughter as she walked away.

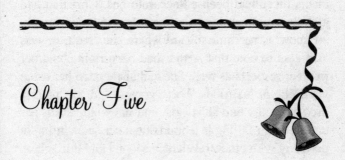

Chapter Five

When Christian arrived at the men's smoking room at half past nine Sunday morning, it was empty, but that didn't really matter anyway. Women weren't permitted in the smoking rooms, and even if they were, it wasn't as if he and Annabel could expect to maintain privacy there. Nor could they linger out in the corridor. As he'd told Arthur, the risk of being seen or overheard by someone who might be in a position to spread gossip was too great for that. So he'd come to this rendezvous a little early to find a more private place for their conversation.

Having obtained a map from the purser, he spent the next thirty minutes inspecting various rooms and stairwells, and by the time he had succeeded in locating a suitable spot and returned to the smoking room, he found Annabel waiting for him.

From what he'd seen thus far, Arthur's assessment of his niece had been an accurate one. Christian had already had occasion to witness her stubborn streak, and now as he came toward where she stood, he was also glad to note that Arthur had been right about her in other respects as well. She had abandoned her usual wardrobe of luxurious Worth gowns, and was plainly dressed in a white shirtwaist and navy-blue skirt, her dark red hair falling in a braid down her back, fitting in perfectly with other travelers in second and third class. The girl had plenty of common sense. She wasn't exercising it in matters of romance, but that was why he was there.

"Good morning," he greeted her, and even though his voice was a low murmur, she put a finger to her lips, stopping him from saying any more. "There's a man in there," she whispered, nodding to the room behind her.

He glanced past her to the mustachioed, military-looking gentleman puffing a cigar and reading the *New York Times*, and he was glad he'd done some preliminary reconnaissance. "People who don't attend church are so disobliging," he whispered back, and turned, taking her by the elbow. "Come on."

He led her down the stairs to third-class steerage and into the storage room he'd selected, which was at the very end of a remote corridor. After taking a peek inside to verify that it was still unoccupied, he stepped back and nodded to her. "Watch your step," he cautioned as she moved to precede him into the room, and she nodded, stepping with care over the coaming and into the room of white-painted steel and gray linoleum, a room littered with stacks of packing crates and cleaning supplies.

Once they were inside, he closed the door and slid a heavy crate in front of it. "I knew the smoking room wouldn't do, so I found a more suitable location. Clever of me, don't you think?"

She sniffed, not seeming impressed. "You've obviously had enough clandestine meetings with women to know how it's done."

"My fair share," he admitted. "But not with young unmarried ladies. That's one of the rules, one to which even blackguards like me adhere. At least," he amended, looking at her, "most of the time."

She looked back at him with a wry smile. "There's a blackguard down in Gooseneck Bend who wouldn't agree with you about that," she murmured, making him think perhaps she spoke from personal experience. He wondered if Arthur knew about it. On the whole, he'd imagine not.

"What happened?" he asked, curious.

Her smile vanished, and an impassive mask took its place. "The usual thing that happens to foolish girls of seventeen," she said with a shrug. "He broke my heart, that's all."

She was trying to pretend it didn't matter, but he studied her expressionless face, and he knew it mattered. To her, it had mattered a great deal.

"Well," she said, breaking the silence, "so far,

London doesn't sound much different from New York. Back home in Gooseneck Bend, we never thought anything about boys and girls being alone together. Even Jackson wasn't like that. Then I came to New York, and it was like a whole different world. Stuffiest place you've ever seen. And cold, too. I don't mean cold like a castle in December," she added, smiling a little. "I mean cold like unfriendly to outsiders."

"I comprehend your meaning." He moved away from the door to lean his back against the wall. "Yet you want to be accepted into this circle?"

She stared at him. "Of course."

"Why?"

The question caught her off guard. She opened her mouth as if to answer, then closed it again and looked away. He waited, and after a moment, she spoke again. "Everyone wants to be accepted," she said without looking at him.

"Even by cold, stuffy people?"

"You don't understand."

"I'm trying to," he confessed, and thought for a second of Evie, so different in temperament from this girl, but just the same in what she wanted. "I've lived in so-called good society all my life, Annabel, and I have absolutely no idea why anyone would want to be part of it."

"But that's because you already are part of it."

"We all want what we can't have? Is that it?"

"I suppose that's true, but that's not what I mean." She looked at him again, her face shining with earnestness. "You were born accepted, so you don't know what it's like not to be. You walk through life always confident of your acceptance in any situation. You don't know how it feels to be shunned. To be laughed at for the way you talk or the place you were born. To be looked down on, to have your whole family looked down on, as if you were dirt on the floor. Nobody," she added, lifting her chin with dignity, "looks down on a countess."

They would. Even if she became Rumsford's wife, there would be many who would look down on her and laugh. If she behaved impeccably, they might not shun her, but it would be years before they would consider her one of their own. She would have to fight and kick and claw and play by every single rule to make a place for herself and her family in society, and along the way, her husband would be of little help to her.

Christian wondered how he could he make her see it wasn't worth it.

"Well, as a countess, you'll have to be willing to act as a chaperone," he said, considering all the various means of changing her mind that were at his disposal. "It's an enormous responsibility. If a scandal happens to a girl you're chaperoning, you suffer censure as well."

"That shouldn't be a problem for me," she said with a touch of humor. "I'm good at seeing when a wolf's in the henhouse."

He noted her pointed glance at him, and he grinned.

"Good chaperones are the reason many unmarried men don't bother going into society at all, until they're ready to find a wife, of course."

"Is that what you're going to do?"

He blinked. "God, no. What put that idea into your head?"

"I—" She broke off, then shrugged. "I just assumed it. I mean, you're a duke. Don't you have to marry?"

"No, thank God. I have a male cousin. And even if I didn't, it wouldn't matter. I have no intention of ever marrying again."

"Some might call that famous last words."

He groaned, his head falling back to hit the wall behind him with an exasperated thud. "Why do women always do this? If they're not matchmaking for themselves, they're matchmaking for everyone else. Listen," he added, straightening again to level a frown at her, "I am not a marrying man."

"But you've been married."

"Yes, exactly." He ignored her sound of impatience at that bit of wit and went on, "Can we return to the subject of your duties as a countess? You'll be expected to entertain lavishly and often. Your level of success there plays a key part in your success in society, but it's an occupation fraught with hazards. You'll have to be sure you don't invite Lord and Lady Ashburton to the same dinner party, for example, because they haven't spoken a word to each other in twenty years. And don't put Mrs. Bedford-Jones anywhere near Viscount Rathmore— they hate each other. But how can you avoid it, since precedent demands they walk in to dinner together? Best to invite Mr. Smythe instead . . . oh, but he's in love with Miss Grey, and if Miss Graham finds out he was at dinner with Miss Grey, the fat would be in the fire . . ."

He paused, noting a dazed quality coming into her expression. "A ball is even worse," he went on mercilessly. "You'll have to give them. Rummy will expect it, but be warned. Ball giving is a very tricky business."

She sat down on a packing crate with a sigh. "You don't have to tell me that. When we first learned we were rich, we moved to Jackson, bought a big, fancy house, and had a coming-out ball for me."

"It wasn't a success?"

"You might say that." She looked down at her hands. "Nobody came."

He stared at her bent head, her hushed admission hanging in the air, and anger hit him with sudden force, like a kick in the stomach. If ever he needed justification of his contempt for society and its rigid class distinctions, this was it.

He crossed the room, moving to sit on the crate beside hers. "What do you mean nobody came? Nobody at all?"

"We were so ignorant," she said, and lifted her head with a laugh. It was a forced laugh, he knew, for there was nothing amusing about what she'd just described. It was appalling.

"We thought giving a ball in Jackson was just like

giving a dance back home," she went on, staring at the blank white wall across the room. "We didn't know you had to send written invitations, two weeks in advance. Heck, nobody in Gooseneck Bend gave a party with invitations, not even the Hardings. We'd never heard of such a thing. So, we just did what anybody we knew would do—we told people about it at church. Yes," she added, shaking her head as if in disbelief, "we really were that dumb."

He didn't know what to say, but he knew a condemnation of society wouldn't be very comforting. "If by that you mean you were stupid, no, you weren't. You simply didn't know."

"Exactly." She turned toward him, the bitter tinge in her voice changing to one of determination, pain hardening into resolve. "That's why I'm here. I want to know all the rules, because I don't ever want to stand in an empty ballroom in London the way I did in Jackson. I don't ever want to feel again what I felt that night."

He looked at her in dismay. This was going to be more difficult than he'd first thought. In agreeing to take this on, he hadn't appreciated that there might be deeper reasons for her ambition than mere social climbing, reasons that stemmed from old wounds. To succeed with this, he'd have to open those wounds, use her own insecurities to plant doubts in her head. And he was tempted, suddenly, to walk away and let the chips fall.

But then he remembered Rumsford winking at him

in the House with the Bronze Door, a memory that revolted even his calloused soul. She did not deserve to be chained to an ass like that for the rest of her life, and he decided he was justified in making her see it by whatever means necessary. Still, he had to be subtle about it. Otherwise, she'd just dig in her heels as she'd done with Arthur.

"All right," he said, breaking the silence. "Very wise of you to want to know as much about the lion's den as possible before you go inside. Knowledge is power, after all."

"Not in New York. I had that place figured out in three months, but five years after moving there, it still hasn't done me any good."

"So that's why you decided go after a British earl."

"I did not go after him!" She straightened up on her seat, seeming quite put out by that accusation. "A woman never chases a man. Ever. Believe me, I learned that lesson a long time ago."

"Ah. From the blackguard in Gooseneck Bend, no doubt."

"My mama told me from the time I was a little girl not to go chasin' after boys." She paused and gave him a wry smile. "I just wasn't very good at listenin'."

"Really?" He glanced down at her mouth, considering. "Have a soft spot for blackguards, do you?"

She jerked to her feet, answering his question without saying a word. "Are you going to behave like a gentleman?" she demanded.

He ignored that. "I'm glad to know this particular

weakness of yours," he murmured, and stood up. "It gives me hope."

She looked at him through narrowed eyes. "There is no hope for you. Not with me. Not even after the shine's off my tiara."

"Now who's using famous last words?"

"I would appreciate it if you'd stick to the subject, please. We were discussing my future life as the Countess of Rumsford."

"Yes, of course." He paused, considering. "You might think," he said after a moment, "that being married means more freedom, but it doesn't."

"It doesn't?" She looked dismayed, and he was quick to pounce on that.

"No. Your every move will be subject to even more scrutiny once you're a countess, especially because you're a newcomer. And the British girls will be the ones who most want to stick the knife in your back. From their point of view, you stole one of their eligible men, and they'd take great delight in seeing you come to social disaster. 'Those Americans,' they'll say. 'So uncivilized.' You'll find it hard to make friends."

"But I have friends of my own. Once I'm settled, I hope to bring some of them over, help to launch them in British society."

"Certainly, but it takes years to have the sort of influence you'll need to do that."

"Years?" she cried. "How many years?"

He shrugged. "Some women spend a lifetime building a position of influence such as you describe. In the meantime, you might technically have more freedom as a married woman, but you don't dare exercise it, even in the smallest ways. You'll be allowed to drink more than a single glass of wine with dinner, for example, but if you show yourself to be the least bit tipsy, it will tell against you."

"No need for me to worry about that anyway," she said, looking a little relieved. "I don't much like the taste of spirits."

He grinned and moved a bit closer to her. "You say that now, but those cold nights in the castle might change your mind. Don't be surprised if you're dipping into the brandy by Christmas. Still, if you don't like spirits . . ." He paused, looking down. "There are other ways to keep warm."

His gaze skimmed over her and his mind began to imagine various methods of applying heat to those luscious curves of hers, a flight of fancy that had the warmth of arousal spreading through his own body quick as lighting a match. But there was no acting on that, unfortunately, not with half a million dollars at stake. With reluctance, he brought his baser nature under control and forced his gaze back up to her face.

She was frowning at him. "Listen, sugar, I don't have much time here, and I don't need you looking at me like you're a cat and I'm the cream jug."

"Sorry," he said. He wasn't sorry, not really, but she did have a point. This might be his only chance to talk her off the cliff she was about to jump from. He couldn't allow her luscious body to distract him.

On the other hand, he reflected, perhaps his best way of changing her mind was by making her see there were more fish in the sea than ever came out of it. A bit of harmless dalliance to show her she was an attractive woman who didn't have to marry Rumsford, who could take her time about marrying. He rather liked that notion. He studied the generous swell of her breasts beneath her pristine white shirtwaist and decided this was an idea worth exploring.

Still, when she folded her arms and he returned his gaze to her face, he knew it wasn't one he could explore at the present moment. She was watching him through narrowed eyes, those full lips pressed in a disapproving line.

He improvised for something innocuous to say. "It's just that I don't know quite where to begin. There are so many ways you could ruin your chances."

Her lips parted and her resentment vanished, replaced by a hint of alarm. "How many ways?"

"Hundreds. Thousands."

"Heavens," she said, her voice a bit faint, the first sign of apprehension he'd seen yet. "Maybe it'd be best if you put these rules in order by importance then. What is the most important rule?"

"Producing a son," he said at once.

"That's hardly something I have any control over!"

"Fair or not, it's in your best interests to see that you have a son. That goes a long way toward social acceptance. And there's also the fact that until you have a son, you are constrained by absolute fidelity. You must remain faithful to your husband."

"Well, I should hope so. I don't need you to tell me adultery is wrong and that a married woman should be faithful!"

"It doesn't work both ways, I'm afraid. You must be chaste, but Rumsford is allowed as many mistresses as he can afford, so long as he is discreet and doesn't flaunt them in front of you."

She didn't react to that quite the way he'd hoped she would. "Men have mistresses sometimes," she said, not seeming the least bit shocked. "It happens."

He lifted his fist to his mouth and gave a cough. "Yes, but Rumsford is allowed to use his income from you to pay for his mistresses. He can use your money to buy them houses, clothes, jewels."

She set her jaw. "Over my dead body."

"How shall you prevent it? Did you put a clause in your marriage settlement cutting off his income if he acquires a mistress?"

Clearly taken aback, Annabel opened her mouth, then closed it again, and it took her several moments to answer. "Of course I didn't! That never even occurred to me. But surely—" She stopped. Her tongue touched her lips, a gesture of uncertainty and apprehension, the most hopeful sign he'd seen yet. "Surely, I don't need to do that. Bernard wouldn't . . . he wouldn't use his income from me for . . . for other women."

Pressing his advantage, Christian gave her a look of deliberate pity. "Believe that, do you?"

"Yes!" She scowled, on the defensive. "Yes, I do."

Christian shrugged, playing this hand as if he had no stake in the game. "He's your fiancé. You know him best, I suppose. Still, what income would he use, if not yours? He has no other. And besides, these arrangements are the norm in Britain, and no one thinks anything of it. In fact, you would be ridiculed if you complained about him spending your money on his mistresses. We British hate a fuss. So you have to bear up and smile and act the part of the contented wife no matter what."

Her chin lifted, a gesture he suspected was quite familiar to her family. "I don't believe you," she accused. "Paying for mistresses with a wife's money is acceptable? It's abominable. It's indecent. Why, it's . . . it's just plain unfair! You must be lying."

Sadly, he wasn't. He might be exaggerating things a bit, but that wasn't the same. "Fair?" he said, forcing amusement into his voice. "Love, if you think there's anything fair about English marriage, you'd best cry off now, while you still have the chance."

"Why?" she countered, one auburn brow arching up in skepticism. "Because you're the sort of man who'd never lie to a girl?"

Strangely, that hurt. It shouldn't, for he'd proved himself quite skilled at lying years ago, but it did. Still, he wasn't going to lose his advantage by showing it. "I'm not lying about this, Annabel. I know I make light of things, and most of what I say is utter rubbish, but not this. If you go into your marriage thinking it'll be different for you—better, happier, more fair than the marriages of the American girls who came before you—you'll only end up being more miserable, because the greatest unhappiness a person can feel in life is unmet expectations."

She sucked in her breath. "Bernard wouldn't spend my money for his mistresses," she said, sounding as if she was trying to believe it. "He would never treat me that way."

Behind the positive words, Christian heard her doubt, and he played it for all he was worth.

"If that's true," he murmured, "then he must love you a great deal."

She winced. He was watching her closely, and he saw it. She turned away, hiding it almost at once, but not before he'd seen it. "He doesn't, does he?"

She didn't look at him. Instead, she started to leave, but she saw the heavy crate blocking the door, and she once again faced him, but she looked decidedly uneasy.

"He doesn't love you," Christian said, pushing his advantage. "And what's more, you know it."

"Bernard," she said primly, "is very fond of me."

"Fond?" He laughed low in his throat. "Well, that's sure to make him treat you with respect."

Pain shimmered across her face, and too late, he remembered the deep need she had for respect. She took a step back and hit the wall behind her, but even hurt, even cornered, she wasn't the sort to admit defeat. "I don't need any mockery from you."

"I'll accept for the sake of argument that he is fond of you," Christian said, gentling his voice. "But it won't stop him from spending your money any way he likes. He can pay for his mistresses and his bastards. He can drink, gamble, and travel the world without you. And he will."

"What makes you so sure?"

"Men are men," he said with a shrug. "Call it another rule."

She glared at him as if he was the one who'd invented all these rules in the first place. "Not all men would disrespect their wives the way you describe!"

"I hate to destroy any romantic illusions you may have about my sex, but for the most part, we do what we want as long as there are no unpleasant consequences to consider."

"Did you?"

Startled by the question, he blinked. "I beg your pardon?"

"You were married to an heiress. Did you spend her money on other women?"

He looked away, an image of Evie flashing across his mind—of an angelic, heart-shaped face and golden hair, and blue eyes that gazed at him with far more adoration than he could ever deserve.

He took a deep breath. "No," he admitted, grateful for that one grain of truth in a marriage based on a slew of lies. "I spent it on a lot of other things, but never on other women. Hard to believe, I know," he added with a laugh, looking at her again, driving the image of Evie back into the past. "I am such a scoundrel. But then, my wife died only three years after we were married, so I didn't have much of a chance to be unfaithful. Eventually, I probably would have been," he added, striving to make himself out as callous a brute as possible. "I did all the rest. Why shouldn't I? I'm a gentleman of the aristocracy, with an enormous income at my disposal, access to a vast array of distractions, and a moral code that is, I regret to say, woefully inadequate to resisting temptation. What was there to stop me? Love? Hell, my wife and I weren't in love. At least—" He stopped, and then for no reason at all, he blurted out the rest, a truth he'd had no intention to reveal. "I wasn't."

"I see." Her animosity seemed to have gone, for she was studying him with a thoughtful, assessing gaze, and he had the sick feeling she did indeed see, that her gaze had penetrated the glib, devil-may-care show he put on and seen the real truth: how much he loathed himself.

"Good Lord," he drawled, forcing out light, careless words to cover the sudden, terrible silence. "How do we keep veering off the subject? We were discussing your future matrimonial success, not my matrimonial failure. Now—"

"Was it a failure?"

There was something in that question—something doubtful. Something reluctant, as if she didn't believe him.

This girl wasn't like Evie. She was strong willed and hard-boiled, without any trace of Evie's soft romanticism, and yet in both of them was the same fatal flaw. Vulnerability.

It was in every line of her upturned face. It was in those big, caramel-brown eyes and that vividly expressive mouth, in the little crinkle of doubt between her auburn brows and in the determination of her delicately molded jaw. Once a chap got past the heart-stopping beauty of it, Annabel Wheaton's face was as easy to read as a book. She cared too much what people thought of her. She believed too strongly that she could make life into what she wanted it to be. She felt too sure that people were intrinsically good and would do what was right. But most important, she believed, in her heart of hearts, that a rake could change. Girls like her were a fortune hunter's dream.

Christian took a deep breath. "Yes," he said at last. "My marriage was a failure. I didn't love my wife. I married her for her money." He paused to let that ugly truth sink in, then he added with calculated brutality, "And that's why Rumsford is marrying you."

He expected her to hurl a spate of furious denial at his head, but she did not. "I know that's partly true," she admitted. "He wouldn't have married me if I'd been poor, that's for sure."

It wasn't just partly true. It was the whole truth. "That doesn't bother you?"

He watched her jaw set. "Not particularly."

That surprised him. Didn't a girl always want true love and happy endings? It went with the castle and the earl like peas went with carrots. "Every marriage ought to be based on love, Annabel. At least at the start. Don't you want love?"

She made a sound of impatience. "You seem to think I'm some naive little fool with stars in her eyes, but I'm not. As I said, I know Bernard doesn't love me, but he's fond of me—"

"What about you?" he interrupted. "Do you love him?"

She paused, a pause that was a fraction of a second too long. "Of course."

"How much?"

She met his inquiring gaze head-on. "Enough to be faithful."

"Which means not at all." He leaned toward her, close enough that his breath stirred the delicate corkscrew curl that grazed her cheek, close enough to catch the elusive scent of her French perfume. Almost close enough for his lips to touch hers. Desire began thrumming through his body again, even as he sensed her hardening resolve and felt his chance to change her mind slipping away. Hanging on to his control, he tried one more time to make her see how wrong it would be to marry Rumsford. "You don't really want to marry him, do you?"

"Of course I do," she whispered, and her tongue touched her lips. "Why wouldn't I?"

"You might be making a mistake."

"Why?" She tilted her head back, her full pink lips curved in a knowing little smile. "Because I ought to marry you instead and give you all my money?"

"I told you, I'm not a marrying man." He strove to think, but lust was quickly overtaking him, coursing through his body, almost impossible to resist, making it difficult to think. "But I'm one of the many men you could enslave if you chose to."

"Really?" Her lips parted. Her lashes drifted down until those dark eyes were half closed. Her voice, when she spoke, was a soft, honeyed hush. "Somehow, I don't get the feeling that's a proposal."

"There are different kinds of proposals." He moved, not even realizing his own intent until she jerked as if coming out of a daze and he felt her palm flatten against his chest, stopping him before he could kiss her.

"What in Sam Hill am I doin'?" she muttered, staring at him in horror.

He smiled. "I think you were about to let me kiss you."

She didn't deny it. "I must be the biggest fool in the entire U.S. of A. Get back," she added, her palm pushing against his chest.

He should. Safest thing all around, and yet, he didn't. His gaze slid to her mouth, but before he could even move, her hand slid upward between them, her fingers pressing against his mouth.

"Listen here, sugar," she said, and despite the fact that his body was on fire, he almost wanted to smile. She was striving to seem confident, as if she had the situation well in hand, but the breathless rush in which she said those words gave her away. "I appreciate the information you've given me, I really do. I'm sure I'll find it very useful. But . . ." She paused, her warm fingertips sliding away from his mouth. "Information's all you'll be giving me, and I hope that's understood."

She ducked past him. "Now," she said as he turned around to find her standing by the door, "kindly move this crate out of my way."

Christian complied, and the moment he'd done so, she was out the door and racing down the corridor toward the stairs.

He didn't follow. He couldn't, not just yet. He was a bit dazed still from her abrupt withdrawal, and he was also fully aroused. A man couldn't go walking around the corridors of a ship in that sort of condition.

He sat down on the crate and leaned his back against the wall, rubbing a hand over his face. How the devil had it happened? he wondered. One minute, he'd been telling her the rules, and the next minute, he was breaking one of his own.

He never made love to unmarried women. Never. The risk a man took for that particular privilege was enormous, the possible consequences far too costly.

He shifted on the crate with a grimace, painfully aware that despite his cardinal rule, if Annabel had stayed one moment longer, he would have willingly taken the risks, and any possible consequences be damned.

* * *

Annabel raced up three flights of stairs, her boots pounding on each steel step in time with the thudding beat of her heart. Scarborough's voice, sleepy and aroused, echoed through her head as she ran down the long corridor of A-deck to her stateroom. Once inside, she shut the door behind her, but she couldn't shut out his words.

Don't you want love?

Breathing hard, Annabel leaned back against the door, wondering what on earth was happening to her brains. Wasn't Billy John enough stupidity for one lifetime? Wasn't one man who could undress a woman with his eyes enough to make her see the truth? Her family always said she was stubborn, and she had to agree, because she just couldn't seem to get one particular lesson through her thick skull.

Men like Scarborough were heartbreak in the making.

Annabel tapped the back of her head against the door three times, wishing she could knock some sense into herself.

Don't you want love?

Love? She made a sound of derision. That man didn't know a thing about love. Lovemaking, for sure, but that wasn't the same thing.

Too bad she seemed to have such a hard time remembering the difference.

But, oh Lordy, when he'd talked about what would keep her warm on cold nights, just his words had been

enough to heat her up. Yessiree, she'd started melting
into a puddle right then and there. By the time he'd got
to the kissing part, she was all achy like she had a fever,
and her knees were so weak she could barely stand up.
How she'd managed to come to her senses long enough
to get out of there without being kissed, she still didn't
know.

When it came to sweet-talking a girl, the Duke of
Scarborough even put Billy John Harding to shame,
and that was saying something, for Billy John was the
sweetest-talking scoundrel in the entire state of Mississippi.

She ground her teeth and hit the door again with the
back of her head. She knew, none better, what it was
like to fall hook, line, and sinker for a pair of blue eyes,
a charming smile, and a line of sweet words. She also
knew what it was like to be literally on your knees, sobbing, when a man who'd just taken your body walked
out on you, and you were left with your pride stripped,
your virtue gone, and your heart in pieces. She knew
how it felt to be used and thrown away.

Annabel caught back a sob of frustration, pressing
her fingers to her still-tingling lips, knowing just how
close she'd come to betraying Bernard and their future
together.

Enough to be faithful.

Her own words came back as if to mock her, words
that she'd made sound so confident, but what she'd felt
when Scarborough had tried to kiss her showed her
words to be nothing more than bravado.

She took deep breaths, working to slow her pounding heart and regain her wits. She hadn't kissed him, she reminded herself. She hadn't done anything wrong. Yet.

She was getting married in four days, and the last thing she needed in the meantime was to test her resolve by being anywhere near the Duke of Scarborough. Annabel wondered dismally if she could just lock herself in her room until the wedding.

Chapter Six

Locking herself in her room was, unfortunately, not possible. She had engagements during the next few days that prevented such a course. The few hours she did manage to steal for herself only served to give her thoughts free rein, and those thoughts dwelled far too much on the man she wanted to avoid. She tried to spend as much time as possible with Bernard, but it seemed as if whenever she was with her fiancé, she found herself reassessing everything about him—his feelings for her, his opinions, even his chin. She began to notice how he avoided answering her more inconvenient questions and how he tended to make decisions for her without consulting her preferences, and these traits began to grate on her already raw nerves. Instead of being reassured by time spent with him, she found that being in his company only caused the whispers of doubt Scarborough had planted in her head to grow louder.

In looking for reassurance that she was doing the right thing, she found that being with her sister served her best, for Dinah was one of the main reasons she was doing all this, but despite that, and despite all Annabel's other efforts to quell her doubts, they persisted. By the time she was twenty-four hours from the ceremony, those doubts had mushroomed into a serious case of cold feet. She could only hope that the prewedding tea would provide the reassurance she so desperately needed.

The wedding gifts had been brought out for the event and placed on velvet-swathed tables in a private dining room, and as she walked with Bernard amid the silver plate, china, and crystal they had been given, she tried to see herself using them. She sipped tea and ate cucumber sandwiches with the ladies of Knickerbocker society, expressing her appreciation to Virginia Vanderbilt for the lovely silver teapot and to Maimie Paget for the unusual screen of Chinese silk with what she hoped was countesslike dignity. As she listened to Bernard and his sisters talk of Rumsford Castle and the beautiful countryside of Northumberland, she strove to regard it as her home, too. As the afternoon progressed, she began to feel as if her efforts were succeeding and she was regaining her equilibrium. But then Maude mentioned the king's visit to Rumsford Castle in the autumn.

Annabel stared at her future sister-in-law in horror, Scarborough's words echoing through her brain.

The king would take one look at you, my delicious little lamb, and start licking his chops.

She felt a knot of dread forming in her stomach.

"Annabel? Annabel, are you all right?"

She gave a start, Millicent's voice interrupting these awful contemplations. She turned to Bernard's second sister, and though she tried to paste on a smile and act like everything was fine, she just couldn't manage it. "I'm sorry, Millicent," she choked out. "I was just . . . just . . ." Her voice trailed off, her mind suddenly blank.

For some reason, all three of Bernard's sisters laughed. "Look at her, my dears," Alice said. "She seems a bit nervous at the prospect of a visit by the king."

I've no doubt he'd make Rumsford step aside.

Nervous? Annabel felt sick.

"There is no need to worry, Annabel," Maude assured her, smiling. "A royal visit is always a bit intimidating, but you'll do very well, I'm sure. The king adores American girls."

Annabel set down her teacup with a clatter and jumped to her feet. She could feel all of them staring at her, including Bernard, but she couldn't seem to make herself sit back down. "Forgive me," she mumbled. "I'm feeling a little faint. I believe I need some fresh air."

She raced for the door and down the corridor toward the stairs, cursing Scarborough and all his stupid talk about rules. If she had the jitters, it was his fault.

Despite her words to her future sisters-in-law about needing fresh air, she didn't go for a walk on deck. Instead, she sought the dubious refuge of her room and spent a few minutes sitting on her balcony, breathing in the bracing sea air and keeping a sharp eye on the promenade deck below, ready to duck out of sight should she catch a glimpse of anyone else she knew, especially Scarborough.

A short time later, feeling much more composed, she was able to return to the tea. Afterward, she strolled on deck with her mother, and though she saw Scarborough out of the corner of her eye walking with his sister, he did not attempt to engage her in conversation, and she was relieved. The last thing she needed was another hot look from that man's blue eyes.

Knowing that, she decided not to risk having dinner in the main dining room, and she asked her mother to reserve a private one. She also asked Mama to make the appropriate excuses to Bernard and his sisters, explaining that she didn't feel well and didn't want them to see her when she wasn't feeling her best. After all, she couldn't tell any of them the truth. She couldn't say she didn't want to face Bernard this evening because she was having doubts about marrying him.

Henrietta complied with her requests, but as they dined that evening, Annabel could feel her mother's thoughtful gaze on her, and Arthur's, too. As a result, she spent the entire meal reminding herself that nothing had actually happened between her and Scarborough. There was no reason to have doubts now, yet she couldn't shake them.

I think you were about to let me kiss you.

Every time she remembered those words, all the aching warmth she'd felt when he'd first spoken them came flooding back, and she found it impossible to sit placidly through the meal. She pushed haricots verts around on her plate with her fork, fiddled with her bread until was it was in bits, and swirled her charlotte russe into a cream and cookie mess. Though she knew her mother and Arthur were watching her, she couldn't seem to stop wriggling in her chair. Before the meal was over, even Dinah noticed something was wrong.

"Sakes alive, Nan, what's wrong with you?" she demanded, frowning at Annabel across the table. "You've been jumpy as a cat on a hot tin roof all night."

"I'm fine, Dinah. Eat your dessert."

"Has she been jumpy?" George, never the most observant of men, looked up in surprise from his charlotte russe. "What's wrong, dear?"

"I said, I'm fine. It's just prewedding jitters, is all."

"Is that all it is, Annabel?" From his place beside Dinah, Arthur leveled his hard, shrewd stare at her. "Or are you having genuine doubts about marrying Bernard?"

"No!" She grimaced at once, that reply sounding far too emphatic to be sincere. "No, Uncle," she said, striving to seem calm, resolute, and sure. "I'm not having doubts."

"Because if you are," he went on as if she hadn't spoken, "it's better to have them now than have them afterward."

"Why would I be having doubts?" she asked, but she could hear the rising timbre of her voice, and she forced herself to bring it down. "Marrying Bernard is the right thing to do," she said in a quieter tone, but she sounded about as convincing as a huckster at the fair, the kiss that had almost happened burning her lips.

Annabel reached for her glass. *Almost doesn't count*, she told herself, gulping down ice water. *Almost doesn't count.*

"You don't have to marry him," George said, and his gentle comment only made things worse. Heavens, if her stepfather was noticing something wrong with her, she was about as transparent as glass. "It's not too late to call it off, Annabel."

The knots of dread that had been in Annabel's stomach all day twisted and tightened. "I can't call it off," she said, suddenly, inexplicably miserable. She glanced around the table, noted the steady gazes directed at her. "I can't!"

Her eyes welled up with tears of frustration and fear and an uncertainty she'd never felt about her engagement before. It was all because of that man. She hadn't felt any doubt at all until he'd showed up, and she was the biggest fool that ever lived if she thought even for a second that getting all weak in the knees over a cad she'd known only a few days was worth throwing away everything she'd ever wanted.

"I don't want to call it off," she said in the most dignified tone a woman could manage when she was on the verge of tears. "And even if I did, I wouldn't dream of doing that to Bernard. He would be crushed."

She didn't miss how Arthur and her mother exchanged glances at that, and she just couldn't take any more.

"I'm not calling it off!" she cried, tossing down her napkin, at the end of her rope. "I know that's what you want me to do, Uncle Arthur, but I'm marrying Bernard and that's that. Now, if y'all will excuse me, I am going to bed. I have a big day tomorrow, and I need my sleep."

For the third time in less than twelve hours, Annabel found herself running away. She returned to her room, and this time, she intended to stay there until the wedding. She had Liza draw her a bath, hoping the warm water would help her relax. As an additional aid to her frayed nerves, she ordered a glass of hot milk and drank it while Liza helped her into her nightgown and brushed out her hair. Afterward, Annabel dismissed the maid for the night and slid between the sheets of her sleeping berth, telling herself all she needed was a good night's rest as she settled her head on the pillow. Tomorrow morning, in the clear light of day, with her mind refreshed and her resolve renewed, these insidious doubts and fears would be gone. In fact, they'd probably seem downright silly.

* * *

Christian was not a disciplined man, but he was a realistic one. He was also a gambler, and a good one. He
knew when his luck was out, the chips were stacked
against him, and it was time to fold his hand. By the
end of the night, he knew he'd reached that point.

A man couldn't talk a girl out of marrying an idiot
if he couldn't talk to her at all. After his conversation
with Annabel down in steerage the other morning,
Christian had tried to find a way to talk with her again,
but there had been none. She had spent the past three
days clinging to her fiancé or her sister like a limpet
or hiding herself away in her room, leaving him no
opportunity to have another go at changing her mind.
It wasn't likely he'd have any chance tomorrow morning, either, since the ceremony was scheduled for ten
o'clock.

He spent the evening before the wedding in the main
ballroom, hoping if he could finagle a dance with her,
he'd have one last chance, but she and her family had
dined in a private room, and Arthur joined him in the
ballroom only long enough to admit defeat. His niece,
he said, had gone to bed.

There was nothing left to do, as far as Christian
could see, unless he was prepared to barge into her
room while she was donning her wedding gown to try
talking some sense into her one last time.

A tempting idea, he acknowledged as he entered
his stateroom suite late that night and closed the door
behind him; tempting in more ways than one. Smiling a little, he allowed himself to imagine her stand-

ing before him in lacy white undergarments as he removed his dinner jacket and waistcoat and loosened his tie.

She'd be surrounded by filmy piles of lace and tulle, he thought, leaning back against the door behind him and closing his eyes. The sun from the window would light up her loosened hair, turning it to fire. As the picture in his mind became more vivid, the arousal he'd felt the other day when he'd almost kissed her, arousal he'd had to work for three days to suppress, came flooding back. Damn, he thought with chagrin, he had a fine imagination.

Still, while barging into her room might be a tempting idea, it was probably a futile one as well. Annabel Wheaton had proved every bit as stubborn as her uncle had made her out to be, and she wasn't likely to see reason at this late date. No, he'd played and lost.

Moving softly so as not to wake Sylvia, who'd gone to bed nearly two hours ago, he crossed the sitting room of the suite to pour himself a cognac. After all, if a man was going to bid farewell to half a million dollars, he definitely ought to have a drink in his hand when he did it.

He sat down in one of the chairs of the sitting room with his drink, trying to contemplate his next move. Upon arrival in Liverpool the day after tomorrow, he'd book a return passage to New York and carry on with his original plans. After all, what else could he do?

A sound outside his room suddenly diverted Christian's attention, a soft click that sounded like a latch being pulled back, followed by the sound of a door opening. He frowned, straining to hear, fancying it was the door to Annabel's stateroom suite that had just been opened.

He'd heard no one come down the corridor, he'd heard no knock or murmur of voices, so no one in her party had rung for a servant or the steward. The door closed again, and when the soft pad of footsteps passed his door, curiosity impelled him to have a look.

He set aside his glass, rose, and walked to the door of his stateroom and opened the door. When he leaned out, he saw that it was Annabel herself who had left her suite and was now walking away from him down the corridor. That dark chestnut hair was unmistakable, long, loose, and gleaming beneath the electric lights of the passage. She was dressed in a loose-fitting satin tea gown of ice blue, and dangling from her hand was a short, squat bottle that she carried by one finger hooked in the glass loop of the bottleneck.

Curious, he waited until she'd disappeared around a corner halfway down the passage, then he snagged his jacket and left his own room. He slipped into his jacket as he followed her, turning where she had just in time to see her vanish through the door that led to the servants' stairwell. Not wanting her to know he was trailing her until he knew where she was headed, he took care to be as quiet as possible as he went through

the same door she had, and he slipped off his shoes
before he followed her down the servants' stairs. He
could hear the clatter of her shoes against the steel,
and by listening carefully, he was able to discern from
the rhythm of her footsteps whether she was going
down steps or turning on a landing, and by the time
he heard the click of a door opening, he knew she had
gone all the way down to E-deck, the bottom of the
ship. He doubted she was going to the engine rooms,
so the only place she could be headed was cargo. Concern began to mingle with his curiosity. What on earth
was she doing?

He quickened his steps, and when he reached the
bottom, he donned his shoes again, opened the door
leading out of the stairwell, and emerged into an
enormous cargo bay. A few of the electric lights had
been switched on, probably by Annabel herself, but he
couldn't see her amid the stacks of cargo.

"Annabel?" he called.

A groan issued from farther along the cargo bay in
reply, but nothing more.

"Annabel, are you all right?"

"Go away!"

He ignored that rather belligerent order, and started
in the direction of her voice, making his way amid
stacks of crates and steamer trunks, and it wasn't until
he'd almost reached the other side of the cargo bay that
he found her, sitting in the back of a cherry-red Model
A Ford.

She was seated in one of the two angled passenger

seats in the rear of the vehicle, her bare feet propped up on the driver's seat. She hadn't turned the lighting on at this end of the bay, and in the dimness, her satin gown shimmered like liquid silver.

At the sight of him, she groaned again, her head lolling back in an obvious gesture of exasperation. "Why, Lord?" she asked, staring at the ceiling overhead as if talking to God. "Why have you brought the plagues of Egypt down upon me?"

Not the least bit discouraged by being the plagues in question, he moved to the back of the Ford. "When a young woman goes wandering about the ship in the middle of the night, someone has to look after her," he said, pulling open the latch to unfasten the door at the rear of the vehicle. He climbed between the two wing seats and sat down in the empty one, giving her a grin. "Think of me as your guardian angel."

"More like devil," she complained, but she didn't sound angry, only rueful.

"Smashing car," he commented, taking a glance over the vehicle as he settled back in his seat, a seat that, like hers, angled inward, enabling the two backseat passengers to converse with each other more comfortably. "Yours, I trust?" When she confirmed that with a nod, he added, "You must let me drive it sometime. I've never driven a Ford."

"No one drives my car but me," she told him. "And Mr. Jones, of course. He's our chauffeur, and an expert motorist. He taught me to drive."

"I'm a rather good motorist myself, I'll have you know. At Scarborough Park, we hold a charity auto race every August, and Andrew and I always enjoyed the privilege of driving the cars entered in the race."

"Well, the Ford wouldn't ever win. It only goes twenty-eight miles an hour."

"Still, I should like to take it for a spin. I'm not bragging about my skill, I promise. I've never yet had a smashup. Not even close."

"No," she said again. "Only me and Mr. Jones. Not even Bernard is allowed to drive my car."

"That'll change after the wedding," Christian assured her. "All your personal property becomes Rumsford's when you marry him."

"No, it doesn't. I kept my stuff separate in the marriage settlement."

"And you think that makes a difference?" he countered. "If Rumsford chooses to take your car out, who's to stop him?"

She gave him that skeptical little frown, the one she always had when she thought he was talking nonsense, but she didn't argue the point. Instead, she shifted in her seat and crossed her feet, a move that slid her skirt several inches up her shins, rewarding him with a view not only of her delectable pink toes and fine ankles, but also of a pair of shapely calves.

Still, as much as he appreciated the view, he also appreciated that the cargo bay was at least fifteen degrees colder than the upper tiers of the ship. He moved to take off his jacket. "Here," he said, offering it to her, surprised when she shook her head in refusal. "Aren't you cold?"

"Nope."

"You must be. It's bloody freezing in here. Humor me," he added when she still didn't take it.

She leaned forward, allowing him to drape it around her shoulders. "Thank you, but like I said, I'm not cold." She reached down to retrieve the bottle he'd seen earlier and held it aloft for him to see. "In fact, I am as warm as toast."

He grinned again, enlightened. "I thought you didn't drink."

"I never said that. I said I don't like the taste, but I'm not a teetotaler. I just can't sleep, is all, and I thought a drink would help." She held out the bottle by the loop handle. "Have some?"

He studied the fat jug for a moment. "You didn't obtain this from the steward," he said as he took it.

"No," she said with a chuckle. "This ship's too grand for that. But George always takes several bottles along when we're traveling. It's handy for medicinal purposes."

He caught the slurring of her S's, and he could tell she was already feeling the effects of this particular medicine. "And what ails you this evening, Annabel? You're not nervous about tomorrow, are you?"

"Cryin' all night!" She made a sound of exasperation. "If one more person mentions prewedding jitters to me, I'll go crazy."

That emphatic reply told him that not only he, but

several other people as well, had hit upon the same theory. He deemed her nervousness and insomnia as very good signs, and he felt a rekindling of hope. Perhaps he still had one last chance to talk her off the cliff she was so determined to jump from. Perhaps.

Chapter Seven

He doubted getting drunk with Annabel was a tactic Arthur would approve of, but it was his last chance. The squat shape of the bottle made it impossible to hold with one hand, so Christian used both to bring it to his lips, but a second later, he was wishing he hadn't. Taking a swallow, he immediately choked, his throat on fire. "Good God," he said, his body giving a convulsive shudder. "What is this?"

She laughed, a low, throaty laugh. "Moonshine, sugar. Pure Mississippi moonshine."

He thrust the bottle back toward her. "It's foul. No wonder you don't like the taste."

She leaned forward, hooked her finger in the handle, and pulled the bottle out of his grasp. Twisting her wrist, she flipped the jug so that its weight rested on top of her elbow, then she raised it to her lips and took another swallow. "Aw, after a few nips, it's not so bad."

He eyed her, doubtful. "And where you come from, that is considered medicine?"

"For near anything that ails you."

He considered that, sliding his gaze to her bare feet for a moment. Then he held out his hand. "Pass that back."

With a chuckle, she did so. He held the bottle as she had done, balancing its weight on his arm, and took another swallow. He choked again, but it burned a little less this time.

"So," she said as he settled the jug on his knee, "Why are you following me around the ship? Couldn't you sleep, either?"

"I could not. When I heard your door open and close, I was curious, and when I saw you with this bottle, I knew I had to follow you." His gaze roamed over her face, a face that would keep any man up at night. "A beautiful woman should never drink alone."

Her lips parted, her tongue darted out to moisten them, and in that heart-stopping instant, he knew both of them were unable to sleep for the very same reason. "Is that a rule?" she whispered.

It shouldn't be, not for her and him. He ought to go, now, because scarcely five minutes in her company, and he was already thinking about what might happen if he stayed. He wanted to do what he'd been hired to do, but he also liked her, and he didn't want to toy with her. And he would if he stayed. He'd toy with her, and possibly a lot more. He moved to leave.

"I couldn't sleep because of the things you said."

Her soft admission had him sinking back into the seat, and he told himself he'd behave. He would. Even if it killed him. "What I said?" he echoed her. "I'm not sure I know what you mean."

"I think it was the part about love that kept me up," she said, and reached for the bottle to take another swallow. "Or maybe it was the chilblains."

He laughed. He couldn't help it. The juxtaposition was too absurd not to laugh.

"Or maybe," she went on in a musing voice, "it's how he likes to order my food for me, and he doesn't like it when I order it myself." She paused, but before he could reply that knowing Rummy as he did, he wasn't surprised, she went on, "You asked me this morning if I want love when I married. I don't think I ever answered you."

"No, you didn't."

She took her feet down and turned to face him. Setting the bottle on the floor, she leaned toward him, reminding him for a moment of a little girl telling a secret. It made him want to smile. "I was in love once."

"Ah. The blackguard from Mississippi."

"His name was Billy John Harding. And he was the son of the richest man in Gooseneck Bend. His family had fourteen hundred acres of prime bottomland planted in cotton. My mama's family sharecropped on their land."

"Sharecropped?"

"Tenant farming, you call it, but that wasn't the only reason the Hardings were rich. They also owned the local bank. Harding Brothers Building and Loan. I knew Billy John all my life. He was seven years older than me, and I was always kind of in love with him. All the girls were, one time or another. He had a way with him, that's for sure. But the summer I was seventeen, I went away to stay with friends in Hattiesburg, and the first Sunday after I came back, I saw him lookin' at me after church. Lookin' at me different."

She met Christian's eyes. "I think you're the sort of man who knows just what I mean by that."

He did. Christian drew a deep breath and let it out slowly. It wasn't something he was particularly proud of, but he knew.

"He looked at me like he'd never seen me in his life before," she went on. "Like all of a sudden, I was the most beautiful girl he'd ever seen."

Christian opened his mouth to point out that the chap had probably felt that to be the absolute truth, but she spoke before he could.

"Like I mattered. Like I was the most important thing in the world. I fell for him that day, right there in church. Fell for him like a ton of bricks. Within a week we were meeting in secret down by Goose Creek. He wanted—"

She broke off, but she didn't have to say the rest. He knew what Billy John Harding had wanted. Hell, he wanted it, too, right now, right here.

"I was such a fool," she murmured, and looked past him to stare dreamily into space. "I was thinking we'd get married. He said he was in love with me, too. 'Course, he wasn't. He had a hankering for the mud is all. Well," she added, her expression hardening as she took a swallow of moonshine, "he got what he wanted."

Christian heard the bitter tinge to her voice, and he wished he could sweeten it somehow, gloss over it, make it into something other than the sordid old tale he was beginning to fear it was. "How do you know he didn't love you?" he asked, and took the bottle from her, feeling in need of a drink. "Did he say so?"

"He didn't have to. Afterward, when I mentioned us getting married, he said . . ." She paused a long moment before she spoke. "He said, 'Marry you? Why would I marry you? A white trash girl like you is only good for one thing, honey, and marriage isn't it.' He wasn't even done buttoning his pants when he said it."

He grimaced at the crude, cruel brutality of it. "Bastard."

With that, he took another drink, a bigger one, thinking a man who said something like that to a girl, especially after taking her virtue, ought to be horsewhipped. He rather wished the fellow was on board so he could administer that particular justice himself.

He watched her for a moment, studying the beautiful face that right now was as hard and smooth as a millpond in winter. "That must have hurt," he finally said.

She shrugged as if it didn't matter, but he knew otherwise. Eight years later, it still mattered. "I wasn't the first girl he'd made a fool of, or the last," she said. "But I think I'm the only one who was ever able to get him back."

"Get him back?" He frowned, not quite understanding the vernacular. "What do you mean? You renewed your acquaintance with him? No," he amended even before she shook her head, "you mean you took revenge?"

She nodded. "Three years ago."

He tried to imagine what sort of vengeance a girl could mete out in exchange for such despicable treatment, but he couldn't even hazard a guess. "What did you do?"

She leaned back in her chair, giving him an unexpected, decidedly tipsy grin. "I bought the bank."

Christian gave a shout of laughter, and she laughed with him. "Billy John had taken over the bank and the farm from his daddy, who had died," she went on, "and he'd messed things up so bad that he had to sell the farm, and he had to bring in an investor to keep Harding Building and Loan from going under, too."

"And you were that investor?"

She pointed to her chest. "Southern Belle Investment Group," she said proudly. "You should have seen his face when I sashayed into the bank to sign the papers and take the controlling interest. He looked like he'd been poleaxed, bless his heart."

Christian smiled, cheered a little by the knowledge that the cur had gotten some punishment, though less than he'd deserved. "What did you say to him?"

" 'I have some bad news, Billy John,' I said, sweet as pie. 'I'd love to keep you on, us bein' such old friends and all, but I can't. I have to let you go. I'm sorry about this, I really am, but there's just too much scandal attached to your name.' "

Christian's smile widened into a grin, for he could imagine the scene with ease. She was a good storyteller.

" 'Scandal?' he said. 'What scandal?' I just gave him my best wide-eyed, innocent look . . ." She paused, suiting the action to the word. " 'Why, Billy John,' I said, 'everybody knows you're the father of Velma Lewis's baby boy—now, don't deny it, darlin'. It's all over this town. And I just can't have someone working in my bank who'd have a child out of wedlock and refuse to marry the baby's mama, so I have to let you go.' " She gave a sigh, shaking her head as if in apologetic regret. " 'A man like you is good for only one thing, honey, and managing a bank isn't it. Best if'n you go back to Velma and put yourself out to pasture. Oh, but . . . that's right. You don't own any pasture anymore, do you?' "

Christian laughed. "By God, you know how to hit where it hurts."

"I do," she confessed, giving him a look of apology.

"Probably best if'n you didn't get on my bad side," she advised, and took the bottle from him to have another drink. "Funny thing, though," she added, settling the bottle on her knees. "Going into the bank that day was supposed to be the perfect revenge, but it wasn't really as sweet as I thought it would be."

"No?"

"No." She paused and grinned again. "But I have to admit, it was still pretty sweet."

"I'll bet it was." He paused, considering. "It all worked out for the best in the end, then, if you ask me," he said. Reaching out, he hooked the bottle with his finger and pulled it off her lap. "If Billy John had come up to snuff, if he'd married you, he'd have got his hands on all that money your father left you. And I can't think of anyone in the world who would deserve it less than a bastard like that. Much better that you never married him."

She considered that as she took back the bottle and took another drink. "That's true. I never thought of it quite like that, but everything did work out for the best. After all, I'm going to be a countess now."

He heard the hint of reverence in her voice and it angered him because he knew she thought being a countess was something special she didn't quite deserve. He could have said she was worth all the countesses he knew put together, but she probably wouldn't believe him. "Yes," he said instead, taking a swallow of moonshine. "You'll be a countess. And Rumsford will get your money instead of Billy John."

She scowled at him, not pleased at having that fact pointed out to her. "We should go," she said abruptly, and stood up. The moment she did, she swayed a little on her feet and gave a moan. "Oh!"

He jumped up, catching the bottle as it slid from her fingers and grasping her arm with his free hand to keep her from falling. "Are you all right?"

She frowned, pressing a hand to her forehead. "I feel dizzy."

"I'll bet you do," he murmured, trying to accept that he'd lost. "Come. I shall walk you back up to A-deck, but we'll have to separate there. You can't be seen wandering corridors with me in the middle of the night, so you'll have to go on alone once we reach the stairs. Can you do that?"

"Of course I can!" She looked quite indignant. "I'm not drunk. I'm just a little dizzy, is all."

"Of course," he agreed, deciding not to tell her the truth. He was decidedly tipsy himself, and he was used to spirits. If he was tipsy, she was three sheets to the wind. "Let's go."

She nodded and bent to retrieve her shoes as he reached behind her and grabbed his jacket. He climbed down from the Ford, and once she'd put her shoes back on, he helped her down. Together, they left the cargo bay and mounted the stairs, and when they reached the top, he opened the door for her to exit the stairwell. She did, but when she started to go the wrong way, he snagged her arm.

"Other way," he said, and turned her in the proper direction. "Halfway down the corridor, turn left."

He stepped back into the stairwell, closed the door, and waited until he thought she'd gotten far enough. Then he opened the door and looked down the corridor to find he'd been a bit optimistic in his calculations.

She wasn't quite halfway down the passage, and she was swaying as she walked, periodically bumping her right shoulder into the wall. Watching her, he grinned, knowing she was going to have one hell of a headache tomorrow. Maybe she'd be too sick to walk down the aisle. It wasn't likely to postpone the wedding, but he liked to cling to hope.

He watched her turn right, and he sighed. Taking a quick glance down the corridor to ensure no one was out for a midnight stroll, he raced after her and turned the corner just in time to see her making another turn.

Where on earth did she think she was going? "Annabel," he hissed, but she didn't stop, and he continued running after her. When he turned the corner, he almost cannoned into her, for she had come to a stop and was staring into what seemed to be nothing more than the closed door of an ordinary stateroom. He skidded to a halt beside her.

"What's a Turkish bath really like?" she asked, turning her head to look at him.

He shook his head, his wits a bit addled by this confounded moonshine of hers. "I beg your pardon?"

Annabel pointed toward the door, where a placard read: LADIES' TURKISH BATHS. GENTLEMEN FORBIDDEN. She started to open the door, but he stopped her, putting a hand on her shoulder. "Annabel," he whispered with a frantic glance around, "you can't do this."

Laughing, she shrugged off his hand and opened the door. "Why not?" she countered over her shoulder, then pushed the door wide and went in.

"Annabel, wait." He started to follow her, but then he stopped, remembering just in time that this room was for ladies only.

The door closed behind her, then opened again a second later. "Well, come on," she urged, frowning at him. "What are you still doing out there in the hall?"

He pointed to the placard, but she didn't seem impressed. "Don't be silly. There's no one in here. Not at this hour. Besides, what do you care?" she added, leaning forward to grab him by the ends of his tie. "You're not the kind of man who plays by the rules anyway."

He couldn't argue with that, especially not when she smiled that gorgeous smile of hers. He'd never been very good at resisting temptations, and he wasn't her damned chaperone. When she pulled at his tie again, he followed her inside, pushing on the button for the electrical light as he entered the room.

The ladies' Turkish bath was a bit different from the one used by the gentlemen. Its floor, ceiling, and walls were not covered in crisp blue and white tiles, but shell-pink ones instead. The potted palms, ferns, and wicker chairs were similar, but dark pink cushions and pots of orchids and African violets made this very much a ladies' sanctuary. The two brass radiators and two pedestal sinks were identical, as were the taps.

"So what are you supposed to do?" Annabel asked, glancing around.

Christian, were he really as bad as his reputation, could have reminded her that Turkish baths were best enjoyed while naked, but instead, he proved he might have a shred of redemption left in him, tossed his jacket onto a chair, set the bottle on the tile floor, and turned to reach for the taps above the radiator nearest him. He turned the taps, and almost at once, steam began pouring into the room. Nodding to the wall behind her, he said, "Turn those."

She did, and within moments the entire room was filled with steam. Laughing, she lifted her face to the jets overhead, holding out one palm as mist swirled all around her. "Good Lord," she said, "this *is* just like church in July!"

He laughed, watching her. She was so different from any woman he'd ever met before, and he'd met many. Her determination and stubbornness were formidable, but they concealed what he knew now to be a very vulnerable heart.

Not that he found her heart the most important part of her anatomy, a fact he proved to himself by slanting a glance over her. The steam was making her loose-fitting tea gown cling to her body, demonstrating that her voluptuous curves were not formed by a corset, since the damp satin showed quite plainly that she wasn't wearing one. Or much of anything else, for that matter.

She didn't seem to realize what the steam was revealing to his gaze. Still laughing, she reached for the bottle and took a swallow of moonshine, but when she set it back down and looked into his face again, she froze. So did he, lust washing over him in a wave.

"We should go," he blurted out, and wanted to kick himself in the head. "Right now."

"I suppose we should. Tomorrow—" She ducked her head. "Tomorrow is my wedding day."

He did not want to think about that, and he opened his mouth to try one last time to talk her out of it, but then, she lifted her head again.

"Christian?"

He took a breath. "Yes?"

"Do you really think Bernard would just step aside if King Edward were to . . . to want me?"

Saying yes would help his cause, and yet, he hesitated, suddenly wanting to tell her not what was convenient, not what was exaggerated, but what was the truth. He considered for a long moment before he gave her an answer.

"Yes," he finally said, "Yes, Annabel, I think he would."

"You might be wrong," she whispered.

He thought of the courtesan at the House with the Bronze Door. "I don't think I am."

Christian took a step toward her, then stopped before he could take another. "We should go," he said

again, getting a bit desperate, fully aware that what
he felt would be blatantly obvious if she were to look
down.

"What about you?" she asked.

"Me?" God, why was it so hard to think? He raked
his hands through his hair. This moonshine seemed to
have turned his brains to flotsam. "I don't understand
what you mean."

She moved a bit closer, clasping her hands behind
her back, a move that pushed her breasts out and
forced his gaze downward. When he saw the hard
outline of her nipples against the thin layer of blue
satin, his throat went dry, and the desire inside him
threatened to burn away the tight leash he had on
his control. "Annabel—" He stopped and swallowed
hard. "I don't think—"

"Would you do it if it was your wife? What if I was
married to you, and King Edward came after me? What
would you do?" She moved another inch closer, and the
tips of her breasts brushed his shirtfront, making him
imagine the satin slick against his bare skin. "Would
you step aside?"

"No," he said hoarsely, every muscle in his body
thrumming with lust even as he looked into her vulnerable, upturned face. "I'd thrash him within an inch of
his life."

"You would?" Her voice was an incredulous whisper, and when she smiled, he felt like some bloody
knight in shining armor even as he wanted to rip her
clothes off.

"Yes. But—" He lurched back, making a belated attempt to retreat to safer ground, his befuddled male brain desperately grasping for control over his aroused male body. "I doubt I'd have the chance. You'd probably have thrashed him yourself, gagged him, and tied him to a chair before I even heard what happened."

She laughed, that dazzling smile lighting up her face, and Christian knew if he couldn't make her see that marrying Rumsford was an idiotic thing to do, it wouldn't take long before she didn't smile like that anymore. Something tight twisted inside him, like a fist squeezing his chest until he couldn't seem to breathe, making him realize that, despite rumors to the contrary, he had a heart, because right now it hurt. For her, for Evie, for all the girls like them who couldn't accept the most basic truth about men.

Rakes don't reform.

"You can't do it." He reached out and grasped her arms, wishing he could shake sense into her stubborn brain, knowing he couldn't. And even if he could, it probably wouldn't stick. How the hell could he make her understand what it would be like? What it would do to her? What she would become? "You can't marry Rumsford. If you marry him, you'll be making the biggest mistake of your life, trust me."

"How do you know?"

"Because I just do." That wasn't a reason, but he didn't know what to say. He couldn't tell her about Evie, how unhappy Evie had been with him, with

England, with the harsh reality of their marriage once her eyes had been opened. He couldn't tell her Evie had hated the rain, the dull tedium of English country life, and him. She'd hated him most of all. For being a deceitful, lying cad and for breaking her heart. He couldn't explain that he hated himself for the same reason, and because he'd been off gambling his way across France when Evie had lost the baby, and because he hadn't arrived home in time to stop her from walking into a pond when she didn't know how to swim.

He couldn't tell Annabel any of those things, but he could tell her about Rumsford. "You can't marry him because he doesn't love you. Because he's a fortune hunter, and he's an ass. Because he orders your food for you without consulting you, without even considering that you might want something different. Because he'll wear you down, him and his sisters and his mother, and all their relations, molding you and shaping you and changing you when there isn't a damned thing wrong with you and you don't need to be changed. Because he doesn't respect you, because he acts as if you're lucky to have him when he ought to be down on his knees thanking God he's lucky enough to have you. And because . . . damn it all . . . because there are things you'll never know with him, things he'll never be able to make you feel."

She groaned and started to pull away. "There you go, talkin' 'bout love again. If you mention love one more time, I swear I'll—"

"I'm not talking about love. I'm talking about something else, a feeling I'd wager my life Rumsford has never given you."

"What feelin' is that?"

He let go of her arms and cupped her face in his hands. "This one," he said, and kissed her.

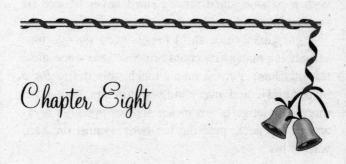

Chapter Eight

She ought to stop him—in the vague, hazy recesses of her mind, Annabel reminded herself that she was engaged to another man and Christian's mouth on hers was wrong. She should turn away, step back, do . . . something. But she was too shocked, too dazed, too dizzy to break free, and it wasn't all because of the moonshine. She was intoxicated, yes, but it wasn't the alcohol that was making her feel this way.

Almost without realizing what she was doing, she parted her lips, turning the warm press of his mouth against hers into a lush, openmouthed kiss that sent shimmers of pleasure throughout her body, pleasure so startling she cried out.

He touched her tongue with his own, deepening the kiss, and as if her body had a will of its own, Annabel grasped fistfuls of his jacket and rose up on her toes, responding to the caress of his tongue with a passion she'd vowed she'd never let herself feel again.

Eight years since she'd experienced the glorious sensation a man's kiss could bring, so long since she'd felt this hunger for a man's touch, this desire for a man's body, and everything within her demanded more. She let go of his jacket and wrapped her arms around his neck, pressing her body against the hard wall of his.

He made a rough, ardent sound against her mouth. His hands slid from her cheeks down the sides of her throat, over her collarbone, to her breasts. He paused there for only a second, just long enough that he must have felt the beat of her thudding heart through the thin satin of her gown. Then he wrapped an arm around her waist and yanked her upward off the ground, bringing her hips against his.

The feel of him, hard and aroused against her, brought her back to reality with painful force. She tore her mouth from his, gasping, and brought her arms down between them to push his aside as he set her down. Wrenching herself free, she stepped back.

He was breathing hard, watching her, and she stared back at him, wordless, as arousal, shock, and dismay coursed through her blood.

Oh Lord, she thought wildly, *I never learn. I never, ever learn.*

That awful admission had barely crossed her mind when suddenly the floor seemed to cave in beneath her, opening up to send her falling down into a dark abyss, and her last thought before everything went black was that she was in serious trouble now.

"Annabel?"

She sat up, sucking in deep gasps of air, her heart thudding like mad in her chest, as if she were a wild rabbit on the run from a hungry wolf.

The room was dimly lit by the oil lamp burning on the table beside her bed, but the pale gray outline of light around the closed draperies of the window told her it was morning.

"Annabel?" her mother's voice came again, followed by a knock on her door. "Annabel, are you in there?"

A dream, she thought, and the sound of her mother's voice sent relief washing over her in a flood. Praise Jesus. She pressed a hand against her pounding heart. *She'd just been having a dream.*

Upon that conclusion came another. She didn't feel well. Her head hurt, her throat was parched and cottony, and she felt slightly sick to her stomach.

"Annabel?" Her mother knocked again, louder this time.

"I'm here, Mama," she called back, and as her door opened, she started to push back the covers to get out of bed. But then she caught the glimmer of pale blue satin, and a vague memory of why she was wearing a tea gown instead of a nightgown flashed through her mind, along with a pair of smoldering blue eyes and swirling gray mist. At once, she jerked the covers back up, barely managing to cover herself before her mother entered the room.

"Rise and shine, sleepyhead," Henrietta said, bustling in. "Today is your wedding day, remember?"

Annabel stared at her mother, and her wedding was the furthest thing from her mind because she was realizing with horror that she hadn't been dreaming at all. She really had sat in the Ford last night getting drunk on moonshine with Christian Du Quesne.

"Why, Annabel Mae," her mother exclaimed, coming to a halt at the foot of her bed, "you're as white as a sheet. What's wrong? Are you sick?"

Sick? Annabel put a hand to her head, which was aching fit to split. "I don't feel well," she mumbled. "Get me headache powder, Mama, would you, please? And some peppermints?"

"Of course, darlin'." Henrietta departed in search of the requested remedies, and Annabel jumped out of bed. Frantic, panicky, she yanked off the tea gown and tried to recall the events of the previous night as she put her nightclothes back on.

She hadn't been able to sleep last night, she remembered. She'd gotten out of bed, taken one of George's bottles of home brew from the liquor cabinet in the sitting room, thinking it would help calm her jangled nerves and make her sleepy, and she'd gone for a walk. She'd gone down to the cargo hold where she'd thought sure she'd be unobserved, and she'd sat in the Ford for a while, imagining herself motoring along England's country lanes with Bernard. She'd tried to envision herself in her new life as his countess, hoping to restore her confidence about her decision to marry him. And then . . . and then . . . Christian had shown up. That, of course, was when the trouble started.

He had followed her down there, which was aggravating enough, but even worse was the incomprehensible fact that she'd let him stay. Christian Du Quesne, the cause of her cold feet, her insomnia, her doubts. She'd let him stay. What had she been thinking?

Annabel strove to remember more. He'd given her his coat to put on, and they'd sat in the car, talking. About the Ford, about love, and . . . oh Lord.

She'd told him, she realized in horror, her hands stilling on the sash of her robe. She'd told him about Billy John.

Annabel groaned, pressing a palm to her forehead, her cheeks burning. She'd confessed her most humiliating moment, spilled her most secret shame to that man. Why?

Taking a deep breath, she shoved aside pointless questions. She had no time for those. All right, so she'd talked water uphill and revealed things even her best friend, Jennie Carter, didn't know to a man she'd just met. What concerned her wasn't what she'd said, anyway.

What had she *done*? Annabel began to pace back and forth across her stateroom, striving to remember the rest of what had happened, trying to ignore the sick certainty in her guts that with moonshine and that man involved, she might have done just about anything.

They'd left the cargo hold together, she remembered that. They'd started back to A-deck, and then, somehow, they'd ended up in the ladies' Turkish bath, of all places.

He'd kissed her. Annabel halted in dismay and shock, wondering what all had happened to her common sense. The night before her wedding, another man had kissed her. And she'd let him do it.

Impelled by that awful realization, she started pacing again, forcing herself to recall other embarrassing details. She remembered feeling faint—from moonshine, she told herself firmly, not from his kisses. She remembered her knees sinking under her, him lifting her in his arms and carrying her back to her room, laying her on the bed, and leaving. And that was all.

The door opened, interrupting these memories, and Annabel turned, pasting a nonchalant look on her face as Liza entered the room. She was carrying the wedding dress draped carefully over her arms, two maids behind her bringing the long cathedral train.

"Good mornin', Miss Annabel," Liza said in her cheerful Irish brogue, giving her a wide smile. "Are you ready to go downstairs and say 'I do'?"

She felt another jolt of panic at that question, and she pressed a hand to her mouth, working to think clearly. She'd done nothing wrong last night—well, not much anyway, she amended, forcing down a pang of guilt. There were more than a hundred people downstairs, waiting to watch her marry the Earl of Rumsford, a man she still wanted to marry. Yes, Scarborough had kissed her, but what was she supposed to do about it now? Call off the wedding because of one night of madness? Humiliate a man she was genuinely fond of by abandoning him at the altar? Ruin all her hopes and her sister's future and relegate her family back to the status of social outcasts because of one kiss from a man she'd known less than a week?

Not a chance. Annabel lowered her hand and drew a deep, steadying breath. "I'm ready, Liza," she said, and tried to mean it. "I'm more ready than I can say."

The moonshine bottle was empty.

Christian frowned, turning it upside down, watching as one last drop of the clear liquor fell to the carpet beside his bed.

For a man who didn't care for the stuff, he seemed to have polished off quite a bit of it during the past few hours. He hadn't drunk enough, however, to blot out the memory of kissing Annabel Wheaton.

The skin of her cheeks was like silk. He could still feel it, warm against his fingers. Her mouth, so soft, like velvet, tasting of the moonshine they'd drunk.

He fell back against the wood-paneled wall behind his bunk, closing his eyes, still able to feel her body pressed against his, smell the scent of her hair, taste her tongue in his mouth. He could still hear their hard, labored breaths afterward mingling with the hiss of steam taps and radiators. And he could still see the desire in her eyes, desire he'd found quite gratifying.

Until she passed out.

He'd caught her before she hit the floor, and even though she'd woken up, she'd had some difficulty standing on her own. He'd carried her back to her rooms, torturing himself during every step with the knowledge that she hadn't a stitch of clothing on under her gown. He'd gotten her back into her suite and into her room— at least, he'd hoped from the empty berth that it was her room—and how he'd managed that particular feat without waking any members of her family still baffled his alcohol-hazed mind. He'd laid her in the sleeping berth without taking even a single peek under her skirt, and sadly, his imagination had been trying to picture what he'd missed ever since.

No, as much as he'd had to drink, it wasn't enough to make him forget all that. Obviously, he needed another drink.

Christian tossed the empty jug onto his bunk, left his room, and retrieved a bottle of whiskey from the liquor cabinet in the sitting room. Not bothering with a glass, he took a couple of generous swigs straight from the bottle, but that didn't help much, either.

His body still ached with desire, ignited by her stunning smile and perfect body and soft vulnerability, desire he'd never be able to act on. And he knew he must truly be an idiot because that fact bothered him a hell of a lot more than losing half a million dollars.

He returned to bed, taking the bottle with him, but he didn't sleep. Instead, he drank, and imagined, and listened to the traveling clock on the shelf behind his head tick away the minutes.

He knew when Sylvia got up, he heard her ring for her maid in the room next door. He thought of ringing for his valet, but then changed his mind. Going to Annabel Wheaton's wedding, watching her chain herself to the Earl of Rumsford for the rest of her days, was the last thing he felt inclined to do.

When Arthur had first approached him, he'd deemed it a perfect, heaven-sent opportunity, but as the minutes ticked by, he also knew what hell it was going to be now that he had failed. He'd planned to be in town for the season, and the possibility of encountering Annabel, of seeing her on the arm of that pompous-ass husband of hers, was a god-awful prospect, one that if he wasn't already drunk, would soon impel him to be. In fact, he might find himself spending the entire London season in a state of perpetual intoxication.

He tried to look on the bright side. He didn't know yet that he had failed. Perhaps some of the things he'd told her had penetrated, and she'd cry off at the last minute. He hadn't been formally invited to the wedding, but the faint possibility that Annabel had come to her senses and that he could see her jilt Rummy at the altar was too irresistible to be ignored. He had to see for himself, and to hell with the niceties of etiquette.

Christian sat up, twisting his head around to look at the clock, which seemed insistent upon dividing itself in two, but after concentrating hard for several seconds, he was able to determine that it was still a few minutes before ten. He swung his legs over the side of his bunk and stood up, a move that had him reaching for the edge of the nearby table, where he held on until everything stopped spinning.

Moving carefully, he bent to retrieve his jacket, which was lying in a huddled heap on the floor by his bed, and as he put it on, the hazy thought crossed his mind that he probably looked the worse for wear. A glance in the mirror of his bathroom confirmed that he looked even worse than he thought. In fact, he looked like hell.

The face that stared back at him showed not only his lack of sleep but also his unshaven face and uncombed hair, and probably his inebriated state as well. He ran a hand over his cheek and grimaced at the sandpapery feel of it, but there was nothing he could do about it. Being late to a wedding was worse than being unshaven and badly dressed.

He did what he could. He splashed cold water on his face, raked his fingers through his hair to comb the unruly strands into some kind of order, and smoothed his wrinkled tuxedo. He also tried to re-form his tie into a bow, but though he didn't know how long he spent on that particular effort, eventually, he was forced to give it up as a lost cause. Letting the ends of his tie fall, he turned away from the mirror, and left his stateroom.

The wedding was already in progress by the time he arrived, and a glance around revealed that there were no empty seats. Annabel seemed determined to go through with it, and he leaned against one of the faux-marble columns at the back of the room, resigned to watching what was sure to be the greatest mockery of matrimony since his own wedding. A few minutes later, however, Christian discovered that it would have been better for everyone if he'd just stayed in bed.

This was the moment every girl dreams of.

As Annabel stood with Bernard before the minister, all the panic and guilt she'd felt earlier eased away. This morning when she'd first woken up, she'd been a downright mess of a girl, and no denying it. But the headache powder and peppermints had done their work, and along with a light breakfast of toast and tea, they had conquered any physical aftereffects of last night. The mental battle had proved a more difficult one, but she'd conquered that, too, and now Annabel felt like herself again, sure, confident, and ready for the future, as she listened to Reverend Brownley begin the ceremony.

"Dearly beloved," the minister intoned, "we are gathered here, in the sight of God and in the face of this company, to unite this man and this woman in the bonds of holy matrimony, which is an honorable estate, instituted by God . . ."

She glanced at the man beside her, and at the sight of his profile, she felt all her fondness and gratitude coming back, along with an enormous sense of relief. Everything seemed to shift back into place, including her common sense.

" . . . and into this holy estate," Reverend Brownley went on, "these two persons present come now to be joined. If any man can show just cause why they may not lawfully be joined together, let him now speak, or else hereafter forever hold his peace."

He had barely uttered that token phrase before another voice followed, the voice of the Duke of Scarborough, ricocheting through the room with the force of a gunshot.

"I have just cause."

Shocked gasps from the wedding guests echoed in the wake of that pronouncement, and people stirred, looking toward the back of the room to the man who had spoken. Beside her, Bernard turned around, but Annabel suddenly couldn't seem to move. She felt paralyzed, stuck in place like a fly on flypaper.

"This wedding is a farce," he went on, derision in every word. "A farce and a lie."

That snapped Annabel out of her momentary paralysis. She turned around, flinging back the tulle that covered her face to stare at the man leaning against one of the columns at the foot of the grand staircase. He was still wearing the same clothes he'd had on the night before, but though he looked rode hard and put away wet, he still managed to be handsome as the devil. And just about as much trouble.

Against her will, she looked at his mouth, and as she remembered it pressed against her own, warmth radiated through her body beneath her pristine white gown. Her own reaction caused tears of frustration and fury to sting her eyes. This was supposed to be the most beautiful and memorable moment of her life, and he was ruining it. Why?

As if hearing her unspoken question, he looked into her eyes, but if she hoped to find any clue there as to his motives, she was disappointed, for his expression was unreadable.

"You have voiced what is merely an observation," the reverend said, speaking to Scarborough. "Do you or do you not have just cause to object to these nuptials?"

His gaze raked over her. "I do."

Oh God, he was going to tell everyone about last night. Dread seeped into her, seeming to penetrate her very bones. When his gaze lowered to her lips, she pressed her fingers to them. *He couldn't. He wouldn't.*

He took a step toward her, but then he halted, swaying a little on his feet. Frowning, he blinked several times and once again moved to lean back against the pillar before he spoke again. "These two people are about to pledge before God to honor, love, and respect each other? Love? Respect?" He made a sound of contempt. "It's the height of hypocrisy, at least in their case."

"Oh!" Annabel breathed, "Why, you low-down, despicable cur of a man . . ."

Her voice trailed away, her dread giving way to rage, rage so great she couldn't say another word, rage that seared away every other emotion she'd felt today, rage that seemed to engulf every part of her—from the toes of her satin-slippered feet to the top of her tulle-veiled head, from her white-gloved fingertips to the ends of her perfectly coiffed hair. Rage that poured through her like lava and felt so hot it seemed to scorch the beautiful white satin of her wedding gown from the inside out.

"But that is merely an opinion," Reverend Brownley told him. "What is the just cause that warrants your objection, sir? You must be specific."

Still looking at her, Scarborough folded his arms across his wide chest, his lips curving in a faint, knowing smile. "Shall I tell him, Annabel?" he asked. "Or would you prefer to do it?"

It was that smile that galvanized her into action. Grasping handfuls of her long gown in her fists, she started toward him, ignoring the avid stares of the guests.

"Tell me what?" Bernard asked behind her as she stalked up the aisle. "Annabel, what does he mean?"

She didn't answer. At this moment all her attention was focused on the man in front of her, a man with mocking blue eyes and the morals of a snake, a man who had made it his business to put doubts about her marriage in her mind, who had made advances upon her person, and who was now managing to humiliate and disgrace her in front of all these people. Somehow, she had to stop him.

As she halted in front of him, she worked to contain her rage and muster her dignity. She might have been born in a tin-roof shack on a stretch of Mississippi backwater, but she was about to become a countess, and a countess always behaved with decorum.

She lifted her chin to a haughty angle worthy of her

future position and opened her mouth to tell him in a coldly polite manner to leave at once, but he spoke before she could.

"Don't you just love those Turkish baths?" he murmured under his breath, and any notions Annabel had of countesslike dignity went to the wall.

"You bastard." Without conscious thought, she hauled back her arm, curled her fist, and in front of more than one hundred members of New York and English society, she punched the Duke of Scarborough right in the jaw.

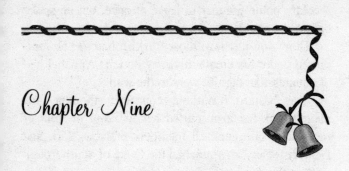

Chapter Nine

"That has to be the most humiliating spectacle I have ever witnessed in my life."

Sylvia stopped pacing back and forth across the sitting room of their suite to look daggers at him. "God knows you've always been cavalier about the niceties of etiquette, Christian, but this is so beyond the pale, I don't know what to say."

She proved that last statement a lie by continuing to talk as she resumed pacing. "Beyond the pale, unforgivable, and downright idiotic as well. What in heaven's name were you thinking?"

Christian pulled the poultice of ice chips from his bruised jaw and opened his mouth to reply that thinking really hadn't had much to do with it, but before he could say a word, Sylvia was off again.

"I know Rumsford is not one of your favorite people, but really! Stepping up and objecting at the man's wedding? Who ever heard of such a thing? That business about 'if any man has just cause' isn't meant to be taken *literally*, for heaven's sake! And what cause could you possibly have? And that poor girl. Dear God, I can only imagine what she must be feeling."

Sylvia stopped again, enabling him to at last get a word in. "Poor girl? She was about to marry Rumsford. Believe me, I did her a favor." He touched his bruised jaw with his fingertips and grimaced. "I think I did him one, too."

"A favor?" Sylvia shook her head, laughing in disbelief. "How is humiliating the bride, the groom, and all the guests a favor? How is embarrassing me and yourself and making the girl the subject of distasteful gossip by your insinuations a favor?"

Christian frowned. Had he made insinuations? He strove to remember, but the entire episode was already becoming quite vague in his mind. All he could recall was standing by the pillar thinking what a farce it was. And how someone should stop it. And Annabel's fist slamming into his face. That part he remembered with perfect clarity. Christian moved his jaw in an experimental fashion, and needles of pain shot through his entire face, making him appreciate that Annabel had a smashing right hook. In his inebriated state, the blow had actually sent him to the floor. He was lucky she hadn't broken his jaw.

She'd stepped over his prone body and walked out, her family chasing after her. Bernard, his sisters, and his best man had vanished by a side door for parts unknown. And Sylvia, with the help of ship's company, had dragged him off for this private set-to.

"How could you?" she demanded, still pacing and still fuming. "How could you do this to an innocent girl and a fellow peer?"

He found it hard to answer that question, for he didn't quite know what his motive had been. Still, he decided now was probably a good time to tell her about the half a million dollars, but she gave him no chance.

"You'll have to go at once and apologize to Miss Wheaton. And to Rumsford. You'll also have to explain yourself and find some way to make amends. God only knows how you'll manage that. What makes amends for something like this, I haven't a clue."

Sylvia was right, of course. An apology would be rather hypocritical, since he wasn't the least bit sorry, but it was required. As for making amends, he knew he'd have to do that as well, though he wished he'd thought of how to accomplish that particular feat before he'd opened his mouth. "Certainly, but I can't do it now. I'm quite drunk at the moment, in case you hadn't noticed."

"Who could help but notice?" she countered acidly. "And even if you hadn't been tilting three sheets to the wind, I would have known you were drunk, because you clearly didn't appreciate the implications of what you were saying."

Christian didn't reply. Sylvia's pacing was making him quite dizzy, especially since there seemed to be two of her. Trying to appreciate the implications of anything was nigh impossible. "What . . ." He paused and swallowed hard. "What implications are you referring to?"

That question brought her to a blessed halt. "Christian, you stood up and declared you had cause to stop her wedding! The only cause you could possibly have is a prior claim on her affections, but since you had only arrived in New York the day before the ship sailed, having never met her before, that claim is barely creditable. And after this morning's events, your names are now linked and you'll be the subject of intense gossip. I've no doubt rumors that the pair of you have been meeting secretly aboard ship have already started circulating through that room. You'll have to deny those rumors, of course."

Guilt slid through him. "Of course," he murmured.

"That is," she went on, staring at him, looking suddenly like a cat ready to pounce upon a hapless mouse, "if they are untrue."

Uh-oh. The fat was in the fire now. He tried to look innocent of any wrongdoing, but that didn't work. It never did with Sylvia.

"Oh, Christian." She groaned and sank into a chair. "You took advantage of an innocent girl? Oh my God."

"I didn't. At least, not really. I mean . . ." He rubbed his hands over his face, trying to think how to explain. "I didn't take the girl's virtue, Sylvia," he said after a moment. "And we have no romantic entanglement. She isn't tainted, for the love of God!"

"Then you'll have to go to Rumsford at once, explain that you were drunk, and that's all. That there's nothing between you and the girl, she's wholly innocent, and you acted out of . . . I don't know! Jealousy or something. Claim a crush on the girl, flatter his ego for having chosen such a pretty one, deny that she had anything to do with it—hell, I don't know what you'll say, but God knows you're glib enough to think of something and make it sound convincing. Somehow you've got to persuade him to go ahead with the wedding, which would halt any rumors in their tracks. You'll also have to apologize to him for your unspeakable conduct, too, of course."

That idea made him more nauseated than he already was. "Apologize to Rumsford? Not a chance in hell."

"Then what *are* you going to do? You have to do something! You compromised an innocent girl."

"I told you, I didn't compromise her." He swallowed hard and closed his eyes, fighting for control over his rebellious stomach long enough to explain. "Arthur Ransom hired me to try and talk her out of marrying Rumsford."

"What?"

"He offered to pay me half a million dollars."

"You stopped that girl's wedding and humiliated her for money?" She gave a disbelieving laugh. "You won't marry a girl for her dowry, but you'd allow yourself to be paid for ruining her? And her uncle hired you to do it?"

"No!" He opened his eyes. "All I was supposed to do

was talk her out of it, and I was trying, but she wasn't listening. She doesn't love him, and damn it all, Sylvia, he doesn't love her, either. He is after her money, and he's not even bothering to pretend otherwise, since he went to a prostitute the night before the ship sailed, right under her uncle's nose!"

"Oh heavens," she murmured, staring at him. "Does Miss Wheaton know any of this?"

"I don't know. I doubt it. Anyway, I was there, watching her, knowing she was about to throw her life away, and I was thinking what it would be like for her married to that pig—and Rumsford is a pig, Sylvia, you know it as well as I do—and all of a sudden, I was objecting without even realizing what I was doing. I wasn't even thinking about the money, although I'm sure no one in her family is going to believe that."

"Probably not," Sylvia murmured. "But I think I'm beginning to understand your motivations." She frowned, still studying him thoughtfully, a scrutiny he was in no frame of mind to interpret, for the room was starting to spin before his eyes, his stomach was wrenching violently, and he began to fear all the alcohol he'd consumed was about to come back up.

"I've got to lie down," he muttered, and suited the action to the words. The settee was too short for his long frame, but just now, his sleeping bunk seemed a long way away. He rested one foot on the arm of the settee and planted the other on the floor. Thankfully, the room stopped spinning.

"Lie down?" Sylvia cried. "You can't. You've got to do something."

Whatever his next action might be, he wasn't going to implement it now. He'd sort this all out and find a solution later, when he was sober. "Leave off, Sylvia," he muttered. "For God's sake, leave off. I'm in no condition to do anything at the moment. But I'll rectify the situation somehow."

"I hope so. For the sake of that poor, devastated girl, I hope so."

Contrary to what Lady Sylvia thought, Annabel was not devastated. She was mad, spitting mad, so mad that she hardly felt the pain in her hand. So mad that she was having difficulty expressing her anger, at least in words that did not describe the low moral character of the Duke of Scarborough.

"That vile man," she muttered, turning at the fireplace and starting back across the carpet. Though she was still in her wedding gown, her steps were not hampered by her train, which had been removed by Liza and taken away. "That low, despicable, dishonorable cad. That bastard. That villain."

Her mother and uncle were the recipients of this assessment of Scarborough's character. Since the awful events half an hour earlier, she had not seen Bernard or his sisters. She assumed they had gone to their staterooms. George, never good at handling difficult situations, had escaped to the smoking room. Dinah had been dispatched to her bedroom with orders to stay there, but though the door was closed, Annabel had no doubt her sister was peeking through the keyhole or pressing her ear to the door. She was too mad to care.

As for the source of her anger, she didn't know his whereabouts, and she didn't want to know, unless, of course, someone had thrown him overboard, in which case she'd have been delighted to hear the news.

"How could he?" she demanded, turning in a swirl of satin and tulle and starting back across the rug. As she asked that question, a fresh set of furious tears filled her eyes, but she blinked them back. "How could he do this?"

Arthur and Henrietta hadn't said a word since they'd all returned to the suite, allowing her to pour out this slew of perfectly justified outrage without interruption, but now, with Annabel's question hanging in the air, Henrietta was the first to respond.

"Well, he must have had a reason. What was it, Annabel?"

Annabel's steps faltered to a stop. That kiss flashed across her mind, more vivid each time she remembered it. She felt a blush of guilt and something more creeping into her face, and she hastily resumed pacing.

"Annabel?" Mama's voice was sharper now, sharp with suspicion. "What reason would the duke have to stop the wedding?"

Annabel was saved having to answer that inconvenient question by Uncle Arthur, of all people.

"Don't be raking Annabel over the coals, Henrietta. It's not her fault." He gave a cough. "It's mine."

"What?" The two women asked the question at the same time. Annabel stopped wearing out the rug, Henrietta turned to her brother, and they both stared at him in shock.

"I . . . um . . ." Arthur lifted his fist to his mouth and coughed again, wriggling in his chair as if he was a naughty schoolboy instead of a grown man. "I hired the duke to talk Annabel out of marrying Rumsford."

"You did what?" Annabel cried.

"Oh Lord." Henrietta fell back in her chair, eyes lifting heavenward. "Oh my Lord."

Annabel wouldn't have thought she could get any angrier, but now, looking at her uncle's shamefaced expression, she knew she'd been wrong about that. She discovered she had plenty of anger to go around. "You paid that man to stop my wedding?"

"No!" Arthur leaned forward, rubbing a hand over his balding head. "I only wanted him to talk with you. Try to explain to you what you'd be getting into marryin' one of these British peers. Maybe get you to postpone the wedding, take more time, think things over. But that was all. I sure didn't hire him to do what he did!"

"Oh, Arthur." Henrietta sighed. "How could you?"

Annabel stared at her uncle, but it was Scarborough she was thinking of. All their conversations made perfect, horrible sense. The way he'd tried to paint British marriage as some sort of awful trap, the way he'd disparaged Bernard, how he'd followed her down to the cargo bay. Even kissing her, she realized, must have been deliberate—to show her there were other fish in the sea, a calculated move with only a pretense of passion. He was good at acting, she realized. Very, very good. But then, bad boys always were. And it wasn't even as if he wanted to marry her himself. No, all he wanted was to stop her from marrying someone else so he could get paid.

That snake.

Her hands curled into fists. "How much?" she asked in a hard voice. Every man, she was beginning to appreciate, had his price. She wanted to know Scarborough's. "How much, Uncle Arthur?"

"Half a million dollars."

Henrietta gasped, obviously shocked by the amount, but Annabel wasn't shocked at all. One thing she'd learned about having money was that most things could be bought, if one was willing to pay enough. "Well, now that my reputation's in shreds because of that man's insinuations," she choked, fighting back tears of fury and pain, "I hope you're satisfied."

"I'm sorry, Nan," Arthur said heavily. "I'm sorrier than I can say. I thought I was acting for the best. But I swear, I just wanted him to talk you out of marrying Rumsford. I had no idea he'd stand up at the wedding! I love you, and I just want you to be happy, and I didn't think you knew what you were doing. I wanted you to take more time, sure if you did, you'd realize Rumsford wasn't good enough for you."

A knock at the door interrupted any reply Annabel might have made. She glanced at her mother, who was looking at her in inquiry, and she shook her head in refusal. She didn't want to face anybody, not yet.

Henrietta walked to the door, and Annabel returned her attention to her uncle. "We'll talk about this again," she told him through clenched teeth. "When I'm not mad enough to spit nails. That man doesn't get a penny of money, yours or mine, understand? And you are just damned lucky I love you so much," she choked, her throat closing up, " 'cause if I didn't, I think I'd have to kill you, Uncle Arthur."

Henrietta opened the door, cutting off any reply her uncle might have made, and at the sound of Bernard's voice, Annabel froze, glad he couldn't see her from this part of the sitting room.

"Mrs. Chumley," he said, "may I speak with your daughter, please?"

"My lord, it might be better to wait," Mama answered. "Annabel, as you might guess, is not feeling well."

"I realize that, but I believe it is best if this matter were resolved as quickly as possible. The guests are all still assembled."

That gave Annabel a spark of hope, trumping all the other emotions that were threatening to overwhelm her. If Bernard had inquired about the guests, perhaps he was here to see if she was ready to proceed. It might be just like Bernard to regard Scarborough's outburst as an appalling lack of good manners, best ignored and forgotten. He might be here to propose that they carry on as if nothing had happened.

She nodded to her mother, and Henrietta opened the door wide for Bernard to come in. Then, murmuring something about Dinah, she went to the girl's room and returned with her younger daughter firmly in tow. "Come along, Dinah. And you, too, Arthur. I think we could all do with some air."

For once, Dinah didn't protest being ordered about. Giving Annabel a wide-eyed look of sympathy over her shoulder, Dinah followed their mother and uncle out the door without a word, closing the door behind her.

Silence followed in the wake of her family's departure, and as she looked into Bernard's face, searching for signs of hope, she found little there to encourage her. He was always inclined to be a bit stiff, but now he seemed more aloof than ever. His expression was unreadable, and the silence seemed unbearable. She wanted desperately to say something to fill the void. "Bernard, I—"

"In light of this morning's events," he said, cutting off whatever she'd been about to say, "I believe we can both agree that the wedding needs to be canceled."

Her heart sank, but she thought maybe she could still head this off at the pass, if only she could find the right words. "Does it have to be canceled? We could . . ." She hesitated, but decided she had nothing to lose. "There's really no reason we can't go ahead."

"Go ahead?" Bernard looked at her askance. "Ignore

that mortifying spectacle as if it never happened? Annabel, you struck a duke in the face."

She grimaced, but decided it was best not to defend herself by pointing out that Scarborough had deserved it. "Everyone is still in the ballroom," she said instead, striving to sound calm and reasonable. "They're all waiting for an announcement of some kind, and if we announced that we're just going ahead as planned, everyone would conclude there was nothing to what Scarborough said."

Bernard stared at her, his appalled face telling her what he thought of that idea even before he spoke. "You can't possibly think I would marry you now?"

Annabel felt the first tear fall, sliding down her cheek, and with it, she felt all her hopes and dreams sliding away, too. She blinked, striving to hold back, as if stopping the tears would prevent what was coming, but his next words proved how futile that notion was.

"Your virtue has been compromised, Annabel. Given that, there is no possibility I can marry you."

Your virtue has been compromised.

Bernard didn't know that Billy John had compromised her virtue long before the Duke of Scarborough had ever shown up. Still, she couldn't just give up. She swiped at her cheeks, wiping tears away. "Bernard, I know you're upset, but—"

"Upset?" He fairly spat the word. "Annabel, *upset* does not even begin to describe how I feel at this moment. I have been grievously insulted, by Scarborough and by you."

"If you'd just let me explain—"

"Explain?" He folded his arms, his pale green eyes glittering with anger. "Yes, Annabel, do be kind enough to explain. What has been happening between you and Scarborough that provides him with just cause to stop our wedding?"

She opened her mouth, but no words came out. After all, what could she say? *Yes, darling, I was alone with another man, got drunk with him, and he kissed me. It all happened on the night before our wedding, but so what? Let's get married anyway.*

That probably wouldn't go over very well, and yet, she couldn't lie and say nothing had happened. She didn't mind putting a little glossy varnish on the truth from time to time, but outright lying to a man to get him to marry you was a line Annabel just couldn't cross.

"I'm sorry," she said instead. That, at least, was the truth. "Bernard, I know I've hurt you, and I'm so sorry."

He unfolded his arms and held out his hand. "The ring, Annabel. Would you kindly give me the ring?"

You can't possibly think I would marry you now.

Thousands of miles and millions of dollars away from Mississippi, she thought, but she was still the girl in the tin-roof shack who wasn't good enough to marry.

She slid the sapphire and diamond engagement ring off her finger and held the ring out to him. Through a blur of bitter tears, she watched him take it, turn away, and walk out without another word. With him went all her family's chances and her reputation, too. Everything ruined because of a sleepless night, a little moonshine, and a disreputable rakehell.

All Annabel's anger and pain came rushing back, and she just couldn't restrain it anymore. She was humiliated, disgraced, and mad as a hornet, and given all that, what else could a girl do but cry her eyes out?

She sank down onto a chair and sobbed until her nose clogged up, her throat was dry, and her lungs hurt. She cried until she didn't have another tear left. And then, when it was over and the tears were dry, she thought about what the heck she was going to do next.

But, really, why did she have to be the one to do anything? She might have been a fool last night, but the Duke of Scarborough was to blame for what had happened today. It was his responsibility to make things right. He broke her life, and she was damned well going to make him fix it.

On the other hand, she could just shoot him dead like a dog.

Right now, the second option appealed to her far more than the first. Unfortunately, shooting him wouldn't accomplish anything except make her feel better for about five minutes. After that, she'd be hanged.

No, her first option was her only choice. He had to repair the damage he'd done. The only question was how.

She thought about that long and hard, and after about an hour of considering and rejecting various possibilities, she began to see a way. But she couldn't do it alone.

Annabel washed her face, powdered her nose, and left the suite to go in search of Uncle Arthur. She was still mad as hell with him for interfering the way he had, but for her idea to work, she knew she needed her uncle's help.

She also knew she had to implement her plan right away. If she didn't, if she sat around much longer brooding about what had happened, she was liable to find one of George's pistols and go in search of Scarborough. And once she had a gun in her hand and that man in her sights, she just might decide shooting him was worth swinging in the wind.

By sunset, Christian was awake and sober, but he felt like death. His mouth was dry as dust, his stomach was still a bit queasy, and it seemed as if a herd of African water buffalo was thundering through his skull.

Sylvia, thankfully, was nowhere to be found, but she'd left him a note confirming that Rumsford had called off the wedding. Though his sister was absent, his valet was in the suite, and McIntyre took one look at him and fetched a Beecham's Powder and a pot of strong tea with plenty of honey and lemon. After consuming those, as well as having a bathe and a shave, Christian felt considerably better. By the time he'd put himself on the outside of a porterhouse beefsteak and a plate of chips, he began to think life might be worth living after all.

While his body recovered from the abuse suffered through alcoholic excess, his mind also began to function again, thank heaven. By eight o'clock that evening, he knew there was only one thing to be done, and by nine, he was knocking on the door of Annabel's stateroom suite, wearing a fresh evening suit and looking, he hoped, penitent.

The door was opened by Annabel's mother, who was understandably not happy to see him. "Mrs. Chumley," he greeted with a bow. "May I have a moment with Annabel?"

"Is there any reason why I should allow that?" she countered, but before he could answer, Annabel's voice floated out to him in the corridor.

"It's all right, Mama. Have His Grace come in. I'm just about done reading this over."

Henrietta opened the door wide, allowing him to enter, and as he did so, he took that opportunity to murmur a request for privacy. Henrietta's brows lifted a fraction, but then she shrugged. "Why not?" she murmured back. "At this point, the niceties don't matter much, do they?"

"No," he answered. "I'm afraid they don't."

"I'll be back in fifteen minutes." Glancing over her shoulder, she added, "Annabel, I'm going out for a few minutes."

"What?" Her daughter, who was standing by a round table in the center of the sitting room, glanced up from the documents spread out before her. "Going out? Where?"

"I just remembered I've got to talk to Arthur. I'll be right back. You two have business to discuss anyway."

She slipped out, ignoring her daughter's sound of protest, and closed the door behind her, leaving them alone.

Christian advanced into the room, halting on the other side of the table. Since there was no time to lose, he wasted none on preliminaries.

"First of all, let me say I owe you my most sincere apologies. My conduct was reprehensible."

"Which part?" she asked in a tart voice. "The part where you agreed to take money for talking me out of marrying Bernard? Or—"

"You know about that?"

"Uncle Arthur told me. Needless to say, he's not feeling inclined to pay you that money now, so is that what you're apologizing for? Hoping he'll give it to you anyway? Or maybe it's breaking up my wedding that you're sorry about? Or maybe it's because you called it a farce and a lie, and hurt my reputation? Or maybe it was the fact that you hauled off and kissed me last night? Which of those reprehensible things is the one you're apologizing for?"

That was rather a damning list, he supposed, but he felt compelled to defend himself on at least one of the charges.

"Well, as to the rest, I'm a rake of the first water, I daresay, but about the kiss, I feel compelled to point out that you did kiss me back."

"I did not kiss you back, you varmint!"

He didn't know what on earth a varmint was, but he suspected calling him one was not a compliment.

"Forgive me," he said and tried to look regretful about the kiss, but he must have failed, for her scowl only deepened. "It's clear we have a cultural misunderstanding. In Britain—and it's important for you to know this if you still want a British husband—when a man kisses a woman and she keeps allowing him to kiss her, when she flings her arms around his neck and pulls him closer, we regard that as kissing back. Perhaps it's different in America."

She was staring at him in horror, a rosy tint washing into her cheeks. "I did not do any of that!"

"Yes, you did." He studied her face, noting the uneasiness creep into her expression, and he couldn't help taking a bit of pure manly satisfaction in reminding her about that. "Don't remember things quite that way, do you? Hmm, it must have been the alcohol. Or perhaps my kiss was so dizzying, it went to your head like alcohol and affected your memory?"

"Don't flatter yourself. And this is turning into a pretty poor apology, if you ask me."

He set all teasing aside. "You're right, of course. The truth is, I was quite drunk, and—"

"So drunkenness is your excuse?"

"No. It is . . . an explanation, if you like, but it is not an excuse. There is no excuse."

"You're right about that," she said through clenched teeth.

"It was never my intent to hurt you or damage your reputation. If that had been my intent, I could have easily arranged for someone to see us together that morning we met in second class. On the contrary, I took great pains to avoid that particular problem, as you recall. And though I did agree to make an attempt to dissuade you from marrying Rumsford in exchange for money, I did not object at your wedding because of that. Believe it or not, I wasn't thinking about the money."

She made a sound of obvious skepticism. "I find that hard to believe."

"I know." He sighed, knowing even if he had an explanation, she probably wouldn't believe that either. "The point is, the damage is done, and there's only one thing that can be done now." He took a deep breath and said what needed to be said. "We should become engaged."

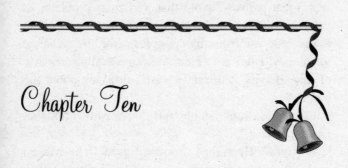

Chapter Ten

Annabel's eyes widened in shock. Her lips parted as if she intended to reply, but no words came out, and she closed her mouth again. She looked away, and when she returned her gaze to his, a frown etched deep between her brows. Christian decided he'd better explain his reasoning before she told him to go to hell.

"The fact that I objected at the wedding implies something between us, and the only way to deal with that now is to acknowledge it as true. By becoming engaged, your reputation would be saved. We'll claim a whirlwind romance aboard ship, that sort of thing. Many will call you mercenary, playing a duke against an earl to see who came out on top, but trust me, once you're engaged to me, they won't hold it against you. In fact, they'll probably consider it quite a well-played coup on your part, and they'll admire you for it."

"Wait!" She held up one hand to halt his flow of words. "You want to marry me?"

"God, no." The moment the words were out of his mouth, he grimaced, cursing his idiotic lack of tact. "Sorry. I didn't mean that the way it sounded."

"Yes, you did. You don't want to marry me, either." She gave a little laugh, shaking her head as if at the irony. "That's pretty much the story of my life."

He sighed. "Hell, all I seem able to do today is either offend you or apologize for offending you. Annabel, the fact that I have no desire to remarry has nothing at all to do with you. What I am proposing is not that we marry, merely that we become engaged. It will put paid to the gossip, and after a long enough engagement—about a year, I should say—"

"A year? Be tied to you for a year in a phony engagement?"

"It has to be long enough to be convincing. After a year, you break it off."

"And look like I've jilted my second fiancé after humiliating my first?"

"A woman is always justified in breaking an engagement, but nonetheless, I shall give you ample cause, something public enough and bad enough that nothing could possibly reflect upon you. God knows," he added, raking a hand through his hair, "that's the least I can do. And with my reputation, no one would be surprised. Of course, your conduct shall have to be impeccable—Caesar's wife, and that sort of thing—so it would probably be best if you steered clear of society. Unless we go out together, of course."

"I see." She looked at him thoughtfully, as if she were thinking it over. He deemed that a hopeful sign. "And what about your conduct?" she asked after a moment.

"Mine?" The question took him back a bit, for he knew she wouldn't like the answer. "Well, my conduct is irrelevant," he said with reluctance, "since my reputation isn't at issue. I suppose it ought to be," he added hastily as her frown deepened. "But it isn't. Not very fair, I grant you. But in circumstances such as these, the same level of propriety isn't expected of a man."

"Really? How convenient." Before he could reply, she went on, "Thank you for your gallant effort to save the day," and the sweet, drawling sarcasm in her voice told him his hope of an easy solution was rather out the window. "I appreciate it so very much, Your Grace. But I think I'll pass."

"You're saying no?" He supposed he shouldn't be surprised. No doubt she felt a bit let down by the idea, for he knew he hadn't made any effort to put a romantic gloss on it. Nonetheless, she couldn't really refuse. "But we have to become engaged. It's the only way to avert a scandal."

"It's not the only way. It's the simplest way, and the easiest way for you because it doesn't affect your life at all."

She caught his slightly guilty shift from one foot to the other, and she pounced on it at once. "How lucky for you," she said, "that you can behave like a cad and get away with it, facing no consequences for what you've done. Other than having to be seen with me once in a while during this supposed engagement, your situation enables you to do whatever you want, while I will have to pretty much stay home, and still be chaperoned when I do go out, with no ability to make friends, have any fun, or meet any other men who might actually want to marry me!"

"That fact that it's convenient for me," he said with dignity, "doesn't make it any less sound an idea."

"First of all, there's no way I'll let the world think I go around humiliating and jilting men. Second, I am not going to waste a year of my life sitting around twiddling my thumbs because of you! And third, I'd have to spend that whole year pretending I want to marry you, and I'm just not a good enough actress to pull that off, since I happen to hate your guts."

"You're angry, I daresay, but—"

"Angry? Angry doesn't even start to describe how I feel about you. The only reason I haven't shot you dead already is because I'd be hanged for it. And now," she added, her rising voice making the sincerity of her words quite clear, "after you've ruined my life, the best thing you can think of to repair the damage is a pretend engagement? Any true gentleman would have offered me marriage for real!"

That was probably true, but any guilt he might have felt was eclipsed by a jolt of pure panic.

"Don't worry, sugar," she said, correctly interpreting

his feelings. "Even if you offered me a genuine proposal of marriage, I'd turn you down. Duke or not, I wouldn't have you on a silver platter!"

Her words should have brought a sense of relief, but they didn't. Instead, they stung, and he felt a bit nettled by his own reaction. "Well, I'm glad we've got that straight," he muttered, jerking at his tie and doing his best to conceal his illogical sense of hurt pride. "Since we're agreed that a true engagement culminating in marriage is out of the question, a pretend engagement is the only option."

"No, it's not. While you've been lyin' around sleeping off your drunkenness, I've been coming up with a plan to save my own reputation, thank you very much."

A woman couldn't save her own reputation, so he ignored that bit of nonsense. "It's hardly fair to criticize me for drinking too much last night, since you were quite pickled yourself," he said instead, "a state you were well on your way to being in before I even arrived. And when you passed out—"

"I did not pass out."

"You weren't unconscious for more than a few seconds, but the fact remains that your knees kept caving every time I tried to stand you on your feet. I carried you back to your suite, snuck you back into your room, and put you in bed, managing not to be seen by anyone in the process, thereby safeguarding you and your reputation."

"And you think that makes you some kind of hero?"

"I don't know. Does it? Where would your reputation be if some Knickerbocker dragon ladies had found you lying in the Turkish baths this morning, passed out with a bottle in your hand?"

"You ruined my wedding!"

"To a man who's an ass!"

She folded her arms, eyes narrowing. "Some might say the man who showed up at a wedding, drunk as a skunk, and stopped the bride from marrying another man without caring two pins for her is the one who's an ass!"

"Well, it isn't as if you were in love with him, Annabel! You wanted to be a countess. And he wasn't in love with you, either, a fact proven by his conduct. Your money was what he was after. Hell, even the fact that you are jaw-dropping gorgeous, with a body like a goddess, doesn't seem to have been important to him, since he went to a prostitute the night before the ship sailed!"

"What?" Annabel's arms fell to her sides, and her eyes widened with astonishment. As he looked into their dark brown depths, he saw the shimmer of hurt, and he wanted to cut his tongue out. He hadn't meant to tell her. He'd hurt her enough already, and even though she hadn't been in love with Rummy, the last thing she'd needed to be told about today was her former fiancé's preference for the company of prostitutes. Still, nothing for it. The cat was out of the bag.

"I don't believe you," she whispered.

"It's true. I saw him at a gaming club that night. Your

uncle was there, too, although he doesn't know Rummy's reason for being there was to see a courtesan."

"Maybe he wasn't there for that. Maybe he was there to play cards."

"No, Annabel, he wasn't. He bragged to me about his reason for being there." Christian drew a deep breath, knowing there was no way to backtrack now. "I saw him go upstairs, and there are no gaming tables upstairs at that particular club. Only prostitutes."

She didn't say anything for several seconds. And then her chin came up, her shoulders squared, and she looked him in the eye. "Even if what you say is true, it doesn't justify what you did."

"No, it doesn't. But because of what I did, your reputation is compromised, and I can't allow that to stand. If we become engaged, honor is satisfied."

"And I've already said no."

"But what else can we do?"

She moved to face him across the table and gestured to the documents she'd been perusing when he came in. "I've come up with a plan, one that doesn't involve us getting engaged." She picked up a sheet of paper. "This is a letter of resignation from Mr. Bentley, one of my trustees. And this," she added, laying that sheet aside to pick up another, "is a contract drawn up by Uncle Arthur, naming you as Mr. Bentley's replacement."

He frowned, not seeing the point. "What does that accomplish?"

"Both of these documents are dated *yesterday*. You

stood up this morning and objected to my wedding, not because there's any hanky-panky between us, but because you have objections to the marriage settlement, and as the new trustee, you couldn't allow the marriage to go through without some renegotiation."

"Clever," he had to admit. "Rumsford broke the engagement, I take it, not you?" She didn't confirm that guess, but the tight press of her lips gave him his answer. "Still, I don't know your family. Why would Mr. Ransom and Mr. Chumley appoint me?"

"You're a duke," she answered promptly. "Arthur met you in New York, and when Mr. Bentley resigned, he and George appointed you to the job because we want to live in England, and they want social connections there for business purposes. You objected because after reading the document aboard ship, you found the marriage settlement unacceptable and not in my best interests, but you didn't know if you ought to object at such a late date. You finally decided you had to speak up, after having a long battle with your conscience, or something like that." She met his eyes. "Most people probably don't think you have a conscience, but from what I've seen, you're a good enough liar to make them change their minds."

Another painful jab, and one he no doubt deserved. "Believe it or not, I was acting in good conscience when I stopped the wedding."

"I don't give a damn what your reasons were." She pulled the pen from the inkstand and handed it to him. "Sign it, please."

He studied her hard face for a moment, and he figured now was not a good time to assure her she'd dodged a bullet this morning. Instead, he took the pen from her hand. "All right, I'll be a trustee. Since you won't agree to an engagement, this is the only thing to do, I suppose. Where do I sign?"

He signed in every place she indicated, glad that the situation was resolved by putting his name to a few documents. "There," he said, handing the sheets back. "All done."

"Not quite." She pulled the papers out of his fingers. "You know, you really should read things before you sign 'em. Uncle Arthur taught me that a long time ago."

He watched with growing apprehension as she held up the contract he'd just signed. "This makes you a trustee, but there are conditions attached."

"What conditions?"

"You didn't really think you'd get off the hook just by signing a piece of paper, did you? After what you did?" She slapped the contract down and leaned forward, flattening her palms on the table between them. "By taking on the job as trustee, you have also become one of my legal guardians, and part of your job shall be to facilitate my launch into London society."

Christian stared at her, appalled. "You can't be serious."

"Oh, I'm serious, sugar. I am as serious as a daddy with a pregnant daughter and a shotgun. I didn't come this far only to tuck my tail and go back to New York in disgrace."

"It still baffles my mind why you'd want to hobnob with our lot, but there's no accounting for taste, I suppose. Still, how am I supposed to make this cherished dream of social success come true?"

"You are going to help your sister to bring me out. Yes," she added, "I've already talked to Lady Sylvia, and she's agreed to introduce me to her friends, make sure I receive invitations, that sort of thing. But to convince everyone that what you did was not a romantic gesture, we need your cooperation."

"I'm to play the role of dutiful guardian? Now that's something no one will believe."

"They have to. If there's the slightest reason to think you have a romantic claim on me, my reputation is still tarnished, and everyone will expect you to marry me. Since you and I both agree that's a horrible idea, you have to help make this story sound convincing."

"Surely you're not still thinking to catch an English husband?"

"My concern right now is my reputation, which you are responsible for blackening! You have to make sure people accept our version of why you did what you did. While I enjoy my season, make friends, and meet respectable young men, you are going to play the role of protective guardian and trustee, whose primary job is to keep the fortune hunters, rakes, and scoundrels away."

He glanced over her delicious figure. "To quote your own words, that's a bit like the fox guarding the henhouse."

"No, it isn't, because you've changed." She gave him a bright, artificial smile. "You've turned over a new leaf now that you're a duke. You've given up your scandalous ways, and you take your responsibility as one of my trustees very seriously."

This was sounding worse and worse by the minute. "But to do what you ask, I should have to go into society myself." One might as well descend into the pit of hell. "I should have to mingle, mix, go to the opera, attend balls. Go to the club and talk dog breeding and politics with men like Rumsford." He shuddered. "It doesn't bear thinking about."

"That fact that you won't enjoy yourself doesn't bother me much."

"Even worse, by doing this I'd be offering a signal to all the unmarried girls in town that I am available for marriage myself. I should have every social-climbing debutante and matchmaking mama in London dogging my heels."

"I reckon you will." She tucked the papers into a leather portfolio, giving him a look of mock pity across the table. "Aw, poor you."

Christian ignored the sarcasm. "Woman, this is the most ghastly idea I've ever heard."

"Too bad." She turned to tuck the portfolio beside the nearby writing desk, then she walked to the door and opened it. "You interfered in my life, and now you deserve what you get. Don't worry," she added. "You'll be paid the same salary Mr. Bentley got as a trustee. Ten thousand dollars a year."

"Are you sure you wouldn't rather we just become engaged?" he asked as he walked out the door. Turning, he faced her across the threshold. "So much easier. Simpler. Less fuss."

"Not a chance. You've been hired for a job, and you're damned well going to earn your salary. It'll probably be the first real work you've ever done in your life."

With that, she slammed the door in his face with a resounding bang.

Christian stared at the closed door, and he wondered in bafflement how this whole interview had changed his perfectly sensible, simple plan into a complicated scheme that would have him gadding about London during the height of the season, safeguarding the reputation of an heiress, protecting her from fortune hunters, and keeping his own hands off her luscious body in the process.

If this had happened to one of his friends, he'd think it a great joke, of course. But since it was happening to him, he found nothing amusing about it. It was going to be torture.

Slamming the door in Christian's face had to be one of the most gratifying things Annabel had ever done. And turning down his offer of engagement had been pretty sweet, too. And, of course, getting him to sign that agreement without reading it first—that had also given her a great deal of satisfaction.

Still, though they made her feel a bit better, a few

gratifying moments didn't make up for the awful events of the morning, or take the sting out of the fact that she now had three men to her credit who didn't want to marry her. And she couldn't even really contemplate what Christian had told her about Bernard. She'd known he'd had mistresses in the past, but a prostitute only a few days ago? It made her sick thinking about it.

Christian could be lying, of course, for that man wasn't to be trusted an inch. But as she studied the closed door after his departure, she had the gut-wrenching feeling that Christian hadn't been lying about that.

Suddenly, an unbelievable weariness settled over her, and she wondered if her new plan was even worth pursuing. Maybe she ought to just go home. But where was home? Gooseneck Bend? New York? She had no home. Not now.

Annabel shook her head, pushing aside despair before it could take hold. She'd already cried enough tears for one day, and she was worn out. Refusing to give in to any self-pity, she went to bed, and the moment her head hit the pillow, she was sound asleep.

Annabel didn't have the chance to feel sorry for herself the following day, either. For one thing, she didn't wake until almost noon. And since the *Atlantic* was scheduled to dock at Liverpool by sunset, the afternoon was spent preparing to disembark. Mama offered to see that all the gifts brought aboard by wedding guests were returned, an offer Annabel was happy to accept.

She spent her time supervising the maids in packing their personal belongings. She was in the midst of that task when a knock sounded on the door of their stateroom.

Annabel herself happened to be the one closest to the door, but she hesitated, not really wanting to face anyone who might have come out of an eagerness for gossip. Still, the maids were in the various bedrooms, occupied with their duties, and when the knock came again, she was left no choice but to answer it herself.

To her relief, she found Lady Sylvia on the other side of the door. A waiter stood beside her with a wheeled tea tray.

"Good afternoon. I hope I'm not disturbing you?" When Annabel shook her head, the other woman gestured to the cart with a flourish. "Since our conversation yesterday, I've been making plans, and I thought we might discuss them over a spot of tea?"

"That would be lovely, thank you." She opened the door wide. "Please come in."

The other woman nodded to the waiter and they entered the suite, following Annabel to the table in the center of the sitting room. "Place the cart there, Sanderson," she said, gesturing to a spot between the two women, "then you may go."

"Yes, my lady."

The waiter departed, and after verifying that the tea had already been prepared and was steeping in the pot, Annabel reached for the strainer. "Lemon or milk?"

she asked as she strained tea carefully into two cups. "And would you like sugar?"

"Milk, please, and two lumps of sugar. You know how to pour out, I see," Lady Sylvia added. "Many Americans don't. Tea isn't something you run much to on your side of the pond. My husband was an American, so I know. He insisted upon coffee every morning."

"Your husband was Roger Shaw, wasn't he?" Annabel asked, passing the other woman her cup. "The architect?"

"He was. How did you know?"

Annabel made a face as she stirred sugar into her own tea. "I know everything about every Knickerbocker family in New York. Not that it's done me much good."

Sylvia paused, her cup raised halfway to her mouth, studying her over the rim. "I'm sorry," she said unexpectedly.

"Sorry?" Annabel stared back, surprised and puzzled. "What are you sorry for?"

"I don't quite know," she confessed, and took a sip of tea. "That my brother can be a complete idiot from time to time. That everyone whose opinion matters to you saw what happened. I think . . ." She paused a moment. "I think what I meant was that I'm sorry I didn't make any effort to become acquainted with you before now."

Annabel smiled a little. "What would you have done? Gone around introducing yourself to all us New

Money outsiders and taken on the job of forcing us on New York society? Besides, you're only saying that because you know me now," she couldn't help pointing out. "Circumstances have forced us together, and now I'm a person." She met the other woman's eyes over the teapot. "I'm no longer just one of the insignificant faces you see in the crowd at the opera from a seat in the Golden Horseshoe."

Sylvia grimaced. "That's truer than I like to think."

"I don't mean to offend you, Lady Sylvia. It's just that I know what I'm dealing with here. I don't have any illusions about it, and I don't want pity. I want help."

The other woman nodded. "Of course. And it is easier for a girl in your position to move in British society than it is in New York, once you have the appropriate connections and entrée, of course."

"And if you have plenty of money," Annabel added with a hint of cynicism. "Because British peers need to marry girls with money."

"Oh dear, you must think we're all so dreadful. But a girl's dowry is one of the most important parts of British matrimony, especially in these days when estates simply cannot recoup their own costs. I would be doing you a great disservice if I pretended otherwise."

"I know. And because I know what it's like to not have money, Lady Sylvia, I don't fault anyone for wanting to avoid being in that situation. Especially now," she added, laughing a little. "Now that I have money,

I don't ever want to go back to not having it, that's for sure."

Sylvia was studying her with thoughtful blue eyes. "It must be so difficult," she murmured, "to be caught between two worlds, a part of neither."

"Yes." Annabel felt a rush of relief to find someone who understood when even some members of her own family didn't. "I want to marry well, have children, and carve out a place in the world. I want my sister to have all the social opportunities I didn't have. I don't ever want anyone to laugh at my family again. But until I met Bernard, I'd just about given up hope." She sighed, setting aside her teacup. "I don't want to go back to Gooseneck Bend. And I can't go back to New York. Not now."

Sylvia patted her arm in a friendly gesture. "You don't have to, Annabel, because now you have connections. I've already begun laying the groundwork, by the way."

"You've started explaining to people our version of why your brother did what he did?"

"Explain? Heavens, no. If one starts explaining, one ends up justifying, and at that point, one loses the battle. No, no. I'm a decade older than you, my dear, and you must trust my knowledge of what to do when a scandal like this happens. One mentions it in passing, laughing a little, sounding quite exasperated with one's impulsive, reckless brother. Since Christian was, of course, acting in his ward's best interest, the fact that Rumsford broke things off rather than talk it out puts the onus of explanations on Rumsford, whom I suspect would rather die than explain anything about the humiliating episode."

"I see."

"By the time we dock at Liverpool, our version of events will have spread to every corner of the ship, and I think most people will believe it. All the earl can claim is that he hadn't been informed ahead of time of Mr. Bentley's resignation and the duke's instatement. He can't sue for breach of promise, and even if he could, he wouldn't."

"You sound very sure of that."

"I am sure." She hesitated, then added, "It's the season, and the earl can't afford to be seen as petty by other young ladies."

"Heiresses, you mean," Annabel said, hearing the cynical tinge to her own voice. "Suing me for breach of promise wouldn't do much to impress them."

"No, it wouldn't. It may not be of much comfort to say you're well rid of him, but I shall say it anyway. You can do far better than Rumsford, if you wish to."

Annabel thought of Rumsford and the prostitute, and she wasn't certain she wished to. "You think my plan will work?"

"Of course it will. It's a sound plan, and I commend you for it, Annabel. I doubt I could have thought of a better one given the situation. Life is like a picture, you know. It's all in the way you frame it. When we arrive in town, Christian and I shall start paving the way, writing letters, paying calls, that sort of thing, and after a respectable waiting period—a fortnight should be long enough, I think—I shall bring you out. To add strength to the story, it would be best if you stay with me at Cinders."

"Cinders?"

"My villa just outside London, in Chiswick. Now, don't refuse, please. I wouldn't dream of allowing you to stay at a hotel when I can offer you the hospitality of my home. It's leased most of the year, of course, because I travel so much, but I always take it for the Season. I've already spoken to your mother about this, and she agrees that having your family staying with me can only lend more strength to the connection between our families."

She drained her cup, set it back in its saucer, and rose to her feet. "I must be off. We've put in a good day's work, but now I simply must pack. We're disembarking in only a few hours."

"Thank you, Lady Sylvia." Annabel also stood up, and she walked the other woman to the door. "I appreciate your help so much."

"Nonsense, my dear. After Christian's abominable display yesterday, it's the least I can do. Besides, I shall enjoy it. I love launching a girl."

"You must also love a challenge," Annabel said with a sigh as she opened the door.

"I told you, my dear, you mustn't worry. You'll do very well in London, despite what's happened. With your pretty face, and American charm, it wouldn't surprise me a bit if you had a dozen suitors before the end of the season."

"Well, I have already had a marriage proposal," Annabel said, bringing the other woman to an abrupt halt on the threshold.

"A marriage proposal already?" Lady Sylvia turned in the doorway. "From whom?"

Annabel was a bit taken aback by the other woman's surprise. "Your brother. You didn't know?"

"I most certainly did not." She shook her head and began to laugh. "Christian proposed marriage to you?" she said as if she couldn't believe it. "Christian?"

"Well, it wasn't a real proposal," she hastened to explain. "Oh no, his idea was that we be engaged for a year, and then he would do something awful to give me an excuse to break the engagement."

"What? And keep you dangling for an entire year with no ability to meet any other men?" When Annabel nodded, she said, "I hope you told him what he could do with that sort of arrangement!"

"I did. I believe my exact words were that I wouldn't have him on a silver platter even if it was only pretend."

Sylvia laughed merrily. "Oh, Annabel, I do like you! We are going to be great friends. I know it."

"I hope so," she murmured, watching the other woman start down the hallway. "To pull this off, I think I'm going to need all the friends I can get."

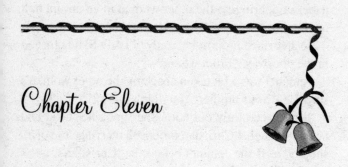

Chapter Eleven

Annabel's first impression of England was simply that it was wet, for they disembarked at Liverpool amid pouring rain. It was also cold, with a biting spring wind, and though it was April, the inclement weather made her appreciate Christian's words about how cold an English castle could be in December.

In addition to being cold and damp, it was also dark by the time hired carriages took them to a hotel near the train station, and Annabel was given little opportunity to study the landscape of the country she had intended to make her home, until the following day when they were aboard the train.

Most of Annabel's belongings had been shipped via cargo freighter and would not arrive for another week, so Arthur arranged for them to be stored in Liverpool before they boarded the train for London. Christian and his sister were also on board, but their compartment was farther down the corridor, and Annabel didn't expect to see much them during the six-hour journey. That was probably a very good thing, she reflected as the train pulled out of Liverpool, at least in Christian's case. After all, only yesterday, she'd had to fight the impulse to shoot him with a gun.

As the train took them south, she was able to have her first real look at the English landscape, and even in the pouring rain, it was every bit as beautiful as she'd imagined. She didn't know if that fact made her feel better, or worse, about everything that had happened.

Either way, she loved the dark green hedgerows, stone walls, and wooden stiles. She loved the statuesque beauty of the ancient churches and priory ruins. She loved the quaint villages, with their half-timbered pubs and thatched-roof cottages.

It was a far cry from what she'd felt upon arriving in New York. Her first view of that city, with its twelve-story skyscrapers, its awe-inspiring Brooklyn Bridge and Statue of Liberty, and its elegant brownstones had seemed far more intimidating to her than this bucolic countryside.

That thought brought a rueful smile to her lips. Despite all her efforts to escape where she'd come from, she was still just a country girl at heart. She didn't know if she'd ever end up living in England permanently, but it was reassuring to know that her first impression of it was a favorable one. After all, staying here was her best option, at least for now, provided that the plan she'd cooked up proved successful.

Even if it didn't, she could probably still find herself some impoverished English peer to marry her, but somehow, that idea no longer held much appeal.

"Are you all settled in, Mrs. Chumley?"

The brisk voice of Lady Sylvia broke into her thoughts, and Annabel turned to find the other woman standing in the doorway to her family's compartment.

"Yes, my lady, thank you," Henrietta answered.

"Excellent. Then would you care to join me in the dining car for a spot of tea?"

"Tea?" Dinah bounded up from her seat. "Can we have scones and jam, too?"

"Dinah Louise, you don't need anything to eat," Henrietta chided. "You just had breakfast two hours ago, and if you eat scones now, you'll spoil your lunch."

"Oh, just one," Dinah pleaded, making Sylvia laugh.

"Don't worry, my dear," she consoled the girl. "This afternoon when we arrive at Cinders, Mrs. West shall have fresh, hot scones ready and waiting for us, I promise you. For now, we shall have to settle for tea alone." She glanced past Dinah to where Annabel sat by the window. "Shall you come, too, Annabel?"

Annabel considered, then shook her head. "Thank you, no. You all go on without me."

They did so, and Annabel returned her attention to the view out the window and thought about why the possibility of finding someone else to marry left her so cold.

The discovery of Bernard's unfaithfulness had left a sordid taint behind. No doubt about that. Also, this was the second undeniable failure of her own judgment when it came to men, and she wasn't sure she could trust herself to choose right the third time around. And though she hadn't been in love with Bernard, she had been genuinely fond of him. She had regarded him as both her friend and her partner, and though that wasn't perhaps a very romantic view of matrimony, she'd thought it a realistic and sensible one. Of course, she'd also thought she and Bernard had mutual affection and respect on which to base a lifelong union, and it was both painful and embarrassing to know those feelings had never been mutual. The brutal truth was if Bernard had a shred of either affection or respect for her, he'd never have gone to a prostitute a week before their wedding.

Respect? He doesn't respect you.

Christian had been right. Right about her, right about Rumsford, right all along. What an awful admission to have to make.

A sound caused Annabel to turn from the window and she found the object of her thoughts standing in the doorway, hands in his pockets, watching her.

"Well, what do you think of England so far?" He sank down in a seat beside the door and nodded to the rain-drenched scenery on the other side of the window. "Is it living up to all your expectations?"

She lifted her chin. "I like it. It's very pretty."

"Prettier than Mississippi?"

"Seems prettier to me." She pointed to some thatched cottages they were passing. "Those cottages are a lot more picturesque than the shack I grew up in, that's for sure."

"And the people that live in them might say the same about Mississippi, were they on a train passing through Gooseneck Bend."

"No, they wouldn't." She made a face. "Not in the summertime, anyway. Our weather would send 'em right back home."

He gave a shout of laughter.

"What?" she asked, turning her head to look at him in puzzlement. "Did I say something funny?"

"Annabel, England is famous the world over for having the worst weather possible. It's dreary and wet and cold nearly the whole year around."

"If today is an example of what you mean, then I have to disagree. I like the cooler weather and I don't mind rain." She leaned back in her seat, smiling a little. "In Mississippi in the summertime, it's so hot you can cook eggs on the sidewalk, rain or shine. And New York City isn't much better, which is why everybody goes to Newport. We used to go to Newport, too, but it was so dreadful that after a few summers, we stopped."

"Dreadful in what way?"

"Oh, I don't know," she said lightly. "The parties we never got invited to. Women sticking their noses up in the air and pretending not to see us when we walked up Bellevue Avenue. Sitting at Polo Field with the other outsiders, thinking we might just as well be in Kalamazoo. You'd think all the outcasts would band together and have our own parties, but that's not how it works. Summer in Newport was awful for us."

"I can imagine. But trust me, Annabel, an English winter is worse. It's dreary beyond belief."

"But you have English Christmas to brighten things up."

He made a scoffing sound. "As much as I adore plum pudding and roast goose, it isn't worth it."

She didn't quite believe him, and her face must have shown it, for he went on, "I suppose a few years from now, when your titled English husband wants to take you to Nice or Juan-les-Pins for the winter, you'll say, 'No, no, darling, I couldn't possibly. I much prefer England's slush, soot, and freezing rain to the heat of the Riviera.'"

It was her turn to laugh. She couldn't help it, not when he talked nonsense like that.

"Ah, laughing at my jokes," he said, smiling back at her. "That's a good sign. After yesterday, I began to fear you hated me."

She should, a reminder that stopped her laughter. "Maybe I do hate you."

His smile vanished. He looked steadily back at her, his eyes sky blue in the gray light, his expression suddenly grave. "I hope not."

For no reason at all, her heart slammed against her ribs, and she looked away, returning to the safe subject of the weather. "But I meant what I said. I like rain."

"I suspect you'd say that even if you didn't mean it. Just to show me I was wrong."

That was so true, she almost laughed again, but she held it back. She didn't want him to make her laugh. She didn't want to like him. Not after what he'd done.

"Anyway," she said, pointing to the window again, "I know the people who live in those cottages are probably every bit as poor as I ever was, but I still think their surroundings are prettier than mine were." She gave him a defiant glance. "I suppose you think I'm making England more romantic than it actually is. I know you thought that's what I was doing with my decision to marry Bernard."

"Weren't you?"

"I reckon I was." She paused, grimacing at the admission. "But I thought I was being practical. Realistic. Completely unromantic."

"That only proves that even though you want to be hard and mercenary, you're not."

She looked at him. "I wish I was."

"Don't wish that, Annabel." His lashes lowered and when they lifted again, she saw in his eyes the same fierce intensity that she'd seen the day they'd first met. "Don't ever wish that. It's hell to have no ideals. I ought to know."

The question she most wanted the answer to was out of her mouth before she even realized it. "You said you didn't stop the wedding for the money, but if that's true, then why did you do it?"

He looked away, staring past her out the window for so long, she thought he wasn't going to answer. "I don't know. I owe you an explanation, I realize, but I have none. As I said, I was drunk, and that's the only thing I can tell you." He tore his gaze from the window, smiling faintly as he looked at her again. "If you did hate me for it, I wouldn't blame you a jot."

Annabel stared into his face, and she knew she couldn't hate him. That was such a dismaying realization, it jerked her to her feet. "I don't hate you," she said, and stepped past him to the door.

"You don't?"

"No." She stopped in the doorway and turned to give him a rueful look over her shoulder. "Don't look so surprised," she said with a sigh. "I've always had a soft spot for bad boys."

As she walked away down the corridor, she began to fear she always would.

When Christian returned to his own compartment, he found Arthur waiting for him, and the grim set of the other man's mouth showed that the visit was not to be a friendly one.

Not that he'd expected otherwise. In fact, the only surprise was that it had taken Arthur this long to rake him over the coals.

"I ought to punch you in the mouth," Arthur said, and stood up from the seat he'd taken by the window. He turned toward Christian, fists clenched. "Do you know why I haven't?"

"I can't think of a single reason," Christian admitted, "except perhaps the fact that your niece already did it for you." He touched his jaw with a grimace. "Did a deuced fine job of it, too, by the way."

"That's not why." Arthur sat down again heavily. "The reason I haven't beat the tar out of you is that I'm the one who's really to blame. I hired one fortune-hunting scoundrel to get rid of another."

Christian, hoping they were now safely past a round of fisticuffs, moved to take the seat opposite the older man. "Mr. Ransom, if you've come for an explanation—"

"I don't need your explanations," Arthur cut him off. "It's obvious why you did it. But if you think I'd pay you a plug nickel for that stunt you pulled, you're mistaken. I'm here," he went on before Christian could correct his mistaken assumption, "because I want to explain some things to you, not the other way around."

Now that was a surprise. "Indeed? What explanations could you possibly wish to make to me?"

"I agreed to Annabel's plan because it seemed the only alternative other than go home, and Annabel wasn't having that. One thing about that girl, she's no coward. And she's not seeming all that het up to find another English peer to replace Rumsford, so that's all to the good. She says she just wants to enjoy herself, and I think she means it. And with you and your sister sashaying them around London, introducing 'em into society and taking them to parties, they're sure to have a good time. So I'm not cutting up rough about it. But," he added, once again looking grim, "I expect this plan to work, and it's up to you and your sister to see that it does."

"I assure you, both Sylvia and I shall do our best to ensure that Annabel is a smashing success."

"Good." Arthur stood up. "Because if you do anything else to hurt or embarrass my niece, I'll do more than punch you in the mouth. I'll kill you."

Cinders was a charming structure of yellow stucco and red brick, with large arched windows and a view of the Thames. When the ducal carriages Sylvia had arranged for halted in the graveled drive just after five o'clock, they had barely stepped down before an elegantly dressed man was opening the front door to them.

"Traverton," Christian greeted him as they bustled into a spacious foyer of black and white tiles, soft yellow walls, and white painted woodwork. "Everything all right while we've been away?"

"The second footman had to be let go, Your Grace," he answered, his ponderous, melancholy voice so much like Christian's imitation of a butler that Annabel almost laughed. "But I am confident his replacement has a better understanding of how things are done in a duke's household."

"Excellent." Christian's voice was grave, but Annabel didn't miss his wink in her direction. He introduced the butler to Annabel and her family, adding, "If there is anything you need, Traverton shall be happy to help, won't you, Traverton?"

"Of course," the butler said with a bow, and turned to Lady Sylvia. "Lady Helspeth and Lady Kayne shall be arriving for their monthly committee meeting with you at six o'clock, my lady."

"The May Day Ball!" Sylvia cried, pressing a hand to her forehead. "I completely forgot I'm on the committee this year. And they're to be here at six? Oh heavens."

"Lady Helspeth," Traverton went on, "shall be bringing her daughter, Lady Edith, with her."

A groan issued from Christian at that announcement. Muttering something about urgent business to see to, he excused himself and started for the wide, curving staircase.

"I shall invite them to stay for dinner," Lady Sylvia called after him, laughing.

Christian did not reply to that. Instead, he continued up the stairs, and within seconds, he had vanished from view.

"You must forgive my brother," Sylvia said to Annabel and her family with a charming smile. "Ladies' charity meetings are not his cup of tea." She returned her attention to the butler. "Now, Traverton, I hope Mrs. Carson has prepared rooms for our guests?"

"Of course, my lady. We followed the instructions in your telegram most carefully."

"I'm pleased to hear it." She turned to Henrietta. "I must speak with the housekeeper about this charity meeting I've got, Mrs. Chumley, but I shall leave your family in Traverton's capable hands. If you will forgive me?"

With that, Lady Sylvia departed, and Traverton took charge. "Mrs. Carson, the housekeeper, will take your ladies' maids to their quarters, and then send them up to you," he told Henrietta. "The footmen will bring in your luggage. Have you a valet with you, Mr. Chumley? Mr. Ransom?"

Both gentlemen shook his heads, and Traverton said, "Should you need anything in the way of valeting, Davis, first footman, and Hughes, second footman, would be happy to assist you. Dinner is at eight o'clock, and guests are always welcome to gather for sherry in the drawing room one hour beforehand. In the meantime, would you care for tea, or would you prefer to be first shown your rooms?"

Dinah, of course, wanted tea. George and Arthur also preferred to have tea, but Annabel and her mother chose to be shown their rooms to change for dinner.

Annabel's room was done up in pale green, with simply carved furniture of cherrywood and vases of early yellow tulips. She liked the room, preferring its elegant simplicity to the oppressive, gilded gaudiness so prevalent in New York.

The footman brought the luggage, and Liza came a short while later with a pitcher of hot water and a basin so that Annabel could freshen up. She exchanged her traveling suit for an evening gown of teal-blue velvet, and with still an hour to go before she needed to go down for sherry, she sat at the writing desk in her room and began the awful task of writing letters.

It had to be done. Thankfully, her mother was arranging for all the gifts to be returned, but it was her duty to write a personal letter to each friend and family member conveying the news that her wedding had been called off, and it was a task that could not be postponed. She kept her letters brief, providing no details, but she still found that it was painful and mortifying news to convey, especially when she thought of how she'd hit Christian in front of all those people. The story would be all over New York in a week, and what people would say about that, she didn't know, but she suspected that striking a duke hadn't done anything to help her gain society's good opinion.

No doubt many would say Rumsford had had a lucky escape, but despite her mortification, Annabel knew she'd been the lucky one. Maybe, she thought with chagrin, that was why she didn't hate Christian. Because she suspected that he had, in a twisted, very wrong kind of way, done her a favor. She had no doubt that she'd have made Bernard a good wife, but would Bernard have made her a good husband?

He acts as if you're lucky to have him when he ought to be down on his knees thanking God he's lucky enough to have you.

Annabel paused, her pen poised over the letter she was writing, Christian's voice echoing in her head, and she knew the answer to her own question about Bernard. The answer was no.

"Face it, Annabel," she muttered to herself, staring out the window at the beautiful beds of boxwood and daffodils. "When it comes to picking men, you are just plain hopeless."

With those words, the gardens of Cinders faded away, and the image of one man in particular came into her mind, a man with vivid blue eyes and dark hair. She could see him clear as day, steam swirling all around him, his damp white shirt clinging to his chest and shoulders, the linen almost transparent against his skin.

During the past two days, she hadn't thought much about what had happened the night before her wedding. Once relief had settled in that nothing more than a kiss had happened between them, she'd pushed it out of her mind. And then, after what he'd done at the wedding, she'd been too damned angry to give that kiss much thought.

But in the two days since then, her temper had cooled, and now, those hot moments in the Turkish bath came roaring back—his arms pulling her close and his mouth coming down on hers in a hard, lush kiss. Her arms wrapping around his neck, and her lips parting beneath his, kissing him back. He'd been right about that, too.

Annabel tossed down her pen in exasperation.

Even now, two days later, she could still feel the thrill of the kiss they'd shared as if it had just happened an hour ago. She knew the best thing she could do was forget it, put it behind her, but as Annabel pressed her fingers to her tingling lips, she had the sinking feeling it wasn't going to be easy.

* * *

Fortunately for Annabel, Christian made forgetting about him a little bit easier, at least for the evening. He wasn't downstairs when she came into the drawing room for sherry at seven. Her mother was there, however, along with three other ladies. One, a rather timid-looking blond of about seventeen, she took to be Lady Edith, and the forbidding, gray-haired matron to be her mother, Lady Helspeth, for there was a distinct similarity to their features. The third, a slender, elegantly dressed lady with touches of silver in her blond hair, had to be Lady Kayne.

"Ah, Annabel!" Sylvia exclaimed when she entered the room. "There you are. Come and meet the other members of the May Day Ball Committee." Sylvia performed the introductions, confirming Annabel's guess as to identities, then she gestured to the place beside her on the settee. "Sit down with us, my dear. We've finished our meeting and it's been the most successful afternoon, hasn't it, Maria?"

Lady Kayne, to whom this question was addressed, nodded in a satisfied fashion. "I do believe we'll raise even more money for the Orphanage Fund this year than last, no doubt because I'm no longer doing it all myself. You ladies have my gratitude."

"Don't thank me," Sylvia protested. "It's all due to Agatha that you've got so many vouchers for the ball. Lady Helspeth," she added to Annabel, "has an amazing talent for raising funds."

"I'm shameless," Lady Helspeth confessed in a

booming voice. "Shameless. I shall be having a contribution from you, Miss Wheaton, before the evening is over. Lady Sylvia tells me that you are American and that her brother is one of your estate trustees?"

"Yes, ma'am." Annabel turned as a footman presented her with a tray of tiny wineglasses filled with sherry, but after what had happened the other night, she decided it would probably be safer if she kept away from alcohol. She shook her head, and the footman moved on.

"Then I hope we can count on you," Lady Helspeth went on heartily. "You'll purchase vouchers for the ball for yourself and your family, won't you?"

"I am always happy to attend a ball," Annabel answered. "And to contribute to worthy charities."

"I am delighted to hear it! Then, in addition to vouchers, can we expect a sizable donation to the fund? It's for the children, you know."

"There, Agatha," Sylvia remonstrated, "don't work on the poor girl in this way. She'll buy vouchers for the ball, but as for additional funds, it's Christian you shall have to work on. As I told you, he's one of the guardians at the gate, and he's being terribly protective about Miss Wheaton's trust fund. The responsibility is enormous, you know. And, of course, becoming the Duke of Scarborough has forced him to become very conscientious about his duties all the way around. I believe . . ." She paused and leaned forward, adopting a confidential air. "Ladies, I believe my brother might actually be turning over a new leaf."

"Is he?" Lady Edith asked, and Annabel caught the hope that brightened the younger girl's expression. "Will he be joining us for dinner tonight?"

"Christian? Heavens, no. He might be turning over a new leaf, my dear Edith, but he's not a whole new tree! It's only your first season, so you're probably unaware of the fact, but even when we're in London, Christian doesn't often go into society. He's at his club this evening."

The girl's shoulders sagged a little, and Annabel looked at her with empathy. It was awful to be seventeen and in love with a rakehell. It was a heartbreak just waiting to happen. Poor Edith.

Chapter Twelve

nnabel had even more cause to feel sorry for Edith a few hours later, after the girl and her mother had departed for home and the rest of the household was going upstairs to bed. Because she wasn't sleepy, she inquired of the footman the location of the library and went in search of a book to read, but when she arrived there, she found someone already there, someone she hadn't expected to see.

"Well, hello," she said in surprise, coming to a halt in the doorway at the sight of Christian, who was sitting at a card table on the other side of the room. "I thought you were at your club."

He gave her a rueful look. "I am playing patience," he answered with a sigh. "In more ways than one."

"What do you mean?" She came in, and as she approached where he sat, she noticed the cards spread out before him. "Ah," she said with understanding. "Is that what you call it? Patience?"

He moved a red queen onto a black king. "I believe you Americans call it solitaire."

"Yes, we do." She slid onto the chair opposite, feeling it necessary to point out the obvious. "We call it solitaire because it's solitary, as in alone, by one's self. It's something a person usually does when he's procrastinating about doing something else, like the job he's being paid for."

He looked up. "Annabel, show a little compassion. When faced with Lady Helspeth's booming voice and her daughter's melting glances, a man has to go into hiding. Please tell me they've gone at last? Is it safe for me to come out?"

She pressed her lips together, trying to look disapproving. "That's not very nice," she said after a moment. "Lady Edith has quite a crush on you."

He grimaced. "If by that you mean a romantic attachment, then yes, I am fully aware of the fact. And as for your accusation that I'm not being nice, I must take issue. By staying up here, I am giving her no encouragement, and I can only hope her crush, as you call it, will pass more quickly if I'm not in her vicinity."

"And how is that plan working?" she asked.

"Not very well, obviously," he was forced to concede.

Annabel chuckled at the glumness in his voice. "Has she always been infatuated with you?"

"Since she was about twelve. Her father's lands are

in North Yorkshire near my family's estate, Scarborough Park, so she's known me all her life. About six years ago, she got this idea in her head that her love could impel me to mend my ways, that I was really only this wild, irresponsible fellow because my wife had died. And that with a new wife, I would be a better man. I'd hoped she'd grow out of this fantasy when her skirts hit the floor, but unfortunately, it seems as bad as ever."

Annabel pushed idly at the corner of a stack of his cards, her heart constricting a little. "Well, it's sort of understandable, isn't it?" she asked in a low voice. "I mean, she is just a girl."

He stopped playing solitaire. She watched his hands still, and then he set the cards down and was reaching across the table. His fingertips lifted her chin. "Annabel, I have never given Lady Edith the slightest reason to hope for my affections."

His hand slid away, but his eyes continued to look into hers, and she could have told him that he didn't have to actually do anything to fire up a girl's hopes and melt her good sense into a puddle on the floor— nothing, that is, except stand there and look at her and smile. But she decided it might be best not to say so.

"So," he said, and picked up the cards, "whenever Lady Edith comes to dinner, I compassionately develop a cold, duck down the back stairs and go to my club, or hide here in the library."

She forced herself to say something. "It's her first season out, and she ought to be having fun, not mooning over you. If you did pay her a little attention, just a little, then other men would notice, and think more highly of her, because you're a duke. And if that happened, she might realize you're not the only fish in the sea. Besides," she added, "according to what your sister was telling them earlier this evening, you've become a paragon of respectability and responsibility now that you're a duke. Pretty soon, you just might find you've lost your fatal fascination and Lady Edith has left you in the dust."

He chuckled. "That's the best argument for respectability I've heard yet. Unfortunately, I can't stop being a duke." His smile faded. "I wish I could."

"Why don't you want to be the duke? Did you love your brother that much?"

"Andrew?" He made a sound of derision. "My brother was a prize bastard."

"You're very judgmental about people, you know that? You don't like Bernard. You didn't like your brother. You don't like Edith. Is there anybody you do like?"

He slid her that look from under sooty lashes. "I like you."

She folded her arms, trying to show she wasn't impressed, trying to hide how that look of his could turn her all soft and warm like butter in the sun.

"And I don't dislike Edith," he went on, thankfully returning his attention to the cards. "She's a very sweet girl, but as you pointed out, she is only a girl, and far too young for me. And yes, it's true that I didn't have much respect for my brother, nor Rumsford, either, but I disliked them both for the same reason."

"Which is?"

Giving up on the game, he tossed down the cards and leaned back in his chair. "They're both snobs who genuinely think they're better than everyone else—"

"But they are better than everyone else—"

"They're not! You're worth a dozen of 'em, Annabel, and I don't give a damn that you were born in a shack! Believe me, Bernard's sisters could take lessons from you on character and kindness!"

She stared at him, a bit shocked by the vehemence of this little speech, and didn't know what to say. "Thank you," she finally managed. "I appreciate that very much, but you didn't let me finish. Bernard, and your brother—and you, for that matter—are better than everyone else in the eyes of society. That's what counts in this world. The day the announcement of my engagement hit the newspapers, I had seven Knickerbocker ladies call on me to offer their congratulations, when none of them had ever spoken a word to me before. By the end of the week, I had invitations to parties I'd never dreamed of being invited to. It sounds frivolous, I know, but . . ." She paused and bit her lip. "It's hell being shut out. It hurts. You can say it doesn't matter what people think, and you don't care, but that's always a lie. It does hurt, no matter how you try not to let it. And more than that, if you can't win the approval of society, it hurts your family, your children."

"But if you hadn't become rich, you wouldn't have

cared what the Knickerbockers thought. It wouldn't have mattered to you."

"But even back in Gooseneck Bend, there was a hierarchy. The Hardings were at the top, my family was at the bottom, and it hurt back then, too. You can say it shouldn't hurt, Christian, but you don't know how it feels. You never will."

"So despite having money, nothing about your life has changed but the setting?"

"Well, I wouldn't say nothing," she said with a smile, leaning back in her chair. "It's nice to have money, believe me. But it sure isn't the road to happiness. When we first got word that Daddy had died up in the Klondike, it didn't seem to matter much. We hadn't heard from him for years, and Mama had already divorced him ages ago and remarried. But when we got the telegram about his death from some lawyer in Seattle, we also found out he had some gold mines and that he'd made a will, leaving them in trust to me. Uncle Arthur went up there to sort it all out, and that's when we found out how prosperous the mines were and that what he'd left me was worth a fortune."

She gave a wry little laugh. "We figured then that all our troubles were over. I mean, we'd have anything you could want, right? Plenty of food, nice clothes, beautiful houses, security. Within a year, we were living in Jackson. Within two years, we were living in New York, but for all the mind anybody paid, we might as well have stayed in Gooseneck Bend. George and Arthur, they were doing business on Wall Street and drinking at the Oak Room and earning everybody's respect—New Money and Old. The men treated them like equals. But the women doing the same for me, Dinah, and Mama? Not a chance."

"No, I should imagine not. It's always the women who decide the social pecking order, and how they decide is often inexplicable. Even here, a title doesn't necessarily gain social position, not by itself."

"But it sure helps." She paused and gave a little laugh. "It didn't take long for us to figure that out. No matter what we did, we didn't fit in."

"Why didn't you go abroad? To France or Italy? The social rules are much more relaxed there."

"We were going to. I told you about my debutante ball in Jackson, remember?"

"Yes."

"I didn't want what happened to me to ever happen to Dinah. And if I ever had daughters, I didn't want it to happen to them. I knew the only way to prevent it was for me to marry a man with a title. I'd gotten a letter from my friend Jennie Carter. She and her family had gone to Paris last spring, and she wrote to tell me she'd become engaged to a French marquess, and she said it was like the whole world just opened up. She invited us to come over once she was married, so I started taking French lessons and making plans for Mama, Dinah, and me to go in the autumn. But then I met Bernard, and before I knew it, we were engaged. If I hadn't met Bernard, I was ready to go to Paris and find myself a French marquess, too."

"Being a marquess is even more meaningless in France than it is in England. There's one on every corner."

"Why do you hate it all so much?"

His reply was immediate. "Why do you love it all so much?"

She shrugged, idly shoving the pile of cards into a stack with her fingertips. "I told you why."

"Yes, and I daresay it's understandable, given your situation, but Annabel, don't you see that none of it really means a damned thing? It doesn't signify anything."

"Most people would disagree with you," she whispered.

"And they'd be wrong. Once upon a time, lands and title were given for deeds bravely done, or some other service to the king, but those days are long over. Now, the aristocracy exists merely to keep existing. I'm not a duke because I accomplished something worthwhile. My brother died. That's all. And God knows Andrew didn't do anything to be worthy of the title, either. He inherited it. As did his father, and his father before him. None of us ever earned a bit of it for ourselves."

"Maybe it's time you changed that family tradition."

"I have to. I don't have a choice. Andrew spent everything we had and left everything in a shambles. The estates don't pay for themselves anymore." He looked at her. "The aristocracy is dying, Annabel. It has to change because it's outlived its usefulness."

"That's easy for you to say," she pointed out, "since your birthright is something no one can take away from you."

He tilted his head, giving her a thoughtful look. "My wife was like you. Oh, not in temperament. Evie was very shy, painfully so. And quiet. But like you, she had money and no pedigree. She was desperate to be accepted, just like you and your family."

"Is that why she married you?"

"Yes, to some extent." He sighed and leaned back in his chair to stare at the ceiling. "She fell violently in love with me. Not the sort of love that would have lasted, mind you. No, it was an infatuation. She fell in love with the man she thought I was." He paused, straightening in his chair and meeting her eyes across the table. "The man I let her think I was."

Annabel understood, and her heart hurt for that girl because she knew a girl could let herself believe anything if it was what she wanted to believe. Her throat constricted, and she forced herself to say out loud what she already knew. "You charmed her, got her to fall for you."

He was silent for several seconds before he answered, "Yes."

"Did you lie? Did you tell her you loved her even though you didn't?"

"No. She didn't ask, believe it or not. I think . . ." He paused. "I think she was afraid of the answer."

"Were you fond of her?"

"I liked her. I—" He broke off, raking a hand

through his hair. "God, this sounds odious, but I felt sorry for her. She wasn't like you, Annabel. She wasn't a fighter."

She smiled a little at that. "Mama says the whole time she was carryin' me, I was kicking, trying to get out. I was fighting even back then."

"I wish Evie had been more like you. Things might have been . . . different." He looked up, and she was startled by the bleakness of his expression. "My wife died by drowning."

She swallowed hard. "I know."

"What you may not know is that she walked into a pond at Scarborough even though she couldn't swim. She was wearing all her clothes and she walked right into the water until it was over her head. A farmer saw her do it, but he couldn't reach her in time to save her."

Annabel gasped. "You mean, she killed herself?"

"Yes. I was away at the time, in France."

She pressed a hand to her mouth, staring at him. He looked back at her, watching as if waiting for her inevitable next question. She had to ask it. "Why?"

"I don't know." His gaze slid away, a shimmer of guilt. He knew, he just didn't want to say. She waited, looking at him, and finally he said, "She had been with child, but she'd miscarried. Sylvia cabled me, and I came back at once, but by the time I reached home, she was dead."

"You blame yourself." It was a statement, not a question, but she held her breath, waiting for what he would say.

"I wasn't there. I wasn't with her because I was off playing. Playing with her money."

It was not only what he said, but the contempt with which he said it, that made her feel slightly sick. "I was barely twenty-one when I married, and because of the marriage settlement, I had a very generous income, so I was always off spending it. Evie and I had quarreled— well, I quarreled, she cried, I left. The story of our lives. I was so immature, and so damned stupid. I went off to the South of France with some friends, and I'd been gone a month when I got the telegram from Sylvia. I hadn't even known she was pregnant when I left. If she'd told me, or later, if she'd written, I'd have . . . oh hell." He sighed, leaning back to stare at the ceiling. "What does it matter now?"

She waited a moment, but she couldn't stop herself from asking more questions. "Is that why you won't ever marry again? Because your marriage was so awful and your wife died?"

"No." His face was hard, uncompromising, filled with self-condemnation. "Because there are no second chances."

Before she could reply, he spoke again. "Do you play cards?"

She blinked at the abrupt change of subject. "I beg your pardon?"

"I said, do you play cards?" He gathered the deck from the table, and as he did, she watched all the self-loathing in his face slide behind the mask of a devil-may-care expression and a charming smile.

It took her a moment to answer. "My daddy was called Black Jack Wheaton for a reason. He taught me to play cards when I was a little girl, though Mama was spittin' mad when she found out. She never did cotton much to cards, probably because she got tired of watching Daddy gamble money away."

"And what about you?" He fanned out the deck across the table. "Are you like your mother or your father?"

"Why?" She tilted her head, smiling a little. "You tryin' to do some gamblin' with me because you didn't get to go to the gaming clubs tonight?"

"Well, you're a damned sight prettier than the men I gamble with. Besides, I like deep stakes play, and you've got money you can afford to lose."

Despite the compliment, she gave him an indignant look. "Pretty arrogant of you to assume I would lose it! I think you're the one who'd lose," she added with a sniff. "And you definitely can't afford it."

"There's only one way to find out." He again gathered the cards and began to shuffle, flipping the edge of the stack to divide the deck in half, pulling the halves apart, then bringing them back together in a fluttering arch between his palms, just as her father used to do. It was the shuffle of a man who'd played a lot of cards. He didn't even watch his hands as he did it. Instead, he looked at her, still smiling a little, and Annabel felt the warm, deep pull of his attraction, just as she had the first day they'd ever met and every day since. She could feel herself sliding down a very slippery slope here, right smack-dab into trouble.

"As for what I can afford·. . ." He paused, his hands suddenly still. His black lashes lowered to the deep neckline of her gown, then back up to her face. "There are things to wager other than money."

He was flirting with her to deflect from what they'd been talking about: how bad a husband he'd been. But reminding herself of that didn't stop what she felt. Her body didn't seem to care that he'd been a bad husband.

She reached for a stack of chips, working to recover her poise. "I prefer money, thank you."

That made him laugh, although she didn't know if the reason was her prim reply, or the fact that she was blushing as she said it. "I usually prefer money, too, but for you, Annabel, I'd make an exception."

Desperate, she leaned over the table and grabbed the deck of cards out of his hands. "Poker or blackjack?"

"Poker, if you're dealing. My odds are better. Besides, I like to watch you blush. I mean bluff," he corrected at once.

Annabel struggled for composure, but it was hard when she knew she actually was blushing. And not just her face—she could feel that flush of heat flooding through her whole body, from the top of her head to the tips of her toes. Even worse, he knew it, too. He was fully aware of his effect on women. Hell, he'd just out-and-out admitted he'd married his wife for money, and here she was, going all moon-eyed over him like Lady Edith. And she knew she had to be the biggest fool from the state of Mississippi if she let him get away with it. But oh my, my, he could look at a girl.

"What's the limit?" she asked, feeling compelled to say something, fiddling with the stack of chips before her.

"Let's keep it simple, shall we? High hand wins the bet. If you win, I shall dance one waltz with Lady Edith at the Marquess of Kayne's May Day Ball. That ought to ensure her success for the entire season. Since I am a duke, I might as well find some useful purpose for my title. Helping debutantes toward social success," he added in a wry voice, "seems to be my main occupation these days."

Annabel could feel herself softening more with every word, sliding a little farther down that slippery slope. "But what if I lose?" she whispered.

"Ah. If you lose . . ." He paused, his gaze lowering to her mouth, and the warmth inside her deepened and spread. "If you lose," he resumed, returning his gaze to her face, "you agree to teach me what you know about Wall Street."

Disappointment pierced her. So stupid to think he'd been about to say, "a kiss," and even more stupid to want him to kiss her and to be disappointed when he didn't.

She took a deep breath, desperate, trying to force her disappointment away. "Why do you want to know about Wall Street?"

"I've been making enough off gambling to support myself, but now that I'm the duke, that can't continue. I have to find another way to earn a living and support Scarborough Park. The only way I can think of is investments and funds. That requires capital, of course, but—"

"Is that why you agreed to Uncle Arthur's idea? So you would have money to invest?"

"Yes. That plan is off the table now, obviously, and although being one of your trustees provides me with a bit of steady income, it isn't enough. Scarborough Park requires triple what you are paying me just to break even. Besides, that income from you will only last the next five years, less if you marry before then."

"But how shall you find the capital you need?"

"The other estates are mortgaged, and will have to be sold to pay the debts against them, with—I hope—a bit left over. I'm also selling everything of value within the estate—jewels, paintings, furnishings."

"Oh no!" she cried, dismayed. "Those things have probably been in your family for hundreds of years. It would be a shame to sell them!"

"It's my only choice. But I know nothing about money—how to invest it, I mean. But you do. Your uncle told me you have become a very shrewd woman of business, and I want you to advise me where I should put my capital."

"Why don't you ask Uncle Arthur for help? He's a lot better at it than I am, and everything I know I learned from him. Why come to me?"

A wry smile curved his mouth. "Your uncle is not exactly in the frame of mind to help me these days. And besides, you're a good deal prettier than he is."

The smile widened a bit. "I told you the first day we met, I like pretty women."

Don't be a fool, Annabel.

"That doesn't surprise me," she answered, her tart reply completely at odds with the sweet, lush warmth she felt inside. "Poker, you said?"

Before he could even nod a reply, she was dealing the cards, face-up since it was just high hand takes all. And when the cards were dealt, she had an ace, and he had a pair of deuces.

"Look at that," he murmured, meeting her gaze across the table, still smiling. "I won."

Her stomach dipped, a weightless, nervous sensation she tried to ignore. "I reckon you did."

"Tomorrow night?" he suggested and gestured to their surroundings. "Same time, same place?"

"Meet alone? After everyone's in bed? Is that necessary?"

"Probably not." He grinned. "But it's much more fun."

She felt a flare of excitement, the same sort of excitement she used to feel when Billy John would ask her to meet him down by Goose Creek.

"And besides," he added before she could think of a reply, "don't you still want to know about the rules of British matrimony? That's not the sort of thing we can discuss in front of your family. It would be terribly inappropriate."

This whole crazy idea was inappropriate. She licked her dry lips, not the least bit fooled by his paltry rationale. She knew just what was really going on in his mind because it was going on in hers, too. And British matrimony had nothing to do with it.

"Tomorrow night, then." She set down the deck of cards and practically ran for the door, trying to tell herself the only reason she was doing this was that she couldn't renege on a bet. But that was a lie. She was meeting him tomorrow night because she wanted to.

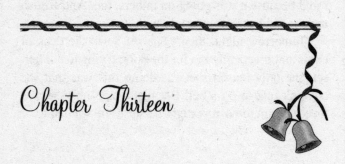

Chapter Thirteen

Christian knew he was playing with fire. He was supposed to be salvaging Annabel's reputation, but what he was really doing was seducing her. He might have felt some guilt about that, if the idea of seducing Annabel wasn't so damned tantalizing.

As it was, by the time of their rendezvous, any inconvenient whispers of his conscience that might have risen up to ruin the moment had been successfully quashed, and by the time she arrived, he was in the midst of a very erotic fantasy involving her and him and the library hearth rug.

Even if Christian had any inclination to curb such wayward, unguardianlike thoughts, the sight of her would have put paid to them. The evening gown she wore might have been considered sedate, with its long sleeves and dark green velvet fabric, except that the scandalously low-cut bodice displayed the full, luscious shape of her breasts perfectly.

Yes, he thought as he stood up to greet her, his gaze lingering on the shadowy crevice between her breasts, he was definitely playing with fire. His body was growing hotter by the moment.

Something of what he felt must have shown in his expression because she stopped just a few feet inside the door, a blush rising in her cheeks. Her lips parted as if she intended to say something, but then she closed her mouth again without a word and looked down. When he followed her gaze, he noticed the sheet of notepaper in her hands.

"This was a mistake," she said, and moved as if to turn and depart. "I shouldn't have agreed to this."

"Wait." Cursing his perfectly honed poker face for choosing such a damned inconvenient time to desert him, all he could think of was finding a way to make her stay. Thankfully, she paused again, and he stepped forward, closing the distance between them.

She wasn't looking at him, and he decided the best thing to do was make innocuous conversation and act as if what he felt was not painfully obvious. "What is this?" he asked, touching the top of the page she held in her hands.

"A list of American companies that you might want to look into for . . . for . . ." Her voice trailed off, and he took a step closer.

The paper crinkled as her fingers tightened around it. "Here," she said, and shoved it at his chest. "You wanted my advice on investments. Here it is."

If he took it, she'd leave. "Would you like a drink?" he asked instead, and stepped away, turning toward the liquor cabinet.

"That's probably not a good idea," she said behind him, but there was a hint of humor in her voice. "Last time I had a drink with you, my whole future got turned upside down."

"At least it's not Mississippi moonshine," he answered as he pulled a bottle of Madeira and a pair of cordial glasses from the interior of the cabinet. "So you're probably safe."

That last part was a lie, and he suspected they both knew it, but thankfully, she didn't argue the point, and when he brought her a filled glass of Madeira, she took it.

"Shall we sit down?" he asked, gesturing to the nearby sofa of black leather.

She moved to the seat he indicated, and he followed her, settling beside her, far enough away that they were not touching, and when she didn't jump back up, his hopes rose another notch.

She held the paper toward him again, but instead of taking it, he simply leaned closer. "What do the asterisks signify?" he asked, pointing to one of several such markings on the page.

"Those are what we call blue-chip stocks."

"Blue-chip? What, like the blue chips in poker?"

"Yes." She glanced at him, smiling a little. "I knew you'd probably like that term. Just like blue chips are the highest chips in poker, blue-chip stocks are the most stable, most valuable stocks."

"You've only marked about half of these as blue-chip stocks," he remarked, trying for the moment to keep his mind on the discussion. "Shouldn't one always purchase stocks that are safe and valuable?"

"Not always. The safest investments don't usually pay very high dividends. They don't have to. A riskier stock can sometimes make you more money, so you want to balance the blue chips you own with a few more speculative investments. Companies just starting out always need capital and they raise it by promising investors a higher dividend percentage per share."

"Like Hiram Burke's transatlantic telephone company," he murmured.

"How did you hear about that?" she asked. "The shares haven't even been offered yet."

"My sister is a fountain of gossip. I hear things. Since you know about this company, what is your opinion of it?"

"Uncle Arthur and I think it's a good idea. Some company is going to make telephones work across the ocean, and if anybody can do it, it's Hiram Burke. We bought fifteen percent. I'd have put that company on this list, but I don't know when Mr. Burke will offer the shares."

"He won't be offering them," Christian said wryly. "At least, not to me."

"Why not you?"

He considered whether to tell her, but after a moment, he shrugged, took a drink, and said, "My understanding is that Hiram's daughter covets a duchess's coronet, but I, alas, am not coveting a wife, so Hiram and I could not come to terms."

"I see."

He gestured to the page, deciding it was best to deflect from the subject of matrimony, since it probably wasn't wise for a man seducing a woman to underscore his adamant opposition to that particular institution. "You recommend quite a few railway companies. Why so many?"

He heard her take a deep breath. "American railway companies are almost always a good investment," she explained.

He paused, easing a bit closer to her, close enough to breathe in the scent of her skin, and the desire he'd been trying to curb flared up again. This time, he didn't try to hold it back. "Why?" he asked, coming closer, his breath stirring the tendril of hair in front of her ear.

"They . . ." She stirred in agitation even though he wasn't touching her. "They're stable," she went on, her voice a breathless rush that gave him hope. "They pay gen . . . generous dividends."

"What about British railways?" He was so close now, almost close enough to kiss her cheek. "Do you have something against the British?"

"Those are probably just as good. I should—" She stopped, sucking in a startled gasp as his lips brushed her cheek. "I should go," she whispered, but she didn't move.

Her skin was like velvet. Had it felt like this that night in the Turkish bath? It must have. He pressed a kiss along her cheek to the corner of her lips, but that move was too much for her.

"I have to leave." Shoving the list onto his lap, she jumped up, and Christian felt a sudden, crazy jolt of desperation. He rose as well, and the list fluttered to the floor as his arms came up around her. She turned toward him, but before she could protest this entrapment, he captured her lips with his.

She made a muffled sound against his mouth—of protest or accord, he didn't know, but he didn't want to know, because her lips were so warm and so soft that pleasure cascaded through his body.

The first time he'd kissed her, he'd been drunk, but this time, there was no alcohol to dull his senses, and the touch of her mouth awakened in him every sensation a man could feel.

The hairs at the back of her neck brushed his fingertips, and her cheeks were soft against his palms. He could hear the swish of silk, feel her leg move against his, smell the delicate orange blossom fragrance of her French perfume. It was an intoxicating mix, more intoxicating than alcohol could ever be.

His body was as enthralled as his senses, for his heart pounded in his chest, his pulses raced, and lust coursed through him like a tidal flood. He felt as if he was drowning in sensation.

He tore his mouth from hers, but not to stop. Instead, he sucked in a deep breath of air, tilted his head the other way, and kissed her again. This time, he parted her lips with his, and his tongue entered her mouth. She stirred, and he felt her hands flatten against his shoulders. Though she wasn't pushing him away, in the vague recesses of his mind, he knew it was his cue to stop. He ought to, he knew, but his need was more powerful than either his good sense or his gallantry, and besides, being her trustee was absurd, unworkable, impossible. He'd known that all along. A trustee had to be trustworthy, and he'd never been a trustworthy chap.

As if to prove it, he slid one hand down between her upraised arms to cup her breast, embracing the full, generous shape even through the layers of fabric.

This time, she was the one who broke the kiss, turning her face away. "We can't do this," she panted, the heel of her hand pushing his shoulder. "We can't."

He knew that, but the sight before him was too tempting to resist. He bent his head to trail kisses along her throat, over her collarbone, and down to the plump curve of her breast. He turned his hand, sliding his fingertips under the edge of her neckline, shoving his hand beneath silk and satin and nainsook to cup her breast fully in his palm.

She gave a startled gasp at the contact, and suddenly, she was pushing against him with enough force to penetrate even his dazed senses. "Stop, Christian," she ordered, her breath coming in quick gasps as her hand shoved his away. "You have to stop."

He did, tearing himself away and stepping back

even as every nerve and cell of his body protested this unthinkable act. He watched her eyes open to stare at him, her dismay obvious. Her dress was wrinkled, the skirt twisted sideways. Her hair was mussed; several locks had come loose to tumble around her face and shoulders. One fell across her breast. He stared at it, heat curling in his groin.

"Cryin' all night," she whispered, sounding miserable instead of glad, her voice bringing his gaze back to her face. He stared at her lips, swollen by his kisses, and he watched her press her fingertips to them with a little moan. "What are we supposed to do now?"

"More of the same?" he murmured, moving toward her.

She flattened a palm against his chest to keep him at bay. "This can't happen again."

"But it will," he pointed out. "Given the arrangement we have, it's inevitable."

"No, it's not. Not as long as we make sure we're never alone together."

He kept perfectly still, fighting the urge to take her in his arms again. "Do you really think that will work?"

"It has to."

"Why?"

She took a deep breath and looked straight into his eyes. "Because you're no good for me, Christian." With that, she stepped around him and ran for the door. "You're no good for me."

She was right, of course. Because of him, all her hopes and dreams had already gone awry. Because of him, everything she'd ever wanted was now at risk. Now, he had to make up for what he'd done by playing the role assigned to him. He owed her that, and his own desires be damned.

Christian sank into his chair and rubbed a hand over his face. Acting the part of the dutiful, protective guardian was proving to be even harder than he'd thought it would be, perhaps the hardest thing he'd ever done in his life.

During the two weeks that followed, Annabel tried not to think about what had happened in the library. Every time she remembered Christian's mouth on hers, the feel of his strong arms holding her close, or his hands caressing her, she shoved those memories right back out of her mind quick as she could.

Thankfully, Lady Sylvia provided her with many distractions—shopping in New Bond Street, motoring around Hyde Park, paying calls on the ladies of the *ton*, having tea at the Savoy, and attending the opera at Covent Garden. Though the setting was different, these activities were just what she and Jennie Carter had always longed for while sitting side by side in the wallflower chairs at charity balls or huddled with the other outsiders at the far end of Newport's Polo Field.

She made several new friends, striking up an especially friendly acquaintance with Lady Edith's older sister, Isabel, who, upon being introduced, had laughingly deemed them "Annabel and Isabel, the two belles of the season," declared her tea gown "simply smashing" and begged her for fashion advice. A shopping excursion the following day cemented their acquaintance into friendship.

During that fortnight, Annabel began to feel as if she was finally living the life she'd once only been able to dream about, and it was every bit as enjoyable as she'd always imagined. There was, however, one fly in the ointment.

Annabel slanted a look down the long dining table at Kayne House to the fly in question. He wasn't hard to find. As a duke, Christian was the man of highest rank present this evening, which meant he was at the opposite end of the long dining table from her, seated at the right hand of their hostess, Lady Kayne. That put him directly in her line of vision every time she glanced toward her dinner companion, which was often, since Mr. Wilbur was not only a passionate birdwatcher and amateur zoologist, he was also a garrulous talker who required an attentive listener. Nor were the table decorations of any help to her, for though the gleaming silver, flowers, and candles made a tall and elaborate display, they could not obscure Christian's face from her view.

During the past two weeks they had donned the façade she had engineered, the façade of ward and guardian, wealthy heiress and conscientious trustee, making every effort to demonstrate to the world that nothing improper had ever existed between them. It was an easy role for her to play during the day, when he was off conducting his own business and she was off paying calls on her new circle of acquaintances or shopping with Sylvia. But in the evenings, whenever she was in the same room with him, memories of the hot kisses they'd shared came roaring back, arousing her, confusing her, and making the fiction much harder to sustain.

Christian, she couldn't help noticing, didn't seem to share her discomfiture when they were together, and though she ought to be relieved by his superb acting skills, she wasn't. She was actually a bit chagrined that he seemed able to play his part perfectly, while she felt as transparent as glass.

This dinner party at Kayne House was a perfect example, she thought, trying to study him as unobtrusively as possible. The candlelight gleamed on his dark hair and glinted off the silver cuff links at his wrists. Behind him, the enormous painting of the English countryside seemed an appropriate backdrop, for within its gilt frame, he looked every inch the proper duke.

This was the world into which he'd been born, she thought with a quick glance around the elegant room, and though he didn't have much fondness for it, that didn't stop him from being completely at ease within it. He sat relaxed in his chair as he conversed with Lady Kayne, amusing her with whatever story he was telling her, making her laugh.

Smiling, he reached for his wineglass, and as he did, he happened to glance up and caught Annabel watching. His smile vanished at once.

She froze, suddenly paralyzed, seeing for the first time in two weeks what she'd seen that night in the library and in the Turkish baths aboard ship, watching his mask slip to reveal his desire for her.

She wanted to look away, before everyone else could observe what he was suddenly, inexplicably making no effort to conceal.

Don't look at me like that, she wanted to shout. *People will see. They'll think something's between us.*

And those people would be wrong. There was nothing between them, nothing important or lasting anyway. All they had was lust, and she knew that was nothing at all, not with a man who wasn't willing to step up to the altar and marry a girl honorably. There was no future for any girl in wanting Christian Du Quesne, no future but a big, fat heartache.

She forced her gaze away and returned her attention to the gentleman beside her, who was still talking nineteen to the dozen about the nesting habitats of the English chaffinch. "Why, Mr. Wilbur," she murmured when she could get a word in, "that is just the most fascinatin' thing I have ever heard."

As she spoke, she pasted on a smile and pretended she hadn't seen naked desire written all over Christian's face, praying he hadn't seen it in hers.

She carried on the pretense, but with each passing day, it proved harder to sustain. She did everything she could to stay away from him, but it wasn't always possible. When she took Sylvia out motoring around Hyde Park in her beloved Model A Ford, he insisted on coming, too, and she couldn't make a fuss without rousing Sylvia's suspicions. When they went to tea with the Duke and Duchess of St. Cyres at their villa in Bayswater, he was also invited, and she had to drag Dinah out for a tour of the splendid gardens to avoid him. But when Sylvia pointed out that she needed to reserve one dance for Christian on her dance card for the May Day Ball, she balked. That was just too much temptation for any girl.

"But Annabel," Sylvia said, bewildered by her flat refusal, "the May Day Ball is the social event that definitively launches the season, and because he is the Duke of Scarborough, a dance with him bolsters any girl's chances of social success. And as your guardian, Christian is a perfectly acceptable dance partner for you. It's a very public way for our family to demonstrate our strong support for your family. Why are you so opposed?"

"People will think there's something in it." She tried to look directly at Sylvia across the writing desk in the study, but she couldn't quite meet her gaze. "Something between him and me."

"They'll be more apt to think that if you don't dance with him, my dear."

Not likely. There was no way she could be in Christian's arms in a room full of people and carry on the farce.

"I said no," she answered, and bolted from the room, leaving a very astonished Lady Sylvia staring after her.

* * *

By the time they departed for the May Day Ball the following night, Annabel had gotten her emotions back under control. Nonetheless, she was glad Christian did not test her renewed resolve by riding with them to Kayne House.

Busy with other engagements earlier in the evening, he made his own transportation arrangements, giving Sylvia use of the ducal carriage to transport them from Chiswick. And when they arrived at the ball, it was such a crush that with any luck, she might not see him at all.

They left their wraps in the cloakroom and took their places in the line moving toward the ballroom. It was a long journey, for each party was greeted at the entrance to the ballroom by Lady Kayne, but Annabel didn't mind. She'd been waiting for an event like this to come her way for seven long years. She could wait a little longer. Anticipation was half the fun.

At last, they were able to enter the ballroom, an enormous, very crowded room decorated with purple lilacs, garlands of fern and ivy, and massive ice sculptures that served to keep the temperature comfortable. To one side, an eight-piece orchestra played and many people milled about the dance floor, but no one was dancing, since Lady Kayne was still greeting guests and had not yet opened that segment of the evening's festivities. Along the back wall behind the dance floor, pairs of French doors leading out onto the terrace were open to catch the spring breeze. Annabel and her family followed Sylvia along the edge of the dance floor, where they paused by the first set of opened doors.

"This is perfect," Sylvia told Annabel and her mother, raising her voice to be heard above the music and conversation. "Take note, ladies, of our location, for this shall be our place to meet should we become separated during the evening. We must be sure to gather here before four o'clock, for it shall take nearly an hour to have our carriage brought around, and I do not intend for anyone to ever say I was the last to leave a ball."

She shuddered as if that were a fate worse than death, then she turned to George and Arthur. "You gentlemen may do as you like, of course, returning with us to Chiswick after the ball or staying in town, as you please. There is a card room and a smoking room, should you not wish to dance. Now, I must have a brief word with Lady Kayne. I'm dying to know how much we've raised for the Orphanage Fund. If you will pardon me?"

Sylvia bustled off. George and Arthur also excused themselves to go in search of that card room, leaving Annabel and her mother alone to study the scene spread out before them—ladies in bright silk ball gowns and glittering jewels strolled about the room with elegant gentlemen in immaculate white linen and black tuxedos.

Watching them, Annabel gave a deep sigh, savoring a social victory that had been mighty long in coming. She'd been to balls before, of course—charity balls mostly, where a person wasn't necessarily required to have high social position to attend. One could usually buy an invitation with a generous enough contribution. But though the Marquess of Kayne's May Day Ball was a charity event, Annabel hadn't had to buy her way in, not this time. She and her family had been *invited* to attend, and that made all the difference.

"Well, Mama?" she asked the woman beside her. "What do you think?"

Henrietta looked at her, and her own happiness grew even stronger at the sight of her mother's smile. "It's mighty fine, darlin', I have to say." She laughed. "We've come a long way from Gooseneck Bend."

"We have, Mama," she agreed, and put an arm across her mother's shoulder for a quick hug. "We sure have."

"At last!"

The sound of another voice entering the conversation had both women turning as Lady Isabel Helspeth came toward them. "I thought you'd never arrive!" she added, giving Annabel a quick kiss on each cheek in the French style.

Isabel was similar to her younger sister in appearance, having the same blond hair and blue eyes, but unlike Edith, Isabel was not the least bit timid or shy. She was lively and self-confident. Even more important, she hadn't seemed to care a whit about Annabel's humble background.

"Mrs. Chumley," Isabel greeted her mother. "It's so good to see you again. Mama is over by the refreshment table, having a fit of the vapors over the lack of strawberry ices. Do you think you might go over and calm her with some of your American good sense? She's quite distraught."

Henrietta smiled, not the least bit fooled. "I know when I'm bein' got rid of," she murmured in her wry way. "Of course you two want to have some girl talk."

Henrietta departed to find Lady Helspeth, and Isabel returned her attention to Annabel, leaning back to eye her ball gown of pale pink silk. "Stunning dress," she pronounced. "I do wish Mama would let me wear the lower necklines! But she simply won't be moved. We Brits are so stodgy, while you Americans are so much more daring, and you have such a way with clothes. Oh, I say," she added with the air of one who just remembered something, "have you any openings on your dance card?"

Annabel was already accustomed to her new friend's quick, birdlike way of flittering from subject to subject, so the question didn't even take her back. "A few," she answered, and glanced at the card dangling from her wrist. "The first one, a Roger de Coverly just before the supper, and . . ." She paused to flip the card over. "And two waltzes right after. Why?"

"My brother, that's why." She rolled her eyes. "Tiger has been pestering me for an introduction to you ever since he saw you at Mama's at-home the other day. Like most men, he avoids at-homes like the plague, but he heard you talking as he passed by the drawing room, and he went absolutely mad about your American voice."

It's a luscious voice, absolutely splendid.

Annabel closed her eyes long enough to force Christian back out of her thoughts, then she returned her attention to her friend.

"Of course, then," Isabel was going on, "he had to have a peek into the drawing room, and when he saw you, he declared you to be the prettiest girl of the season. I fear he's got a crush."

"Oh!" Annabel laughed, flattered. She'd never been the recipient of a crush, at least none that she knew of. "I see."

"When he found out you were to be here, he asked me to discover if you had a waltz open, the idea being that I'll introduce you just before and then he can ask you to dance. Brothers are such a bother." She frowned, looking vexed. "I was hoping you'd be fully engaged."

Annabel felt a pang of alarm, fearing the worst—that she might have been mistaken in her newfound friend's opinion of her. "Do you not . . . want your brother to take an interest in me?"

"Darling!" Isabel looked stricken. "That's not it at all, you silly goose. Quite the opposite. It's Tiger. He's awful, a thorough scapegrace in every way, and not to be trusted by any girl. I hate to say such things about my own brother, but there it is. Even girls with brains go moronic over him. I've seen it happen time and again. It's inexplicable, and quite nauseating. I should hate to see that happen to you."

Annabel laughed, relieved. "I think I can handle

your brother. I've no intention of forming any serious attachments, at least for a while."

"Quite right of you!" Isabel said with approval. "I feel the same way myself. I shall go to Italy, paint, and have dozens of lovers. But I shall never fall in love myself! Of course," she added, "I might feel differently if I were staying at Cinders. The Duke of Scarborough is divine. Too bad he's so unattainable." She sighed. "Poor Edith."

They both glanced at the far wall where Edith sat with the other wallflowers, gazing hopefully—too hopefully—over the gathering crowd.

"I wish she'd give it up," Isabel went on. "It's well known Scarborough won't ever marry again, and she knows that. What she needs is a few suitors hanging about to distract her. Oh, here's Mr. Wentworth to claim me, for I promised him the first dance. I must go." She started forward to meet the young man approaching them, adding over her shoulder, "I'll bring Tiger to you right after the supper, then?"

Isabel went off to dance with Mr. Wentworth, and Annabel glanced back to the row of faces along the wall. Lady Edith was still in one of the wallflower chairs, looking less hopeful now, and more resigned.

Such a shame, Annabel thought, that she hadn't won that bet three weeks ago. It would have been such a boon for the girl's chances and a boost for her self-confidence to dance with a duke.

She returned her attention to the couples swirling about the floor, seeing some faces that she knew— Lady Kayne, of course, dancing with a grand-looking fellow who had an enormous mustache and medals all over his chest. Lady Sylvia was dancing, too, with Uncle Arthur. Now that was a surprise. How on earth had she persuaded him? Uncle Arthur hated to dance.

Another couple swirled past her line of vision, catching her attention. It was Bernard, dancing with a girl Annabel knew from New York, Rosemary Lucas. Rosemary was the daughter of Midwest dry-goods king Jeremiah Lucas, another New Money outsider, just like herself.

Watching them together, Annabel felt no pang of regret. Christian might have stood up at her wedding for the wrong reasons, but despite the embarrassment caused by it, Annabel was glad now that he had.

Her change of heart was hard to define. It wasn't only because Bernard had gone to a prostitute just before their wedding, demonstrating that her affection for him had been both transient and misplaced. No, it really had nothing to do with Bernard at all and everything to do with her.

She wasn't willing to settle for the deal anymore. Maybe that was because she was making new friends here in London and enjoying herself. Or maybe it was because she now had the chance to improve her family's social fortunes without having to marry. Or maybe it was because some of the things Christian had told her about British marriage had soured her on trading her money for a title. Or maybe, she thought with chagrin, it was because of that man's smoky blue eyes and smoldering kisses.

"Why won't you dance with me?"

The low voice by her ear made her jump, and she turned her head to find the object of her thoughts standing right beside her. "Heavens," she gasped, pressing a gloved hand to her chest as she turned toward him, "how you startled me!"

"Sorry." He smiled at her, hands in his pockets, looking rakishly handsome in his tuxedo. "Woolgathering, were you?"

"I was just watching the crowd and thinking."

"Of me?"

She lifted her chin. "How conceited you are!"

"It's not conceit," he corrected, giving her a rueful look. "It's wishful thinking."

"In this case, it's not. I *was* thinking of you. And," she added to keep him from guessing why, "I was also thinking about Lady Edith. It's her first season and her first ball, and instead of dancing, she's sitting over there with the other wallflowers."

He groaned, moving as if to use Annabel as a shield between him and the chairs against the wall. "Well, don't let her see me."

"It's probably already too late. And since you are already here, and the first dance is ending now, it's a perfect opportunity for you to make the poor girl's evening a success. Go over and ask her for the next dance."

"No." He shook his head. "I don't want to give the poor girl any false hopes."

"That won't happen. She has a crush on you, yes, but to get over it, she needs some real suitors. If you danced with her, all the young men would see that, and want to dance with her, too."

"Possibly," he allowed, "but why do I have to be the one to lead the way?"

"Because you're a duke. It's your job to lead the way."

He made a face. "You want me to dance with Edith, but you refuse to dance with me yourself? Annabel, I can't tell you what a blow that is to my vanity."

She smiled sweetly. "Twenty blows to your vanity wouldn't make a dent."

"Ouch," he said with a grimace, and then his expression once again grew thoughtful. "You really are serious about this."

"Yes, because I know how she feels. I've been her, Christian. The wallflower who doesn't get asked to dance is just like the girl who never gets invited to the party. The reasons are different, but the feeling is the same, and it's miserable."

He leaned a little closer. "If I did dance with her, would that please you?"

She caught her breath. "Why should that matter?"

"It matters to me, Annabel."

Her heart slammed against her ribs. "You should do it because it's a nice thing to do."

"Ah, but I'm not a nice man." As if to prove it, his gaze lowered to her mouth, and he said, "I'll dance with Edith, if you dance with me first."

"No."

"Why not? Afraid once you're in my arms, you'll succumb to my charms?"

That was exactly what she was afraid of. "No," she countered at once. "I can't dance with you because I'm engaged for the next dance."

At that moment, she spied Mr. Wilbur approaching to claim her, and she eyed the bespectacled bird enthusiast with relief.

"Later then?"

"Sorry," she said, adding the lie before she could stop herself, "but I'm engaged for all my dances."

She joined Mr. Wilbur, not feeling the least bit guilty about her lie. Confirming Christian's guess that she was afraid to dance with him because she wanted him was the last thing she needed. As for how she was going to fill up the rest of her dance card, she'd worry about that later.

Chapter Fourteen

Annabel's relief at escaping Christian was short-lived. It lasted about ten seconds.

She walked the few steps onto the dance floor, turned toward her partner, and took one glance back, just in time to see Edith's hunched, dejected pose and Christian's pause beside her chair. Annabel watched as he held out his hand to the girl. And when Edith lifted her astonished face to see just who was asking her to dance, Annabel felt a pang of happiness twist her own heart.

The music began, and as Mr. Wilbur swirled her across the floor in the first waltz of the night, Annabel tried to force that burst of happiness into its proper perspective. Though he had done it to please her, it was still just a gesture, one that cost him nothing and changed nothing. Yet, despite these efforts to prop up her protective walls and keep him at bay, Annabel could feel her determination to stay away from him softening a little more with each moment.

Desperate, she dragged George out onto the floor when her next free dance came up. She didn't know if Christian was watching, but she didn't want to give him any opportunity to claim her for a dance and shred the last of her resolve.

After the supper, she was introduced to Isabel's brother, Edward, and she could see at once where he'd gotten his nickname of Tiger. He had a tawny, wind-blown handsomeness that was impossible to ignore. In addition, even without Isabel's warnings, she'd have seen the wandering gleam in his eye and the dangerous charm in his manner. Still, though she enjoyed look-ing into Tiger's roguish blue eyes while they danced, laughing at his jokes, and happily accepting his brazen compliments, she felt nothing beyond the simple plea-sure any girl felt at a man's admiration. There was none of the melting sweetness and hot desire she felt every time she was with Christian. It was a relief, she sup-posed, to discover she wasn't susceptible to *every* bad boy who came her way.

Afterward, as Tiger started to escort her back to her place, she caught a glimpse of Christian through the crowd, standing with her family, watching her, wait-ing to see if she did indeed have a partner for the next dance. She didn't, and she was seized by sudden panic that made her stop dead in her tracks.

"Miss Wheaton?" Tiger stopped beside her, hover-ing solicitously. "Are you unwell?"

She cast another glance toward Christian. He was looking at her as he had that night at Lord Kayne's dinner party, his desire for her plainly written on his face, and she could feel an answering hunger for him pulling her like a magnet. She took an involuntary step toward him, then realized it and stopped again, turning abruptly toward her dance partner. "I need some air," she said to Tiger. "Will you excuse me, please?"

Without waiting for an answer, she turned away and ducked out the nearest set of French doors onto the terrace. She went down the steps and into the gardens of Kayne House, gulping in deep breaths of cool night air as she made for the back of the gardens and ducked into a boxwood maze that would obscure her from anyone's view.

She walked, turning corners between the tall hedges without any thought to where she was going as she tried to compose herself, but she soon felt hopelessly lost, not only within the maze, but in her own heart. What did she really want?

As if in answer to that question, she emerged into the center of the maze, and found Christian there, leaning back against the edge of the fountain behind him, as if waiting for her, as if knowing she would find him, as if it was all inevitable. Perhaps he was right.

She took a step toward him, desire drawing her, but then she stopped. "We're supposed to be staying away from each other," she said, reminding them both.

He straightened away from the fountain. "That's

what you keep saying, but I can't . . ." He paused to take a deep breath. "I can't stay away from you."

"I don't think you're trying very hard."

"No," he agreed, and started walking toward her. "I'm not."

She felt another jolt of panic, but she could not seem to make herself turn and leave. She stood there, held by his gaze like a butterfly on a pin, shaking inside as he came closer, fighting not to step forward and meet him halfway. "If anyone sees us—"

"Dance with me. I know you already have a partner for every dance," he added, smiling faintly, demonstrating he'd seen right through her lie, "but that's too bad. As your trustee, I shall tell him to sod off."

"It's just a dance," she whispered as he halted in front of her. "Why do you want it so badly?"

"Isn't it obvious? I want any excuse to touch you. Even if it's in a room full of people." Slowly, ever so slowly, as if he feared she'd bolt again, he reached out, taking her hand to entwine their gloved fingers. His other hand settled on her waist. "This is better, of course."

"We shouldn't be out here."

His hands tightened, pulling her closer. "I know."

Desperate, she tried one last time to fight the inevitable. "I don't want to dance with you."

"All right," he said, and let go of her hand, bending his head. "We won't dance."

He kissed her, and at the soft, warm contact of his mouth, pleasure bloomed in her like a flower opening to sunshine, pleasure so great that her lips parted at once. Tacit permission, and he took advantage of it, cupping the nape of her neck as his other arm tightened around her waist. He deepened the kiss, his tongue entering her mouth, tasting her again and again.

The kisses were slow, deep, drugging kisses that melted away good sense and lessons learned. She felt as if she were sinking down, down, down into a sweet, blissful oblivion.

With one arm around her waist, he slid his other hand from her nape, gliding down her spine and over her hip. He grasped folds of her skirt, working his way beneath layers of silk and muslin.

Stop him, she thought, but even as that thought passed through her mind, she curled her fingers around the lapels of his jacket, drawing him closer.

Under her skirts, his hand touched her hip, his palm so hot that his touch seemed to sear her through his glove and her thin nainsook drawers. She moaned against his mouth, and he stirred at the sound, his arm tightening around her waist, his hips pressing against hers. She felt the hardness of him, the need, and in a momentary flash of sanity, she remembered where they were, and what she would lose if they were caught. If she was going to stop him, she had to do it now, before every shred of her resolve and her pride were gone and she made another very bad choice.

She broke the kiss, turning her face away, feeling as if the move were ripping her apart.

"I don't want this!" She brought her arms between

them to push his apart. The moment he released her, she stepped back, shaking her head. "I don't want you."

He didn't move. He simply looked at her, breathing hard, and it seemed forever before he spoke. "That's a lie, Annabel. And we both know it."

The tenderness in his voice was almost her undoing. "I don't want to want you! Is that a better way of putting it?"

He rubbed his hands over his face as if trying to clear his head and think. "I'm not sure I understand the distinction," he muttered.

"Wanting you is pointless." As she spoke, the euphoria and desire of the past few stolen moments began giving way, bringing back the painful reality. "There's no future in it."

He took a step forward, reaching for her, but she evaded the move and his arm fell to his side. "Why does there have to be a future?" he asked.

"Because there does!" She took a deep breath, striving to be clear with him and with herself about what she wanted in life. "I want marriage. I want a husband and children. I want a man who respects me. A man who thinks I'm good enough to be his wife."

"And you believe I don't think so?" He shook his head as if in disbelief. "If I did marry you, how would that prove I think you're good enough? Did Rumsford prove it by proposing marriage to you? If you don't already believe you're good enough—whatever the bloody hell that means—then nothing I say or do will make a difference. Don't you see that?"

"What I see is that men want certain things from every woman, but I want—I deserve—a man willing to offer me more than that. And we both know you aren't that man."

He didn't deny it, and that confirmation of what she already knew hurt more than she would have thought possible. She took another step back, knowing she had to leave before she did the most embarrassing thing of all and started to cry.

"Stay away from me, Christian. I've made plenty of mistakes in my life, Lord knows, but I try real hard not to make the same ones twice. Please, please stay away from me."

She whirled around, grasping fistfuls of silk in her fists, and ran away. Running seemed to be the only defense she had left.

Christian stared after her, lust raging through him, his body rebelling against what had just happened, even as his mind fought to accept it. He felt torn apart, bereft, and worse—he felt helpless. Because what she said was true.

Her words ringing in his ears, he watched her go, striving with everything he had not to follow her, grab her, kiss her until she didn't have the strength to fight him anymore.

But he knew he couldn't do what he wanted. It was perfectly right of her to want a husband and children, to want the respect that society would confer on her if she made a good marriage. He might think marriage a meaningless institution, but most people didn't, including Annabel. And because of his actions, she'd been deprived of one chance at marriage already, and though in his opinion Rumsford had been no prize, the fact remained that he'd interfered in her life when he'd had no right to do so, and he still had the obligation to right that wrong.

On the other hand, this damnable situation could not go on, or he would lose his sanity, and he knew there was only one course open to him.

He had to find her a husband. It was the only decent thing to do. He drew a deep, steadying breath and hoped doing the decent thing didn't break him.

Annabel didn't see Christian for two days. He stayed in town, slept at his club, and sent no word of when he would return to Cinders.

After what had happened at the May Day Ball, she ought to be relieved by his absence, but she wasn't. On the contrary, she missed him, and the fact that he was only doing what she'd asked him to do just made her feel more miserable about it all.

"Now, Annabel," Sylvia said from her place at the foot of the dining table, "I thought we might go to the theater tomorrow night."

Annabel stirred, lifting her gaze from her plate of bacon and eggs, trying to drum up an interest in going to the theater. "What's the play?"

"They're doing *A Bit South of Heaven*—that's Sebastian Grant's latest play—at the Old Vic. Sebastian is the Earl of Avermore, you know, and a very good friend of Christian's. It's a bit late in the day, but Sebastian always keeps a few tickets in reserve for his friends. Or we could go to the opera. Which would you prefer, Annabel?"

"Either one," she answered politely, and returned her attention to pushing eggs around on her breakfast plate. "Whatever you'd like."

"It's Wagner at Covent Garden," Sylvia went on, as if that might persuade her to form an opinion. "Which is always good, but I do wish they would perform something modern—Puccini, perhaps."

"Oh, Mama," Dinah cried, entering the conversation, "may I come, too? It's bad enough that I can't go to balls, but I'd love to see a play or go to the opera."

"You're only eleven, darlin'," Henrietta reminded. "Way too young for the theater.

Annabel felt impelled to speak for her sister. "Oh, let her come, Mama. One late night won't hurt her."

"I agree with Annabel," George said. "Why shouldn't Dinah come if she likes?"

"I agree, too," Uncle Arthur put in. "We're in London. Might as well let the girl see some things and enjoy herself while we're here."

"Many girls do attend the theater in London, Mrs. Chumley," Sylvia said. "Not the opera, though, I'm afraid, especially not Wagner. The Ring operas make for too long an evening for a young girl. So, the theater it is, then?" She glanced around the table, and at the nods of agreement, she went on, "I shall write to Avermore this morning, and see if he has tickets to spare for tomorrow night."

Whether Sebastian Grant had tickets, however, became immediately irrelevant, for the discussion was interrupted, and by the last person Annabel would have expected.

"Sorry, Sylvia," Christian said, entering the dining room. "But I fear I must usurp your plans. Good morning, everyone."

Annabel straightened in her chair, watching as he strode past the dining table to the sideboard where breakfast had been set out in warming dishes, but though he nodded politely to her mother and gave Dinah's hair a tweak as he passed them, he didn't glance toward her side of the table at all.

"Usurp my plans?" Sylvia echoed as he helped himself to bacon and eggs. "We haven't seen you for two days," she reminded him with mock severity. "And now you come waltzing in at breakfast, daring to usurp my plans?"

He paused to give her an apologetic glance over one shoulder. "I am the duke," he said, and went back to filling his plate. "I'm entitled."

"Well, I have to admit I'm delighted by this sudden interest in the social whirl, dear brother," Sylvia said, laughing. "But what's in the wind?"

"I've invited the Duke of Trathen to dine with us tomorrow night, and I've reserved a dining room for us at the Savoy."

"Trathen?" Sylvia stared at her brother in surprise. "But we barely know the man."

"You barely know him," Christian corrected as he brought his plate to the table and sat down. "I've known him since Oxford. Fine fellow. Wealthy, influential, honorable." He reached for the jam pot. "Unmarried, too."

What was he up to? Annabel stared at him in bewilderment, but if she hoped for any sort of explanation, she was disappointed. He didn't even look at her.

"And that reminds me," he went on as he spread jam on his toast, "are we free on the seventh? I saw Sir Thomas Duncan at my club last night, and he invied us all to a picnic at Kew Gardens."

"Did he, indeed?" Sylvia said, sounding as bewildered as Annabel felt. "I wasn't aware Sir Thomas was in town."

"Arrived a few days ago, I understand. Spied Miss Wheaton the other night at the ball, and was quite bowled over. Said she was the prettiest girl there, and he begged me for an introduction, so we've arranged a picnic. I hope you don't mind, Miss Wheaton," he added without looking at her.

"I think we're free on the seventh," Sylvia murmured. "Any other plans you've made on our behalf, dear brother?"

"Well, there's Lord Pomeroy," he went on. "Ran into him at Cook's. I happened to mention our guests, and he asked if we'd be attending his mother's water party on the fifteenth. I won't be able to go, but I'm sure you'll be able to do so. Pomeroy seemed very interested in meeting our guests, particularly Miss Wheaton."

He was shoving other men at her, Annabel realized. But why? The question had barely crossed her mind before the answer came, and in her own words.

I want marriage. I want a husband and children.

He was giving her what she'd told him she wanted, she realized with a pang of dismay. Was this some horrible attempt to punish her for those words?

"Did he?" Annabel murmured, staring at him, trying not to believe it. "I suppose he's single, too?"

"As a matter of fact he is." Suddenly, he looked up, and in his face was something she'd never seen there before. Anguish.

He wasn't punishing her, she realized. He was trying to be honorable. The look in his eyes ripped her heart apart, shredding all her desires but the one that was impossible. The desire to be with him.

"You saw Pomeroy at Cook's?" Sylvia asked. "What on earth were you doing there?"

"Thought I'd go back to New York in a week or so," he told his sister, his gaze on Annabel.

"New York?" Annabel and Sylvia cried at once, with equal surprise.

"Why not?" he countered, giving a careless shrug and tearing his gaze from hers to look toward his sister. "You've got things well in hand here, Sylvia, and I've got to continue with my own plans at some point."

"I see," his sister murmured, sounding disappointed. "But—"

He shoved back his chair and stood up, cutting off any more questions. "I do have my own life, you know,"

he said, and walked out of the room, his breakfast un-
finished, leaving Annabel, Sylvia, and everyone else at
the table staring after him.

Christian left the house at once, but it took him all day
and most of the evening before he felt sufficiently in
control to return to Cinders. When he did, he picked
up his letters from the tray by the door, stopped by the
drawing room where Annabel and her family were
gathered after dinner to issue a quick, polite good night
from the doorway, and then he went straight upstairs to
his bedroom.

Avoiding Annabel was the only decent thing to do.
It was also the safest thing. If he was all the way on the
other side of the house from her, she might be safe from
him until he could leave London.

He occupied his time by reading his letters, which
only served to depress his already glum spirits. The
latest report from Saunders about the deteriorating
condition of Scarborough Park was disheartening.

Even worse, Hiram Burke had sent him an invitation to dinner. Yesterday, he'd called on the American,
who had arrived in town a few days earlier with his
family and was leasing a house in Grosvenor Square.
During their conversation, Christian had happened
to mention those shares, and this request to dine was
obviously Hiram's answer. He had no doubt that if he
accepted the invitation, Miss Fanny Burke would be
at dinner, too, and since he could not accept either
dinner or Miss Burke, he clearly had no chance of

buying any shares in Hiram's transatlantic telephone company.

Still, there was one bright spot in an otherwise thoroughly depressing slew of correspondence. Trathen had other plans for the following night, and would be unable to join them for dinner.

It made no sense to be relieved about that, since he'd gone to such pains to arrange it, but he was. His fellow duke was everything a girl wanting marriage could ask for—wealthy, of good character, amiable, and in search of a wife—everything, in other words, that Christian was not. And now that Trathen had declined his invitation, he was glad beyond all reason that he would not have to sit through dinner watching the other man begin courting Annabel and pretending he was happy about it.

He leaned back in his chair with a sigh. Trying to marry off a debutante when you wanted her yourself, when you wanted her so much that you felt sure you must be emanating lust every time you looked at her, was a hellish business.

He tossed Trathen's letter aside and rose. Not bothering to ring for McIntyre, he stripped, tossed his clothes aside, and went to bed. Going to bed, however, didn't mean he could sleep.

He didn't know how long he lay there, but it was long enough to hear the other members of the household go to bed. In the distance, footsteps sounded on the stairs, good nights were said, and doors closed, but even after the house was utterly quiet, he was still wide awake.

He stared at the ceiling, listening to the mantel clock click away the seconds, one by one. He had to resign this ridiculous position as one of her trustees, for he couldn't bear any more of this torture. As he'd told Sylvia, he had to get on with his own life.

The trouble was, he didn't know what his life was anymore. He could go back to New York, as he mentioned this morning, carry on with the plans he'd made before becoming entangled with Annabel.

Just the thought of her made him ache with need, and he tossed back the sheets with an oath. This was ridiculous. There was no point in even trying to sleep.

He got out of bed. Naked, he walked over to window and pulled back the drapery a little. The moon was waning, but there was enough light for a walk, and it wasn't raining. He turned from the window and reached for the clothes he'd tossed aside hours ago, the moonlight that spilled in between the draperies enabling him to find them in the darkened room. He pulled on his trousers, but before he could reach for his shirt, the possibility of either a walk or sleep was taken entirely away from him.

The click of the door had him looking up, and when he saw Annabel slip inside his room, carrying a lamp and dressed for bed in a white nightgown and robe, he thought he must be asleep after all, because this had to be a dream.

"Annabel?" he said, frowning as he watched her close the door behind her. "What the devil are you doing in here? What are even doing at this end of the house?"

She pressed a finger to her lips. "Shh, not so loud," she admonished in a whisper. "Someone might hear you. I came because I wanted to talk to you."

"Talk?" His gaze slid down from her face, over the long braid of dark red hair that fell across her shoulder and down over her breast, all the way down to her bare toes peeping out from beneath the nightgown. Heat began pouring through his body.

"Christ have mercy," he muttered, and turned to jerk the drapery beside him completely closed. If she expected him to stand here in his bedroom and hold a conversation, he'd have to hurl himself out of a window to avoid the torture. "Don't you know the consequences of sneaking into a man's room in the middle of the night? And carrying a lamp, to boot? What if someone was still awake and saw you?"

"I was very careful."

"I daresay, but God, woman, don't you know the risk in coming here?"

"Maybe . . ." She paused and licked her lips, looking suddenly nervous. "Maybe I thought you were worth the risk."

He wasn't. He ought to be noble and tell her that, but he didn't. Instead, depraved soul that he was, he kept mum, hope rising inside him that this visit wasn't a dream.

"I want you to tell me why," she whispered. "Why are you pushing these men at me?"

That made him realize there was no way this could be a dream. In his dreams, Annabel would never come to his bedroom in the middle of the night to talk about other men. He wasn't that far round the bend yet.

"What does it matter at this hour?" he asked, trying to make sense of out of these nonsensical circumstances. "And Trathen declined my invitation anyway. Prior engagement."

"I'm glad. Because I don't want him."

"You haven't even met him. You might like him," he added a bit wildly. "He's quite a decent chap."

She made a sound of impatience, set the lamp on the dressing table beside his unlit one, and crossed the room to stand in front of him. "Will you answer my question please?"

He would if he could remember what it was, but she was standing in front of him in her nightgown, for the love of God, after he'd spent hours—days—thinking about her like some lovesick boy. How was a man supposed to answer questions of any sort in a situation like this?

He looked at her, unable to think, unable to move. In the silence, she stirred, coming closer, close enough that he caught the scent of orange blossoms. Its effect on his body was immediate. Just that, just the scent of her perfume, and all the desire he'd been keeping in check for three days came roaring back as if no time had passed since that night in Kayne's gardens. Desperate, he took a step back, grasping at some shred of gentlemanly honor. "Annabel, you shouldn't be in here. If anyone saw you come in—"

"No one saw me. Everyone's in bed."

He looked down, and his throat went dry at the creamy expanse of skin exposed by the open vee of her nightgown. "You have to go. Now."

He lifted his hands to put them on her shoulders, thinking to turn her around and propel her toward the door, but he changed his mind at once and lowered his hands to his sides. Touching her was never a good idea. It always got him in trouble.

Unfortunately, she didn't seem inclined to depart his room on her own. Quite the contrary, for she eased even closer to him.

"Why are you playing matchmaker?" she asked.

He stared into her upturned face, shaking inside with the effort of holding back. "You know why," he said, his voice a harsh whisper in the quiet room.

"Yes, I do." She moved another step closer. "I know you're trying to do the right thing here," she murmured, "but I don't want any of those men, Christian."

He was growing more desperate and more hopeful with each passing second. "You said you wanted marriage. A husband."

For some inexplicable reason, that made her smile. "Well, the wedding doesn't have to be next week."

She closed the last bit of distance between them, coming so close that the tips of her breasts touched his chest, and he felt himself coming apart. He tried to step back, but he immediately hit the armoire behind him. "Annabel, for God's sake—"

"I've been thinking things over, and I do want to get married. I meant that. But I also think I need to wait a bit between fiancés and just enjoy myself." She rose up on her toes, still smiling, her lips so close, they almost brushed his. "Don't you?"

She kissed him before he could answer, and he knew he'd lost. Any notions to do the right thing went out the window, his arms came up around her, and he broke the kiss only long enough to say, "God, yes," before he captured her lips again and pulled her hard against him.

There was no sense trying to be honorable. He'd never been that sort of chap, and with her mouth on his, he saw no reason to change his ways now.

Chapter Fifteen

od, yes. To Annabel's ears, Christian's words sounded like the sweetest sweet talk she'd ever heard. His kiss was full, open against her mouth, and instead of fighting what she felt, she savored it, tasting him as deeply as he tasted her. This was what she'd come for, the hot, blissful beauty of his kisses. She wrapped her arms around his naked back, and his muscles felt hard beneath her palms, his skin scorching hot.

He broke the contact with her lips. "You're sure about this?" he muttered, cupping her face, pressing kisses to her cheeks. "I've been trying to right the wrong I've already done you. This isn't going to help."

She smiled, hearing the note of desperation in his voice. "I know," she whispered back. "But right now, I want you to stop trying to be heroic."

"This isn't a joke." He pulled back enough to look

straight into her eyes. "You know what it means if you stay the night with me."

"I know what it means." Her big, dark eyes looked steadily into his. "I'm no innocent virgin, Christian."

She heard him catch his breath. "God damn us both for fools then," he muttered. "We can't make any noise," he added, reaching for the sash of her robe. "If anyone were to find out, you'd be thoroughly ruined."

Even as he said it, his fingers were tugging at the sash, and she gave a soft, shaky laugh. "I thought I'd have to work harder at seducing you after you tried shoving me at those other men."

"I was seduced the moment you walked in here." He pulled the robe apart, slipping it off her shoulders. It fell to the floor behind her, and he reached for the top button of her nightgown. He slid the tiny pearl buttons through their holes all the way down to where they stopped at her navel. Then, bunching the soft muslin in his fists, he dragged the nightgown off her shoulders, down her arms, and over her hips, letting it fall to the floor around her feet.

He stepped back, taking a moment to just look at her, and the sight of her lush, perfect breasts, her small waist and gorgeous hips made his throat go dry and his head spin. Her skin in the lamplight was the color of cream, and the sight of the dark curls between her thighs made him feel primal and savage.

He wanted to pull her down and take her without any of the time-consuming preliminaries. But he took a deep, steadying breath, striving to keep his own desire firmly in check, reminding himself that given the man she'd chosen her first time around, her previous lovemaking experience had probably been ghastly. He knew what she needed, and a quick, hot, primal coupling wasn't it.

He kissed her mouth once more, then he wrapped an arm around her back and bent down to hook the other beneath her knees. He lifted her into his arms.

"Oh!" she breathed, a sound of surprise, as she entwined her arms around his neck. "Where are we going?"

"Well, making love on the floor is a bit uncomfortable. The bed would be better, don't you think?"

He carried her to the bed, where he laid her in the center. But she glanced away when he reached for the top button of his trousers, and he decided he'd better keep them on for now. He stretched out beside her, and when his hard cock pressed against her thigh, she shied a bit, confirming his suspicion that despite her declaration of a moment ago, she was nervous.

"When I . . . when I did this before, it was on a dirt floor," she said as if reading his mind, but she still didn't look at him. Instead, she stared at the ceiling. "In a deserted shack down by Goose Creek. I could see . . ." She paused again and swallowed hard, laughing a little. "I could see the sky through the holes in the roof."

"Not very romantic."

"No, it wasn't. In more ways than one."

"I shall endeavor to do better." He reached out,

turning her face toward him so that he could kiss her again. He did it slowly—slow, soft, deep kisses, over and over, just as he had in the maze, until at last he felt her body relax. Then he pulled back to look into her face as his hand strayed to her breast. He cupped it, relishing the full, round weight of it against his palm. He toyed with her, smiling as he watched her eyes drift closed and her lips part, listening as her breathing began to quicken.

He bent his head, parting his lips over her breast, pulling her nipple into his mouth. She moaned softly as if in reply, and though he didn't lift his head, he pressed the fingertips of his free hand to her lips as a reminder, for they could not afford to be overheard.

She nodded in understanding, and his hand slid down to her other breast, toying with it as he suckled her, relishing the way she shivered as his tongue gently drew the tip of her breast against his teeth again and again.

Her hips stirred, brushing against the tip of his erection through his trousers, but this time, she didn't shy away. Wanting to see her face again, he lifted his head as his palm slid over her body, from her breast, down over her ribs and her stomach and even further down, until his fingertips grazed the soft triangle of hair at the apex of her thighs. He eased his hand between her legs, and she gave a shocked gasp, making it clear that while she may have loved that boy from Mississippi enough to let him deflower her, love play had clearly not been part of the experience. "Christian," she whispered, a remonstration in the word and a plea in her eyes. Her hand encircled his wrist as if to push him away.

He wasn't going to let her. "What is it, love?" he asked, pressing kisses to her face. "He never touched you here, did he?"

When she shook her head, Christian felt a fierce protectiveness rise up inside him, a hot, savage emotion every bit as primal as the lust coursing through his body.

"But I want to touch you here," he said tenderly. "Let me do this."

He waited, and at last, her hand released his wrist, and he resumed his task, gliding his finger back and forth along the crease of her sex. Despite her apprehension, she was already wet and deliciously hot, but it wasn't enough. He was compelled to make her hotter, wanting to arouse her so fully and satisfy her so completely that this night would vanquish any memory of her previous experience. He stroked her, gliding his finger back and forth along the seam of her sex, watching her face as she again relaxed. Her eyes closed, her breathing quickened, and her hips began to rock in rhythm with his touch. Words, he knew, could be as erotic as a kiss or a caress, and he used those, too.

"Do you like this?" he whispered, watching her face, relishing the excitement he saw there as he toyed with her.

Annabel heard his question, but she could not reply, for she was too overwhelmed by what he was doing to say anything. This wasn't like anything she'd ever experienced. She wished she could tell him that, but though her lips parted, she could say no words.

"Do you like this?" he repeated, and when she still didn't answer, he started to withdraw his hand. She arched up, her body following the move.

"Don't stop," she gasped before she could stop herself. "Don't stop."

"So you do like it?" he murmured, laughing softly as she nodded. "Want more, do you?"

He was teasing her, she knew it. Carnal, unbearable teasing, and yet, she wanted it. "Yes, yes," she told him, her hips stirring again. "More, please."

Those were the only words she could manage, for the tip of his finger was already touching her again, sliding back and forth over her most intimate place, and each tiny move brought another throb of sensation.

She could feel her body moving in response, movement over which she had no control. He was the one in control, and as he caressed her over and over, her pace quickened until she was moving in frantic, helpless little jerks and she had to press her hand over her mouth to stop the moans of pleasure that hovered on her lips. The tension of it was almost unbearable as the glorious sensations built, one on top of the other, growing more intense with each stroke of his fingers. She felt as if she were striving toward something, needing something he could give her, but she didn't know what it was.

He knew, though. "That's it, love, that's it," he murmured. "You're almost there."

And the only thought she had time for was to wonder

where "there" was, and then, suddenly, she knew. She felt it, a burst of sensation. Her hips arched up, and this time, she couldn't stop the startled cry that tore from her lips at the pure, melting ecstasy of it. He caught the sound in his mouth even as she made it, and he continued to caress her even as her thighs clenched convulsively around his hand again and again and the ecstasy washed over her in wave after wave. His fingers continued to pleasure her even as the waves subsided, and she collapsed, panting, against the mattress beneath her.

"Annabel, it's time." His voice was harsher than before, and she noticed that his breathing had quickened. "I can't wait much longer, and you are so wet and soft, so ready." His finger eased inside her. "You are ready for me, aren't you?"

Ready? Lord have mercy, she was on fire, that's what she was. This wasn't like anything she'd ever felt in her life. But she knew what he meant. She knew about this part. "Yes," she managed, nodding. "Yes."

He slowly withdrew his hand and stood up to unbutton his trousers. His eyes met hers, but she couldn't hold his gaze. Instead, she looked down his body, from his wide, muscular chest, along his flat abdomen and his narrow hips, to his shaft. She felt a jolt of panic at the sight of it, jutting and erect, and she couldn't help remembering the last time she'd done this and with whom.

"Christian?" she whispered, seized by sudden doubt even as she said his name.

He stepped out of the trousers, tossed them aside,

and moved back down beside her. "It's all right," he murmured, kissing her, his hand caressing her stomach, moving lower, over her hip, across her thigh. "Part your legs, love. Open for me. It'll be all right."

She complied, but her panic increased as he moved on top of her, as his weight settled onto her and she felt that hard, relentless part of him pushing between her thighs. The pain and disillusionment of the first and only other time she'd done this came rushing back, and she could almost feel her heart breaking all over again. She caught back a sob of panic, but still, he heard it.

"Annabel, Annabel. Look at me." When she opened her eyes, he was poised above her, his weight on his arms, his face grave, a lock of his black hair falling over his forehead. His gaze riveted her in place. "I'm not him. It's all right. I promise. I'm not him."

As he spoke, she caught the unsteadiness in his voice, heard the labored pace of his breathing, and she realized it was the strain of holding back for her. "Do it, then," she whispered, spreading her legs apart, wanting him to have what he'd already given her.

He moved his hips, and she felt his hardness brushing her opening, but not entering her. "Take me in your hand," he told her, and when she did, wrapping her hand around his thick shaft, she was startled by the scorching heat of it. "Bring me inside you."

She did, feeling terribly awkward, using both hands to guide the tip of his shaft inside herself, and she couldn't look at him as she did it. And when she felt him pushing further into her, she moved her hands out of the way and kept her gaze on the ceiling, bracing for the pain. But there was no pain, only a stretching sensation as he slid fully into her. She inhaled deeply, a gasp of pure surprise.

He stilled. "Are you all right?"

"Yes." She nodded, all her panic of a moment ago ebbing away. "Yes, Christian, yes. I . . ." She paused, stirring her hips, considering. "I like this."

That made him laugh, a low, pleased, breathy laugh that felt warm on her face. "Do you, now?" Still poised above her, he flexed his hips, rocking against her, a controlled motion, despite the strain of holding back. "What about this?" he asked, and did it again. "Do you like this?"

"Cryin' all night, Christian," she wailed softly, wriggling impatiently beneath him, wanting to quicken the pace. "Are you tryin' to torture me?"

"This sort of torture . . ." He paused, his breathing labored. "Has rewards."

She grabbed a handful of his hair. "You talk too much," she said, and pulled his head down to kiss his mouth. "We don't have all night here."

That reminder must've done the trick, for he began to move within her again, his shaft caressing her from the inside, a deep, luscious caress over and over. He quickened each time, thrusting harder, deeper. She relished it now, matching the pace willingly, and as she did, she felt again that rising, thickening pleasure. When the waves came over her, even more intense than before, she had to bite her lip to keep from crying out.

Her muscles contracted, instinctively tightening around his shaft again and again, increasing her pleasure as she felt him follow her to the peak. His body sank down onto hers, his arms sliding beneath her to hold her tight. His moves became rough, frantic, until finally, he reached the same climactic moment she had already experienced. Shudders rocked his body, and his hoarse groans of release were buried in the softness of the pillow, until at last, he stilled on top of her.

After a few moments, he stirred, and she felt her legs tightening around him, foolishly reluctant to let him go, suddenly afraid of what was sure to happen now. But as he lifted his hips to slip free of her where they were joined, he took her mouth in a soft and tender kiss, and Annabel pushed that pang of fear away.

This night would not happen again, she knew that. This time, she wasn't expecting marriage or even declarations of love. And she certainly wasn't expecting him to want her to stay, to linger here with him.

But Christian, in regard to the last, at least, surprised her. He rolled onto his side and his lashes drifted down in that sleepy look as he gazed at her naked body. She would have been embarrassed by such thorough scrutiny, but as he looked at her body, his hand glided over her in long, slow caresses of her face, her breasts, her stomach, her thighs, and back again. He kissed her—pressing his lips to her cheeks, her chin, her mouth, and her hair.

He whispered how beautiful she was, and when he

pulled the covers over her and cradled her in his arms, she suddenly, stupidly wanted to cry, because she'd never thought a man could be tender. Maybe a little, before the act, but certainly not afterward. Not like this.

And as she lay there in Christian's arms, she knew she was starting to fall in love with him. This was what she'd feared all along, and she worked to stop it, to harden her heart and protect herself before it was too late. Christian had shown her what tenderness was, and if she fell in love with him and he didn't love her back, she didn't think she'd be able to bear the heartbreak.

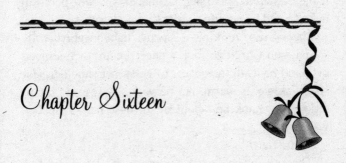

Chapter Sixteen

She was asleep. The lamp on the dressing table had gone out and the room was pitch dark, but though he could see nothing, he could discern that she slept by the deep, even cadence of her breathing.

She felt lusciously warm and soft lying naked in his arms like this, and he would have liked nothing better than to kiss her awake and repeat their experience of an hour ago, but they could not afford to take that risk. He had no idea of the time, but it had to be coming on for dawn, and he had to get her back to her room before anyone woke up.

Christian carefully eased out from under the covers. He dressed in the dark, deciding he could better trust the more honorable side of his nature if he were dressed. Then he found her nightgown and robe, and tried not to think about how he'd stripped her out of them.

Instead, he moved to stand by the side of the bed and leaned down to wake her. "Annabel," he whispered in her ear, and he couldn't resist kissing her there.

She stirred, making a sleepy, unbelievably erotic sound, and Christian took a deep breath, then slipped his hand beneath the covers to grasp her shoulder. Her silken skin was warm, but he valiantly resisted temptation. He shook her shoulder to rouse her. "Annabel, wake up."

"Christian?"

The instant he heard her voice, he let go of her. Touching her was far too tempting. "You have to go back to your room before you're found here."

"Of course." She sat up, pushing aside the covers, and he stepped back as she swung her legs over the side of the bed and stood up. Now that his eyes were adjusting to the dimness—or perhaps because he had such a fine memory—he fancied he could see the faint outline of her exquisite body, and he took another deep breath. "Here," he said, thrusting her nightgown into her hands.

He heard the swish of fabric as she donned the garment, but he allowed himself the luxurious torture of assisting her with her robe. "Turn around," he said, and when she did, he held the robe as she slid her arms into the sleeves. But before she could wrap it fully around her, he couldn't deny himself the opportunity to slip his hands inside the still-unbuttoned placket and cup her full, luscious breasts in his hands. She made a faint sound of surprise, then leaned back against him with a little sigh, and he took the pleasure of toying with her for a bit longer, even as he told himself he was flirting with disaster.

He gave himself five—and only five—seconds of this agony, then, reluctantly, he withdrew his hands, pressed a kiss to her hair, and turned her around, drawing her robe around her and tying the sash firmly into place.

"C'mon." He led her to the door, where he fumbled in the dark for the oil lamp she'd left on the dressing table, and handed it to her. "We can't light it," he said, keeping his voice low. "I've no idea of the time, and if any of the servants are already up, they might see the light moving about when you pass the stairs. Can you find your way back in the dark?"

"Of course. You seem to know quite a lot about this sort of thing," she added, a wry note in her whispered words. "People sneaking in and out of other people's rooms and all."

"Of course," he replied at once, striving for the flippancy that would mask what was nothing but the rather sordid truth. He didn't want to think of all the women who'd padded down the Bachelor's Corridor at country house parties to visit him over the past dozen years. Resting his forehead against hers, he went on, "Gorgeous young women come sneaking into my rooms, flinging themselves at me all the time, don't you know? Happens every night of the week. I've simply got to start locking my door."

She made a choked sound—a laugh, and though

only he knew it wasn't really something to laugh about, he didn't say so. Pressing one last kiss to her mouth, he opened the door.

She slipped out into the corridor, and he closed the door behind her. He undressed again and got back into bed, and this time, he had no trouble falling asleep. In fact, he did it with a smile on his face.

"Christian, wake up."

He was in such a heavy slumber that his sister's insistent voice barely penetrated his consciousness—just enough to make him determined to stay asleep. But then, she started shaking his shoulder, and though it woke him, he tried to pretend otherwise, his usual practice in this particular situation.

"Christian, you must wake up. Right now."

He didn't want to. He felt as if he'd just fallen asleep. "Leave off, Sylvia, for God's sake."

"I can't. I have to talk to you immediately."

He rolled away, onto his stomach. "This is why I secure my own rooms when I'm in town," he mumbled into the pillow. "Your habit of barging in on me at an ungodly hour of the morning to hold a conversation is so damned annoying."

"It's not an ungodly hour. It's half past nine, and besides, this is important." She shook his shoulder again, this time with considerable force. "Damn it all, brother, wake up!"

There was a sharp edge to her voice, an urgency well beyond her customary morning cheer. It sounded almost like . . . panic. It penetrated his sleep-dazed, very reluctant senses and told him something serious actually was afoot. Instantly awake, he rolled onto his back.

"What's happened?" he asked, but his question was answered the moment he looked into his sister's eyes. She knew. Dread settled into him at once, like a stone in his guts, and it must have shown in his face.

"Oh my God, it's true." She sank down on the side of the bed, staring at him as if she'd never seen him before. "I actually thought at first that it was just gossip. That even you . . . could not . . . would never . . . even after that ghastly debacle at the wedding . . ."

Futile to pretend, but he tried anyway. "I can't imagine what you're talking about."

"Oh, Christian." It was a sigh of disappointment that cut him to the heart.

Reminding himself that lying to Sylvia was always a tricky business, he gave up any further attempts at deception. "How did you know? Did Annabel tell you?"

"Of course not! Annabel is still in her room, and I haven't seen her."

"But then, how—"

She arrested him in midsentence with a gesture to the dressing table and the china shepherdess lamp that stood there, a hurricane lamp that was similar to his, but not the same. His mistake hit him with the force of a lightning bolt. In the dark this morning, he'd handed Annabel the wrong lamp. Of all the stupid, careless, idiotic mistakes a man could make.

"You took up the wrong lamp in the dark when you left her room, I assume? What were you thinking to take a lamp at all? Didn't you realize—never mind," she added acidly. "Thinking obviously played no part in this."

Sylvia had it the wrong way about, but he didn't correct her. Better for Annabel that way, and more blame for him. He didn't look at his sister. Instead, he stared at that lamp on his dressing table as the inevitable consequences of its presence there sank into his brain, and it occurred to him that he would probably remember every detail of that lamp, its exact proportions, its undulated glass shade, its delicately painted pastoral scene, for the rest of his life.

After a moment, he schooled his features into the most unreadable expression he could muster and forced himself to look at his sister again. "So now you know," he said with a touch of defiance.

"I'm not the only one who knows, Christian. The servants knew before I was even out of bed."

"What?" He sat up. "How?"

"Givens told me the gossip raging belowstairs when she came to help me dress."

"But how the devil did the servants find out? They are trained never to come until we ring."

"Yes, but that's our wish, Christian. Our guests often have other preferences. Annabel's preference is to be awakened with coffee at half past eight, so Mrs. Wells sent the coffee up with Hannah, as usual. Hannah saw the lamp—your lamp—on Annabel's dressing table when she put the tray there. Being a sweet but not particularly bright child," his sister went on, "she mentioned the lamp to Mrs. Wells, who knew exactly what it meant and discussed it with the head housemaid at length—and I'm sure with considerable relish. That conversation was overheard by the footman, and so . . ."

"And so, all the servants know," he finished as her voice trailed off. He paused, trying to think, trying to hope that this didn't mean what the knot in his guts was telling him it must mean. "What about her family? Do they know?"

"I don't think so, but—"

"Will they be discreet, do you think?" he cut in, afraid they wouldn't. "The servants, I mean?"

"I've gone down and made a little speech about the evils of gossip, and the harm it can do, but I can't guarantee their silence. But that's not really the point, is it?" The incisiveness of her voice as she asked that question cut through irrelevancies and excuses and ways to duck consequences. "You bedded an unmarried woman in my house, a woman under your trusteeship. The point is not whether her family knows, or the servants know, or even if I know. *You* know, Christian. That is the point."

He drew in a sharp breath, the truth of her words and the condemnation in her eyes hitting him like a blow to the chest.

He tilted back his head, staring at the intricate plasterwork on the ceiling, a view very different from the hole in the roof of a dilapidated shack, but for Annabel, it would seem like exactly the same view if he didn't do what was right. Slowly, he let out his breath. "You're quite right, of course."

"You know what you have to do."

He looked at Sylvia. "Yes."

His clipped reply didn't seem enough for his sister. She waited, grim-faced, for him say the rest, and he forced himself to say it. "I'll talk to Annabel straight-away. And her stepfather and uncle, too, of course. You'll have to assist Annabel and her mother with making the arrangements, setting a date, sending out the invitations, that sort of thing. We'll have to present the entire business to the scandal sheets in the best light possible. Loved her madly all along," he added, grimacing at how much it sounded like a penny dread-ful. "Got carried away at her wedding to Rumsford. Couldn't bear to see her marrying another man. She refused me, quite rightly, but after a discreet waiting period, she finally consented to marry me. That sort of thing. You know what to say, of course."

"I shall make it sound as if it's the love match of the century."

The dry note of her voice was not lost on him, but he chose to ignore it. "I'll go to Scarborough," he went on, "see the vicar, and make things ready. We'll hold the wedding there. When you and Annabel have set the date, let me know. A fortnight from now, per-haps?"

She nodded, satisfied, and stood up. "It'll have to be more than a fortnight. You need to be in residence at

Scarborough for fifteen days, or you have to apply for a special license here before you go."

"Which will increase the possibility of gossip. And we'd have to make up a reason. No, I'll leave for Scarborough straightaway and we'll post banns the old-fashioned way and everything proper. I'll go today. If we wait too long . . ."

"Quite," she said when he paused. "But there's one other thing you must consider." At his puzzled look, she sighed. "Hasn't it occurred to you that there might . . ." She paused, biting her lip, hesitating a moment. "Christian, there might be a baby, you know."

A baby. He hadn't even thought of that. He leaned forward, cradling his head in his hands, his dread deepening into pain.

"Evie wasn't your fault," Sylvia said at once, seeming to read his mind with ease. "And Annabel isn't Evie. Nothing like."

He nodded without looking up. He knew that, but it didn't ease the sick knot in his guts.

"You'll have to find a way to forgive yourself for Evie, my dear. Or a happy marriage is doomed from the start."

"I don't . . ." He paused, Evie's adoring face flashing before his eyes. "I don't think I can."

"You have to. For Annabel's sake, for the sake of your marriage to her and the children you'll have, and for your own sake, you must lay the past to rest."

Sylvia gave his shoulder a comforting squeeze and departed, and he got out of bed. He tugged the bellpull to fetch McIntyre so that he could shave and dress and face the consequences of what he'd done. Facing his past, he feared, was going to be a lot harder.

Annabel sat on the edge of her bed, staring at the hurricane lamp on her dressing table, a lamp with a plain milk glass base and frosted shade, a lamp that, except for its shape, looked nothing like the one she'd carried into Christian's room last night.

The servants knew. She'd seen the reflection of Hannah's puzzled gaze in the cheval mirror as the kitchen maid had set the coffee tray on the dressing table. She'd looked at the lamp, looked over her shoulder at Annabel, who was sitting up in bed waiting for her coffee, and then back at the lamp again.

Annabel hadn't attached any particular significance to the maid's puzzlement. Only after Hannah had departed had she realized that the lamp on her dressing table was not the one she'd taken to Christian's room last night. That was when the implications of the horrible mistake that had been made finally struck her, but it was too late by then. An hour later, when Liza had come to help her dress, she'd learned from her little Irish maid what was being said about her and His Grace downstairs.

They all thought Christian had come to her, that somehow they'd arranged it between them, and he'd taken the wrong lamp away with him, but the details didn't matter. The servants knew she had lain with the master of the house. They knew she was unchaste.

She also appreciated another hard reality, one that she was chagrined to admit she hadn't even thought about last night. There could be a baby. With Billy John, she hadn't understood, not really, that lovemaking was how babies came. She'd seen farm animals all her life, and yet her understanding had been rather incomplete, until Billy John had shoved himself inside her, and total comprehension had come in a painful flash. Luckily, she hadn't become pregnant that day, but this time, she might not be so lucky. And this time, she couldn't claim any lack of understanding whatsoever.

Annabel stared at the lamp, and fear made her feel a bit light-headed, a little bit sick to her stomach. But she didn't feel shame. She ought to, she supposed. For the second time in her life, she'd fornicated with a man who wasn't married to her, and she ought to be all teary and full of shame about her wanton behavior as she'd been the first time around. She ought to regret going to Christian's room and the hot, passionate things they had done, but she didn't regret it. She wasn't sorry she'd behaved like a strumpet. She was just sorry she'd been caught. Because if her family got wind of the gossip downstairs, or if she was with child, it would hurt and shame them. That was the part she regretted.

But the rest? No. How could she regret the most beautiful thing that had ever happened to her?

Annabel stared at the lamp, seeing past it to Christian's room last night, remembering the hard thud of her own heartbeat as she'd tiptoed across the house, down the long corridor, hoping she remembered the correct door from the brief tour of the house Sylvia had given them the day after they'd arrived. She remembered how her hands had been shaking so badly that she'd barely been able to open his door, and how the sight of him standing there without his shirt on had set the butterflies to fluttering in her stomach so hard they might have been stampeding cattle. Even now, she got all fluttery again, just thinking about that man's bare chest. Oh my Lord.

She closed her eyes, going all warm and achy as she remembered how his hands had caressed her, how he'd evoked such hot excitement in her. Even now, it made her catch her breath, how he'd kissed her and touched her and drawn those unbelievable sensations out of her, sensations she'd never known she was even capable of. Never in a million years would she have dreamed fornicating felt like that, like . . . bliss. It sure hadn't been like that the first time around.

The episode at Goose Creek when she was seventeen had been short, painful, and heartbreaking. But last night, Christian had wiped that slate clean. He'd erased Billy John Harding from her soul in a way that getting rich and taking revenge and getting engaged to an earl hadn't been able to do. Christian had made her feel beautiful and vibrant instead of used and thrown away. Christian had given her something beautiful to replace something sordid. How could she ever regret that?

Facing the servants today would be embarrassing, and she wondered if perhaps they ought to just avoid all that and move into town. Make some excuse to Lady Sylvia, and go stay in a London hotel. Or maybe they ought to go to the Continent, something she'd have to do anyway if she were pregnant.

It wasn't as if there was any future with Christian. She knew there wasn't. And he was such a long, tall, tempting drink of water that if she stayed here, what happened last night might happen again. In fact, when she thought of his bare chest, she realized wryly there was no *might* about it. And even if she wasn't pregnant now, she couldn't afford to keep tempting fate on that subject. Europe was probably best. France, maybe. From what Jennie had written, those people seemed to take fornicating right in stride.

The knock on her door made her jump.

"Annabel?" her mother's voice came through the closed door. "Are you all right?"

"I'm . . ." She paused, striving for an excuse. "I'm fine, Mama. I . . . umm . . . I just . . . have a headache, is all."

"A headache?" The door opened, and her mother came in. Annabel jumped up, turning toward the door and striving to look as if everything in her life hadn't just gone all topsy-turvy again because of a bad boy with blue eyes.

Her efforts at nonchalance didn't seem to work. "You look like you've got more troubles today than a headache."

She felt a jolt of nervousness, the same apprehension she always felt when she lied to Mama—the fear that

she was as transparent as a windowpane. "No, no. I'll
be all right. I just need some fresh air." She strode past
her mother and out into the hallway. "I think I'll go for
a walk in the garden."

Henrietta followed her, and Annabel could feel her
mother's gaze boring into her back. "I think you should
eat some breakfast. That'll make you feel better."

"No," she called back, quickening her steps as she
went down the hall, relieved that Mama hadn't asked
any probing questions, glad the fact that she'd been a
strumpet didn't seem to be discernible from the outside.

She wanted to be alone, to think, to make plans, to
consider where to go and what to do. The best place
to do any serious thinking like that was Lady Sylvia's
garden. It was quiet there, and pretty, and the fresh air
would do her good.

But she wasn't destined to get to the garden, at least
not on her own. When she came out of the hallway, she
stopped dead at the tall, dark figure standing by the
stairs.

She smiled. She couldn't help it. Despite the circumstances, the sight of him brought with it a feeling of happiness she couldn't hide if she tried. "Good
morning."

He lifted one brow as if surprised by such enthusiasm, and he didn't smile back. Annabel felt a sudden
twinge of uneasiness.

"What's wrong?" she asked, but even as she asked,
she knew the answer. He must have heard the talk, too.

Men back home didn't hear anything servants said, but maybe England was different.

He gestured to the stairs. "May I speak with you in the drawing room for a moment? A private interview?"

With those words, her heart gave a sudden, illogical leap of hope and joy. "A private interview?" she echoed, scared to believe she'd heard him right. Men wanted a private interview to propose.

"Yes." Christian glanced past her. "If that is acceptable to you, of course?"

Annabel glanced over her shoulder to find her mother only a few feet behind her, but Henrietta wasn't looking at her. "Of course, Your Grace," she answered, her eyes on Christian.

She looked at him, too, and saw him gesture to the stairs. "Madam?"

Henrietta preceded them down. Annabel and Christian followed, descending the stairs side by side. As they did, she tried to quell any of the hopes she felt bubbling up.

He wasn't a marrying man. She believed men when they said that, at least nowadays. But maybe he'd fallen in love with her. The moment that thought came, she tried to squash it, not daring to even consider it. He must have heard about the servants, and he was trying to suggest that silly pretend engagement business to quiet things down. That was it. Had to be.

Henrietta was waiting by the doors when they reached the drawing room. She gave Annabel a reassuring smile as she and Christian went inside, but

when Henrietta moved to close the doors, Annabel realized the drawing room probably wasn't a good idea.

"You know what?" She turned to Christian. "Would
you mind if we talked in the garden instead? I really
need some fresh air this morning."

"Of course."

They retraced their steps out of the drawing room
and past Henrietta. "No need for you to tag along after
us, Mama," Annabel said brightly. "The duke's a gentleman. Besides, you can watch us in the garden from
the drawing room window."

"I reckon I can, darlin'," Henrietta called to her in a
wry voice. "And you better believe I will."

"I hope the garden's all right with you," she said a
few minutes later as they exited the house and started
across the lawn to the rose garden. "You said you
wanted a private interview, and with Mama that close
by, nothin' is private."

"What?" he asked, opening the garden gate for her.
"You think she would eavesdrop on our conversation?"

"Ear to the keyhole," she countered as she walked
through the gate. "I guarantee it."

That made him chuckle, and she felt a bit relieved.
As they started along the paved path amid the bloom-
ing roses, she decided to take the bull by the horns.
"Look," she said, stopping on the path, obligating him
to stop as well. "I know what you're going to do, and
while I appreciate this attempt to be noble and all,
I think I'll save you the trouble. I won't enter into a
phony engagement to stop the talk in the servants' hall.

Yes," she added, "I know about it. My maid told me they're all talking about it."

"Is that what you think I wanted to propose? A phony engagement?"

She wished he'd smile. She didn't like the gravity of his face. It made him seem so distant, and she didn't like it, not after the beautiful intimacy of the night before. "Well, you didn't ask to talk in private to propose for real," she said, trying to laugh as if that would be silly. "We both know you're not a marrying man."

"Yes," he agreed. "We both know that, don't we?"

There was an odd inflection in his voice, and though the day was warm, she suddenly shivered. "What's wrong? You seem . . . I don't know. I can't explain it. So grave."

"Should I not be?" He met her eyes. "All the servants know, Annabel. Sylvia knows as well. She would never tell, of course. My sister adores gossip, but she also knows how to keep a secret. It's the servants that are of concern to us."

"Yes, I know. That's why I think it's best if I leave."

"Leave?" He looked at her askance. "That's not possible."

"Why not? I'll go abroad, or—"

"My God," he interrupted with a laugh, though he didn't seem amused. "Do you think so little of me as that? On the other hand," he went on in a musing way before she could answer, "why shouldn't you?"

"I don't think little of you at all! I seduced you, remember? It's not like any of this is your fault."

"Isn't it?" He faced her, and any glimmer of relief vanished at his uncompromising expression. "Annabel, I am not suggesting a phony engagement. I am suggesting a real one."

"What?" She supposed if she were good at all this high society business, she'd have agreed on the spot and secured herself a duke, but she proved her lack of skill as a social climber by gaping at him in complete astonishment. "You think we should get married?"

"We have to marry. That is the reality of our situation."

"Because of a little gossip among some servants?"

"Gossip can blacken a girl's reputation in a heartbeat. Why do you think I try to avoid unmarried women? Present company excepted," he added with a grimace. "I've done everything I could to put myself in your path from the beginning."

"This is my fault, too. If I'd thought more about it last night, I'd have stayed away. No," she added at once. "I can't lie. I wouldn't have stayed away, Christian. Last night was . . ." She paused, mortified that she was choking up and getting all sentimental. "Last night was the most beautiful thing that's ever happened to me," she whispered, even as her confession made her feel like a lovesick fool of a girl all over again.

He didn't smile, but something flickered across his face, something that might have been a smile if his lips had moved. But then he looked abruptly away, staring out over the roses. He swallowed, and his lips parted, but for a long moment he didn't speak. "And," he finally said, "I don't think I've . . ." He paused, then gave a cough, shaking his head, laughing a little as if at himself. "I don't think I've ever had a more beautiful compliment. I'm unworthy of it, I assure you."

"That's not true. But let's not argue about how wonderful you are, all right? I know you don't want to marry me. And I—" She stopped, for Lord help her, she didn't know what she wanted from him now. Did she want to marry him? She didn't know the answer to that, but she did know she didn't want it this way, because he felt an obligation. He didn't give her the chance to decide.

"Yes, well," he said, turning to her with startling abruptness, "we're well past what either of us wants, I daresay. We're down to what we must do. Even I, scoundrel that I am, cannot shirk a duty like this one. We exercised no precautions, and as a result, you might be carrying my child."

My child. Annabel hadn't thought of a baby in that way until this moment, as his baby, too. She hadn't allowed herself to consider that her future might be aligned with his in such a way. Happiness flickered up again, but again, she squelched it. She didn't want to be his duty. "There might not be a baby. Isn't it better to wait and see before we worry about that?"

He was shaking his head before she'd even finished. "It isn't possible. In circumstances such as these, time is of the essence, and I cannot compound my wrong by delay."

"No," she said again, while she still had the nerve. "I

won't force you to marry me because of a baby when I know you don't want to marry at all. Besides, we both know that you don't love me, and I—" She stopped, unable to say the rest, unable to force out the words that she didn't love him.

"Listen to me, Annabel." He grasped her shoulders, preventing her from turning away and ending the conversation. "We have no guarantee the servants won't talk to others outside this house."

Fear rose up inside her again, more powerful than before—stark, cold fear evoked by the harsh realities. She'd had servants long enough to know that what he said was quite possible. "You mean they might talk to their friends who are servants in other houses," she said, her heart sinking.

"Word will quickly reach ranks far higher that Sylvia's kitchen maid and housemaid. When that happens, rumors will spread like plague. Eventually, journalists from the scandal sheets will pick up the story. Once they do, they'll print it, in all its lurid detail. They'll lay out the story of your whole life for public consumption, including Billy John Harding, who I'd wager would be quite happy to tell them all about your promiscuous ways."

"Promiscuous ways?" she echoed, suddenly struck by what he must think of her. "Christian, I never . . . only you and him, I swear to you—"

"I know that," he cut in. "My brains may be on holiday most of the time these days, but I can discern when a woman is not practiced in the art of lovemaking. God knows," he added, sounding suddenly tired, his hands falling to his sides, "I've practiced enough to know."

His words hurt her, not because of the other women he'd had, which didn't surprise her in the least, but because of the bitter tinge to his voice as he confessed the fact.

"Unfortunately," he went on, interrupting this line of thought, "though I may be a rake of the first water, that isn't the way it will be regarded by others. You are an unmarried woman, and the servants know that. It's every bit as much my fault, and I won't be anyone's favorite dinner guest for a while, but the consequences for you are far more grave. You'll be—"

He stopped, but she finished his sentence for him. "I'll be ruined."

He grasped her shoulders. "No, you won't. If we're engaged now, today, that cuts the juiciness of the gossip down considerably once it leaks out. Our engagement must be confirmed at once and banns posted. Our marriage must follow as quickly as possible, three weeks later at most. If we're lucky, the story won't spread far until after we're wed, and after that, no one will give a damn."

She felt dazed, bewildered, and panicky. This was all part of a world she'd thought she wanted, but she was realizing just how unprepared she was to move in it. "But what about the next three weeks?"

"Sylvia and I shall do all we can to ensure that the scandal sheets are too full of stories about our joyful wedding news to print more sordid rumors. Stories will appear every day rhapsodizing about the lovely young heiress and the handsome duke who captured her heart, a duke so carried away by passion that he protested her marriage to another man. They'll talk about our obvious and undeniable love and our fairy-tale romance, a fiction we must do our best to make as convincing as possible."

A fiction. Of course.

It would be silly of her to think for a moment that love had anything to do with this. Her heart clenched with unexpected pain, and she fought back, reminding herself that she didn't want to fall in love anyway. She was fighting very hard not to. So why did it hurt so much to hear him speak of the possibility of love with such contempt?

"A story of scandal," he went on, "isn't nearly as interesting or believable if it's told after the engagement is announced. It will be put down to rumors created by malicious men or envious women who resent the fact that you, a New Money nobody from Mississippi, who has barely entered good society, captured the heart of a duke and married him."

A New Money nobody.

She knew that's how most people thought of her, of course. She'd been called that many times in the New York press. But somehow, it hurt to hear it on Christian's lips.

"Once we're engaged, I doubt the papers would grant any stories of scandal enough credence to print them. Especially since everyone knows I usually stay well away from unmarried women. Anyone who doesn't believe the story of true love will still applaud both of us for choosing each other. But I think most people will believe it's a love match, after the way I stood up at your wedding to Rumsford."

"Then we are the perfect transatlantic marriage," she said flatly.

"So it would seem."

She nodded, feeling the inevitability of her future sinking in, and even though it was exactly the sort of future she used to believe she wanted, she didn't feel the least bit happy. Instead, she felt sick. "Christian, I'm sorry."

A muscle worked in the corner of his jaw. "It takes two," he said after a moment. "That's why they call it coupling."

Abruptly, he looked away. "We'll be married at Scarborough, in the ducal chapel, three weeks from now. I hope that's acceptable to you." He gave her no chance to express an opinion.

"I have to find your stepfather and your uncle," he said and started back toward the house. "Tell your mother, and see Sylvia about wedding plans."

He left her without another word or even a backward glance. Annabel stared after him, but even after he'd disappeared into the house, she stood in the garden for a long time, trying to take it all in.

She certainly was moving up in the world, she thought with a hint of cynicism. She was engaged again, to a duke this time, a fact the Knickerbockers would probably discuss with grudging admiration and plenty of envy, saying that she'd played her cards boldly but well, throwing over the earl to secure the duke. As Christian had told her the first time he'd proposed, they would probably tip their hats to her and say well done. And she'd be a duchess, accepted everywhere, by everyone.

She now had everything. A handsome, charming, titled husband, estates on two continents, wealth, position, power, and fame. Everything a white trash girl born in a tin-roof shack on a Mississippi backwater could want. Everything but love.

Annabel sat down on a garden bench and burst into tears.

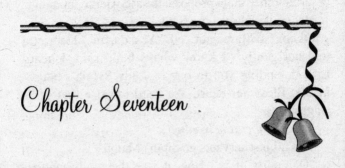

Chapter Seventeen

Annabel?"

Her mother's voice calling her name stopped her tears at once. She would not cry in front of Mama, not again, not like she had after Billy John, and she couldn't bear to see the same disappointment and pain in her mother's face that she'd seen last time she'd confessed a lapse of virtue. No, she'd have to lie. And from what Christian had said, she'd be doing a lot of that for the next few weeks.

She wiped her eyes, glad she hadn't cried long enough for them to be puffy. She pasted on the smile of a happy bride, and turned around to greet her mother, who had crossed the lawn and was now entering the garden.

"Oh, Mama," she breathed, striving for just the right amount of modest astonishment and bridal happiness.

"So he did propose." Her mother's voice sounded

flat, not nearly pleased enough. "Was it real this time, or just another sham proposal to save your reputation?"

Her smile faltered just a bit.

Of course Mama noticed. "Yes, darlin'," Henrietta told her gently. "I know what's bein' said. I heard Liza defending you to one of Lady Sylvia's house-maids. Bless her heart. We need to raise that girl's wages."

Lie, Annabel. Lie like hell.

"It's all just servants gossipin', Mama."

"Of course it is." Now it was there—disappoint-ment. In her, not for what she'd done, but for lying.

A sob came out. She tried to choke it back, but when her mother opened her arms, Annabel went running into them just as she had eight years ago.

"He says we have to get married," she said against her mother's shoulder. "He says I'll be ruined if we don't."

"Hush," Mama soothed, patting her back. "Hush now. Everything will be all right."

"It won't. He doesn't love me."

Her mother's arms held her a little tighter. "Are you sure about that?"

She thought of his face, so distant and unreadable, and his voice, so contemptuous when he'd talked about the charade they'd have to put on for everyone, how they'd have to pretend an undeniable love.

A fiction we must do our best to make as convincing as possible.

"Yes, Mama," she answered miserably. "I'm sure."

"But what about you? You love him, and that must count for somethin'."

Annabel lifted her head. "What?"

"Don't look so surprised." Henrietta gave her a sad smile, cupping her chin with one hand. "You never can fool me, Annabel Mae, even when you try to fool yourself."

"I guess not," she sighed, wretched at the admission she was about to make to her mother and to herself. "I do love him, Mama. And that's the worst part."

Upon leaving Annabel in the garden, Christian went in search of Annabel's male relations to acquaint them with the situation—a carefully edited version of it, at least. Mrs. Chumley's manner indicated she was already aware of what was being said belowstairs, but since neither of the men had a valet, Christian could only hope the gossip had not reached their ears.

He found Chumley in the library, and though Ransom was not with him, Christian decided not to wait. He sent a footman in search of Annabel's uncle and asked her stepfather for a few moments of his time.

Upon news of the engagement, Chumley seemed delighted and gave his consent quite happily. "I thought that might be the way the wind was blowing," he said, smiling as he leaned back in his chair. "Even drunk, a man doesn't just stand up at a weddin' unless he's smitten."

Smitten? That, Christian thought wryly, was a very apt description. He had to be smitten, for there was no other explanation for why he'd been acting like a prize ass of late.

"We'll get hold of Arthur," Chumley went on, "and the three of us can draw up a prenuptial agreement."

He nodded. He would have liked to refuse it, but he couldn't afford that luxury. Ransom was sure to think the worst about his motives no matter how much or how little the amount he received, but that couldn't be helped.

"My solicitors are Hutton, Bayhill, and Ross," he said, scribbling down the address on the back of his own card. "I must go to Scarborough and make arrangements there, but—"

"You son of a bitch!"

At the sound of that voice, both men turned toward the doorway of the library to find Arthur standing there, Annabel and her mother right behind him.

"Now, Arthur," Mrs. Chumley began, but Ransom shook off the restraining hand she put on his shoulder.

Christian stood up, turning toward the other man as he entered the room with Annabel and her mother hard on his heels. "You're not getting your hands on her money," Ransom said as he came toward Christian, fists clenched, his usually benignant face red with fury.

"Uncle Arthur, you're getting this all wrong," Annabel said, but Ransom gave her no chance to explain.

"You won't get a dime out of this," he told Christian. "Not one dime, you mercenary, fortune-hunting son of a bitch."

Christian, not being drunk, was more prepared this time for the fist that came toward his face. He managed to evade the blow, and before Ransom could try again, Chumley stepped between them.

"Whoa, gentlemen," he said. "There's no need for a fight. I'm sure we can work everything out."

"There's nothing to work out," Ransom said with disgust. "He's nothing but a fortune hunter, and if you agree to this, George, I swear I'll—"

"Uncle Arthur," Annabel cut in, stepping forward, "George doesn't have to agree. I agreed. I want to marry Christian."

Annabel was a better actress, Christian realized, than he'd have given her credit for. Her voice was calm, her words uttered with assurance, and when she moved to stand beside him, she took his hand in hers in a manner that was thoroughly convincing. "I'm marrying Christian, Uncle Arthur, and that's all there is to it. I want this with all my heart."

"Lord," Ransom muttered, staring at her, "that any niece of mine could be such a fool."

Her expression didn't falter, and only her hand, squeezing Christian's hand tight, indicated the strain she was under uttering such outright lies and being thought a fool by her uncle, whom she loved and respected, because of him.

Shame consumed him, causing a hot, tight pain that twisted his chest.

When she let go of his hand, he forced himself to speak. "I shall leave it to Annabel and you two gentlemen to draw up whatever agreement you desire, and I shall instruct my solicitors to accept on my behalf any terms you have laid down. All I ask is an annual sum for the maintenance of Scarborough because it shall be Annabel's home, and an amount to be set aside in trust upon the birth of each of our children. As for the rest, Annabel may do whatever she likes with her money. I don't want it. I know you don't believe that, Mr. Ransom, and you have every reason not to, but it is the truth. Now, if you will forgive me, I must go. There's a great deal I must do."

He pressed a quick kiss to Annabel's hair and departed the room, but as he stepped through the doorway, he paused for one look back at his bride-to-be.

She was looking at him, and as their eyes met, he vowed to himself that she would never, ever, have cause to regret this day, or the night that had made it necessary. This was his second chance, and he was taking it.

Christian went upstairs and instructed McIntyre to pack his things for Scarborough Park, informed Sylvia everything was settled with Annabel and her family, and ordered his carriage brought around. He went into the City and met with his solicitors, outlining what he'd told Annabel's family and ignoring their well-meant advice that he should ask for much more.

He arranged for announcements to be sent to the press, and personally paid a call on Viscount Marlowe, who was not only an acquaintance of his, but also the owner of the *Social Gazette*, London's largest and most reputable society paper. Marlowe was in, and happy to accept his offer of an exclusive interview. When he explained he had to leave for Scarborough on the evening train, a journalist was called up to the viscount's offices at once, and Christian spoke with the fellow for more than an hour, playing his part with far more ease than a man ought, but as he discussed his devotion to duty, to Annabel, and to Scarborough, he found himself wanting it to be true and not just a necessary façade.

When he felt he'd said enough to be convincing, he ended the interview. After bidding good day to Marlowe and assuring the viscount that he and Lady Marlowe would be receiving an invitation to the wedding, he left Marlowe Publishing and met up with McIntyre, who was waiting for him with the luggage at Euston Station. The two men boarded the evening train for Yorkshire, and by late evening, they were at Scarborough Park.

He had only three weeks to make things ready, and given the condition of his ancestral home, that wasn't much time. The following morning, he made an announcement to the staff, and he was both surprised and pleased by how excited they were at the news that there would once again be a duchess at Scarborough. They'd never taken much to Min, Andrew's wife, who, after her husband's death, had stayed only long enough for the funeral before sailing back to the States. Christian couldn't blame her for escaping this place as soon as she'd been able. He'd spent most of his life wishing he could do the same.

And yet now, as he toured the house with Mrs. Houghton, the housekeeper, as he ordered a thorough airing of the ducal apartments and discussed the condition of the nursery, he began to see Scarborough not as the depressing place he'd grown up, nor even as the place he'd brought his first bride fifteen years earlier. Perhaps it was the silent vow he'd made to Annabel, but he began to think of how Scarborough might become a home, if the effort were put into it.

As he surveyed the wine cellar and the silver with Morgan, the butler, as he walked the grounds with the gardeners and inspected the tenant cottages with his land agent, he began to feel a spark of hope for the future build inside him. The future was something he hadn't dared to believe in for a long time, and hope had always been just a word. Yet, now, in the work he did and the decisions he made, he felt it in himself, faint at first, but growing stronger each day as he took over management of the property left in his care, as he called on his neighbors and toured the village, walked in the gardens and rode through the woods, he felt as if he were climbing inch by inch out of a dark abyss.

He tried not to think of Evie. Whenever he was forced to traverse the gallery, he didn't look at her portrait, he never went to her rooms, and when he rode the grounds, he avoided going anywhere near the pond where she had taken her life. But there were times here at Scarborough when he'd see her face, fleeting and insubstantial, like a ghost. Perhaps he always would. He'd made her a part of Scarborough, and he had to live with that.

Marrying Annabel would never make up for the wrong he'd done Evie, but every day, in everything he did, he renewed his resolve that his second wife would have all the consideration and care he'd been too immature and selfish to give to his first. As the days passed and the day of his wedding approached, Christian worked hard every waking moment to not only accept the position he'd been given by fate, but also be worthy of it, for Annabel's sake. His sister had often told him to let go of the past and banish his guilt, but for the first time since Evie's death, Christian began to feel it was actually possible.

For Annabel, the days after Christian's departure went by in a blur.

Lady Sylvia took her to the dressmaker Vivienne for her wedding gown. "I know you adore Worth, my dear," Sylvia said, "but we haven't time. They take forever nowadays. Vivienne is actually Vivian Marlowe, the sister of Viscount Marlowe, and a personal friend of mine. She will put you at the top of her list, and we'll have a splendid gown in a matter of days."

When Annabel found herself in the showroom of London's most fashionable dressmaker, being assessed by the slim, willowy Vivienne herself, she felt as if the other woman's keen green eyes would find her full-figured shape a difficult one to work with. Fashionable dressmakers, she'd learned a long time ago, preferred slender figures without many curves. But she soon realized she'd underestimated this particular dressmaker.

"Not satin," Vivienne said at once. "Silk chiffon for you, Miss Wheaton, no doubt about it." She waved a hand. "The ivory silk, Claudette, the one with peachy undertones."

Moments later, one of her assistants was bringing a bolt of that fabric, and Annabel was being swathed in it.

"I'm thinking a sort of Grecian, draping effect for the skirt and a bodice that wraps the bosom." Vivienne spoke through a mouthful of pins, wrapping and pinning fabric to Annabel's underclothing as she spoke. "I hope you didn't have your heart set on satin. Most brides are still wearing it, but it's not right for you at all. It would cling to you in a most unforgiving way."

Annabel bit her lip, remembering her first wedding gown had been exactly like that, and how she'd ignored the feeling of being encased like a sausage for the sake of fashion.

"This will flatter your figure much better. What do you think?" Vivienne inserted the last pin and stepped aside to allow her to see her reflection in the long mirror. "Before you answer, I must warn you, and your mother, too," she added to Henrietta, who stood a few feet behind them, "this silhouette is not yet in vogue. Only the most daring girls wear the very latest fashions."

Daring? It was more than just daring. It was unlike any dress design she'd ever seen, and yet, as she studied her reflection, she realized the dressmaker was right. Already, even when it was just yards of silk pinned in place, she knew the draping folds and soft fabric flattered her shape and skin tone far better than the bright white satin and swan bill shape of her previous gown.

"So, how daring are you, Miss Wheaton?" Vivienne asked her. "Are you willing to trust me and allow me to design for your figure, or do you simply want the current mode and none of my pert opinions?" Vivienne's eyes met hers in the mirror, and Annabel saw in them both a hint of amusement and a challenge.

"I'm already considered a fish out of water," she answered ruefully. "Might as well be modern, too. Besides," she added, smiling at her refection, feeling that exquisite thrill of knowing she'd found a beautiful gown, "I love it already."

"Excellent! I so adore dressing women like you." She turned to Sylvia. "Fitting a week from today, darling? Two o'clock?"

Sylvia pulled her appointment book and a pencil out of her handbag, flipped a few pages, and gave a nod. "Two o'clock."

"Excellent. Claudette will take out all these pins and measure you, Miss Wheaton, and I will see you next Friday." Vivienne gave Annabel's shoulders an encouraging squeeze. "Many brides come to me, and I can say from experience that you will feel quite overwhelmed during the coming weeks, but don't let that feeling ruin things for you. After all, this is one of the happiest times of a woman's life."

With that, she turned away, waved farewell to Henrietta and Lady Sylvia, and with a swish of her greenish-bronze silk dress, she departed.

"Easy for her to say," Annabel muttered, staring at her reflection in the mirror. Swathed and pinned into pristine bridal silk, she suddenly felt like a complete hypocrite.

"Don't worry, Annabel," Sylvia said, putting an arm around her shoulders. "You're not doing this alone, you know, and though all this might seem overwhelming, I intend you to see that you enjoy yourself."

Annabel appreciated the kindness that lay behind Sylvia's intentions, but enjoying herself wasn't easy. The newspapers were full of the engagement, and though, as Christian had told her, the stories were mostly positive, some were unbelievably vicious. But it was Christian's interview that was hardest of all. He spoke of being carried away by his feelings, and how fortunate he was that she'd at last accepted him. He agreed that to marry for love as well as duty was a splendid thing indeed, and he emphasized several times how ecstatic they both were. Reading that interview only made the knot of misery in her stomach even heavier, because even though she knew it was all just lies for the press, she wished it could be true. After that, she stopped reading the newspapers.

She went in to Vivienne to be fitted for her gown as

scheduled, and the moment she put it on, she wanted to cry. It was beautiful, perfect, but what did it matter? It didn't make the wedding less of a farce.

She tried not to think. With Lady Sylvia's help, Mama's encouraging hugs, and Dinah's not always tactful opinions to make her laugh, she got through the choosing of invitations, the guest list, the flowers, the menu for the wedding tea that would follow the ceremony, and the dozens of other choices that had to be made. Having done it all before, she ought to have found it easier this time around. But it wasn't easier. It was much, much harder.

Nonetheless, the days rushed by. Journalists followed her everywhere, and her jaw ached from smiling, her heart hurt from acting happy, and sometimes, she just wanted to run away.

The wedding was set for May 26, and it was arranged that Sylvia would bring her and her family to Scarborough a week earlier, but so much was still undone that she, Henrietta, Dinah, and Sylvia were forced to stay in London longer than they'd expected. Arthur and George went on ahead to tour Scarborough Park, sign the marital agreements, and decide what needed to be done to the place. Arthur was only slightly mollified by Christian's flat refusal of an income, especially after Annabel made him slip in funds for Christian anyway. A duke, she insisted, had to have an income. She could afford it, and she could only hope Christian wouldn't read the thing before he signed it. He was trying to do right by her, and in the marital agreement, she intended to do right by him.

They arrived at Scarborough in the early afternoon with only two days to spare before the wedding. Christian, an entourage of journalists behind him, was waiting for them as they descended the platform of Harrowgate's tiny train station, and he bustled her, her mother, and sister to a waiting carriage at once while his valet dealt with their luggage and Sylvia deftly took charge of the journalists.

"Lord," Henrietta said, falling back in her seat as the carriage jerked into motion. "These reporters! I've never seen the like."

"They are relentless," Christian agreed. "They've been prowling around, skirting the edges of Scarborough Park for days, hoping to catch me out. They've become so brazen that I should advise staying near the house as much as possible. I fear we shall have to save any grand tours of the estate until after the wedding."

He turned toward her. "How are you, darling?" he asked, picking up her gloved hand and pressing a kiss to her knuckles. "Holding up all right?"

"Of course," she lied. "I'm just fine." After all, what else could she say?

Scarborough was a vast structure of gray stone accented with crenellated parapets, octagonal turrets, and climbing green ivy. It seemed to sprawl in all directions, wings sticking out and chimney stacks popping up without any consideration of architectural beauty, a fact that gave it a haphazard appearance.

Christian laughed, watching her face as the open landau pulled into the graveled drive. "A bit fantastical, isn't it? Sylvia's husband always said a restoration of Scarborough Park would be an architect's dream or nightmare, depending upon how much money was involved."

She studied it for a moment. "I kind of like it," she told him.

"Like it?"

"Yes. It looks . . . a little tipsy."

That made him laugh again, an easy, relaxed-sounding laugh. He didn't seem to share any of the worry that niggled at her. That was a good thing, she reminded herself. Wasn't it?

The staff was gathered by the doors awaiting their arrival, and as the carriage came to a halt, a footman stepped forward to roll out the steps for them. Christian presented her and her mother to the staff, introduced Morgan, the butler, and Mrs. Houghton, the housekeeper, and escorted them inside. "We'll have tea, Morgan," he said over his shoulder as he led her across a vast hall to a wide, sweeping staircase of limestone and wrought iron. "In the drawing room. And watch for Lady Sylvia's carriage. She'll be a bit behind us."

He led them up to the drawing room, where George and Uncle Arthur were already partaking of scones and jam. Afternoon tea was one of things about England Arthur genuinely liked, a fact made clear by the dab of strawberry jam Annabel noticed on his chin. She tapped her own chin meaningfully with her finger, and he took the hint at once, scrubbing away jam with his handkerchief.

Henrietta poured tea, as Arthur and George told them all about the estate. Even Arthur sounded enthusiastic as he recounted tales of all the trout fishing they'd been doing. When he began to rhapsodize about the pheasant hunting they'd be able to do in the fall, she shot Christian a look of surprise across the tea table. He merely smiled back and gave her a wink.

Sylvia arrived a few minutes later, and Annabel had no chance to ask Christian anything about Arthur's change of heart until they were able to steal a few minutes alone together, and only then because Christian insisted upon taking her for a walk in the rose garden.

"How on earth did you manage it?" she asked him as they walked arm in arm amid rose beds edged by low boxwood hedges. "Did you cast some sort of spell on Uncle Arthur or something? He's talking as if he actually likes England!"

He stopped as if to admire the fountain, causing her to stop beside him. "Well, it is rather a nice place, you know," he said, letting go of her arm and turning toward her as he reached into his pocket. "I have something for you."

She was too amazed to be diverted by a present, especially now that she seemed to be the only one with apprehensions about the wedding. "Uncle Arthur was all prepared to hate it here. When Bernard and I called things off, he wanted us to go straight back home, and it was only because of my reputation that he went along with staying here and having you as a trustee. Now he's talking like he wants to stay awhile. I never thought I'd see—"

"Annabel," Christian interrupted, and picked up her hand. She looked down, watching as he slipped a ring of diamonds and platinum onto her finger.

"It was my mother's," he said. "Min—that was Andrew's wife—didn't like it. The main diamond's only two carats, and she thought it too small for a duchess, so it's been sitting in the vault for years. I know it's rather late in the day for an engagement ring, since our wedding is the day after tomorrow, but still, I thought you might like it all the same."

"It's beautiful," she said, and meant it. Seven years ago, she'd never thought in a thousand years she'd wear diamonds of any size, and though now she had a treasure trove of jewels, she never forgot where she came from. So to her, this ring, one that had been handed down in Christian's family for generations, seemed far more beautiful than any of the Tiffany or Cartier jewels she owned.

She turned her hand, watching the diamond wink at her in the sunlight. An engagement ring was a circle, a symbol of eternal love. But what did it mean when the love was one-sided? Suddenly, the diamond began to blur before her eyes.

Remember, this is one of the happiest times of your life.

Annabel blinked, bringing the ring back into focus. She swallowed hard, and tried to believe that was true. After all, a girl didn't need a man's love to be happy. She'd figured that out a long time ago.

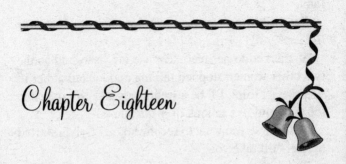

Chapter Eighteen

The following morning, the men had already
breakfasted and left the house by the time
Annabel came downstairs. Christian, she was
told, was going about estate business, while Arthur and
George had, not surprisingly, gone fishing. Dinah, too,
was gone. "Exploring," Henrietta explained in answer
to her question as she sat down at the table.

"Dinah seems a very adventurous sort of girl,"
Sylvia commented.

"That's one way of putting it," Henrietta said in her
wry way. "I worry sometimes that she's too much of a
tomboy."

"She is a bit of a hoyden, certainly, but she is only
eleven. And girls are much more independent and ath-
letic nowadays. I've no doubt she's destined for all sorts
of adventures."

Annabel looked down at her hand, watching the

result of her own "adventure" winking at her in the light.

Remember, this is one of the happiest times of your life.

She jerked to her feet. "Excuse me," she said as the two other women stopped talking and looked at her in surprise. "I think I'll be adventurous and go exploring, too. I should like to look over the house."

"Of course you want to see the house." Sylvia started to rise. "I'll take you."

"No," she said, grimacing at the curtness of her voice. "Please, finish your breakfast. I just want to wander a bit, on . . . on my own, if that's all right."

"Of course, my dear. This is your home, you know."

Her home. As Annabel spent the day walking the long hallways, studying the watered-silk wall hangings, glittering crystal chandeliers, and gilt-framed portraits, she wanted to think of it that way, as her home, but she couldn't quite make her mind form the picture.

It wasn't the house. On the contrary, she loved the place, with its sprawling wings and endless corridors, its overcrowded gardens, enormous fireplaces, and creaky floors. It was a bit threadbare in places, showing wear and tear and a lack of upkeep from the previous duke, but she had more than enough money to change that.

The problem was that whenever she tried to see this as her home, she felt a strange heaviness descend on her, a sinking feeling of dismay that this would never be her home, not if Christian didn't love her enough to stay in it with her. Wasn't that what she was really afraid of? That he'd go off to Paris and she'd be like Evie, walking in the gardens and wandering the corridors alone?

She stared up at his portrait, one of many that hung along a long, wide corridor by the library. He looked so young—about twenty, perhaps, and the lines at the corners of his eyes and mouth hadn't yet made their appearance. Despite that, he seemed more handsome now than he had as a youth, but men always did seem to age well. Annabel, like most women, found that awfully unfair.

Flanking his portrait were portraits of two women. One was unmistakably Sylvia. The other was an angelic blond in pink silk so pale it seemed almost white. This, she knew at once, was Evie.

Footsteps echoed in the distance, a soft thudding on the carpets, and Annabel glanced up as a maid in striped gray dress, white apron, and cap passed the gallery. The girl happened to glance sideways, and backed up at the sight of her, stopping in the doorway. "May I help you, miss?" she asked.

"No, no." Annabel smiled. "I'm just exploring."

The girl glanced at the wall, then back at her. A fleeting expression of—uncertainty, perhaps?—crossed her face, but she gave a curtsy and went on, leaving Annabel to her contemplations of Christian's first wife.

Evie Du Quesne had been pretty, rather like a porcelain doll was pretty. Her chin was down, her eyes almost peeking at the artist, not in a coquettish way, but tiredly, as if the diamond tiara and earrings she wore were too heavy for her slender neck. Against a backdrop of white draperies, with her almost colorless dress and fair hair, she seemed to fade into complete insignificance.

Annabel's heart constricted with compassion and that hint of fear. She wasn't timid or shy like this girl, but without Christian's love, what would she be? Bitter, she thought at once. Angry. That seemed almost as bad.

This time, the sound of footsteps made her jump, and this time, it wasn't a maid who paused in the doorway. It was Christian, looking grave. He glanced—a quick, furtive glance—at the wall, then back at her. "I heard you were in here," he said slowly. "Anna—she's the head housemaid—came and found me, asking me to come to you. She seemed concerned to see you wandering about alone." He paused, looking at her. "Was she right to be concerned?"

She hesitated, then joined him by the door. Glancing around to be sure no one was within earshot, she asked, "Are we doing the right thing? What if . . ." She paused, but heartache, she feared, hovered over her whether she expressed her doubts aloud or kept them to herself. "What if we're making a mistake?"

"It isn't as if we have a choice, Annabel."

That didn't help reassure her. It only made her want to know even more how he really felt. He didn't love her, but he did have some regard for her. She knew that. Not because he'd bedded her—she wasn't naive enough to think that—but because of what he was doing now.

But was it enough? Did he respect her? Could love come later? Did he think that was possible? She turned away, staring down the long portrait gallery, to the pale girl on the wall. He came up behind her, put his hands on her shoulders, and turned her around.

"Maybe we haven't known each other long enough," she said as he gently, slowly pulled her through the doorway and out of the room. Standing in the hallway outside the gallery, she searched his face, looking for anything that would give her a clue how he felt and what he thought. "Maybe you were right before to suggest a pretend engagement, then at least we might have gotten to know each other better before this happened."

Unexpectedly, a smile curved his mouth. "I think we already got to know each other quite intimately, don't you? That's the reason for the rush, remember?"

She colored up at once. "I'm serious, Christian. What if we make each other unhappy? I don't . . . I don't want to ever make you unhappy."

He studied her, still smiling a little. "Are you getting cold feet? And if so, do you do this with all your fiancés?"

"I've only had two. And my cold feet the first time around was your fault."

"I'm starting to worry you'll abandon me at the altar."

"Oh, Christian, don't tease. This isn't funny. I'm—" She broke off, wanting to tell him she loved him, and too afraid of hearing that her feelings weren't reciprocated. That galled her, that she was afraid, because though she had her faults, cowardice wasn't usually one of them. She sighed, giving up. "Never mind. It doesn't matter."

He studied her for a moment, head to one side, then he took her hand. "Come with me."

"Where are we going?" she asked.

"I want to show you something."

He led her all the way to the other end of the house and up a dark, tucked-away staircase. At the top, he took her down a long, equally dark hallway, opening doors into small, plain, empty rooms as he went. Each had one window with a view of the stables, a carpet on the floor, and walnut paneling below faded floral wallpaper.

"Why did you bring me here? What is the purpose of these rooms?"

"This is the nursery."

"What?" She stopped, looking around the dismal little room, a room that stood in absurdly stark contrast with the lavish guest chamber she'd been given. Her first impression was of *lack*. Windows not big enough or plentiful enough to let in light, carpets not thick enough for stumbling toddlers, not close enough proximity to the parents' rooms for the soothing away of bad dreams. She looked back at him, appalled. "This gloomy place, tucked back in a remote corner of the house? You're not serious?"

But he was. She could tell that by his face.

"You . . ." She paused and swallowed hard. "You were raised back here? You and your brother and sister?"

He nodded. "Once a day, if our parents were in residence, we'd be toddled down all the corridors and hallways to the drawing room, where we'd be dutifully kissed on the cheek by Papa, held and petted by Mama, and admired by any of their friends—until we cried or fussed or asked an awkward question, of course. Then Nanny would come to the rescue, and we'd all be whisked back here again. That was our lives until the age of ten. At that point, each of us was sent off to school. Sylvia to finishing school in France, Andrew and I to Eton, then Oxford."

"For an education?" she asked, unable to keep the acid out of her voice. "Or to be got out of the way?"

He met her eyes. "Which do you think?"

"No." She shook her head. "If you brought me here for my opinion, I shall give it gladly. I say no, to all of this. School, yes, I know that's important, but they don't go until they're twelve. And in the meantime, they are not going to be stuck back here in this dark place, unimportant and forgotten. We'll use these rooms for something else and find a new nursery closer to our rooms, one that has lots of windows to look out of, that has toys and games as well as books. And none of this being seen once a day and sent back to the nanny. No!"

"It's called a daily viewing."

"I don't give a damn what it's called! No, Christian! Not our children."

He looked at her. Not a muscle of his face moved, but she saw a smile in his eyes, and she felt sweet, fierce tenderness welling up within her, a bubble of emotion that pressed against her heart until it ached.

Until it demanded her to say what she felt.

"I love you," she blurted out before she could stop herself, reaching up to touch his face, brushing back a lock of his hair. "I love you."

Her hand fell away. The silence in the room seemed deafening, and although Annabel didn't feel that sickening knot of fear she'd felt the first time she'd told a man that, she still wondered if she'd made a mistake. Christian was marrying her because of obligation, he wasn't marrying her for love. Given his choice, he'd never marry anyone ever again. So in blurting out what she felt, what in tarnation did she expect him to say?

The silence lengthened, and it seemed so long and felt so awful, she had to speak again, say something, anything to break it. "I just wanted you to know," she mumbled. "In case you were troubling your mind about it."

She tried to tell herself it didn't matter, but it did, and the fact that she was the only one talking confirmed they both knew it. She turned as if to go, but suddenly, he caught her arms, pressing her back against the walnut paneling behind her.

He kissed her, a hard kiss that stole away her ability to think, or even breathe. His weight pressed her to the wall, and she could feel him, hard against her abdomen. His hands moved between them, working her shirtwaist open. He slid one hand inside to cup her breast through her corset as the other frantically pulled up skirts and petticoats, jamming fabric between their bodies, slipping inside her drawers.

She broke the kiss with a gasp, for she needed air, but she had time to suck in only one breath before he captured her mouth again, almost as if he were afraid she would say something to stop him.

His mouth kissing hers, and one hand at her breast, his other hand slid between her legs to caress her in that special place. Again, she broke the kiss, a moan escaping her. Her head tilted back against the wall and she closed her eyes, feeling hot, sweet pleasure rising within her as the tip of his finger spread her moisture, preparing her, she knew now, making her ready.

"I want you, Annabel," he said against her ear. "Right here, right now."

She nodded, making a wordless sound of accord, powerless to refuse him. He left off caressing her breast, using both hands to untie her drawers and push them down her legs. He pressed kisses to her throat as he unbuttoned his trousers, his breathing harsh, his moves rough and frantic. And then, his hands were cupping her buttocks, lifting her as she instinctively spread her knees apart. He entered her, pushing deep, taking her in hard, purposeful thrusts, and she hit that peak almost at once. She cried out, clenching around him as the waves broke over her. Over him, too, for his body shuddered with the pleasure as he thrust deep several more times, and then was still, breathing hard against her neck.

He kept her there, pinned to the wall, for several

more moments, and then slowly pulled back, slipping free of her and easing her back down until her feet hit the floor. He lifted his hand to touch her face, smiling as his fingertips glided along her check, his expression so tender, she almost believed he had said he loved her. But he hadn't said it, and the past few minutes, however passionate they were, didn't change that. He might never say it.

He raked his fingers through her hair to cup her face, and he kissed her one more time, a soft, tender kiss, a kiss so loving, it made her declaration of a few minutes ago even harder to bear.

"You'd best go back first," he said as he stepped back, releasing her. "If any of the servants see you, you've gotten lost."

"A believable lie. In this house, anyways."

She retraced her steps, finding her way back to the drawing room. Everyone was there, her whole family, having tea with Lady Sylvia, and she knew she couldn't join them. Not now, not with her clothes all rumpled and her body in a state. She could feel the moisture still between her legs and the sweat on her skin. She probably smelled of sex, she thought with a grimace, and instead of joining the others for tea, she went to her room. She used the water in the pitcher on the washstand to take a spit bath, then she tipped the basin, drenching herself with the water just for an excuse to change her clothes. Servants, after all, noticed everything.

Dressed in fresh clothes, and feeling a bit fresher all around, she called for a maid to clean up the water she'd spilled, then pinned back the stray hairs that had come loose from her chignon and powdered her nose. In the mirror, she watched the maid mop the floor, remembering there'd been a time when she mopped floors herself. And scrubbed clothes on a washboard. Now, here she was, half a world away, about to be a duchess.

A duchess. In a marriage without love.

Annabel leaned forward in her chair, plunking one elbow on the table, resting her forehead on her hand. This was sort of becoming an obsession with her now, that word. Why?

She hadn't cared about love before. She'd been ready to marry Bernard and join up with him for the rest of her life, but she hadn't loved him. She winced, looking back on it, remembering the lack of love between them, and she couldn't help wondering what on earth she'd been thinking to agree to marry him when she hadn't loved him.

That was it, right there. She hadn't loved Bernard, and in her crazy, mixed-up way of looking at everything, she'd wanted it that way. No love was easier. Safer. Less painful.

Nothing hurts more than unmet expectations.

Christian's words that day on the ship came back to haunt her now. So true, those words. The best thing she could do was go back to being the girl she'd been two months ago, a girl who'd been happy to get married without love, and without any expectation of it. That girl couldn't get hurt.

But she wasn't that girl anymore. She loved Christian, and she was fooling herself to think that the fact that he didn't love her was all right. It wasn't all right. It would never be all right. It would hurt her all her days, bruise her heart every time she wanted him to say it and he didn't. Cut her every time he left her and went off to amuse himself without her.

And he would. That's how marriage was with a charmer. She knew that. Her daddy had been going off places all the time, and Mama used to cry for days. And then, one day, he'd gone off and never come back.

Bernard had told her, straight out, that they'd be expected to live rather separate lives, each having duties to perform that kept them apart for days or weeks at a time. Strange how that had been okay for her and Bernard, but it wasn't okay now.

With Christian, she didn't want separate beds, separate lives, and freedom. She wanted him, every day, every night. Right beside her, doing things together. His first wife had wanted that, too.

Annabel watched the maid in the mirror, and she thought back to a girl in Gooseneck Bend who'd scrubbed floors, who'd worn shoes too tight or no shoes at all because she couldn't afford new ones, and whose heart had shattered into a million pieces because she wasn't good enough for a Harding boy to marry. Through all the pain and hardship, the happiness and heartbreak of her life, never once had the thought of ending it even occurred to her. It probably never would. She wasn't made that way.

But you couldn't make a man love you. You could

just accept the fact that he didn't and try to be content. Annabel knew she'd never been very good at being content. She probably never would. And she had no reason to think Christian would be any different in his second marriage than he'd been in his first.

Her life loomed before her, wearing a duchess's coronet and opening fetes and doing charity work and sleeping alone most of the time. Married women told you it was better that way. She used to agree with them. Now, she didn't.

Without love, none of it means a thing.

Christian was right about that, too. He seemed to know a lot more about life than she did because he had no expectations. She was full of 'em.

With a sigh, she stood up and left her room. She went downstairs for tea, and dinner, and cordials afterward in the drawing room, listening as Christian and Sylvia told her family stories of life at Scarborough, and she tried to cushion herself against expecting anything more than what was right in front of her.

She went to bed early. She didn't need to invent an excuse. After all, she was getting married tomorrow. Back in her room, she rang for Liza, and as the maid undressed her, she looked at the luxurious furnishings around her—furnishings another American heiress's money had paid for—and she felt the duchess's coronet getting heavy. Lord, the shine was off the tiara and she hadn't even put it on yet.

She donned her nightgown and slid between the sheets of her bed, but she didn't sleep. Instead, she lay in the dark and tried to console herself with the hope that he might not love her now, but maybe, someday, he would. That seemed a very small consolation and a very faint hope, but it was all she had.

Funny how she used to think love wasn't what she wanted. Now, it was what she wanted most, and it was the one thing money couldn't buy and position couldn't guarantee. Tomorrow was her wedding day, but without Christian's love, tomorrow was really just another day on the calendar.

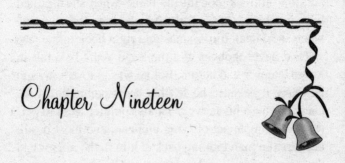

Chapter Nineteen

*I*t was almost time. Christian paused in front of the mirror, listening to the chapel bells ring in the distance for a moment, then he met his own eyes in the mirror, as Annabel's words from yesterday went through his mind.

I love you.

When she'd said that, he hadn't really believed her. He'd put her declaration down to desire and the need many women had to equate that with love. But this morning, he'd woken with those words ringing in his ears, and he decided, quite consciously, that he was going to believe those words were true every day from now on. He'd *make* them true, he vowed, even if it took his whole life to do it. This was his second chance, and hers, and he wanted it. He wanted Annabel. He wanted her beside him every day and every night for the rest of his life. He loved her. He'd probably loved her ever since that night in the Ford when she'd given him a tipsy grin and told him she bought the bank, when she'd pulled him, laughing, into a Turkish bath, even the next day when she'd dealt him a smashing right hook to the jaw.

He'd never thought in a thousand years he'd fall in love. He never had before. But he was in love now, and he knew it because he felt his heart pounding in his chest, because his nervous hands couldn't seem to perform the simple act of tying a cravat, and most of all, because the man looking back at him in the mirror had the sappiest grin on his face that Christian had ever seen. Men, he reflected, always looked ridiculous when they were in love.

They did ridiculous things, too. Like stand up, sodding drunk, and stop a wedding. If anybody stopped his today, he'd kill the bastard.

Behind him, McIntyre gave a cough. "Would you like me to do it, Your Grace?"

That brought him out of his reverie. "No," he answered and wiped the grin off his face, returning his attention to the task of tying his white silk cravat. When he finished, he lowered his hands and studied it for a moment. Satisfied, he turned around.

McIntyre, not satisfied, tweaked it a bit before inserting the tie pin. The valet then reached for the knee-length wedding coat he'd laid out on the bed earlier, brushed away a speck of lint that had dared to rest on the lapel, and held the garment open for him. Once Christian had slid his arms into the sleeves and shrugged the garment on, he turned around so that McIntyre could button it. The valet pinned the spray of white rosebuds and lily of the valley to his lapel, and then handed him a pair of white gloves.

"Thank you, McIntyre," he said, as he donned the gloves. "Have Carruthers bring the carriage. I'll be down shortly."

"Yes, Your Grace."

The valet departed with a bow. Christian didn't follow, for he knew that there was one more thing he had to do before he departed for the chapel. He left his rooms and went down the stairs, but instead of going to the entrance hall, he turned to walk in the opposite direction, his steps taking him to the gallery.

He paused at the entrance, took a deep breath, and walked down the long length of the room, passing ancestors and relations until he came to one portrait in particular, the portrait of a pale, slim girl with golden-blond hair, an image he hadn't looked at for twelve years.

Evie's portrait was the only tangible trace of her life here that remained, and he'd avoided looking at it for long enough. He forced himself to look at it now. He forced himself to study that shy, timid smile, to meet straight on those blue eyes that had gazed at him adoringly so long ago, and made himself remember the events that had transpired. His father's death, Min's vanished income, and Andrew hammering away at him about family honor and duty to Scarborough. The London season with all its balls and parties and pretty heiresses from America, and Evie looking up at him as if he was king of the earth when he walked over to her chair against the wall and asked her to dance with him.

He forced himself to remember the summer they'd spent in Philadelphia when he'd asked her to marry him. To remember the reassurances that he'd given her parents and the cynicism of his own soul when he'd thought how extraordinary Americans were to hope love played the major part in the business arrangement called matrimony.

He looked at Evie and forced himself to remember the lies he'd told her, and the ones of omission, too. The lies that had been in his smile and in his eyes and in his voice during their courtship. The lies in the vows of love and honor and comfort he'd made to her on their wedding day.

He forced himself to remember the man he'd been when he made those vows, a young and callow man who, though never technically unfaithful in the three years of their marriage, had never been much of a husband, a man who'd continued to gamble and drink and fritter away his time on useless pursuits and shallow companions, neglecting the girl he'd promised to cherish as he'd lived his own life and spent his allotted share of her money. He'd never stopped to appreciate the depth of her loneliness, and he hadn't been with her in her darkest moment of despair.

Today was his second wedding day, and as he looked up at his first wife's portrait, he endured the pain of saying to her what he'd only said in his mind, what needed to be said out loud, here, as he looked into her eyes. "I'm sorry, Evie." His voice was a quiet hush in the empty gallery. "Please forgive me."

He didn't deserve to be forgiven. He knew that. But standing here now, thinking of the man he'd been then, he knew he wasn't that man any longer. Somehow, in the intervening twelve years since her death, he'd grown up without even realizing it. The man he was now could appreciate what he had, take care of his responsibilities, and love one woman with his whole heart.

Today, the vows he made would not be a lie. He loved Annabel, he wanted to love and honor and cherish that woman forever, he wanted to spend his life with her and only her. He wanted her love in return, and he wanted, every day, to make her happy. He loved her in a way the shallow, immature youth he'd been all those years ago had never been able to love Evie.

The grandfather clock chimed the half hour, and Christian knew it was time to go. Slowly, with infinite regret that he knew would never quite leave him, he laid the past aside and reached up to touch his wife's pale, painted cheek. "Evie," he said gently, "I have to say good-bye."

The dress fit her like a glove. The flowers were beautiful, the chapel hushed and lovely as Annabel walked in on George's arm. As she came up the aisle, she was glad for the veil. It hid the doubts she felt railing inside and made her seem ethereally calm as she walked toward Christian.

He watched her as she came closer, his handsome face so serious. As she separated from George and moved to stand beside him, her doubts, instead of easing, grew louder.

"Dearly beloved . . ." the vicar began, while Annabel's mind raced.

Could she do it? she wondered. Could she spend her life loving him and not being loved in return? She began to fear that she couldn't. But she had to.

"If any man has just cause," the vicar intoned, "why these two should not be joined in holy matrimony, let him speak now or forever hold his peace."

This was it, the moment of truth. Now or never.

"Wait." Annabel held up her white-gloved hand, palm toward the vicar. "I can't."

Ignoring the gasps and groans of the guests, she yanked back her veil, thrust her bouquet into Sylvia's hands, giving the other woman a look of heartfelt apology, and turned to Christian. "I can't do this," she said, forcing herself to look up into his astonished face. "I can't marry you because of what other people think, or because you want to do the right thing by me after what happened before. I can't do it."

He was staring at her as if unable to believe what he was hearing, and she couldn't blame him. She hardly believed it herself. "I'm sorry, Christian. I know I'm the hardest-headed woman in the world, and it takes me forever to admit when I'm wrong, but I'm admitting it now. I was wrong, and you were right."

"Right about what?" He shook his head in bafflement. "Annabel, what are you talking about?"

"You said no one should get married without love." She paused, feeling her throat close up, and it took everything she had to force out the words that had to be said. "And you were right," she choked, gesturing to the glittering opulence of the chapel, "that without love, none of this means a thing. I love you, but I know you don't love me, so I can't marry you, Christian. I'm sorry."

Tears stung her eyes, tears of real heartbreak this time, and she turned away before he could see them, before he got any more silly ideas in his head about doing right by her.

Grasping handfuls of her silk skirt in her fists, she ran down the aisle, ignoring the astonished faces of the guests and Christian's voice calling her name. She ran for all she was worth, out of the chapel and across the weedy lawn. She didn't know where she was going, but all she wanted now was to get away before he tried to be noble again and do the right thing.

"Annabel, wait!"

She could hear him behind her, and she ran faster, but there was no way she could outrun him, especially not in her corseted gown. She tried, but within moments, she felt his arm wrap around her waist, pulling her against him, and he stopped, bringing her to a stop as well. "Did you mean it?" he asked, his voice a fierce whisper against her ear. "Do you love me?"

She struggled, but his arms wrapped around her to

keep her there, his chest pressed to her back, his breathing hard and quick against her cheek.

"Let me go, Christian," she cried with a sob, shoving at the arm he had around her waist, unable to free herself or stop the tears that began rolling down her cheeks.

"Did you mean what you said in there?" he asked again, holding her tight. "Do you love me?"

She couldn't say it. "Why does it matter?" she said instead, and she was glad he couldn't see the tears falling down her face. "We can't get married. Don't you see that? I can't be your second chance."

"Is that what you think?" He let her go then, but only to turn her around, her fingers gripping tighter when she tried to turn away. "That by marrying you, I'm trying to make up for Evie?"

"Aren't you?"

"No. And I'm not marrying you to 'do the right thing,' as you put it, although I don't blame you for thinking so. Even I thought that's what I was doing. But this morning, I finally realized the truth, and I'm afraid it's far more selfish than that. You see, I've never been very good at doing the right thing. I'm marrying you because I want to. I love you, Annabel. I realize it's a bit late in the day to say it, but it's true."

She stared at him, terrified, not able to quite believe him. "You mean it?"

"Yes, I do." He tightened his hold on her arms, giving her a little shake. "And I don't care where you came from. I don't care how you talk—I adore your voice, and always have. It's a smashing voice, and if you ever take diction lessons, I shall sue for divorce. And I'm not marrying you because of what people would say if I didn't. I'm not saving your reputation or being heroic. I love you. I've loved you almost from the beginning, but I just didn't realize it. Call me thick, but I believe it only started to sink in when I came home."

"Home? You mean—"

"I mean here. At Scarborough. While I was here without you, making everything ready for today, it made me think about what all this really meant. Marriage, you know, and children, and how we'd be caretakers here, not owners, and how we'd be taking care of all this not for ourselves, but for them, the next generation. That's why I took you to the nursery yesterday, and I've never been happier in my life than I was at that moment when you said you didn't want our children to be stuck back in those dark, gloomy rooms, and how you just weren't going to let it happen."

"I feel pretty strong about that. So—"

"I know, and that's why I love you. You're a fighter." He paused, looking at her steadily. "I never thought you'd try to try to duck your responsibilities."

She sucked in her breath. "That's not fair."

"I never thought," he continued, "that you'd run away, or take the easy way out." He spread his arms wide, a sweeping gesture that encompassed the vast estate all around them. "I thought you'd fight for this, and for us. That's what I want to do."

She caught back a sob, wanting with all her heart to believe him. "Christian—"

"I don't want to duck my responsibilities. For the first time, I feel as if there's a purpose to my life, and that purpose is to be your husband, live here with you and our children, and do what I can to take care of this place and the village and the farms. I'd never thought about things that way before. I'd regarded marrying Evie as a duty I was expected to perform, but I never saw any need to change my life because of it. I was only twenty-one when I married, far too immature to know what love or even duty really meant. But I know now. I love you and my duty is to you and us, and our children."

"And I—"

"I'll be honest," he cut in, "I'm glad you've got money, because we'll need it for Scarborough. I wish I could have made the grand gesture and said I won't take a penny from you, but I couldn't afford to do that. There really wasn't any other way, but I swear to you, Annabel, on my life, your money has nothing to do with why I want you to marry me. It's because I love you, and—"

"Cryin' all night," she shouted, forced to raise her voice to get a word in, "when you decide to sweet-talk a girl, you just don't know when to stop! Can I say something, please?"

He straightened, letting her go, and gave a little cough. "Of course. Sorry."

"I meant what I said. I do love you." As she spoke,

she began to laugh, the joy bubbling up inside her impossible to contain. "And I'm not trying to run away or duck out. Honest. But I knew I couldn't marry you without your love in return. I love you, Christian. And now that I know you love me, you'll never get rid of me. If you decided to give up your title, if you decide to go wandering off to Paris or America or even the Klondike, you better be prepared to take me with you, 'cause I'm not gonna sit at home alone and cry over you."

"Annabel, a duke can't give up his title. There's no means of doing so, and I don't want to. I want the job." He laughed, as if in disbelief. "Deuce take it, I really do. But only if you are my duchess."

"I want it, too."

"Do you, really? I know far better than you what you're in for. Maybe . . ." He paused and swallowed hard, then added diffidently, "Maybe you ought to take another minute and think it over."

She did. She looked into his handsome face and thought about it long and hard. She looked in those smoky blue eyes with their devil-black lashes, noted all the faint creases of too much high living at the corners of his eyes and mouth, and remembered how that mouth could form its wicked yet charming smile. It was a rake's face, that was for sure. But, like her daddy, she must have a gambler's heart, because she was going to put her money and her future on the line for a rake.

She frowned at him. "Are you goin' to reform once we get married?"

He didn't even blink. "No."

"Good." She wrapped her arms around his neck. "Because I love you just the way you are."

"And I love you, so don't change. Ever." He kissed her, a long, lingering kiss, but then, he pulled back, smiling at her. "I might be a rake and you might be just a girl from Gooseneck Bend, Mississippi, but we have two hundred and forty-two guests in there, waiting for us to carry on with this. So . . ." He paused, gesturing to the chapel behind him, "Shall we?"

"I think we have to. It is our duty."

"Quite right, m'dear," he said, his voice so highbrow it made her laugh. "Quite right."

As they walked back toward the chapel, he unexpectedly threw back his head with a shout of laughter. "God, me doing my duty. Who'd have thought it?" He paused outside the chapel doors. "Maybe I am reforming after all."

"Well, stop it, would you?" she ordered. "I knew the first moment I saw you that you were trouble, and I wouldn't have you any other way."

Christian and Annabel went back inside, and this time, when the vicar reached the part about any man having just cause, nobody said a word. Annabel's family was probably mighty relieved about that.

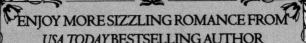

978-0-06-184132-3

978-0-06-202719-1

978-0-06-206932-0

978-0-06-204515-7

978-0-06-207998-5

978-0-06-178209-1